Darlene and Jean-Jaques are getting to know each other—sort of . . .

"I am French, but actually, I was born in Br-r-r-azil," he said, trilling his *r*s. "So I have dual citizenship: French and Br-r-r-azilian."

"I dated a French guy once—he loved garlic—but I never dated a Brrrazilian. How *do* you make that sound? I can never get it right."

"It's all with the tongue. To be very good with the tongue takes a lot of practice."

"Yes, I know."

"Try again."

"Br-r-r-azilian."

"Spoken like a native. You have a great tongue. Did anybody ever tell you that you have a great tongue?"

"Not on a first date."

"I love your earrings," he said, fingering one.

"Emeralds. I have them in all colors. Are you in cof-

ee?"

o, my brother, Ricar-r-r-do, is in coffee. I am in tin."

how interesting. There must be millions of tin
ade every day."

tually, *billions*."

very fascinating."

HEADHUNTERS

♡

Jules Bass

JOVE BOOKS, NEW YORK

13024377

HEADHUNTERS

A Jove Book / published by arrangement with
the author

PRINTING HISTORY
Jove advance reading edition / February 2001
Jove edition / June 2001

The Penguin Putnam Inc. World Wide Web site address is
www.penguinputnam.com

JOVE®
Jove Books are published by The Berkley Publishing Group,
a division of Penguin Putnam Inc.,
375 Hudson Street, New York, New York 10014.
JOVE and the "J" design
are trademarks belonging to Penguin Putnam Inc.

PRINTED IN THE UNITED STATES OF AMERICA

10 9 8 7 6 5 4 3 2

For Jeannine, dreamer of my dreams

ACKNOWLEDGMENTS

The author also wishes to express his sincere appreciation to the following:

La Belle Otéro, Edward VII, Czar Nicholas II of Russia, Leopold II of Belgium, Reza Shah, William Vanderbilt, Ivana Trump. The designers Hanae Mori, Christian Lacroix, Givenchy, Balmain, Valentino, Yves St. Laurent, Victor Edelstein, Ungaro, Zandra Rhodes, Stéphane Kélian, Charles Jourdan, Pollini, Sonia Rykiel, Chanel, Escada, Christiana Stambolia, Dior, Jacques Fath, Oscar de la Renta, Gucci, Galliano, Lagerfeld. Producers, writers, actors, and directors of the stage musicals and motion pictures *A Little Night Music; La Traviata; Dangerous Liaisons; The Man Who Loved Women; Breakfast at Tiffany's; Pennies from Heaven; Moonstruck; Sleepless in Seattle; Thelma and Louise; Divorce—Italian Style; Tea and Sympathy; Casino Royale; The Wizard of Oz; Cinderella; The Great Gatsby; Ready to Wear; Victor/Victoria; Dr. Zhivago; The Age of Innocence; Casino.* The owners and staff of the Hotel de Paris, the Louis Quinze Restaurant, the Monte Carlo Casino and Les Thermes Marins, Restaurant La Salière, the

Hotel de la Voile d'Or, the Monte Carlo golf club, Jimmy Z's, Hotel Royal–San Rémo, *Playboy* magazine, Le Cirque, Turnbull & Asser, Borsalino, Rolls-Royce, Bentley, Sulka, Cartier, Tiffany, Van Cleef & Arpels, Bulgari, Lobb. And to those who inspired me along the way: Richard Gere, Charles Aznavour, Scott and Zelda Fitzgerald, Ernest Hemingway, Anthony Quinn, Deborah Kerr, Tom Hanks, Meg Ryan, Daniela Rocca, Stefania Sandrelli, Jacqueline Bisset, Jacques Brel, Simone Signoret, Martin Scorsese, Felix of the Tahiti Beach Restaurant, Madame du Barry, Madame de Pompadour, King Louis XV, King Edward VII, Henry Charpentier, Henry Mancini, Olympia Dukakis, Vincent Gardenia, Marcello Mastroianni, Catherine Deneuve, Chopin, Pierre Goujon, Jean Lorenzi, David Niven, Troy Aikman, Michael Irvin, Richard Burton, Elizabeth Taylor, Omar Khayyám, Shel Silverstein, Ava Gardner, and to my friend Mickey Rooney (who probably to this day wonders how he got so lucky so many times).

"Women love the lie that saves their pride, but never an unflattering truth."

—Gertrude Franklin Atherton,
The Conqueror (1902)

CONTENTS

"We are the Movers and Shakers,
We are the dreamers of your dreams,
We are the headline makers,
For all of the world, it seems,
We'll do your living for you,
Just read your magazines.
We are the Movers and the Shakers,
The dreamers of your dreams . . ."

PROLOGUE

F OUR ELEGANTLY GOWNED and dazzlingly bejeweled
women, well past the age of consent, about to descend
the marble staircase into the rococo entrance hall of the
grande dame of European hotels: the exquisite, exclusive,
very expensive, Hotel de Paris in Monte Carlo.

Crêpê Suzette was invented here.

In the era of La Belle Époque, when men wore white
tie and tails in the evening and gambled away fortunes at
the casino across the square, the women might have been
mistaken for a covey of courtesans. In those halcyon days,
at the turn of the century, "expensive" ladies were kept
in grand style by the rich and royal; delectable damsels
like the notorious La Belle Otéro whose lovers included
Edward VII, Czar Nicholas II of Russia, Leopold II of
Belgium, Reza Shah, and William Vanderbilt, to name but
a few. Monte Carlo was a man's playground; a protected
sandbox where he could flaunt his caprices with impunity.
It was designed for the moneyed uppercrust and catered
to their every whim. There were no "slots" or "craps" at
the casino; that didn't come until much later. Carefree,

tax-free Monte Carlo—still the crowning jewel of the Côte d'Azur.

Where else is it against the law to drive a dirty car?

Four women, taking their first hesitant, synchronous steps into the future.

Make no mistake, these are not women of the sidewalk sisterhood; no damsels of the *demimonde* on the hustle, this quartet.

FOUR MEN, HANDSOME in their evening attire, comfortable in their surroundings, crystal aperitif stems in hand, *habitués*—of the clubby wood-paneled cocktail lounge of the hotel, waiting for their luck to change. No tourists, these.

All of the chairs in the room face front. To enter is to have your moment onstage—to be openly appraised. The four women are so evaluated as the pianist starts his set; a soft progression of chords leads to Michel Legrand's romantic main theme from *The Umbrellas of Cherbourg:* "If it takes forever, I will wait for you . . ." (In the film, the beautiful star, Catherine Deneuve, didn't wait, as she had promised, for her young garage-mechanic lover to return from military service; she married the first rich man who came along.)

As the *maître d'hôtel* parades the four women to a table, they float as one past the four men, in a soft cloud of duty-free perfume, Guerlain predominating. A scene from *Hello, Dolly!* The women barely register the presence of the men within their periphery; their facial expressions projecting studied serenity. The men, in response, offer token half smiles and mini-nods of acknowledgment.

The combined pulse rate of the four women is four hundred and seventy-eight; of the four men, three hundred and twenty. The amateurs versus the professionals. The stage is set. This is the way it was planned. Each has what the other wants. Or so it would appear.

Fortunately, we will hear the story from both sides.

PRELUDE
"The Tango"

When we are dancing and you're dangerously near me,
I get ideas, I get ideas,
I want to hold you so much closer than I dare to
Because I care, oh yes I care, more than I care to
And when we kiss . . .
—Cochran and Sanders, "I Get Ideas"

*Y*OU'RE WALKING ALONE *by the sea. Music. A house up ahead, set back from the beach. People laughing, swimming, dancing, having fun. A man. He calls out your name. You run toward his open arms, desperate to be embraced by them. But no matter how fast you run, he's always the same distance away. You awaken, out of breath and wet—everywhere.*

You lie there, thinking about the routines you will follow, like the automaton you have become. Mindlessly, one day becomes another. Yesterday you brushed your teeth twice because you couldn't remember the first time; forgot to put sugar in your coffee because you thought you already had. More of the same every day. Repetition damages, bores, depresses. Everything used the same way every day eventually breaks down, wears out. The brakes on your car, the toaster, lightbulbs—your brain.

You check in with the world: radio, television, Internet, e-mail. You telephone the same friends, at the same time. Look at the mail with anticipation, knowing it can't possibly contain anything interesting.

Tension mounts. You take the same pills the other women do. They serve only to break the surface tension; the deeper pools are left unplumbed. The day looms before you. Why is this day different from any other day? No answer comes to mind. Lunch with a friend. A reason to get yourself together; avoid the void.

You're like the others, in your third life span: youth, marriage, and family, divorce, and death. Alone. Thoreau wrote that most men live lives of quiet desperation. Assuming that by men he meant mankind, this includes you. But why quiet desperation? Why not raging desperation? Simple. Because raging is not acceptable behavior. Suppress the rage, deal with it. The phone will ring, things will change.

No, they won't. Do something. Anything, a dumb thing—an ad in the personals, an Internet romance, put yourself out there. Bullshit, it never works. It's not out there. Desperate seeks desperate for ugly sexual encounter. Condoms. What an ugly word. Why don't they think up another word? All the words are ugly: spermicides, diaphragm, vagina, penetration. Where is love in all of this? Desperate seeking desperate for understanding, comfort, stroking, kindness, friendship, affection, laughter, fun, togetherness. Anyone will do for a start. Only in your dreams.

Not like your college days when everything . . . no, don't dwell on that, on the past. Stop reading those books that cause the dreams. No wandering photographer of old bridges is going to show up at your door. There will be no shattering, explosive orgasm that you remember for life. It's all science fiction, the stuff of romance novels, being swept off your feet to never-never land. Don't buy into the myth, because that's what it is—a myth. But you buy more of them.

At the hairdresser. You read the latest copy of W magazine. Do these people really exist or are they hired for the photos? They shout out at you from the pages, toasting you with their champagne, in their tuxedos and perfect little black dresses. "We are the movers and shakers, the dreamers of your dreams, we'll do your living for you, just read your magazines . . ."

There is another world going on, without you. The woman you pay to listen to you twice a week tells you that you have to stop thinking of yourself as a victim. Get out there, network, emphasize your strong points. Be aggressive. Break the cycle, the mold. Do something different.

You decide to take tango lessons. How's that for different? It's been so long since you danced with a man who was "dangerously" near you. The image takes your breath away . . . and gives you ideas you haven't had in a long time.

ACT ONE
MAKING THE PLAN

I

"The Support Group"

Somewhere in New Jersey.
Tuesday evening.
At a table, in a coffee shop.

DARLENE OPENS THE meeting. It is her turn to be leader.

"Who wants to start?"

No one ever wants to be first. After the first few minutes it gets easier.

"Irene?"

"I started last week."

"Eleanor?"

"I'm having my period."

"Why don't you say what you mean? Carla?"

"Pass."

"This is not a bridge game. We're here to talk, not to avoid talking."

"Good, then you start."

"Okay. I had my first tango lesson last night."

"Why?"

"That sounds like a pejorative and judgmental 'why.' We're not supposed to be judgmental with each other. That's the whole point of these meetings, isn't it? Otherwise we couldn't call ourselves a support group, right?"

"This coming from Ms. Judgmental? Do my ears deceive me?"

"I'm trying to change, as you all know. It hasn't been easy."

"Anyway, I was just being curious."

"How'd it go?"

"It was—interesting. Very sexy, as a matter of fact."

"A lot of contact, huh?"

"You'd probably think it was a lot."

"Okay, we're even. Claws in."

"You know, it's a proven fact that skin-to-skin contact, on a regular basis, can lessen tension and prolong life."

"So can stroking a cat."

"What percentage of single women have cats?"

"Who gives a shit!"

"Thirty-eight-point-six percent."

"Are you making that up?"

"Yeah."

"Some guys don't like cats."

"Fuck them."

". . . and my instructor asked me out to dinner. I never know what to eat. I always order something stupid—like a lobster."

"That's the worst. It has be something you can eat with one hand."

"Why?"

"Figure it out."

"I always order filet of sole; amandine, if they have it."

"Perfect."

"How about a pizza and a cold-six, in bed watching *Monday Night Football*?"

"On a first date?"

"Think about it. It's really original. He calls and says, 'Where would you like to go?' and you say, 'Why don't you come over and we'll get in bed with some cold beer and pizza, and watch the game?' And, as an added incentive, 'I'll suck your cock during halftime.' "

"And *he* says?"

"Will you marry me?"

Good-natured laughter. The ice is broken.

"Last guy I went out to dinner with, he spreads a napkin on his lap and puts my hand on it. Then he asks me to reach under, unzip his fly, and play with him."

"Did you do it?"

"What do you think?"

"I think you probably did."

"With the headwaiter standing right in front of us waiting to take our order?"

"Yeah."

"You really think I'd do something like that?"

"Yes."

"It was kind of exciting. Until he came in my hand."

"In front of the headwaiter?"

"No, while a busboy was pouring water in my glass."

"Ugh! Gross."

"That wasn't the problem. I went to the ladies' room and washed up."

"What was the problem?"

"He was so fucking boring for the rest of the meal. You know how guys get afterward?"

"You can always tell in a restaurant if a couple has done it before dinner. Never, never do it before."

"Tell me about it."

"When I was a kid, guys used to do stuff like that."

"How old a kid were you?"

"Old. Fourteen."

"You had your hand on some guy's penis under a napkin in a restaurant at fourteen?"

"No, in a box of popcorn at the movies."

"That's a new one for me."

"I've heard about it but it never happened to me."

"How's that work?"

"Well, he's got the box of popcorn on his lap and you reach in for a handful—and that's what you get. A handful—of him."

"I'm still not getting it."

"I'll draw you a picture. He cuts a hole in the bottom of the popcorn box and shoves his dick—"

"I think I've got it."

"What did you do then?"

"Well, it was all buttery and it was my first time, so I did it."

"And he came—in the popcorn?"

"Really fast."

"That's hysterical."

Another long moment of silence.

"I'm not placing any more ads. I'm still recovering from last week. Another dentist."

"I dated one, once. Every time he stuck his tongue in my mouth all I could think of was that he was poking around for cavities."

"I know what you mean."

"It's all so ordinary."

Irene sings: "Is That All There Is?"

They all join in: "Let's break out the booze and have a ball . . ."

"We should name our group The Lemmings. Get jackets and caps."

"What is a lemming, anyway?"

"They're those little animals that migrate in huge groups from the mountains to the sea—mindlessly following each other until they all drown."

"That's us, all right. Once a year we plan a vacation—somewhere we stand a chance of meeting Mr. Right, right? And where do we geniuses go? Where every other bored, lonely, single, divorced, widowed wonder goes. With the herds, on cruise ships, to the mountains, to the beaches."

"So, last year I diet and go to the gym religiously. I think I'm looking pretty good, you know? So I decide to unveil my new bod in Miami. I walk out to the beach in front of my expensive hotel—underline 'expensive.'

There are lots of cute guys around, so I ask one of the boys for a lounge. He says they're full up for the day— I should try tomorrow. Do you believe it?"

"New Year's Eve, I'm in a nice bar in Acapulco? Good-looking guy walks in and sits next to me. Smiles. I smile. Figure he's going to ask me to have a drink with him, something like that. No chance. For openers he says, 'Why don't we go up to my room—I'll make you come so hard you won't be able to make a fist for a week.' "

"Original."

"I couldn't believe it. So I say, 'I'm not that kind of a girl.' It was all I could think of. And he says, 'If you're not that kind of a girl, what are you doing sitting in a bar, alone, at two o'clock in the morning on New Year's Eve all dressed up showing your titties in that sexy low-cut dress?' And he takes off—just when I was thinking about what it would be like not to make a fist for a week."

"He did have a point."

"Nothing makes sense, anymore. However you act these days it's wrong."

"So, what's right?"

"The frogs never turn into anything but pricks."

"What you see is what you get."

"Maybe the whole problem is that we don't have an original thought in our heads. Maybe we've become very boring women."

"We've convinced ourselves that just talking about our problems will help us find a solution. But let's face it, you don't get solutions without taking action."

"Lemmings."

"Lemmings!"

"I can prove it. Who has an interesting and original idea?"

"About what?"

"Anything but *them*."

The longest moment of silence yet.

"I hate my fucking trainer."

"Everybody hates their trainer."

"Mine's a les."

"So's mine. All the guys hit on her—right in front of me. It's depressing. She's up-front with them right off that she's gay. They say that doesn't matter."

"Fucking men."

"Yeah. Let's face it, guys only want three things."

"What are the other two?"

"The woman they're *not* with and money. Anybody see that article in *People* magazine?"

"No."

"Lead story's about the richest women in the world. What they want they get. Make that, they *take*. They're not sitting around waiting for the phone to ring. They're not placing personal ads or surfing for chat rooms."

Eleanor takes a copy of the magazine out of her pocketbook and tosses it on the table.

"Take a look. There are people out there doing the things that we sit home and read about. They are living our dreams, realizing our fantasies. Without them, these magazines wouldn't exist. It's like they do our living for us—all we have to do is read the magazine. And what's the difference between them and us?"

"Money—pure and simple."

"Maybe pure but not so simple."

"Money is a state of mind."

"Money is sexy."

"*Very* sexy."

Eleanor picks up the magazine and starts to read.

"How about this lady: Greta Harmon-Cates, the former Mrs. Harrington Harmon-Cates—he of the armaments business. Reputed to be worth in excess of four hundred million dollars. Six houses, cars, blah, blah, horses—"

Irene grabs the magazine from Eleanor.

"Listen to this. The Baroness Natasha Karmanov owns two yachts, houses in Marbella, Palm Beach, Beverly Hills, and Corfu. She wears the Star of Jedda Diamond—fifty carats—husband died last year leaving her two hundred and fifty million and all the real estate—blah, blah, blah . . . Look at her—she's not so hot. Take away the houses and the money and what have you got? Me!"

Darlene was next to read, adding an exaggerated, little-girl Texas accent:

"Lou Ann Barlow, Houston Texas. Never been married. Oh, poor thing, she's still Daddy's little girl, which is not terrible since Daddy is Dexter Hunt Barlow, owner of Barlow Industries—oil. Lou Ann has a trust fund reputed to be worth close to a billion dollars. And get this: Her big complaint is that she's never sure if men are interested in her or her money. Oh, how awful for her."

"We shouldn't read this trash—it's not healthy."

"But don't you just love it?"

"Let me see that," said Carla. "I think really rich women are fascinating. How about this one? Contessa Stephania di Romanesco. Poor thing, she's been in mourning for her husband for three years—never seen in public. Former Italian film star; her husband was a big Mafia guy—owns an island off the coast of Sicily. The usual ton of money, et cetera, et cetera, et cetera."

"Let's face it, girls, if you wanna sell you gotta be in the marketplace. Think these women ever sat around doing what we're doing? No fucking way. They're in the world's playgrounds, being treated like royalty."

"Rich people—they have that aura. Does Ivana Trump get a coat check when she comes into a restaurant? Fat chance. The manager rushes up and takes care of it."

"That's because everyone knows her."

"I don't think so. It's the smell of money."

"Money smells?"

"You bet your sweet ass it does."

"Headwaiters can smell it from across the room. Hotel reservation clerks can smell it through a thousand miles of phone line. Jewelers are taught to smell it through plate-glass windows."

"The aura?"

"The aura."

"Maybe we should go where the movers and shakers go. Where the money is—instead of just reading about it in magazines."

"First we'd have to figure out how to smell like money?"

"Great. Anybody got any ideas how we do that?"

A pause to allow for the thought to sink in and for the cloud of dejection that usually precedes the end of the weekly group sessions to pass.

"Who had the butterscotch brownies?"

"I had two cappuccinos. That's six-eighty, plus the tip; call it seven-fifty even."

"You're the diet Coke, two *biscotti* . . ."

The four women divide the check. The regular Tuesday-night support group session has ended. But it will be discussed and debated over the phone, all week, until next Tuesday's session—which all the women look forward to with great anticipation. Exploring the yin and yang of each other's lives has become an addiction.

Nothing is ever decided. Nothing is ever resolved. Nothing is ever changed. That's the way it is—that's the way it's always been—and that's the way it will always be.

Unless . . .

2
"The Four Women"

God created women,
And boredom did indeed cease from that moment . . .
—*Nietzsche*

Darlene

Darlene, amid her hoard of gold and silver—like the dragon Smaug in his lair—surrounded by trophies won during her younger days. Pictures of her as homecoming queen at Texas A&M, her alma mater.

Photographs of a bright, beautiful, and shapely young woman who had the world at her feet. Each award that she carefully dusted (for she was passionate about keeping her memorabilia in pristine condition; smoking was never allowed in this room) brought back sweet memories, treasured moments from her past. An array of photos set on glass shelves against a mirrored wall in her den showed Darlene's progression from winner in a beauty contest for five-year-olds to the pinnacle of her career as Miss Texas in the Miss America Pageant too many years ago. Very carefully, she lifted this last photo of herself in a bathing suit down from its place of honor. Shrugging off her terry robe, she stood in her bra and panties, shifting her eyes between the framed photo and her present mirrored image. She held the photo at arm's length, pulled in her stomach, and tightened her buttocks. Leaning forward, she created extra cleavage by pressing her upper arms against her breasts, and sucked in her cheeks, making a moue of her generous lips.

Not so bad, she thought. A few extra inches around the hips, the abs could use a little attention (she'd work with her trainer on that), a few fine lines here and there—nothing a good makeup job couldn't hide—a wrinkle here, a crinkle there—*character*. A patch of cellulite that no one would ever see, roots that could use a touch-up; the color was a bit dull (easily fixed). All in all, not bad considering the passage of time and two pregnancies. She felt pleased with herself. Her careful diet and thrice-weekly workouts at the gym had paid off. True, her figure was now a bit less than Greek, but she was not unhappy with what the mirror revealed. Maybe she wasn't "trophy" material anymore but dressed-to-kill she probably still could. She was just out of practice. During a recent school break her sons had brought home two of their male friends and she had overheard them talking about her as they looked at her pictures and awards.

"For my money, she's still a great piece of ass."

It had made her smile. She hadn't heard herself referred to like that in a long time.

Darlene slipped back into her robe and sat down in a poofy lounge chair next to a cocktail table that held her college yearbook. She opened it to the bookmarked page: *most likely to marry a rich guy,* the editor had written under her picture. It all seemed like yesterday, she thought as she leaned back and surveyed the room, seeing for the umpteenth time the short lifetime of documented accolades for the fresh-faced blonde that stared back at her from every angle.

When Darlene turned eighteen she began to think about—make that *obsess* about—getting married. She refused to date any boy who didn't measure up to her marital standards for looks, money, intelligence. Furthermore, they had to be "serious" about dating her. Whatever that meant to a college boy. Most of the guys at school either fantasized about bedding her or had actually tried. None had even come close to succeeding.

If a boy had potential, she tried out his name by doodling it endlessly after hers: *Mrs. Darlene Wright, Mrs. David Wright, Darlene Wright....* Darlene daydreamed about her wedding, planning every detail carefully in her head. It would be the highlight of her life. *Most likely to marry a rich guy.* It was a joke that became a reality.

TWO YEARS AFTER graduation she had gone from trophy winner to trophy wife, marrying the thrice-previously-tied Hamilton Stillwell, Jr. He liked her body, 38-24-36, her model's face, and her baby-talk voice. But to him, she was just a trophy—and there would be many other trophies in his life. When they first met, Darlene was a virgin, much to her future husband's disappointment. He was sure she had fucked half of the football team—at least, that was the rumor—and would be able to teach him a few new tricks. He had no idea who his wife really was— and didn't care. As long as he had the best-looking and youngest wife in his social and business circle, that's all that mattered. He didn't care much about sex with her anyway—preferring, like many masters of the universe, to mind-fuck his staff and pay for his extracurricular sex on a whimsical basis. They had two children, both boys. After ten years of marriage Darlene was replaced by a new contestant, and left with fading memories of stardom.

Funny thing was that Darlene was an A student and graduated with a 3.9 average, having majored in the history of Western civilization. But her face and figure were what got her where she thought she wanted to go and so she acted the part of Little Miss Sunshine until she wasn't sure where her adopted persona stopped and the real Darlene began.

She hadn't dated, after the divorce, when the two boys were small, but now that they were away at college she found herself wondering where all the time had gone and if it was too late to start again with another man. One thing was for sure—her old act would not suffice this time around.

She had the house—a smallish old Tudor on two acres—and the alimony gave her just barely enough to get by on, given the rate of inflation since the divorce. Her ex was generous when it came to providing for the boys, but there were never any extras for her. So after the kids went off, she signed up as a salesperson for Avon. This gave her enough for small indulgences and yearly vacations with "the girls."

She enjoyed talking to the others at the support-group sessions even if they really didn't ever accomplish much. It was a break in the day's occupations . . .

Eleanor

Eleanor always told you exactly what was on her mind. She was loud and she was funny. No one ever put anything over on Eleanor. She told it like it was, as in: "I threw him the fuck out and stripped him for all he was worth. I burned one of each pair of his shoes in the fireplace and cut one arm off of every one of his jackets. The pants? I took the zippers out so that he wouldn't have to waste time in the office when he wanted to whip it out and show it to his new bitch—not that there was that much to show, the putz. What an a-hole, thinking he could screw me and that fluff of a secretary at the same time. It's not like we were married! I had the poor sucker on his knees begging forgiveness—and me, being bighearted like I am, I gave it to him. 'I forgive you, dickhead—now get the fuck out of my life.' Too bad—in a way I really kinda liked the schmuck."

The way Eleanor looked at life, you were either part of the problem or part of the solution. Lead, follow, or get out of the way. She made lots of mistakes—but she was a doer. A born leader. Nothing and nobody intimidated her. She may have had a heart of gold, but if she did, no one ever got a chunk of it after she dumped Harry.

Eleanor had met him at a hockey game. She was on the ice, in goal. He never realized that the goaltender was a *she* because of all the equipment a goalie wears—so when Eleanor stopped his slapshot from blasting into the net, he was startled by the obviously feminine voice that screamed at him: "No fucking way through me, asshole."

Harry's fantasy, from that day on, was to bang her on the ice, with all her equipment on. He told her exactly that—the next time he slammed into her with a missed shot. Oddly, she was up for it. Talk about a sport-fuck! It turned out to be an unfeasible event, but they had lots of laughs and that started it all. Problem was, Harry would fuck a snake—and often did.

As the years passed, Eleanor resigned herself to the fact that she would never get married. Her energy was divided between her job in the public defender's office, as a lawyer handling women's rights cases, and her varied sports activities, which included gym work four nights a week, jogging, biking, tennis, skiing, and—her passion—horseback riding. Lots of opportunities to meet men—but most were intimidated by her and became "friends." Yes, Eleanor had lots of male friends—gay, straight, old, young, married, single, divorced. She was a den mother to them all.

Eleanor never showed her vulnerability—except when she was indulging in her second-greatest passion, the study of classical piano. She took lessons two nights a week and practiced religiously for four hours a day on weekends. To listen to Eleanor playing Chopin with such an exceptional depth of feeling and precision was to be allowed a peek into a very private part of her complex psyche, into her second self. But she allowed few such entrée and rarely played for friends, preferring to keep that part of her shut off from the rest of the world. When she played she was completely vulnerable; all defenses were down. Only the gay men knew her for what she really was—she couldn't hide it from them—but the others never even guessed there were any soft spots and so treated her like one of the guys.

During the years when her biological clock was winding down to zero, she often thought about having a child ... especially on evenings when she was alone in her small apartment playing Chopin. She would do it, she thought, by simply choosing her best-looking, smartest friend and making a deal with him to lend her his chromosomes. But at the crucial moment she always got cold feet. She liked the others girls in the support group and wanted for them all the things that she knew she would never have for herself.

Of course that's not absolutely true—nor could it be— of any woman.

Irene

Thoreau also said that "man basically only hits what he aims at." We can only assume, once again, that by "man" he meant mankind, i.e., women included. Or maybe he didn't. Maybe he was a nineteenth-century male chauvinist pig, or maybe he never considered the issue at all— which is the more likely. After all, he was living in the woods, *alone*! From the moment she first considered men, Irene took careful aim at them. But when throwing an ax at a heavily wooded spot, one frequently hits the wrong tree. Three "nearby tree" marriages; three divorces. Never mind who divorced whom—that always varies depending upon which side of the aisle you sat on, whose story you believe (assuming you get to hear both sides). No one wants to be the, ugh, discarded.

Although Irene had suppressed the facts, and the issues that provoked the divorces were now irrevocably convoluted, one thing she did admit to: the basic fact that each time she stood at the altar and felt that ring gripping on her finger like one-half of a pair of mini-handcuffs, she knew she was headed for eventual failure. But, like many, she chose togetherness. Spending her life alone was not an option. Why did she always convince herself that she was in love? And, anyway, what did that mean? Wild passion? Intense desire? A warm glow? Do people marry people they don't love? *Unquestionably.* Irene was an intelligent and literate woman. She knew what she was getting herself into each time. She knew that others before her had had the same experience, the same unspoken terror and disbelief that they were actually making an untenable, supposedly lifelong commitment. Irene was always reminded of what Philip Roth wrote in his autobiographical novel, *The Facts,* of the woman he abhorred, who lied to him, whom he had struggled to avoid, and who was, by his own description, his worst enemy. "Reader, I married her," he shouted out from the page (words Charlotte Brontë had used one hundred and fifty years earlier in Jane Eyre). His decision was unbelievable, even to himself. It was as if he was seeking solace, understanding, telling us that he, too, was fallible (stupid) in matters of the heart. Irene was simply more fallible than most.

Some women (some men) can live alone and cope; Irene was not one of them. To the contrary, she obsessed about the possibility of a fourth marital venture. But there were no takers.

Irene's problem was that she was still as snobbish and aloof as she'd been when she was a top runway star. Fashion modeling had been a job well suited to her talents and disposition. Back then she'd had more marriage proposals than she could handle. For a decade an endless stream of men had lined up at her door pledging money, marriage, and fidelity. It seemed all they required of her was that she continue to look haughty, elegant, and unapproachable. And she had said yes three times. But now what beauty she still possessed (and make no mistake, Irene was still considered a most handsome and elegant woman—menopause notwithstanding) faded with each sentence she uttered, revealing, beneath the external veneer, not truth or character, but simply more veneer; lay-

ers of it. The very superficiality she had worked so hard
to project as a model was now hard to discard. She was
like an actress who couldn't slip out of her part after the
play was over. Two years of expensive psychiatric hours
hadn't succeeded in scraping away any of it. Indeed it
may have added a protective layer or two. As anxious as
many men were to bed her, most fled before the onslaught
of her banality.

Now, working as a booker in her old modeling agency,
her formerly successful snobbish-aloof act simply made
her appear cold and hard, and outside the door to her
perfectly decorated two-bedroom condo there was no
longer a crush of men down the block and around the
corner begging an audience with the Ice Princess. In the
evenings her phone stared back at her reproachfully, eerily
silent except for the occasional voice of a newly widowed
or divorced man who called hoping for a mercy-fuck-for-
old-times, a sad sport in which, from time to time, out of
desperation, she found herself indulging.

As the years passed she slowly retreated into a solitary
life. She knew she was still young enough for another
grab at the ring and a part of her felt she would be able
to reveal her true self to the right man. But instead of
making the effort, she devoted more and more of her time
to her job and had recently been promoted to assistant
manager of the office. She was efficient, precise, and hardworking—and everyone hated her.

In her computer Irene had a file named MISTAKES.DOC,
and in it she had listed all of the reasons why she felt her
marriages hadn't worked; what mistakes she wouldn't
make again. There were one hundred and fifty entries.
That alone should have told her something, but given that
she was a Taurus, it only strengthened her resolve. She
continued to aim, but for the past five years had not even
come close to hitting anything. She lied to her intimate
friends in the support group, telling them that she preferred living alone. To herself she admitted nothing. When
her metaphorical ax did graze a potential tree, she held

back and told a modified story: her first husband was gay, her second much older, and her third she greedily married for his money. None of her friends believed any of her fictions, but that did not keep them from sisterly commiseration. Women lie differently than men, considering their lies to be comforting, supportive.

Irene knew that next time, if there was a next time, she was going to have to open up and let it all hang out—reaction be damned. It was the only thing she hadn't tried. Somewhere, deep down, there was a really wonderful person. Problem was, it was too deep down for anyone to reach. And if she waited much longer, even she wouldn't know how to access it.

When the group played "if you could be anybody, who would you be?" Irene always fantasized herself as a beautiful Russian princess, in the days of the czar, living in St. Petersburg. Icy-cold, sought after by men, filthy rich, furred, and bejeweled. Playing that part in real life would not be a stretch for her.

Carla

Carla was two generations removed from her Italian roots. She neither spoke her native language, cooked Italian dishes, or related in any way to the land of her ancestry. Her mother had succeeded in removing every ethnic trace from her beautiful daughter's persona, except one: Carla looked like a *Madonna* painted by Raphael; a Madonna with a New Jersey accent. She had flawless olive skin, dark, shiny long hair that was almost black, large brown eyes, a generous bosom that she always showed to advantage, and a pleasingly rounded figure. Carla attracted a lot of the wrong kind of men. She finally settled on the one decent man she knew—Giovanni di Benedetto. He was not only Italian, but a professional Italian who knew a *vongola verace piccola* from a little-neck clam, a Versaci from a Valentino, a Barbaresco from a *Barolo*.

He was an excellent cook. His *risotto alla Milanese* was superb. He tried to teach Carla but she had no knack for *la cucina*. He complained, in a gentle way, that she either stirred the rice too much or not enough, that it was too hard or too soft, too sticky or too runny. In ten tries she never came close to getting it right, even though he eventually pretended that it was good. *Molto buono*, he said. Good. But it was a qualified, soft *molto*, a strained *buono*, a halfhearted *buono*, a weak *buono* at best. She never realized there were so many ways one could screw up a bowl of rice.

Fortunately, in life there are cookers and eaters. He cooked. She ate. She was a good eater. She made Giovanni smile when she offered her approval. *Molto buono, amore*.

He bought her clothes, he went with her to the hairdresser (an Italian, of course), got her a private tutor to instruct her in the language, and, when she had learned the requisite words for bedroom activities, taught her how to make love, Italian-style. Giovanni knew how to really love a woman. He treated her like a Madonna and she worshiped him. They had a cassette of the movie *Don Juan DeMarco* and watched it endlessly, making love to the title song; it was their theme:

> *When you love a woman you tell her that she's*
> *   really wanted*
> *Let her hold you until she tells you she needs to*
> *   be touched*
> *You've gotta breathe her, really taste her*
> *till you can feel her in your blood*
> *And when you can see your unborn children in*
> *   her eyes.*

They decided to wait another year before starting a family—but it was not to be. When he died suddenly, of a heart attack, after only two years of blissful marriage, Carla was devastated. No one would ever be able to measure up, much less replace her beloved Giovanni. As the years passed she forgot all of the language she had learned and went back to her plain style of microwave cooking. Mama was secretly happy. Carla joined the support group.

3
"The Smell of Money"

Things are seldom what they seem,
Skim milk masquerades as cream.
—Gilbert, H. M. S. Pinafore

Q: What is the difference between a vein, an artery, and a capillary?

Carla wrote the answer in the blank practice box of her study manual:

A: Arteries carry blood from the heart throughout the body. Veins carry blood to the heart from throughout the body. Veins: blood in. Arteries: blood out. Capillaries: the smallest blood vessels connecting arterioles with venules forming networks throughout the body. Veins, then, carry blood from arterial capillaries to the heart, where it is pumped out through the arteries into capillaries into veins and around again. So, an injection into a vein, i.e., intravenous—

Carla put the study book down. The exam was only a week away. If she passed she would be a nurse at Passaic General. When her husband collapsed in her arms, she had felt helpless. All she could do was panic and call the ambulance. By the time the EMS people got there, it was too late. If she had only learned CPR. Now, after all these years, she had decided to do it, and more. She couldn't just sit home and think about the husband she'd lost, the children she'd never had. The pain was still there along with memories that refused to fade, but it had all softened and retreated to a positive distance and Carla had known for some time that she had to discard her widow's weeds and move on to a new life. A job was part of it. Getting back into circulation was the other more difficult decision, but she had made it, was committed to it, had started to do the things that *mature* single women did (or were supposed to do)—read all the how-to books (learning nothing), took all those tests in the women's magazines (and learned what she already knew), went to mixers but didn't mix, pretended to be interested when she wasn't.

The phone rang. It was Eleanor.

As a lawyer, Eleanor was used to getting right to the point of the conversation—no hellos, no opening small talk.

"I figured it out. I know how we get to smell right."

"What are you talking about?"

"Get with the program, willya? Smell right. Rich. Smell *rich*."

"Is it a perfume? Eau de Rich?"

"Hint: It's a state of mind. Gotta go—tell you all about it tonight."

Eleanor hung up before Carla could say another word. Carla instantly called Irene at her office.

"I just spoke to Eleanor."

"So did I, so if you're about to ask me what she said, forget it. I don't have a clue."

"Well, see you tonight. Seven, at Darlene's?"

"Right."

* * *

PART OF DARLENE'S job as an Avon Lady was to give makeup demonstrations as many evenings a week as possible. It wasn't a bad deal. The ladies all got free makeovers, sample products, watched a video, and heard about all the latest products she was trying to sell. Tonight she was giving a private demonstration at her house, to the support group. Eleanor had spelled out part of her plan and was pressing for a commitment. She paced, as if in front of a jury, as Darlene applied Skin-So-Soʳ ...ʋɪsturizing suncare to Irene's cheeks.

"If we all think positively, we can make it work. So who's in? I'm looking for a few good women, here."

"Where do we get the money? I hear Monte Carlo is one of the most expensive places in the world."

"Plastic."

"You've go to be kidding."

"Spike Lee made a *movie* on plastic. And look where it got him. He had guts."

"None of us has the right clothes."

"Details. I've got that covered," said Eleanor. "There's a place on the West Side of Manhattan where they rent everything: gowns, furs, jewelry, shoes, even wigs. It's fantastic, and best of all it's cheap as hell. Most of it comes from TV, movies, the theater, and people who sell their designer clothes every year."

"There are women who really do that?"

"Rich women. That's how they stay that way."

"You think they can make us smell rich?"

"*Stinking* rich."

"Well, what have we got to lose by looking?"

"Good. Twelve-thirty tomorrow. They're expecting us."

Hollywood CastAways was on the second floor of an old building on West Forty-eighth Street. There were literally thousands of gowns, suits, and cocktail dresses hung on racks that filled the big loft space. Shoes, costume jewelry, wigs, and other accessories were arranged along the far wall, in boxes that rose up to the ceiling. Despite the disarray, the owners, Rob and Dennis McCall, knew exactly where everything was. The four women rummaged excitedly through the crowded aisles and saw labels of Hanae Mori, Christian Lacroix, Givenchy, Balmain, Valentino, Yves St. Laurent, Ungaro, Oscar de la Renta, Galliano, Lagerfeld, among others. In the show-business section there were costumes purportedly from *Amadeus, A Little Night Music, La Traviata, Dangerous Liaisons, The Great Gatsby, Ready to Wear, Evita, Victor/ Victoria,* and more. And everything was for sale or rent at prices the women could afford. Irene immediately snatched a gown that Rob said was worn by Glenn Close in *Dangerous Liaisons.*

"What do you think, girls?" she said, holding it up in front of her.

"Great, if you're thinking of seducing Louis the Fourteenth," Eleanor said.

Rob pinned some Russian braids on Irene's head, intertwining them with thin ropes of fake diamonds. In the "pre-owned" quilted czarina dress he suggested (supposedly from *Dr. Zhivago*), she looked every inch the Russian royal she would soon pretend to be.

Dennis found Carla what he called a "gently used knock-off" of a gown for "a certain princess." Originally by Victor Edelstein, he whispered, as if that should mean something to her. It was a midnight blue, made of a velour-like material, off the shoulder, floor length, and very sexy.

Eleanor tried on a number called the "Elvis dress"—a white sheath topped with a high-collared jacket—but she looked too much like Elvis in it, so Rob convinced her to try on a gown he swore was worn by Mary Beth Hurt in *The Age of Innocence,* and then suggested a preowned Balmain—a black sheath decorated with diagonal swirls of rhinestones. She looked every inch the wildly wealthy widow she would pretend to be.

A petaled and feathered dress for Darlene made the final list, as did a gray, glacial number with frosty buttons and icicles of crystal beading and a figure-hugging sheath made of a patchwork of pearly lace, and a heavily embroidered Zandra Rhodes in white satin, an off-the-rack preowned Christina Stambolian above-the-knee cocktail dress, deep cut at the bosom, in black shirred silk and chiffon—and more, and more, and still more.

Hour after hour the women, their arms full of frocks (does anyone say *frocks* anymore?) staggered into makeshift dressings rooms that were nothing more than draperies hung on wooden rods to divide and privatize the space. Rob and Dennis collected accessories for them: phony diamond necklaces, ruby, sapphire, and amethyst rings, an emerald pendant, pins, pearls, wigs, shoes, purses—the whole nine yards of formal dressing.

Each time the curtains were pulled aside, rather spectacular women materialized who only vaguely resembled their former selves. None of them had ever worn clothes like these and were shocked by how different they made them feel. But after each try-on, the women called out "more!" to Rob and Dennis.

"More? You want more? I think they want *more*!" they mimicked, from a scene in *Oliver!* "Well, you shall have as much more as you want."

Carla modeled a black-beaded, skintight Dior gown with a deep neckline, her creamy cleavage framed by a strand of huge sparkling "emeralds." Darlene wore an off-the-shoulder white sequined floor-length gown with a tight bodice, by Grès, with diamonds at her throat, wrists, ears, and drifting down her bare back. Irene looked regal in a Jacques Fath creation: an elegant gold lamé sheath with ropes of pearls. From the waist up Eleanor looked like Victor in *Victor/Victoria*, in a Nina Ricci tuxedo top, and Victoria, from the waist down, in a black satin floor-length skirt slit high up on both thighs.

Twenty-four dresses in all; six each, plus matching shoes, rhinestones up the wazoo, boxes of sparkly earrings, rings, hairpieces, and enough other whatnots to cover any blank spots.

There was no question that these women *looked* rich!
Smelled rich! They stared at each other, in amazement,
for a long moment, before Eleanor broke the silence.
"Fucking great."

One by one the women stepped in front of the mirror.
If anything, their reflections in the mottled glass added to
the effect. As Carla twirled, Eleanor announced their new
personas.

"CARLA, FORGET ABOUT emptying bedpans, from now on
you are la Contessa Stephania di Romanesco. Irene, imagine yourself from now on as the Baroness Natasha Karmanov. Darlene, you're Daddy's little rich girl, Lou Ann
Barlow from Houston, Texas. That shouldn't be too much
of a stretch for you."

Darlene looked at Eleanor as she took her turn in front
of the mirror. "Then you must be that filthy-rich-bitch
Greta Harmon-Cates?"

"You got it, babe. Armed and ready to fly."

"It's crazy."

"It'll never work."

"We'll end up in jail."

Eleanor shook her head in dismay at their attitudes.
"Nothing like thinking positively, is there? Chickenshits."

"They look like a million dollars," said Rob.

"Two million five, minimum," said Dennis.

"Make that a hundred million," said Eleanor.

Still, despite their altered exteriors, three of the women
were not convinced.

"Where are you all *going* in these creations?" Rob
asked.

"Monte Carlo," Eleanor answered, as if the question
were settled.

"I think we should run this by Margo. Tonight's her
night, isn't it?" said Carla.

Irene and Darlene agreed; Eleanor had no choice but
to go along. Margo, an old friend and the group psychol-

ogist, attended every fourth support meeting and helped the women work through whatever problems had come up during the month. Eleanor was sure she'd dump on the idea—and she was right.

4
"Group Therapy"

They sailed away in a sieve, they did,
In a sieve they sailed so fast . . .
                              —*Edward Lear*

Unlike others in the mind-over-matter game, Margo Gardner was a very opinionated and vocal psychologist. Three years before, she had introduced the women to each other after they had each consulted her separately. It was she who had suggested the support group and was pleased that the women had all become close friends as a result. From time to time she met with them together. During these sessions she always felt free to say whatever was on her mind.

"Let me go over what I've just heard so I'm sure I understand. Eleanor is suggesting a one-week trip to Monte Carlo, which none of you can afford, staying at the very expensive Hotel de Paris, which none of you can afford, all the while impersonating four of the richest women in the world, which is illegal, immoral, and ridiculous—all of this in order to meet rich, exciting men who will sweep you off your feet—until they find out you're conning them, which will cause them to dump you faster than a door slam. Have I got this right?"

"Let me restate the situation in other terms," said

Eleanor, who began her usual courtroom pacing. She was
prepared and had rehearsed her summation. "The plane
fare and the hotel we can spread out over eight credit
cards—AmEx and Visa, we each have both. Eventually,
we'll pay it out. What are they going to do to us? Think
of it as a long-term mortgage. As for the impersonations,
they're just an extension of what every woman does every
day when she puts on her makeup. By the time she makes
her entrance into the world, she doesn't look like what
she really looks like, smells like. Maybe she's had a few
nips, tucks, lipos, augments, implants, caps, dye jobs—
whatever. It's been part of the game ever since Cleopatra
seduced Antony, ever since the Olympian gods assumed
guises to seduce mortals—and each other, for that matter.
All we're doing is taking it a step further. Borrowing a
few personas, like actors do every day. 'All the world's
a stage, and all the men and women merely players. They
have their exits and their entrances; and one *woman*, in
her time, plays many parts,' as he should have said. What
is a persona anyway? It's a *mask*. Check your Latin. If
we cause any men to be hopelessly smitten—how about
that word? Shit, when was the last time a man was *smitten*
with you? We'll deal with smitten when the time comes.
In the meantime, we live like royalty for a week. Live
like movers and shakers, instead of reading about them.
Let them read about *us*. Hell, maybe we'll even learn
something. It sure as shit beats Club Med again. I rest my
case."

The three women looked to Margo for a response. She
realized that a new tack was called for. "It is obvious that
you feel your depression can be cured by this journey.
You see yourselves as heroines on a quest. Slaying drag-
ons, overcoming dangers, darkness, fears, climbing mountains, the rain in your face, the wind at your back, seeking
treasure. The plane is your wings, the hotel your castle,
your costumes your armor. Penetrating impenetrable barriers to win the hearts of valiant Knights of the *Craps*
Table."

Eleanor slow-clapped her appreciation. "I have no time to blow smoke rings up your collectives asses. So here's the way I see it—down and dirty: You're right that this is a quest, but it's more than that. Even if we don't score, think of the goddamn adventure. If we stick together and treat it like a kids' treasure hunt, a scavenger hunt, a sorority initiation, we can probably have the time of our lives. Or, we can predict and anticipate all the terrible things that *might* happen and stay rooted in New Jersey. I'm for the hunt."

Again no one responded as all heads turned toward Margo—the *authority*. Margo stared at the ceiling and in her best bored teacher's voice intoned: "Death and rebirth. It's classic. A rite of passage. Who am I to hold you back? Fuck this crystal-balling the future; if I weren't in the middle of a divorce I'd probably go with you."

"Then we have your blessing?" said Darlene.

"You don't need my blessing; what you need is to get lucky at the casino before they bust you."

"Let's bring this to a vote," said Eleanor, not wanting to break the positive tension of the moment.

"Carla?"

"Why not?"

"Irene?"

"It's a mistake, but I'm in."

"Darlene."

"*Mais oui.* Let's do eet. *Cherchez les* men."

"Wait a minute," said Carla, "suppose they ask for our passports?"

Irene answered—in Russian-accented English: "But, babushka, they wouldn't dare ask the four richest women in the world for their passports. *Nyet.* Especially not after they receive my request for reservations. Leave that to me."

"How about credit cards? They'll see our real names?" said Darlene.

"Not until we check out—and by then, who cares?" Eleanor had all the answers.

*   *   *

THE NEXT DAY Irene set to work on her office computer. She quickly found a Russian Web site and printed out a coat of arms that she intended to reprint at the top of a piece of bogus stationery she was creating. The coat of arms showed a two-headed triple-crowned eagle with red beak and talons and spread-out wings holding a golden scepter in its right talon and the golden imperial orb in its left. On the eagle's chest was an etching of St. George on horseback, driving a spear into a dragon. It was impressive, but most important of all, it looked official. She was certain that no reservations manager would realize that it belonged to Tsar Ivan III of Moscow, circa 1497. The eagle symbolized the imperial pretensions of the Russian Tsar; now it would represent the imperial pretensions of the Baroness Natasha Feodorovna Karmanov.

After positioning the crest at the top center of a blank sheet of paper with her laser printer, Irene proceeded with the balance of the forgery. Under the majestic eagle she printed her assumed name, in commanding Gothic bold:

BARONESS NATASHA FEODOROVNA KARMANOV

The letter, addressed to the manager of the Hotel de Paris, was brief and simple, giving dates and requesting "accommodations" for the baroness and her dear friends, la Contessa Stephania di Romanesco, Mesdames Lou-Ann Barlow and Greta Harmon-Cates, and herself. It was signed by the Baroness's "secretary," one Adaliunda Onkudinov, and requested an immediate confirmation by return fax (the number given was Irene's home fax machine).

So much for passports. *They wouldn't dare ask.* But to be doubly certain, she had confirmed this with the French concierge of a prestigious New York City hotel. She told him she was a writer who was researching some information for a novel. He assured her (money having changed hands smoothly in advance) that neither his hotel nor the five-star hotel he had previously worked at in Paris would *ever* ask a "recognized" baroness for her passport—especially after receiving a letter such as she had exhibited to him.

Thus fortified and assured, Irene sent off the letter by fax that evening and the following morning found a confirmation in her machine. Done.

5
"The Four Men"

How cheerfully he seems to grin,
How neatly spreads his claws,
And welcomes little fishes in,
With gently smiling jaws.
        —Lewis Carroll

Maurice Gerard

Maurice Gerard had always lived on the edge. When his finances were negative he won at the gambling tables; when the rent came due for his luxurious suite at Monte Carlo's famed Hotel de Paris, he could always pawn one of his hoard of gold watches. If his aged classic Bentley cabriolet cried out for expensive repairs, well, his credit was good.

Everyone knew that he paid his bills after the season—in October at the latest—when he was usually flush with cash.

Maurice lived like a squirrel, hunting and gathering when the pickings were good and hoarding for the long winter when business was slow and he exchanged his grand suite for a small room at the back. He could have moved with the social somebodies, as they gathered for the seasons in Gstaad and Palm Beach, but Gerard loved Monte Carlo—his two morning breakfasts, one in bed and the second at the Café de Paris on the square opposite the casino, where he could watch all the action as the day began. A double *noisette,* his first cigar of the day, a Monte Cristo number seven, and four newspapers—the *Herald Tribune, Corriere Della Serra,* the London *Times,* and *Le Monde,* brought to his room every day promptly at eight by the head hotel concierge, Pierre Goujon, his friend and "business associate."

Women described Maurice as debonair, a word hardly used anymore, but debonair was the perfect choice, for Maurice was impeccably dressed by Savile Row's best, shoed by Lobb, tied and shirted by Turnbull & Asser, with accessories by Cartier (although these he rarely bought for himself). He was tall, in good physical shape for a man of his age, had a full head of silver-gray hair, and was classically handsome in the manner of a Douglas Fairbanks, Erroll Flynn, Omar Sharif, or Christopher Plummer. Women gravitated to him, loved to be seen with him.

His secret? Simply this: He adored women! He knew how to compliment them. He was elegant and, most of all, discreet. Important attributes if you were the most expensive gigolo in the south of France. But the word "gigolo" did not fit Maurice Gerard; he was no Richard Gere. Maurice rarely solicited business; it was mostly all by referral. Friends sent friends. They called in May, or wrote. They would be in the principality for a week and would he be available for certain social functions? They knew that Maurice fit in everywhere. He was gregarious, well read, fluent in five languages, and, as we have mentioned, so very discreet.

But Maurice Gerard had fallen off the edge. Today was to be his last as a resident of the luxurious Hotel de Paris. In short, he had been evicted for nonpayment of rent, three months in arrears. Of course the French would never use a word as harsh as "evicted." In fact, Gerard was the one to say that his last day would be today. The management had breathed a Gallic sigh of relief. Confrontation had been avoided and in France, especially in the principality of Monaco, confrontation was to be avoided at all costs.

Suite 100, overlooking the main square, the grand gambling casino, and the Mediterranean Sea beyond. Ah, if
walls could talk.

Maurice picked up a picture of an attractive woman,
in a silver frame. "Barbara," he said aloud, "maybe I
should have accepted your offer." But he had never taken
any of them seriously. Summer romances, at best. How
could it have happened? he thought as he carefully folded
the last of the six identical black silk robes custom-made
for him by Sulka. "Two ways; gradually and suddenly,"
as Hemingway had so aptly put it in *The Sun Also Rises*.
"Gradually and suddenly." Men had committed suicide
with that phrase in their minds as they—

Gerard's thoughts were interrupted by a knock at the
door. The movers had arrived. There was little to take
save a few trunks filled with personal items—and these
last six robes. In the past twenty-five years he had given
away (or allowed to be stolen) two hundred and ninety-
four of them.

Curricula vitae of his "clients," all dutifully logged in
a Gucci leather notebook kept in a locked drawer at his
bedside table. Maurice opened the book and glanced at
the last entry: Barbara Darworth, Palm Beach, Florida.
They had dined at the famed three-star restaurant Louis
Quinze; he had recommended the baby vegetables in a
black truffle-flavored broth followed by a perfect risotto
with *white* truffles, the filet of daurade with crisply fried
zucchini blossoms, and, of course, a magnum of Roederer
Cristal. Magnums were so perfect, even if you didn't finish them—and the wine was better, as well. Few realized
that. Who ordered a magnum for two anymore?

Barbara had loved being guided through the meal and
not having to deal with the *carte* and make choices. Of
course, that was his job. When the check came (and here
is where Maurice Gerard shone) he took out a checkbook
and wrote a check; it had been presigned by her, of
course. The tip was in cash; all *maîtres d'hôtel* preferred
it that way and Gerard was generous, but not casual, with

Barbara's money. It all looked so right—the way Barbara's friends had told her it would be.

They danced under the stars at the open-air Monte Carlo Sporting Club and then drove back to the hotel, past the glittering yacht harbor, in the open Bentley. Back to his hotel suite for a nightcap—ice cold vintage Krug in chilled Baccarat flutes. Barbara had changed into something more comfortable—one of Gerard's black silk monogrammed robes, of course, as had the two hundred and ninety-three before her.

As Aznavour sang "*Je t'aime*," Barbara presented Gerard with a token of her appreciation: a gold watch from Cartier, inscribed on the back. (He dearly wished that they wouldn't always have them inscribed; it was costly having the letters removed.)

A gold watch for a silk robe, more than a fair trade, *n'est-ce pas*? He pawned them all—except this last, which he had decided to keep for sentimental reasons, at least for a while. Memories.

A waiter brought in a tray that held a note and a bottle of vintage Moët in a crystal bucket, from the management. The French had class. Eviction accompanied by champagne. But, after all, he had been a paying client for twenty-four years and nine months. He checked his watch. Noon. Departure time, as agreed. One last look, one last sip of the bubbly, one last Aznavour before they took away the tape recorder: "*Après l'amour*," one of his favorites.

> *Yesterday, when I was young and many, many*
> *songs still waited to be sung . . .*

Misty eyes scanned pictures in silver frames. A lifetime, waiting to be packed away in moments. Beginnings. Endings. The cycles of life. So easy to view, with distance, like a rainbow far out at sea.

*   *   *

FOR MAURICE GERARD, it had all ended several years ago; that much, with distance, was now very clear. Today was merely the *delayed* ending. He should have left the game years ago. As the gambler said, "You gotta know when to hold, know when to fold . . ." It was not an ending he had ever envisaged; not in the best of times, not in the worst of times. He was a fixture in Monaco. Permanent. But he should have known that nothing is permanent, least of all an image. Smoke and mirrors. The years had brought fewer and fewer opportunities for him to perform his classy magic act. Those who did seek him out were of a different stripe: they wanted to know the price of everything, in advance, complained about the amount of gas consumed by the Bentley, and were not averse to tossing their platinum plastic on the tablecloth. Wilde was right: some knew the price of everything, the value of nothing.

Gerard never charged for his services. The ladies simply knew what he was worth and discreetly left envelopes where they would easily be found. In recent years the envelopes had contained less and less. One lady had the temerity to ask what his "hourly rate" was. He would have told her, but he had no idea. He just knew that he was three months behind in the rent—for the first time in a quarter of a century.

He had been married, once. No point in going into that. Suffice to say he had a child; a girl, a woman now, who lived in California. A grandchild, three years old; a boy whom he rarely saw, except once a year at Christmas— in a photo enclosed with the ritual card. It was his own fault.

Gerard had been head steward on the world's most elegant cruise ship, the *Île de France,* when an attractive, very wealthy woman made him an offer he didn't refuse: would he be interested in accompanying her for the next year on a world tour? Gerard was, at first, confused and somewhat taken aback. He was no gigolo. But when she explained her situation he became more sympathetic to her circumstances. She was simply not acceptable, as a single woman, in the circles in which she traveled, or wished to travel. She dreaded the prospects of her friends' ever-constant search for suitable dinner, theater, and travel companions.

She wanted a man with her. One who would be elegant and discerning. And she was willing to pay handsomely, more than double what Maurice was making at the time. Plus, there would be a generous allotment for expenses, clothes, etc. They would share hotel suites but he was given to understand that he would have his own separate room. She was not hiring a sexual partner.

The year had been very exciting. At its conclusion, he received the first of the Cartier watches and a note from one of her dearest friends asking if he could spare the time to show her the sights in Monte Carlo and escort her to the elegant Red Cross ball. No mention was made of "hiring" his services. After a quite enjoyable month, Maurice received his first "envelope" and his second Cartier gold watch. He had also given away the first of his silk Sulka robes. And, so it went. Maurice became an *available man* who could afford a suite at the Hotel de Paris, in Monte Carlo, and a new Bentley. He considered them to be business expenses, which, in effect, they were.

Was there sex involved? you ask. Sometimes yes, sometimes no. But there was always romance.

GERARD'S RETROSPECTIVE WAS interrupted by the clearing of a throat. No one could clear his throat like the head *concierge*, Pierre. But this time it was because Pierre was truly choked up. He and Maurice had been friends forever, it seemed.

"Ah, les vieux temps quand nous étions si malheureux," Pierre said as he kissed Maurice on both cheeks, in the classic French manner.

"I've always loved that expression of yours. 'Ah, the

good old days when we were so unhappy,' " said Maurice.
"Too bad they're over."

"Some reservations you may be interested in," said
Pierre. "I know you don't solicit business, but considering
how things are at the moment . . ." Pierre shrugged and
handed Maurice a large envelope. "They are—how do
you say?—heavyweights. Four of them."

"Thank you, *mon ami*, I've been thinking of retiring,
but one never knows, does one? The exigencies of life
have a way of changing one's priorities."

"Where will you be living?"

"I've found a decent flat—with a small view of the
sea, on Avenue Bouchard. Just within walking distance."

"Please, come for the newspapers," said Pierre. "At
least allow me to continue to do that. It would be my
great pleasure."

The two men embraced, both holding back tears.

"Can I drive you to your apartment?"

"No, I'm keeping the old Bentley until I can find a
buyer—which I probably never will."

Pierre Goujon nodded. Maurice Gerard nodded. What
more could one say? A cycle had ended. A cycle was
beginning.

Trevor Weymouth

Trevor Weymouth guided the silver Rolls Corniche up the
gravel path lined with majestic thirty-foot high cypress
trees, toward the gate of the magnificent Villa la Fortunata
on the Cap Ferrat. The damned gravel played havoc with
the car's mirror finish and got stuck in the tire treads, but
there seemed no alternative other than ugly paving or
hard-packed dirt. Problems of the rich and famous. Trevor
parked by the fountain at the bottom of the marble stairs
and walked up onto the terrace. The unobstructed view
over Beaulieu Harbor, and the Italian Alps beyond, never
ceased to make him smile. The grounds of the villa were
perfectly manicured; planted in mimosa, eucalyptus, olive,

orange trees, palms, and umbrella pines. Isolation and privacy, that's what the hundred or so villa owners cherished about the Cap Ferrat—a tiny six-hundred-acre peninsula jutting out into the Mediterranean between the coastal villages of Beaulieu and Villefranche, a fifteen-minute drive to Monte Carlo, a half hour to the Italian border.

Trevor glanced at his gold Rolex watch; he still had a free hour before people were expected, part of which he spent swimming in the fifty-meter heated lap pool. Today's guests would be arriving by boat. Twenty for lunch, a small party by Cap Ferrat standards. Trevor toweled off and strode into the house. Maids scurried about, nodding to him as he passed. One gave him a bit more than a knowing smile, which he ignored.

The kitchen was enormous, bigger than most restaurant kitchens in the area. The chef and his two assistants worked calmly, preparing the lunch. Trevor glanced at the printed menus, which would be set at each place. They would start with a cold vichyssoise, garnished with fresh snipped chives. Following would be chilled *langoustines*, tiny baby lobsters, grilled *loup*, sea bass; vegetables; a platter of cheeses; and, for dessert, chocolate soufflé. Trevor nodded his approval to the chef and left to dress.

A half hour later he stood on the villa's private dock dressed in a dark blue blazer, a white sea-island cotton shirt, with a pale yellow silk ascot instead of a tie. White pants and blue boating shoes completed the ensemble. He watched through binoculars as the invited guests alighted from a graceful hundred-foot sloop into the tenders that would bring them ashore. Trevor hadn't heard the approach of Prince Ibn Saud until he spoke.

"Is everything in order, Weymouth?"

"Yes, sir, of course. I'll be serving the '87 Corton Charlemagne with the *loup,* if that is agreeable? And the ninety Chateau Yquem with the soufflé?"

"Perfect. Did the Havanas arrive in good condition? The last shipment was a bit dry."

"In excellent condition. I've filled the humidors," said Trevor.

AT COCKTAILS, BEFORE the dinner, Trevor assumed another persona—that of pianist, for he was quite an accomplished player. Many of Ibn Saud's friends had tried to steal him away with offers of more money, but Trevor knew he had the perfect situation and was never tempted, at least not by any recent offers. Ibn Saud had stolen him away from his previous employer, for whom Trevor had worked on a three-hundred-foot yacht. So he knew the game. Stealing household help was an active sport in the south of France.

The party was, of course, a complete success. The prince expected no less from his butler and majordomo, Trevor Weymouth, and Trevor always delivered—flawlessly. He knew exactly how the rich liked to live and be served because he had once been rich himself. His one demand to his new employer was that he not have to dress in the traditional white jacket, black bow tie, and gloves of a servant; hence this afternoon's blazer outfit. On the other hand, if the occasion was black tie, he dressed accordingly. He always looked like one of the invited guests. In fact, that was his disguise. Without the butler's garb he felt more a part of his old life than his new one.

His family had owned homes in London, St. Moritz, and Palm Beach. Trevor was schooled by private tutors from his earliest days. His father was an inheritor. He loved to answer the question "what do you do?" with the response "Nothing. I'm an inheritor," and laugh his fool head off.

Trevor became what is locally known on the Côte d'Azur as a "Riviera layabout." He screwed around at university and, after graduation, decided to follow in his father's footsteps. After all, an inheritor wasn't such a bad thing to be. He bought a catamaran, his own villa on the sea at La Garoupe, a Harley, a Porsche, and tried to outdo the old man. His mother and father had no common interests and led separate lives. There was nothing in their relationship for him to covet, admire, or want to emulate. At times he wondered about how he was conceived; if they'd ever found the need to "do it" again after that. He assumed his father had numerous affairs, and for all he knew his mother had hers as well. The English were so circumspect that anything was possible. Although Trevor's home life had not disposed him positively toward the state of marriage, all that changed when he was twenty-five. He fell madly in love with and married an internationally famous and beautiful Norwegian supermodel; his collection of "toys" was now complete. Together they set out to imitate the frivolous escapades of the lost generation; of Scott and Zelda and their friends in Juan-les Pins. At age thirty, after five years of living in high style, the bottom dropped out. His father died and his inherited fortune dried up and blew away on a passing mistral. Not only was there no money but there were piles of bills—mountains of bills, under which Trevor found himself buried. When they dug him out he found himself homeless, boatless, carless, worthless, and wifeless. The supermodel divorced him the moment the "For Sale" sign went up in front of the villa. "What's love got to do with it?" Apparently, for her, nothing. She sued him for everything he didn't have. Trevor was devastated. She was the one thing in his life that mattered. He didn't realize the extent of his love and need for her until she wasn't his anymore. Notwithstanding the fact that Trevor was penniless, the court awarded her a heavy judgment for her years of devoted service. His plea of poverty went unanswered. It appeared as though his "salary" would be garnished until the end of his days—and it was. This episode would forever color the way he saw women—as predators to be feared . . . and taken advantage of at all turns.

After five years of living off friends, he decided to bite the bullet and get a job. His background prepared him

amply for a position as a butler (he preferred the term
"majordomo"). It wasn't so bad. His employers rarely
used their villas, so Trevor merely had to demean himself
for fewer than sixty days a year. Quite acceptable, all
things considered.

When the last guest had finally departed at six (on the
Côte d'Azur, lunch sometimes went right into dinner, if
you weren't careful), Trevor Weymouth walked onto the
terrace, poured himself a glass of champagne, and inhaled
the smell of the pinewood and wisteria. He raised his glass
in a toast to the view, which was magnificent. On clear
days he could see the hills of Italy rising behind the mountain peak called Tête de Chien, the head of the dog, which
sheltered Monte Carlo.

He had the best of everything, and nothing of his own.
The something that was missing wasn't women, he had
plenty of those. Rich, errant husbands frequently parked
their wives at a rented villa for a month or a top hotel
like La Reserve, La Voile d'Or, or the Grand while they
"traveled on business." His problem was the gold-and-
silver itch—money to cater to his still unforgotten sophisticated tastes. Occasionally, he worked with Maurice
Gerard. Amusing work, and sometimes a good dollar to
be made into the bargain. But he had never achieved his
aim—finding a rich woman who would treat him according to his elegant, carefree, pre-bankruptcy style. All of
the women would have married Maurice Gerard in a
heartbeat, but they saw through Trevor at the first pop of
the cork. They loved being escorted by this handsome
man who could be counted upon to observe all the formalities flawlessly—and they loved the sex, when there
was sex. But beyond that, all they saw beneath his elegant
exterior was the heart and mind of a cad who would seduce and abandon at the drop of a *chapeau*—and so they
treated him much like they knew he would one day treat
them, given half a chance. They took what they wanted,
paid him handsomely for it, and dumped him. Not that
there wasn't the occasional wealthy woman who was

tempted to give him his due in exchange for the superficiality of his company, but never tempted enough.

One would have thought that Trevor's shield of invulnerability against the charms of beautiful (but in his terms, poor) women who had offered themselves to him after his divorce—at times rather shamelessly—would at some point have cracked. But Trevor had steeled himself against that inevitable consequence and never let his emotions rule his head. Sex was great and to be sought after, but once he felt an *attachment* growing he was history.

Was there a softer, gentler, kinder, loving man lurking beneath the surface? If there was, his doppelganger had yet to make himself known.

Trevor stood on the villa's dock and looked westward. In the far distance he could see the Esterel Mountains that sheltered St. Tropez and, above them, the tiny dot in the sky that was Delta flight 89 from New York as it banked lazily over the sea, past Cannes and Cap d'Antibes, and began its descent into Nice airport.

The phone rang.

Julio Benvenuti

Julio had hardworking parents whose goal in life was to retire early and buy a coffee bar; the dream of so many Italians. Why was a coffee bar a fantasy? It meant long hours on your feet, standing behind the bar in the cold, the damp, the hot, the smoke. The upside was that you had intercourse with people. You were the gossip center of the neighborhood. You knew everyone and everyone knew you. *Imprenditore*: entrepreneur. Better than feeding the pigeons.

Julio was born when his mother was forty-three and his father was fifty-four—a happy accident. And so, he grew up in the bar and worked there part-time when he was a teenager in school and full-time when he graduated. He hated everything his parents loved, and dreamed of going to Rome to work at the film studios of Cinecittà—

doing anything. He loved the cinema and was a walking encyclopedia of film trivia.

"The music score for *Death in Venice* was written by . . . ?" he would ask, if the opportunity arose. (Few, if any, knew the answer.) "Mahler, of course," he would say, with an exaggerated shrug of his shoulders, the palms of his hands turned upward, his eyebrows raised.

Finally, an uncle who was "connected" got him in. Unfortunately, the job was in the studio cafeteria, so Julio had the same job as the one he left, with one exception: he was in the film business now. After a year of pleading with anyone and everyone he thought might have pull at the studio, Julio finally got a weekend job as an extra on the Lina Wertmuller film *Pasqualino Settebellezze* (*Seven Beauties*). It would prove to be the highlight of an otherwise rather unfulfilling career.

JULIO WAS VERY handsome and, therefore, popular with the ladies—especially the young starlets who couldn't afford decent meals. Within five years he had progressed to head chef at the cafeteria and was on a first-name basis with most of the executives, crews, directors, and stars who worked there. If fame can be said to be achieved by brushing up against fame, then Julio had indeed achieved a small measure of it. He catered meals on location for the crews and there was always an actress with whom he could hone his lovemaking skills while she was "on the picture." When he was twenty-eight he married Olivia, an English actress ten years his senior. Outside of the opportunity to perfect his English, the marriage was a disaster and lasted only a year, but that year was long enough for Julio to be further smitten by show business. He landed his second role when he was thirty; a one-line speaking part in a spaghetti western. It wasn't "they went thataway," but close enough to be forgettable. It was to be Julio's last appearance on the silver screen. When he was thirty-five he was in charge of catering a small Italian film being shot in the village of La Mortola, a stone's throw from the glamorous principality of Monaco. On his first day off he took the bus there—and never came back.

FOR JULIO, MONACO was a living, breathing movie that never ended, replete with a fairy-tale prince, princess, castle, and court. On that first day's visit, as he strolled around the main square, his jacket hanging idly around his shoulders, he had the odd but nevertheless very strong and sure feeling that somehow his life would be changed that day. Every Italian fiber in his body cried out for a chance encounter that would send him spinning in a new direction; some primeval instinct told him that this was to be an important day in his life—a turning point. While the streets he walked down were seemingly chosen at random—since he had never been in Monte Carlo before and knew only vaguely where he was—he felt he was being led. He looked down at his feet and, for some odd reason, decided to take exactly a hundred and fifty more steps before looking up. He was the camera; shooting his point of view: 147 . . . 148 . . . 149 . . . 150. Stop. Pan up slowly to frame, in medium close-up, an elegant woman of a certain age, la Contessa Maria de Largo, sitting alone at a table on the outdoor terrace of Le Louis Quinze, Monte Carlo's most expensive and most prestigious restaurant, at the world-famous Hotel de Paris. She was dripping with jewels, even though it was only lunchtime. Julio was dripping with charm, even though he had not a clue as to what he was going to do or say next. Her table was set for one. He would start again. Julio walked around the square in front of the hotel, mentally preparing for take 2. Stopping in the exact same place, he caught her eye, doffed his hat, and bowed. He had no idea what or who she was, but as he bowed grandly, he spoke the first words that came into his mind, as if the cameras were rolling: *"Contessa . . . buon giorno."* Her smile was enough to embolden him and he continued, in Italian, *"Mi chiamo*

Julio di Benvenuti. Will you do me the honor of joining me for lunch?"

She answered, casually, rather regally, in perfect Italian, *"Aspetto degli amici"*—I'm waiting for friends. But her body language told him that she was allowing him the opportunity to continue.

"A beautiful woman like you should not be kept waiting. Whoever he is—let *him* suffer."

There was no way he could afford the wine, let alone the cost of the lunch. It was doubtful that he even had enough for the tip. What he did have were *cojones*—balls. Julio knew he looked good that day. White suit, blue shirt, red tie, white Borsalino hat. He would play Rossano Brazzi in *Summertime,* for a few hours. Why not? Who would be hurt?

The contessa smiled and raised a finger at the waiter: *"Garçon, s'il vous plaît. Un couvert pour le monsieur."* The waiter quickly set another place at the table as Julio wended his way toward the contessa. "Not so fast. Slowly," whispered the imaginary director. "Don't get there before the waiter finishes setting your place. Good. Now kiss the air an inch over her hand. Perfect. Now sit."

Julio sat, snapped his fingers at the sommelier, and ordered a bottle of Saran Nature, a champagne that had no bubbles. "Much easier on the digestion, I find. Especially at lunch," he said to her. The contessa was impressed with his approach, even though she knew he was a fraud. There was something so positive and happy about him. Yes, she would allow him to entertain her. Julio wanted her to think that the bill would be his. What the hell. He'd deal with that when the time came. He needed to be in control.

"How did you know I was a contessa?" she said.

Julio spread his hands, in the Italian manner, as if to say, "What else could you be?" He smiled. She smiled. They smiled. She was in Monte Carlo for the month. She had just arrived that very day. He was a film actor, in between pictures. She paid the bill. Actually there was no bill ever presented. She had a five-room suite. He had his own room—sometimes. She knew many people in the film business; he was anxious to meet such people. Fortunately, for Julio, she was a bona fide contessa. Nevertheless, they were two kindred souls, each in need of what the other could offer—for a month. When she left, he applied for a job at Lino's Ristorante Elegante on the sea and was accepted as the number-two pasta chef. Within the year he was number one. On his days off he studied acting—the part of a gigolo, which he slowly perfected. It paid more than films, the work was steady, the surroundings perfectly suited to his newly acquired tastes. As years passed he knew that he was getting older and thought about a wife and *bambini*—but there was time for that. He didn't want to end up owning a coffee bar in San Remo.

Jean-Jacques Lacoste

Jean-Jacques (never called just Jean or Jacques, but sometimes "The Count," for reasons we shall learn about later) woke up promptly at six A.M., on a day that began like every other day, with a morning ritual that never varied. As he washed his face with cool water, after shaving, he inspected every inch of himself in the mirror. Hair was still fairly thick, streaked with gray; no thin spots, yet. Skin: a few wrinkles about the eyes that he hadn't noticed before—to be expected. Teeth in good shape; he was religious about their care. Body: he worked out every other day at the Monte Carlo Grand Hotel gym. He could still afford to take his clothes off with the lights on. Plumbing. He hefted it. In working order. He was tall, over six feet, and, depending upon how he dressed, could pass for a banker, a boat captain, a lawyer, a doctor. He wasn't any of these things—not by a long shot. While he was growing up, his father, who was a concierge at a hotel in Lyons, had tried to interest his son in the hotel business. He sent Jean-Jacques to the best hotel school in Lausanne,

Switzerland, and his son did well at his studies until he became interested in soccer. It became a passion with him; and he was good. So good that he was signed by the prestigious Marseilles club for a very handsome bonus and salary. He became well known for his exploits on the field scoring goals, and off the field scoring with the ladies. He was a success with women because he had time for them. He listened to them and truly (if only for a time) loved them deeply. Like the hero in Truffaut's *The Man Who Loved Women*, he had seemingly limitless passion. Six years later he had quickly (not quickly enough, as it turned out) glanced at a woman in the stands—causing his career to come to an abrupt end (blindsided by an opposing player; breaking his leg in six places). His entire world fell apart. He bought a small hotel with his savings and married a local girl from St. Étienne. Neither attempt at a normal bourgeois life succeeded, and after three months spent in an alcohol rehab center, he found himself divorced, and in bankruptcy. He simply could not adjust to the real world outside of the soccer stadium. He desperately missed the spotlight, the sound of the crowd chanting his name when the ball came his way. How would he ever find anything to compare with that? He had never considered what life would be like without the adulation, excitement, and the money—all for being good at kicking a little black-and-white ball. He began to think about a regular home life, becoming a nine-to-five man, because truth was, he felt incomplete without a marital partner. But it never went further than the thought that maybe he could find a *rich* woman to marry.

Jean-Jacques began to dress, carefully. Black socks, crisp white shirt, black bow tie. He was intelligent, spoke English as well as French. He could survive a shallow discussion about art, politics, finances, or talk in depth about his *main* topic: the weather. The Count, as he was called, only by close friends, pulled on a pair of well-pressed blue trousers and a matching blue jacket with gold epaulets and three gold stripes near the cuff of each sleeve. A gold lapel pin completed his attire.

When he put on his peaked cap, he could have been mistaken for an airline pilot. It was when Jean-Jacques checked himself in the mirror one last time that he had the revelation. For the first time in his life he looked at his reflected image and realized who he was, what he was, and what he would always be. That he'd gone as far in life as he would ever go. That this was the top. It would be level and then downhill from here. He believed in balances in life. He knew he was now paying for those years when he was ambivalent about the future. In fact, he had never considered the future for a moment. He was the Count, he was young, handsome, a sports hero—it would go on forever. He spent everything; saved nothing for rainy days because in his life the sun would always shine—until one day it didn't—and he had been walking under his personal cloud for what should have been the best years of his life.

Men, or women, who have this revelation at some point in their brief journey on earth must either deny or suppress it because the reality would not be acceptable to most. Jean-Jacques took a deep breath. "You have finally risen to the absolute highest level of your incompetence," he said aloud.

He willed his facial muscles, which had relaxed into deep sadness, to give his woeful countenance its usual outward appearance of placidity. Turning smartly on his heel, he walked out of his tiny room at the top of the hotel, down one flight of stairs, where he took the elevator to the lobby. Jean-Jacques Lacoste, a.k.a. the Count, was always prompt; you could set your watch by the time he started his morning shift as a doorman at the Hermitage Hotel.

6

"Sailing into the Wind"

All great changes are irksome to the human mind.
—*John Adams*

No MATTER HOW closely you look at an apartment or a house before you take possession, the reality of living there is always different from what you expected. Small things that you didn't notice the first time now take on new and oddly important dimensions. Moving a person can be compared to moving a tree: roots are dug up, carefully wrapped, and replanted in the new location. But in the act of transplantation, a profound disturbance occurs. Leaves on certain branches wilt as the roots struggle to reorient themselves in the foreign soil—and hopefully, although some roots die, the tree usually survives. But it has undergone a change and will never be exactly as it was. We don't realize the extent to which we are creatures of habit until we relocate ourselves. Suddenly everything is wrong; nothing's in the right place; every action that was automatic must now be considered, until new imprints are stabilized. For some, this never happens, and that person remains a stranger in his own home. In fact, it never becomes a home, but merely a transitional location, both mentally and physically.

Such was the case with Maurice Gerard as he took the tiny, old elevator to his floor and walked down the dingy hallway to his new abode. Was it this dingy when he first saw it? The door opened to reveal a one-room studio apartment badly in need of . . . everything. His few possessions did nothing to make him feel at home. He walked to the single window and opened it. Leaning out and turning to his left, he could see a sliver of the sea; otherwise the room faced another gray building. It was a far cry from his sumptuous suite at the Hotel de Paris. He felt like a man, used to a hundred-foot yacht, now having to make do with an old twelve-foot Boston whaler. It was a place to come in out of the rain—no more. A bed without breakfast. All of his daily energy would have to be spent in planning his escape.

He sat down on a hard chair by a small table that was serving as a makeshift desk. It held a telephone. The pictures in silver frames looked out of place and he removed them to make room for a large folder that contained *curricula vitae* on four women. Four very rich women. In fact, four of the richest women in the world. But that could wait. First he had to finish the unpacking of his wardrobe—or as much of it as would fit in the small, rickety armoire.

There were no pictures of the women in the file, but Maurice had arranged for them to be taken at the airport. He checked his watch. The photographer he had hired would be doing that shortly.

As he worked, Delta flight 89 from New York was on its final approach into Nice airport.

Now, reader, you obviously know that the four women are going to meet the four men, but that was preordained and you've known for some time. In that regard, you are ahead of the women, who knew nothing, and the men, who thought they knew everything. It is when we are absolutely certain that we let our guard down, that we make mistakes.

At that very same moment, Inspector Georges Delarue,

of the Monaco police, and his number one, Bernard La-
combe, were sitting in the café opposite the Hotel de
Paris. Neither was in uniform. Both, from time to time,
between sips of coffee and bites of croissants, traded
sheets of paper—all from a dossier on four of the richest
women in the world. Delarue had arranged for photos to
be taken at the airport. That would be occurring shortly.

Monte Carlo was known as one of the safest places on
the globe (unless you take into consideration that the
wearing of seat belts, while driving, is not mandatory),
and Delarue intended to keep it that way. They would
keep tabs on the four women, unobtrusively, of course,
just to be sure that their visit to the principality was without incident. Delarue was not in the least suspicious about
the women; his department gave the same attention to
every wealthy, high-profile person who visited. Most
times it was cursory; business as usual.

7
"The Quest"

To dream the impossible dream
—Darion and Leigh, "The Impossible Dream"

FOUR HYPERVENTILATING WOMEN entered the arrivals terminal at Nice airport. As they headed toward the customs area to claim their luggage, three things happened in quick succession. Two photographers using identical 300mm Nikon telephoto lenses took their pictures from fifty yards distant. They were unseen either by each other or by the four women. At the moment the cameras clicked, a uniformed emissary from the Hotel de Paris walked up to the women and doffed his hat. He carried a small leather-encased notepad from which he read: "Mesdames Barlow, Harmon-Cates, Baroness Karmanov, Contessa di Romanesco—*oui?* Yes?"

Not expecting this, all of the women had the same thought at the same time: they had been caught, were being arrested.

Eleanor was the first to speak. "Is there a problem, Officer?"

"Not at all. If you will please follow me."

"Shit," said Irene. "Fucking paddy wagon and we haven't even seen Monte Carlo. These guys are good."

"Let me do the talking," said Eleanor.

The man led them past the luggage claim area and outside.

Eleanor caught up with him. "Hey, what about our luggage?"

"That will be taken care of. Everything is arranged, madame."

Just as Eleanor was about to pull out her passport and demand to be taken to the American consulate in Nice, a huge black Rolls-Royce Phantom V slithered to a silent stop before them. The uniformed emissary quickly opened the rear passenger door. "Courtesy of the Hotel de Paris. Madame Barlow," he said, looking past Eleanor.

As he put his hat back on, Eleanor saw, for the first time, a band on the brim that read HOTEL DE PARIS— MONTE CARLO. Needless to say, she was floored. "Helluva taxi," was all she could manage as Darlene swept past and into the car. When Carla started to follow her, the man held up a hand and gestured toward a second identical Rolls that had pulled up behind the first. *"S'il vous plait, Contessa."* Irene's turn was next as yet another Rolls Phantom materialized. She entered, majestically, chin raised. Eleanor deflated and tumbled into the last of the black British behemoths, realizing she had been holding her breath for over a minute, as she sometimes did unconsciously when juries filed back into the courtroom with their verdicts.

All of the women had ridden in limos before, but calling these stately sloped-back, vintage Rolls Phantom V limos was like calling a castle a ranch house. A Phantom V was not simply transportation, it was built to be a unique experience. Cocooned in skin-soft Connolly cream-beige glove leather upholstery, Wilton carpets with lambswool overrugs (in which to bury their stockinged feet), and flawless burled walnut-and-silver fittings, the women felt like they were in a special world—a private bubble that separated them from the common people motoring past in their endlessly numbered Mercedes and Japanese wannabes. Absolute quiet; the loudest sound, the ticking of the clock, as the famous ads used to proclaim. The Rolls is certainly the least economical car to drive, hence its appeal to the very wealthy, the pretenders to wealth, and film producers. Glass separated the huge rear section; contact with the liveried driver was by intercom. A hidden bar was furnished with crystal and silver. All of this splendid, unaccustomed luxury was a perfect way to begin their adventure into this foreign land.

Irene realized that her neck was tired from holding her nose in the air as the chauffeur exclaimed, in cultured British tones, "Would the baroness care for a glass of chilled champagne; excellent after the long flight."

Irene really didn't want champagne, but she was dying to see how the driver intended to accomplish the feat of serving her while traveling at seventy miles an hour on the autoroute.

"Oh, maybe a splash . . ."

The driver touched a button that opened the bar built into the rear of the front seat. A champagne bucket was revealed, holding a bottle of Roederer Cristal. The rear of the bar opened into the front seat so that the driver could reach down, without taking his eyes from the road, and deftly pour out a glass, which Irene took with a smile. She decided to try her first word in French. What better time? *"Merci,"* she said, with what she hoped was a Russian accent, as the bar slid silently closed and a small table upon which to rest her glass magically glided out to her right. At that moment she noticed the car carrying Carla to her left and the other two behind it. As the triplet Phantoms passed, Irene raised her *coupe de champagne* and toasted them all; her noblesse oblige in full bloom. This isn't too difficult, she thought.

The three others thought the verboten C-word, but said nothing.

The drive from Nice to Monte Carlo took about forty minutes, along the lowest of the three roads known as *corniches*—the *basse, moyenne,* and *grande;* low, middle, and high—that were cut into the cliffs of the Alpes Maritimes. All of the women had their guidebooks out as the Phantoms passed the harbor of Nice, following the coastline toward Villefranche, Cap Ferrat, Beaulieu, Cap d'Ail, and into Monte Carlo, around the yacht harbor and up the hill to the main square, which held the gambling casinos, the café, the Hotel de Paris, and a magnificent park, planted with exotic specimen trees. The women were overwhelmed with the beauty of the coast and petrified at the thought of making a mistake in this exotic fairy-tale world they were entering.

They had all read up on their history of the Riviera and knew that when the casino was built, in 1868, there was no lower road access; one rented a horse and carriage and climbed endlessly, on packed dirt roads, up to the *moyenne corniche* and then down into Monte Carlo. A wearying journey that many were willing to make because, at that moment in time, Monte Carlo had the only gambling venue in France and Italy. Others arrived by yacht or had local fishermen ferry them in from Beaulieu Harbor. A favorite ruse of the fishermen was to "accidentally" tip a passenger's trunk into the water (they knew exactly where the shallow shoals were). After apologizing profusely and agreeing not to take their usual exorbitant fee, the crafty fishermen deposited their enraged clients in Monte Carlo and returned to claim their pirated booty. When the railroad line was built a few years later, one could travel from Paris through to Monte Carlo, and the casino flourished. It is almost impossible to comprehend the wealth of some of the royal visitors; for example, the reprobate King of the Belgiums—Leopold II—personally owned all of the rich Belgian Congo. Yes, personally. Buying diamonds for casual acquaintances or building grand villas for mistresses was pocket money to him and his royal Euro-cronies, the dukes, marquesses, barons, princes, counts, and especially the crazed blue-blooded aristocracy from Russia. It was not uncommon for clients of the Hotel de Paris to rent apartments or even entire

floors for the winter season and have them redecorated
with their own store of furniture. The kitchens of the hotel
were open twenty-four hours a day and had chefs from
all over Europe and Asia catering to every taste. During
the lunch and dinner hours one chef made soufflés continually so that they would be ready at a moment's notice,
if ordered. The nobility never waited for their soufflés to
rise; that was for the proles (Irene was determined to order
a soufflé at the earliest opportunity and time its arrival).
Nor did they eat in the public dining rooms but, rather,
in *salles à manger privées* or in their vast suites. Contact
with the staff of the hotel was made through their couriers,
aids, and majordomos, who traveled with them and stayed
at the hotel in rooms reserved as *chambres des courrier*.
Royalty rarely spoke directly to anyone and vice versa.
The start of the First World War in 1914 brought an end
to such caprices, and when the war was over, Monte Carlo
became a haven for the *nouveau riche;* the industrialists
and those who had actually worked to attain their fortunes.
Though the principality has undergone many changes
since then, it is still one of the favored tax havens of the
world and a magnet for the rich and wanna-stay-rich. It
is worth reflecting upon the fact that citizens of Monte
Carlo are not allowed to gamble. It was F. Scott Fitzgerald
who wrote, "The rich are different from us," and Ernest
Hemingway who was reputed to have answered, "Yes,
they have more money."

Outside of the imposing entrance of the hotel was a
small parking area that held dozens of the world's more
expensive and exotic motorcars. Little mini-buses were
parked nearby, for use by clientele of the hotel. They
made continual round-trips to the beach, where private
cabanas sheltered topless beauties of both sexes. The
beach complex held several restaurants, the Monte Carlo
Beach Hotel, and a huge Olympic swimming pool where
the *haut monde* swam. Most everything that made money
was run by the Societé Bain de Monaco, owned by the

prince and his partners, and their emblem, SBM, was everywhere.

Security in Monte Carlo is very tight, with television cameras that survey activity at most intersections and borders that can be sealed in seconds. It is one of the few places in the world—maybe the only place—where women can wear all of their jewels at night without fear.

Monte Carlo, a scant square mile that contains one hundred and thirty restaurants, is unlike any other on earth. It is two different towns; the old town of Monaco, with its palace built on the top of a flat rocky promontory, and the new town of Monte Carlo, sloping down to the sea, where it meets the huge yacht harbor. Skyscrapers sit cheek by jowl with old palaces. The women found the tiny jewel of a city rather startling to come upon after passing the sleepy seaside villages.

As the caravan bearing the four Cinderellas pulled up in front of the marble columns framing the entrance of the hotel, four footmen, their liveries covered with gold and silver, raced up immediately to open the doors of the black coaches, while doormen, assistant managers, and the staff of the *conciergerie* stood at attention; truly a turnout fit for royalty. This is how Cinderella must have felt, thought Darlene as she grasped the white-gloved helping hand of one of the footmen and stepped forth into the rarefied air reserved for the fortunate *Monégasques,* as natives of Monaco are called. Irene took a deep breath to steady her nerves. Prince Charming, I'm here, she said to herself. Carla felt like the former Italian film star she was pretending to be. All Eleanor could think was that if they got through the next few minutes they were in the game.

Pierre Goujon, the hotel's redoubtable concierge, rushed to greet them: "Welcome to the Hotel de Paris, mesdames. We are honored to have you with us. Please allow me to show you to your apartments." He pronounced it *ah-par-tah-mont,* with a soft *t* at the end. "Your luggage has been delivered. I took the liberty of having the housekeepers

Eleanor summed it up with: "Money talks—bullsh
alks."

"Let's hope not," concluded Irene.

DARLENE WAS IN the tub, up to her neck in bubbles, wear
ing earphones connected to a Sony Walkman that held he
Berlitz French language cassette. She had been studying
French ever since the plan was made, and was determined
to learn at least a bit, even though it appeared that everyone in the hotel spoke English. Actually, they spoke
French first and then immediately translated themselves
when they saw the first hint of the blank stare; like the
maid who had just left. "*Bon soir, madame. Je vous ai
apporté un peignoir en tissu-éponge:* I've brought you a
warm robe for after the bath." Darlene decided she would
do the same, just in case, and so after she said, "*Vous
êtes très gentille,*" she followed with the translation—
"You are very kind"—even though one never said that to
a maid. Anyway, it was the thought that counted. The
French appreciated foreigners who made an attempt at
their language, even if the syntax or accent was invariably
wrong. It amused the French that Americans held up two
fingers to ask for two of something, while the French held
up a thumb and forefinger. This meant that Americans
always got three when they wanted two and two when
they wanted one (since one is just a thumb). Many Americans had learned to order either one or three croissants
to avoid the embarrassment of not being able to pro-
nounce the French word for two. Darlene practiced—
"*deux:* two"—but the maid always asked her how many,
causing her to hold up two fingers, for which she got
three! *Très* goddamn complicated, she thought.

They say the French are chauvinistic, meaning they are
unduly partial to things French—but why not? Isn't that
the reason Americans love to come to France? Surely it's
not to go to another McDonald's—or MacDo, as the
French call it—which have proliferated in France like rab-

steam and hang everything. I hope you find it all in good
order."

At mention of the word "apartments," the four women
exchanged terrified glances, but managed to hold their
tongues as they all forced smiles. Eleanor was the first to
speak. "Well, it is *wonderful* to be back in Monte Carlo.
It's been *too* long." And with that, she swept up the marble staircase.

"I guess you won't be wanting to see our passports?"
said a nervous Darlene, smiling sweetly and causing the
others to hold their collective breaths.

Irene broke the tension: "Oh, isn't she amusing? Passports. Oh, Lou Ann, you *are* a caution . . . as the Americans say." Pierre just smiled. He was used to the
eccentricities of the super-rich.

Hurdles one and two having been passed, the women
were on their way to their rooms—make that apartments—
without having had to show either their passports or credit
cards. At the moment they entered the elevator, the sur-
reptitious photos taken of them at the airport were being
processed, enlarged, and printed in two separate locations.
The ones destined for Maurice Gerard were, by far, the
better, while the police photographer's images lacked cre-
ativity and were badly composed. Nevertheless, both versions served their purpose and both were being perused
with great interest.

THE FOUR APARTMENTS were approximately identical in
size—living room, dining area, bedroom, dressing room,
two enormous bathrooms with all the gold-plated bells
and whistles, a butler's pantry, and entrance foyer—and
all had large balconies that faced the yacht harbor and the
sea beyond. Each was decorated with different fabrics and
a tasteful selection of antiques and art. Crystal chandeliers, *trompe-l'oeil* paintings on the ceilings, marble floors
covered here and there with rare Oriental carpets. Ornately
framed mirrors, fireplaces, and those three buttons familiar

to every stayer in *luxe* French hotels: housekeeper, floor waiter, bellman. There were no mini-bars. There were masses of flowers in painted vases and several sterling-silver ice buckets holding bottles of champagne, Perrier, Evian, and diet Coke. The linens were by Portault, the fabrics by Pierre Frey, the paintings by Picasso, Matisse, and Braque. The four suites took up the entire third floor of the hotel. Eleanor immediately called an urgent meeting of the support group in what she insisted on calling her "room."

"Ladies, we are in deep *merde*."

"I don't have enough credit on my plastic to cover an hour here, let alone a week. What do you think this floor costs?" said Carla.

"Whatever it costs, my Visa card is going to self-destruct. I say we call down and ask for four single rooms or two doubles," said Irene.

Silence greeted that suggestion. No one wanted to start over again now that they were safely ensconced.

"Maybe one of us will meet a rich guy," said Darlene.

"You think some affluent asshole, some moron Midas, is going to pay for all of this? Maybe you give great head, sister, but not this great," said Eleanor, sweeping her arms around the room. "We're here to meet rich guys, sure—but let's not be more ridiculous than we already are. This is supposed to be fun, right?"

"So, how do we pay for it all?" said Carla.

"How much are we talking about?" said Darlene.

"I saw a sign on the back of my bedroom door; 17,500 francs a day. How much is that in real money?" said Irene.

Eleanor scribbled on a pad and came up with $3,500 a day, each. "For the four of us, that's about seventy thousand total, minimum. Seventeen thousand five hundred apiece."

"I say we go for it. What can they do to us?" said Irene.

Eleanor was running the numbers on her pad. "I make

it, with the interest, around a hundred bucks pay it out over four years."

"No problem. We get rid of our trainers. We anyway," said Carla.

"You think it'll work, Eleanor? I mean, legal Darlene.

"I had a case like that once," Eleanor said. "card company gave my client a hard time and then s for the long payout. They didn't have much choice. It either that or sue. Costs them too much to sue. So, bet says they'll give us a hard time and then take payout."

"We don't really have any other choice, do we?" said Carla.

"There's always cut and run. At the end of the week we leave all the clothes and luggage in the room and go home. After all, they don't even know who we are," said Darlene.

"Somehow I think they'd find out in a hurry," said Eleanor.

"Maybe we'll get lucky at the tables," said Carla.

"We can't think about this or we'll screw up," said Irene. "Just remember that we're all very rich—so rich that they'll give us anything we want. So act rich."

"Any ideas?" said Darlene.

"Rich equals eccentric. The more normal we act, worse."

"When you don't know what to say," said Eleanor, "just smile and say clever things like: 'Oh, that so interesting,' or, 'Oh really,' or, 'That's fascinating.'"

"What do we do next?" said Carla.

"I suggest we all go back to our rooms and get d to kill."

"Kill or be killed," added Irene.

"It's just as easy to marry a rich man as a poor from Carla.

"Money goes to money," said Darlene.

bits (over eight hundred at last count). They come to enjoy the patrimony of France—which includes the architecture, art, food, and ambience of things uniquely French. When the U.S. government sends ambassadors to European countries, those chosen rarely speak the language of the host country, while European ambassadors to the United States always speak English. The reason for this is quite simple: U.S. ambassadorial positions are awarded as a form of political patronage, many times to those with little or no diplomatic experience. In Europe, France especially, diplomats are educated as such, as a career, from the time they enter university. Darlene remembered all this from her college courses. Maybe she'd get a chance to use her brain instead of her bosom over here. Doubtful. Maybe, in addition to. In any event, she would prepare for both eventualities.

There seemed to be champagne everywhere in France. There were even two bottles of Moët by the tub—amid the bath oils, and what appeared to be at least a half-gallon bottle of Chanel No. 5. Darlene wondered if she should use it; if it was included in the price of the room or was an extra—not that it mattered how much she couldn't afford. She poured a thimbleful in the water. What the hell.

NONE OF THE women had managed to sleep on the overnight flight from New York and after luxuriating in their respective baths, they were seriously jet-lagged and opted for a nap, which lasted until early evening. Refreshed but still tired, they contacted each other to plan the evening. When Carla suggested room service in her apartment, the others quickly agreed. Tomorrow they'd have a look around, do some touristy things, and prepare for the evening, which had been arranged: cocktails in the famous hotel bar, dinner, and show at the Sporting Club—Julio Iglesias was performing—followed by a visit to the casino. Monte Carlo has three venues for gambling: the venerable original, with its rococo turrets and green copper cupolas, housing many gaming rooms; slots in the Salle Blanche, roulette and *trente et quarante* in the Salle Europe, craps and blackjack in the American Room, *chemin de fer* and *banques à deux tableaux* and pai gow poker in the Salons Privés (for high rollers only; one had to be formally attired and pass inspection to gain entrance). These were hushed, glittering, chandeliered gaming rooms decorated in ornate style, with exotic marble flooring, soaring onyx marble columns, huge gilt-framed mirrors, bronze sculptures, and enormous allegorical paintings. One could, on the other hand, try the slick, modern, noisy, new Las Vegas–style casino behind the Café de Paris, where slots, electronic games, blackjack, and crap tables predominated, or the summer casino at the beach. The four women would be where the heavy hitters were—at the old casino, in the Salles Privés for high rollers.

The arrival of the most elaborate room service they had ever seen or even imagined, accompanied by a *maître d'hôtel* and two waiters, was yet one more surprise in a day of surprises. No wheeled-in cart; linen was laid on the dining table, vermeil tableware and a selection of elegant stemware at each place, huge white napkins that looked like they had never been used, a selection of silver serving pieces, four heavy crystal finger bowls with miniature orchids floating in them, and, finally, the food, artfully arranged on a side table.

As the *maître d'hôtel* announced each dish as it was placed, Eleanor whispered to Carla, "I thought you just ordered some munchies and sandwiches?"

"I did."

"*Des petites langoustines*—cold baby lobsters—caviar de beluga, blini, *saumon fumé*—smoked Norwegian salmon—*des sandwichs aux truffes blanches*—white truffle sandwiches—*mini-soufflés au fromage,* steak tartare, *taramosalata, des huîtres belons*—oysters—*barquette de champignons*—mushrooms—and *bourekakia.* I hope everything is adequate. And to drink? Some wine?"

"I don't suppose there's any chance of getting a beer?" said Eleanor.

"*Bien sûr, madame*—certainly," he said as he walked over to a huge ornate armoire and pressed a button at the side. The doors opened, revealing a well-stocked bar complete with a rack of fine red wines and a glass-enclosed, temperature-controlled refrigeration unit for the whites. A separate section held a wide selection of mineral waters, soft-drinks and beer.

"Budweiser?" said Eleanor, knowing she'd have to settle for one of the imported brands, which were, of course, domestic here—but she was wrong.

"Would Madame prefer lite or classic?"

Eleanor had a lite beer—several, in fact—while Carla drank a *cassis blanc de blanc,* a lovely, fruity white from the coastal town of Cassis, just west of Marseilles, that was excellent. Irene asked for a shooter of frozen Stoli and Darlene had a Perrier—which came served with Perrier ice cubes, of course.

Most surprising to them was that one of the waiters stayed until the women had finished—serving, pouring, but otherwise invisible. Day one: perfect.

Long ago and far away,
I dreamed a dream one day,
And now that dream is here before me . . .

. . . and the four women dreamed of fairy-tale romance and storybook love . . .

8
"Double Jeopardy"

*The world will never learn to beware
of these stately gentlemen . . . which is why
the confidence trick is still running.*
—*William Bolitho*

INSPECTOR DELARUE SAT in an unmarked minivan across the street from Lino's Ristorante Elegante by the Sea. It was ten o'clock in the morning, well before opening time. His assistant, Bernard, operated the video camera, shooting through the one-way glass. One by one, the four men arrived. Julio Benvenuti was the first to be captured on tape.

Delarue spoke into a microphone, narrating the video for possible future use. "Ah, the infamous Julio Benvenuti. Claims he was a movie star in Rome. More like an out-of-focus extra. Although we've had complaints lodged against him from several women for theft of jewelry and nonpayment of loans, none of them ever stayed in the principality long enough to press charges. We'd like to throw him out if we had a reason that would stand up in court."

Ten minutes later another man appeared and entered the restaurant.

"This one is French, Jean-Jacques Lacoste—former soccer star, arrested several times in the last few years for possession of stolen goods, extortion, and illegal gambling. Plea-bargained his way out by implicating and giving testimony against others, so he has no arrest record. It was, as they say, *effacé*—expunged. He used to repair one-armed bandits but now he's a part-time doorman at the Hermitage Hotel, and, good-looking devil that he is, works for Maurice Gerard from time to time, during the season.

"Ah, Mr. Trevor Weymouth. Tells the ladies he is an inheritor. A would-be inheritor is more like it. Ha. So far they've all seen right through him. The rich women he chases all love his good looks and charm, but he's never managed to worm his way into their fortunes. We almost had him a few years ago when he was working on a yacht. An investment scam, but the investigation led to a dead end in Liechtenstein. Poof.

"Here we have Maurice Gerard, also known as the King of Hearts, for good reason. An old friend of mine for many years, a true gentleman. Calls himself an 'adviser.' Women of a certain age apparently find him irresistible. So far he has never done anything illegal, but now that his circumstances have changed . . . one never knows what a desperate man will do, does one? This meeting, for example. Why? Certainly they are not having pasta at ten in the morning?"

"Why does he need these other men?" asked Bernard.

"They handle, as it is called, his overflow. Whatever women he has no time for he passes along to them and takes a percentage of their take."

"Nothing illegal there that I can see."

"Nothing illegal, *yet*. But one can never be too sure of anything in Monte Carlo."

MAURICE GERARD, TREVOR Weymouth, and Jean-Jacques Lacoste sat at a table in the otherwise empty restaurant, waiting impatiently for Julio Benvenuti to join them.

"Julio," Trevor shouted, "what the hell are you doing in there? We don't have much time."

"I'm coming—two seconds," Julio answered, from the kitchen.

As Maurice opened his large folder, Julio walked in carrying a steaming dish of *spaghetti aglio e olio peperoncino,* which he put in the center of the table.

"*Uno spuntino*—a little snack—it will help us to think better, no?" said Julio.

"Please, Julio, not at ten o'clock in the morning. It is making me ill, take it away," said Maurice. "Just bring some coffee."

Julio spread his hands and shrugged. *"Va bene, presto,"* he mumbled as he reluctantly took the platter back into the kitchen, forking a few twirled strands into his mouth as he went. "Vincenzo," he called out to his second, *"quattro cappuccini."*

After the coffee with steamed milk was brought to the table, Maurice passed photos of the four women around the table.

"I hope these are better than last year. One of mine actually asked me for her change after I paid the bill," said Trevor.

"È vero, è vero," said Julio. "I had exactly the same problem."

"I think you'll find these women quite different. I've done a little research. They're four of the richest women in the world. I don't think they'll be asking for change. Now, this time I have something a little different in mind. Here's how I see it working." The others listened—a bit taken aback—for what the classy King of Hearts was describing was pure con, all the way. For the first time in Maurice's long career, money was to be the objective, the sole objective, and they would do whatever it took to get it, even if it meant pretending to be in love.

"You should have married the last one, Maurice," said Jean-Jacques. "We all wondered why you didn't; knowing you were in trouble. She was quite an attractive woman, not to mention very rich."

"You're probably right, but I had been so used to putting up automatic defenses against marriage that, as usual, I hid behind my façade of prepared banal excuses. Marriage has always seemed like defeat to me. Something one agrees to when there are no other options, something that young people are compelled to do. As well they should, I imagine. But I've fought that war once, and lost. Not a reason to disparage the rite, true—but when one has been a bachelor for so long, just the thought of it is almost paralyzing. Complete independence is addictive. My problem is that I have never had the time to be lonely, but now I see that prospect looming before me. Possibly I could cope, but loneliness combined with poverty is an event I would rather not entertain. What I am saying, in too many words, is that I find I am out of excuses, and options. I should have left the table long ago while I still had chips to cash in."

"So, we try to break the bank," said Trevor.

"Yes, with the perfect crime of love."

"Looks like we have four good chances? Winner take all?" said Julio.

"No. That has to be part of the arrangement. Think of it as sharing four lottery tickets; the chances of winning are increased significantly," said Gerard. "Let me give you some of my thoughts."

AS GERARD SPELLED out the details of his plan, the four women were spending their first morning at the hotel spa, Les Thermes Marins, housed in a super-luxurious setting of pink marble and light woods.

The four impostors had shown up in their American-style gym gear. Eleanor wore gray sweats; Darlene, skin-tight green-and-gold spandex and leg warmers; Carla, an L.A. Gear outfit that made her look like an aging cheer-leader; and Irene, gym shorts and a printed tank top that

read UNDER THIS I'M NAKED, a gift from Eleanor that she
wore reluctantly. After being relieved of their unsuitable
outfits by the spa staff, the four women were dressed in
official white spa outfits and given a list of treatments that
were available. Eleanor told them that they all wanted "the
works," head to toe, which consisted of a light workout
in the fully equipped gym, followed by a thermal bath, a
sea-mud bath and seaweed treatment, and a full ninety-
minute body massage. After a refreshing swim in one of
the two magnificent azure-blue filtered-seawater pools that
were partially open to the air, and lunch on the spa terrace
overlooking the yacht harbor, their makeup was redone
and hair styled. What all of that cost we will not know,
for the moment, since they weren't given a bill to sign.

"See," said Eleanor, "just like Ivana."

AT POLICE HEADQUARTERS, Inspector Delarue was just com-
pleting instructions to his men. A still video image of
Maurice Gerard lingered on the screen in back of him as
he spoke.

"Gerard has lived in Monte Carlo for twenty-five years.
He does what he does. I don't think he's involved in anything shady, but the others, we cannot be too careful." As
he spoke, the screen changed to a picture of the other three
men. "The rich people who come here must be made to
feel that they can wear their jewels, spend their money in
the casinos and shops, and feel protected. So keep an eye
on these three. We get something, anything, we may have
a reason to throw them out of the principality once and
for all. Meanwhile I will have a talk with the King of
Hearts myself."

WHILE THE WOMEN were having their lunch at the spa,
Maurice Gerard ordered a *salade niçoise* and a glass of
chilled rosé at the Café de Paris, on the outdoor terrace,
just as Inspector Delarue wandered past.

"Inspector, won't you join me? Have you had lunch? I've just ordered."

"Ah, Maurice, how are they hanging, *mon ami*?"

"As well as can be expected, at our age," Maurice answered as Delarue took a chair opposite him. "A salad? No, I forgot—you're a *croque monsieur* man. Grilled ham and cheese, right?"

"Only if it's properly made and here they happen to be excellent," said Delarue. Bread from Poilâne in Paris, ham from Bayonne, Swiss Gruyère cheese—perfectly melted—not too long under the broiler or the natural oil in the cheese evaporates and it becomes dry. In most places a *croque monsieur* is just packaged white bread with cheap boiled ham and those processed cheese slices wrapped in plastic. Dreadful.

"Rosé? They have a good Bandol."

Delarue concurred with the choice of wine and the waiter rushed off to the kitchen with the order.

The obligatory chitchat over, Delarue nosed around the subject that was on his mind. "The usual preparations for the beginning of the season, Maurice?"

"The same. And you?"

"The usual."

"Keeping the flies away from the honey?" said Maurice, smiling.

"Precisely. So many people being too casual—leaving their money and jewels about, cars unlocked. It's the same every year."

"Is it?" said Maurice. "Either it has changed or I have."

"Probably a little of both. We see the same scenes through different eyes," said Delarue.

"You mean older eyes," said Maurice.

"That, too. People are less formal, more relaxed. More concerned with how much money they spend."

"One has to be. You know what it costs these days to fill up my old Bentley with gas? Four hundred and fifty francs! And my American clients, they want to know the price 'up front,' as they say. Impossible."

Delarue nodded in commiseration. He truly liked Maurice and was uncomfortable prying into his affairs, especially at lunch. Nevertheless, it was his job.

"One hears, a rumor of course, that you are not living at the hotel anymore."

"All rumors are usually true, as is that one. It became impossible. The price of a suite? Poooof! At the end of the month I had nothing left."

"But you are not leaving us, are you? Monte Carlo without the King of Hearts? Unthinkable." Delarue laughed. He was probably one of the few who could call Maurice by his nickname to his face.

"I think this is going to be my last season, Georges."

"What will you do?"

Now it was Maurice's turn to laugh. "Who knows? Maybe I'll marry a rich woman."

"You know what they say . . ."

"Yes, but it's not true—unless, of course, one has no scruples, and no list of qualifications; unless money is the only requirement."

"You must have had many opportunities. All those women—all those years?"

Maurice nodded and shrugged. What could one say? With hindsight every man is clairvoyant. They finished their meal in silence. Maurice offered to pay but the inspector reminded him that it was against the rules, so Delarue paid his share and departed while Maurice ordered another coffee and lit one of the last of his fine pre-Castro Cubans. The coffee was brought to him by Sophie, the café manager, a woman who reminded many of the French actress Simone Signoret in her forties—an attractive, somewhat buxom blonde with sad eyes that denied her always cheerful demeanor.

"Man talk?" she said to Maurice as they exchanged the obligatory kisses on both cheeks.

"Ah, voilà—my sunshine has arrived."

"Having a bad day?"

"You're incredible. Even when I'm smiling you can see right through me."

"It's in the eyes. You can make the mouth happy but not the eyes. They will always betray you."

"You know how it is? We got to talking about the old days, when suddenly I heard myself saying that this was going to be my last season. It just came out. But when I heard it, I knew it was probably the truth."

"August in Monte Carlo without Maurice Gerard? Are you sure?"

Maurice smiled. This time the eyes smiled with the mouth. "Of course not," he said. "What in this world can one really be sure of?"

"If I had the money I'd keep you."

"As a lover?" said Maurice, enjoying the friendly banter and feigning surprise.

"As a friend."

"I've got very expensive tastes, you know."

"As I said—*if* I had the money."

They both laughed, as only very old friends can laugh, with and at each other. Maurice tried to keep his eyes from giving him away again, but he failed. Sophie reached for his hand and pressed it. A tear escaped despite her willing it back. It was true: *if* she had had the money she would have made the offer long ago, despite everything she knew about the notorious King of Hearts. "Anyway, what would you want with an old hen like me?"

"Sophie, you're a very attractive woman."

"Once. I can't count the times I've watched you driving away in your car with a new 'client,' or whatever you call them—and I've played a game, fantasizing about where you were going, what you were eating and drinking, whether it was for money, love, sex, or all of the above, or none. Lonely women send you their dreams on paper, and you make them come true in real life. I know that men who do what you do are called gigolos or walkers or some other pejorative terms, but none of them describes you. You bend with the wind, never row against the current. Whether the woman is beautiful or not, whether it is for a night or a month, with or without intimacy—make that *sex*—they all become passing ships in the night for you, don't they? A means to an end."

"What end?" said Maurice. "A studio apartment on the Rue Bouchard? Is that an end result worth the investment of a lifetime?"

"You tell me."

"I don't know. What else could I have been? A ship's steward with a pension?"

"You could have done anything," said Sophie.

"But I didn't."

"Would you call yourself a happy man?"

"There were times, yes."

"Now."

"This is not one of those times."

"*Tant pis*. Too bad. It should be the best year of your life."

"And you," said Maurice. "You were married, once."

"Yes. But I was not in love."

"Why did you do it?"

"It was time. Past time."

"Have you ever been in love?" asked Maurice.

"I don't know. I've worked since I was twelve. Love was not something anyone I knew talked about. They spoke of marriage and children, but not love."

"What can one say that hasn't been said, that is not a cliché?"

"Nothing. Another coffee?"

9
"The Acid Test"

A rose is a rose is a rose.
—*Gertrude Stein*

DARLENE, LIKE THE others, toned, buffed, and coiffed, was a nervous wreck at the thought of the group's "coming out" that evening. This was the acid test. Would they be able to pass? Would anyone believe that Darlene was Lou Ann Barlow, one of the richest babes in the whole effing world? She decided to have a drink, and was in the process of grappling with a recalcitrant champagne cork when the doorbell rang. Champagne bottle in hand, Darlene opened the door to an immaculately tailored young man holding a large briefcase.

"Yes?"

"Armand Lescault, of Van Cleef and Arpels. We spoke earlier today?" he said, handing Darlene his calling card.

"Oh, yes. You had something you wanted to show me? Isn't that right?"

"If I may?"

"Oh, come in. I've been having a battle with this cork. Ornery little sucker."

"Allow me," said Armand, putting his briefcase aside

and taking the bottle from her. He opened it quickly, with a flourish.

"I'll bet you're French, aren't you?"

"Oui, madame."

"I just knew it. You French are so handy with things like champagne corks and peeling garlic."

Armand tried to maintain his composure as he poured the champagne into one of the glasses on the cocktail table. Darlene gave him the once-over—and not very lightly. This was her kind of guy. Slick, ultrasuave, handsome. She was overwhelmed. "I hope you'll join me?"

"Thank you," he said, pouring out a second glass—of what they both thought was champagne, but was actually Dom Pérignon Bubble Bath Oil that Darlene had taken from the bathroom.

The competition to sell jewelry in Monte Carlo is fierce. Within a stone's throw of the hotel there is Cartier, Van Cleef & Arpels, Bulgari, and Tiffany, to name but a few. All in close proximity to the casino. Salesmen from these establishments are part of the social fabric of the principality, always ready to do whatever is necessary to make a big sale. Lending fabulous necklaces, earrings, and rings worth millions to rich prospective clientele is part of the game, on the theory that the women will receive compliments and hate to part with the items; ergo, a sale. Also, they are walking advertisements for the shops. It is not uncommon for wealthy yacht owners to take a dozen or more necklaces on consignment, hoping to hand them out as gifts to certain young women in exchange for their "favors." Very few sweet young things looking for thrills on the Riviera and confronted with a box of glittering ten-thousand-dollar necklaces, can resist the line "Choose one that you like."

Armand recognized Darlene's interest in him and tried to turn that to his advantage. He knew, instinctively, that she would be agreeable to wearing his company's jewels, on loan. He also was smart enough not to make any moves on her until after the sale was closed and the check cleared the bank. Then she was fair game, but not before. Before, he must maintain his sophisticated façade. He got a lot that way. But he wasn't prepared for Darlene.

"To us—I mean, to you, *and* to us," she stuttered.

"And to a pleasant holiday in Monaco."

"Yes. That's what I meant to say. You'll have to excuse my bad French."

Armand blinked off this non sequitur. As he took his first sip of the champagne, he knew that something was badly amiss. He did not swallow, watching with incredulity as Darlene drained her glass and smiled. He held his breath and swallowed slowly, hoping he could keep it down. A few small bubbles escaped from the corners of Darlene's mouth and she giggled. Armand smiled and a bubble forced its way between his two front teeth.

"Now I know why they call it 'bubbly,' " she said. "I've never had this one before, have you?"

Armand glanced at the champagne bottle that held the bath oil and admitted that he hadn't.

"Now, what was it again that y'all were sellin'?" Darlene had automatically affected her little-girl Texas accent. Between that, the bubbles, and Darlene's creamy voluptuous cleavage peeking out of her dressing robe, Armand was mesmerized. Should he break his own rules? No. Be firm, and he was; that was the problem. Very firm indeed.

"The world's finest jewelry, Madame Barlow."

Armand opened his case, which folded out into three sections and contained an assortment of little drawers lined in silk and velvet. Diamonds, emeralds, rubies, sapphires, rings, necklaces, earrings, the odd brooch. Darlene was stunned.

"They're real, of course."

"Of course," he said. "If I might suggest—to go with your eyes . . ." Armand reached for an incredible necklace of green emeralds set off by clusters of diamonds. "May I?" he said, indicating that he would like to put it around her neck.

Darlene's nipples hardened with the thought and she
lost her voice. All she could do was nod yes. She felt the
cool white gold of the settings nestling down in the cleft
of her bosom and the light touch of his hands on the nape
of her neck as he fastened the clasp.

"Magnificent. Let me show you how you look. Don't
move—the light is perfect where you are."

Armand walked over to a large gilt mirror that hung
above a table, unhooked it, and held it in front of Darlene.
All she could manage was: "Oh, these are really cute.
What's something like this go for?"

"Go for? Ah, *excusez-moi*, 'go for.' In francs, they go
for—*cinq cent mille quatre-vingt-dix-neuf.*"

"Well, that seems reasonable, now doesn't it."

"In today's market it's most reasonable, I assure you."

"Well, I would have to think on it a bit before I laid
out that kind of money, if you know what I mean. You
think they'd go good with red?"

"They were *made* for red."

"I was thinking of wearing red tonight. You don't think
red's too, you know, *loud* for around here?"

"Not at all."

"If you've got a little time, would you look at it? It'll
only take me a minute to put it on."

"Please, don't rush."

Darlene put on the red dress. Armand, of course, said
the obligatory French word used by every salesperson in
France: *ravissant*—ravishing. You could have on a cotton
wraparound that sells for forty bucks and makes you look
like your grandmother on a bad day and they'd say *ravissant.* So, *ravissant* did it and Armand went in for the
easy kill.

"Why not keep it for the weekend and we'll talk more
on Monday?"

"Oh, I really couldn't," said Darlene, lying through her
teeth. "If anything happened to it, why, I'd be devastated."

"We are fully insured, madame. Please don't concern

yourself with such details. I have matching earrings that I think you'll find very suitable. Now, may I show you something that looks simply exquisite with green? You do wear green, don't you? With your eyes and all that gorgeous blond hair . . ."

Darlene started to swoon, her breath coming in gasps. He came toward her; she reached out to him, as her dress slipped from her shoulders. She was completely nude except for a fortune in emeralds around her neck . . .

No, none of that happened except in Darlene's brief mind flash of a daydream. It was real up until "You do wear green, don't you?" Darlene was really into it now. Act eccentric. They expect rich people to act eccentric.

"Why don't you just leave all of it, darlin', and I'll call you first thing Monday—and we'll talk. Okay?"

"Perfect. Until Monday, then. *Au revoir.*"

"Well, *au ray-voir* yourself. See ya."

Armand bowed himself out. A major score, he thought. He was already planning how he would spend the commission when the elevator arrived bearing a competitor from Cartier. Armand watched him walk past Darlene's room and ring the bell of an apartment at the end of the hall. Armand took a small leather-covered notepad out of his breast pocket and opened it. Suite 307—the Baroness Natasha Karmanov.

"Oh, well, can't get them all," he said aloud to himself as he entered the elevator, "Don't be greedy." In the hotel lobby he noticed a salesman from Bulgari walking in, and another from Tiffany's talking to the concierge. That was to be expected. Luckily he'd found his client first.

Meanwhile, Darlene had ordered several bucketsful of ice cubes, which she now emptied into the bathroom sink, and filled it with water. Holding her breath, she slowly lowered her breasts into the icy water and began to count to a hundred. She repeated this several times, until she was satisfied. She had read that many French women did this. It was supposed to firm the breasts and give them a rosy glow. It seemed to be working. She had told the others about this trick, and at that moment six other breasts were undergoing the same icy treatment.

10
"Blitzkrieg"

FOUR ELEGANTLY GOWNED and dazzlingly bejeweled women, well past the age of consent, about to descend the marble staircase into the rococo entrance hall of the grande dame of European hotels: the exquisite, exclusive, very expensive, Hotel de Paris in Monte Carlo.

Four men, handsome in their evening attire, comfortable in their surroundings, crystal aperitif stems in hand, habitués—regulars—of the clubby wood-paneled cocktail lounge of the hotel, waiting for their luck to change. No tourists, these.

EACH WOMAN HAD the same thought in her head, but had never divulged it to the others: a night of revelry and sex with her jewelry salesman. But each was smart enough to know that their prey were elsewhere. After all, a jewelry salesman was just a salesman, no matter how handsome or smartly dressed, or sexy, or—never mind. To the battle at hand.

All heads in the lobby turned to watch the four expensively baubled women hesitantly take their first steps, hand in hand. Imagine the sight: millions of dollars' worth of diamonds, sapphires, topaz, rubies, emeralds reposing upon glowing, recently iced, uplifted bosoms—courtesy of the world's foremost jewelers.

As the concierge, Pierre Goujon, looked up from his post, he saw: Lou Ann Barlow (Darlene), stunning in a red low-cut gown of organza enhanced by a cascade of green emeralds; Baroness Natasha Karmanov (Irene) looking regal and imperial, in a tight white floor-length sequined sheath, diamonds set in platinum flashing everywhere; Contessa Stephania di Romanesco (Carla), movie-star magnificent in black silk with a noose of stunning bloodred rubies at her throat; Greta Harmon-Cates (Eleanor) in bold yellow chiffon set off by a rare yellow topaz necklace and matching teardrop earrings. Pierre rushed to greet the ladies and escort them into the bar.

"*Vous êtes tout ravissantes:* you are all ravishing," he said. "To the bar for cocktails?"

"Please," said Irene, practicing her newly acquired icy, regal Russian baroness's voice.

Pierre escorted the women into the bar and handed them over to a waiting *maître d'hôtel.*

ALL OF THE *chairs in the room face front. To enter is to have your moment onstage—to be discreetly appraised. The four women are so evaluated as the pianist starts his set; a soft progression of chords leads to the tinkle of the score of* The Umbrellas of Cherbourg. *As the* maître d'hôtel *parades the four women to a table, they float as one past the four men, in a soft cloud of duty-free perfume—Guerlain predominating. A scene from* Gigi. *The women barely register the presence of the men within their periphery; their facial expressions reflect studied serenity. The men, in response, offer token half smiles and mini-nods of polite acknowledgment.*

The combined pulse rate of the four women is four

hundred and seventy-eight; of the four men, three hundred
and twenty. The amateurs versus the professionals. The
stage is set. This is the way it was planned. Each has
what the other wants. Or so it would appear.

The blitzkrieg begins.

AS THE WOMEN pass, Trevor Weymouth dons a pair of
large black glasses, pretending to read a bar menu, but
actually using them to better evaluate the jewelry. When
they are out of earshot, he whispers to his cronies, "Unbelievable—they're wearing millions, and it's all the real
stuff, of that I can assure you."

"Maurice, you are a genius," said Jean-Jacques.

"I am already in love. I don't even think I will have
to pretend," said Julio.

"We can't miss. We won't miss," said Trevor.

"We'd better not," said Jean-Jacques. "This champagne
and caviar is costing us a fortune."

"Do we really need to send over *white* caviar?" said
Julio. *"Mama mia."*

"Don't be petty, when you're trolling for big fish you
don't use worms," said Trevor. "Think of it as an investment for the future."

Maurice said nothing. This was all new for him.

IT WAS HARD not to stare at the four women, as most of
the patrons were doing as casually as possible. Nevertheless, casual staring is still staring and the women were
uncomfortably aware they were the cynosure of every eye.
They were as skittish as opera divas on opening night.

"Do you believe it?" said Darlene.

"Not only do I believe it, I'm starting to get used to
it," said Carla. "I *feel* like an Italian contessa."

"Stop looking back at those guys, Irene; you'll jinx it,"
said Eleanor, trying to stay in character as the wildly
wealthy Greta Harmon-Cates.

"They're looking at us," Irene answered

"Do they seem interested?" Eleanor whispered.

"Do you want me to look again? You just told me not to look."

"Be blasé about it. Sort of look around the room, like you're searching for a waiter."

Irene did as she was told and two waiters scurried over. She dismissed them with an imperious wave of her hand.

"We are definitely on their radar screens and they are scanning," said Irene, out of the side of her mouth. "We should expect an attack at any moment. I can feel it. Get ready girls. Suck it in."

Four sets of abs were tightened and four rosy bosoms raised just as the missile launched from the men's table hit its target, in the form of a silver-and-mahogany cart being wheeled in the women's direction. It held a magnum of Taittinger Comtes de Champagne; four flutes, thin champagne glasses chilling in ice; a crystal bowl of white caviar reposing in a silver tureen, and all the accouterments: the thin crisp toasts, the mini-linen serviettes, the mother-of-pearl spoons, and the delicate china plates.

"Mesdames, compliments of Monsieur Gerard," the *maître d'* said, making a small gesture toward Maurice, who nodded and raised his glass in a mock toast. The women now had the opportunity of looking directly at the men, resplendent in their evening attire, and they liked what they saw. In this gambling town, you might ask, what were the odds of four available women meeting four available and attractive men from the git-go, as they say in Texas? If the women had considered this, our story might have ended here or made a sharp right turn, but the four women all believed that they were on a roll, and since their trip had been one surprise after another, they simply took this one in stride. They'd rolled another seven.

"Well, isn't he nice. We should ask him and his friends to join us."

"Darlene, that just isn't done," said Irene.

"Eleanor said we should act eccentric. Wouldn't that be eccentric?" asked Carla.

Eleanor took a long look at the men. "Let's face it, girls, when was the last time anyone sent us champagne, and whatever that white stuff is?"

"My last husband once brought me a bottle of champagne. It was lukewarm and domestic," said Irene.

"So was he, as I recall," said Darlene.

"I vote yes. Anyone against?"

Terrified silence prevailed for a long second before Eleanor said to the *maître d'hôtel*, who was busily pouring and spreading, "Bring four more glasses, please, and ask the gentlemen to join us."

"Certainly, madame."

"That was pretty direct," said Carla.

"You don't ask, you don't get. Now don't blow it, girls."

Each woman couldn't help mentally choosing the man she hoped would be hers, but that didn't matter because the coupling, so to speak, had been prearranged: Maurice would take the baroness (Irene), since he spoke some Russian; Julio would, of course, take the Italian contessa (Carla); Jean-Jacques had drawn Lou Ann Barlow (Darlene); the Texas lady; and Trevor was left with the tough-assed lawyer, Eleanor, a.k.a. Greta Harmon-Cates.

Let the games begin.

MAURICE STRODE OVER to the table. The headwaiter pulled up another chair. For the moment Maurice remained standing, as Pierre Goujon rushed up to handle the introductions. "May I present my good friend Maurice Gerard."

"Good evening, ladies. I highly recommend the white caviar. It is very rare, from the albino beluga sturgeon of the Caspian Sea."

"Oh, is that fascinating," said Darlene, in her best Texas drawl, "simply awesome."

"Madame Lou Ann Barlow," said Pierre. Gerard took her hand lightly.

"Madame Barlow, it is a pleasure."

"And the Contessa Stephania di Romanesco."

"Madame Greta Harmon-Cates.

"The Baroness, Natasha Karmanov."

While Maurice had simply taken the hand of each woman, when he held the Baroness's he leaned over and kissed it lightly, causing Irene nearly to collapse.

The other three men watched Maurice's machinations with nothing less than awe. The students observing the professor. "The man's a fucking genius," said Trevor.

"The son of a bitch never misses," said Jean-Jacques.

All Julio could say was, *"Madonna,"* as he stared in obvious passionate hunger at the radiant Contessa Stephania di Romanesco.

Meanwhile, Maurice was orchestrating the service of the white caviar. "Never anything with fine caviar, I say. Just microscopically cut light toast, or better yet just a chilled spoonful, *au naturel,* don't you agree, Baroness?"

"In St. Petersburg, my grandmother always served it just like this. Personally, I've always preferred the white. The black is so, so—*black.*"

"I WILL LEAVE you in the capable hands of Monsieur Gerard. *Bon soir, mesdames,"* Pierre said as he slithered off, his part in Act 1 of the play concluded.

"Well, I must say, this is marvelous. It must go for a bundle," said Darlene.

"It owes its value only to its scarcity, like many things in life; if they were abundant they would decline severely in value."

"And this champagne, I've never tasted anything like it," oohed Carla in her newly acquired pseudo-Italian accent. "Is it your favorite, Mr. Gerard?"

"Call me Maurice, please. Yes, one of my favorites,

although I must admit I prefer the Krug eighty-eight for breakfast."

"I couldn't agree more. It's so much lighter," said Eleanor.

"So, Maury," said Darlene, "do you come here often?"

"Actually, I live here, in the hotel." A lie that would be covered up by the concierge, if necessary.

"All the time?" said Irene.

"Yes, for the past twenty years."

"It must set you back a ton," said Darlene. "Wouldn't a condo be a better deal?"

"It's a matter of style, I guess."

"Of course," said Irene, "style is everything."

Carla decided to try out a few of her newly acquired Italian words: *"Assolutament, Non possiamo."* She smiled broadly, like a student that had just received an A for her oral test, while the other women stared at her in amazement. Eleanor almost applauded.

"È vero, è vero. Io concordaro, Contessa. I agree. It's the one thing you can't pretend to have, isn't it? I pride myself on being able to judge a person's style the moment I meet them," said Maurice.

"So, then, how do you judge us?" said Irene, tilting her nose a bit higher.

"Konechno," Maurice replied in perfect Russian. "It goes without saying."

"Oh, you are all so multilingual. I'm embarrassed to use my French," said Darlene.

"A trick of headwaiters and dilettantes. My favorite language is Russian. I love the way it rolls off the tongue, don't you, Baroness?"

Irene had anticipated this type of question and was ready for it. "If you don't mind, when my husband died I promised myself not to speak Russian for five years. Unfortunately, I have six more months to go; but yes, I think in Russian and I can't wait to use it again. It's so, so—*Russian,* if you know what I mean."

"I understand. Pity, I love the sound of it. Now, will

you ladies be going to the casino this evening?"

"Oh, definitely," said Eleanor. "After dinner, I suppose."

"Regrettably, I won't be able to join you because I am entertaining some important guests this evening," he said, indicating the table with the three men. "But I wish you all good luck at the tables and hope our paths cross again."

Maurice rose from his chair, took two steps, and turned back. "I know this is very impromptu, and a bit bold of me to suggest, but if you would consider joining us for dinner at the Louis Quinze Restaurant and for some baccarat at the casino afterwards . . . ?" He let the question hang in the air and fade away as the women restrained themselves from responding too quickly.

Darlene thought that baccarat was a bitter red cocktail drink that she hated, but would drink if she had to. Irene knew it was the name of fine French crystal and thought he was offering snifters of brandy after dinner. Eleanor thought it was the name of that music guy, Burt—maybe Maurice was offering to take them to a club where he was playing? Carla thought it was a game she had seen in Florida—like jai alai. Fortunately, all of them kept these thoughts to themselves. None of them knew the first thing about high-class, high-stakes gambling, except for a weekend in Atlantic City where they spent all of their money on the slot machines and never played any of the other games.

"Oh, that sounds fascinating," said Darlene, going with a safe answer.

"If you prefer, we could try our hand at blackjack or roulette? Well, we don't have to decide now, do we? What do you say? Yes?"

"Of course. How generous of you to offer," said Irene, rising and taking his arm possessively. Seeing this, the men at the other table rose to await formal introductions to their companions, which were duly made by Maurice. The pairing-off seemed very natural; everyone was satisfied.

11
"Getting to Know You"

"We know how to speak falsehoods which resemble real things . . ."
—Hesiod, c. 700 B.C.

IF A RESTAURANT can be called grand, imposing, opulent, and majestic, then surely the Louis Quinze in the Hotel de Paris rates those descriptive adjectives and more. One would be hard-pressed to find its match. Named after King Louis XV, who reigned from 1710 to 1774, it is decorated in the extravagant and exaggerated rococo style that defined the period of his rule. Approaching it from the outside, one is confronted by two larger-than-life-size cast nudes that soar out over the terrace windows of the façade, like twin figureheads on the prow of some old sailing schooner. The interior room is ringed with a frieze of ornate arches embracing painted cameos and interspersed with plaster cupids—supported by twenty-four square marble columns with gilded Ionic capitals. Four crystal chandeliers hang from the extravagantly painted ceiling; a dozen wall sconces shed a most flattering peach-colored light upon the pampered complexions of the seriously dressed women. Damask draperies frame four large *trompe-l'oeil* paintings and the French mirrored doors. On gold pedestals sit two ormolu clocks and two sculpted

marble busts of women. The round tables, sitting on a
leaf-patterned Aubusson carpet, are covered with fine
linen (look closely at the tablecloth; you won't see a fold
line or a wrinkle because they are ironed on the table
before the service begins). The presentation plates and the
table settings are vermeil; next to each woman's uphol-
stered chair is a low stool for her handbag. There are fresh
flowers everywhere. The tables are far apart and the food
and service are impeccable. The restaurant's own bakery
provides a variety of over twenty-nine different kinds of
bread and rolls.

Certainly the four women are in for a culinary treat, if
they can pay attention to the food. If they order the *menu
de dégustation,* they'll be able to taste a selection of the
famed chef's specialties. Leave the choice of wine to the
sommelier and they'll savor some of the finest wines of
France kept and served under optimum conditions, for the
hotel's vast cellar is world-renowned. There are no no-
smoking areas, but the tables are so far apart that even an
adjacent quartet of cigar chompers will not be trouble-
some. In any event, cigars are only allowed after dinner.
This is definitely a restaurant to dress up for, as far *up* as
you can afford.

A fly on the nearby wall (of course there are no flies
allowed in the principality!) would have heard some of
the following snatches of getting-to-know-you conversation:

Between Darlene and Jean-Jacques

"I am French, but actually I was born in Br-r-r-azil," he
said, trilling his *r*s, "so I have dual citizenship: French
and Brrrazilian."

"I dated a French guy once—he loved garlic—but I
never dated a Brrrazilion. How do you make that sound?
I can never get it right."

"It's all with the tongue. To be very good with the
tongue takes a lot of practice."

"Yes, I know."

"Try again."

"Br-r-r-a-zilian."

"Spoken like a native. You have a great tongue. Did anybody ever tell you that you have a great tongue?"

"Not on a first date."

"I love your earrings," he said, fingering one.

"Emeralds. I have them in all colors. Are you in coffee?"

"No, my brother, Ricar-r-r-do is in coffee. I am in tin."

"Oh, how interesting. There must be millions of tin cans made every day."

"Actually, billions."

"Oh, *very* fascinating."

Between Carla and Julio

"Don't tell me—it was *La Strada*, Fellini. No, *aspetta*— wait, *La Dolce Vita*—"

"No, no. It was *Divorce—Italian Style*, with Mastroianni."

"Yes, of course. I remember. You were *magnifica*," he said as he took her hand and kissed her ruby ring.

Carla breathed a sigh of relief; she had gotten away with it.

Julio smiled inwardly. He knew she was lying, of course. The female leads of *Divorce—Italian Style* were Daniela Rocca and Stefania Sandrelli—not to mention the fact that the film came out in 1962 (Carla wasn't *that* old!). But who cared? If she wanted to pretend that she had been a movie star, that was fine with him. Silly rich ladies—they could get away with anything.

Between Eleanor and Trevor

"Ah, topaz—what a perfect match for your eyes."

"And yours," she said, entranced.

Between Irene and Maurice

". . . and you spend most of your time in the United States?" he said.

"Yes, Palm Beach, New York, the Hamptons, Beverly Hills, Aspen . . ."

"It must be difficult to keep up so many residences."

"Actually not, if you have a good staff, as I do. I've been thinking of buying a tiny *pied-à-terre* in Paris. A dozen rooms or so in the sixteenth, nothing extravagant."

Between Eleanor and Trevor

"You look like you're in pretty good shape, Trev. Do you work out?"

"Yes. I have a small gym on my yacht. It's very convenient."

"Constant repetition until muscle failure, that's what works for me," she said, jerking her hand up and down with an imaginary barbell.

"Have you tried using low weight and increasing the reps? I'm very into Zen. I like to take my time—up-down-up-down-slowly-slowly, until . . ."

Between Carla and Julio

"You look wonderful in black. *Meraviglioso*."

"It's mourning black."

"Well, it looks fantastic in the evening."

"I meant that my husband—"

"He is here with you?"

"Not any longer—and yet . . ."

Between Irene and Maurice

"What an incredible room."

"Fit for a baroness."

"Thank you."

"They should have a more strict dress code here," Maurice said. "There was a time when this room, with its elaborate Louis the Fifteenth decor, was considered the epitome of sophisticated elegance. Men in business suits and women in day dresses were barred from entering. It was reserved for well-groomed and discerning people who came to see and be seen while they indulged their Epicurean fantasies. But times have changed. Look at that man over there. Can you believe he's standing on the chair taking a flash picture of the food on his plate? And look at the way they're dressed; for an afternoon at the racetrack. Where is the *savoir faire*, the *savoir vivre*?"

Maurice allowed his hand to graze Irene's for the briefest of moments as he continued. "When I first saw you I was suddenly transported back to that other time. Who is that stylish, graceful woman, dressed so exquisitely? I had to know, to meet you. And so I was rather bold, and for that I hope you'll forgive me."

"Consider yourself forgiven," she said, taking the opportunity to touch his hand as he had touched hers. "It is a wonderful room; and it does need us, doesn't it?" Irene said, looking around. "I love the decoration. Those sculptures of the two women; do you know who they were?"

"Yes. Two of the king's mistresses. Madame du Barry and Madame de Pompadour."

"Rather odd choice for here, isn't it?"

"Not at all. After all, they were great courtesans. Courtly love was acceptable in those days, and it was public knowledge that both of these ladies were mistresses of the king. Why not? They were simply using a man to advance themselves and achieve a lifestyle that they could not hope to attain any other way."

"And you find that acceptable? Women using men?"

"Perfectly acceptable. It's the way of the world, why deny it?"

"How about the other way around?"

"Of course the queen had lovers, but her liaisons were more discreet, not as public, although everyone knew."

"In that case, a man was using a woman—for the same reasons."

"Yes."

"And you find that acceptable? That someone would be using you to further their goals in life?"

"As long as I knew about it, I would find nothing wrong with that scenario. Don't you agree?"

"I don't know."

"Look, it's a fact that powerful men and powerful women are very attractive to each other. It's a natural law of human nature. Take her," he said, pointing to the statue of Madame du Barry. "She started out life as an assistant to a hatmaker. Then she became a prostitute. By using men effectively, she ended up as the mistress of a king. Everybody had their eyes open; she even sought and gained her husband's complicity. And the other one, Madame de Pompadour, was also raised in simple circumstances and did the same. One day she visited a fortune-teller who told her that she would someday be 'almost a queen.' And that prophesy came true. She lived at court and eventually was awarded a royal title—Marquise de Pompadour. Certainly the king was not laboring under any misapprehensions. What he wanted he got, and paid for royally, as was the custom. Take yourself; I'm sure there's been the odd man who has tried to insinuate himself into your confidence for reasons other than pure love."

"Yes, and it's so tiring. I always know within the first fifteen minutes. They're usually so transparent. Don't you agree?"

"Completely. But that doesn't mean it can't be amusing, for a time."

Irene looked at this handsome, sophisticated, articulate man. Could he truly be interested in her? Or was he attracted to who she seemed to be. Of course it was the latter. She began to fabricate a story in her mind, one that she would eventually have to tell him. She would say that she was of royal Russian birth but that her father gambled away the family fortune, and she was down to her last ruble. He would understand. It wouldn't matter to a wealthy man like him. Or would it?

Between Darlene and Jean-Jacques

"Have you ever been to a soccer match?"

"No. Is it exciting, like football?"

"There's much more action. I will fly you to Marseilles in my private jet. My old team is playing this week."

"You were a soccer player?"

"Yes, I started in Brrrazil when I was very young."

As the *maître d'hôtel* approached with the menus, Julio held his hand up. "Contessa, may I have the honor of ordering your dinner for you? I assure that you will be in good hands."

"Of course."

Julio turned his attention to the headwaiter, who stood ready.

"La contessa and I will begin with risotto and white truffles, followed by the veal sautéed with porcini mushrooms. The chef is French," he said to Carla, "but he loves Italy, so we have the best of both worlds," he said, ignoring the *maître d'hôtel*'s pained expression.

Jean-Jacques also refused the menus. "Will you join me in eating Brazil's national dish, *feijoada*?" he said to Darlene. "It's made with black beans, beef, sausage, pigs' feet, and tongue. You do like tongue, don't you?"

"You seem to have a fixation on that particular organ," Darlene whispered.

"*Feijoada* for two—and tell the chef not to overcook the tongue."

Before the *maître d'* could recover, Trevor made things even worse. "The last time I was in Munich I had a marvelous sauerbraten at Walterspiel's. Are you in the mood for sauerbraten?" he said to Eleanor. By now Eleanor was in the mood for anything and quickly agreed. The headwaiter looked imploringly at Maurice, whom he knew

quite well, quietly pleading for help, but Maurice added
the *pièce de résistance* with a request for Russian chicken
Kiev, which he ordered with its full Russian appellation:
kotlety po-Kyivskomu, adding *kartoplia solimkoi*—straw
potatoes—as an afterthought.

The *maître d'hôtel* smiled weakly and trudged off into
the kitchen, like a convict taking his last steps toward an
execution chamber. A headwaiter's position in a restaurant is like that of a general on a battlefield; he doesn't
do the fighting but he's responsible for the outcome of
the battle. If his team of waiters doesn't pick up their
orders fast enough, he gets heat from the head chef. If a
dish is late coming to table because of a mistake in the
kitchen, he gets heat from the patrons. If he makes a mistake on an order or agrees to a substitution without consulting the chef, he hears about it, long and loud. On the
other hand, if the food and service are perfect, the chef
receives the accolades. While everyone tells the truth to
the *maître d'*—the service was slow, the soup was salty,
the potatoes cold, the beef too rare, etc.—everyone lies to
the chef, when he makes his rounds at the end of the meal,
telling him how wonderful everything was. Maybe it's
that uniform or the white *toque* that makes him a foot
taller, forbidding and imposing. No one ever says to his
face: "Your cooking sucks, Where was your last job,
McDonald's?"

Maybe there's something about the person who cooks
your meal that demands respect and requires lies. When
a friend cooks a poor meal at home, he or she is nevertheless complimented graciously. So maybe it's not just
the hat. Maybe it's dining convention.

Alain Dumont had been a dining-room general for
twenty years, working at many of France's top restaurants.
But never in all that time had he walked into the kitchen
to call out an order with such trepidation. Surely he risked
being fired. Nonetheless, shoulders squared, he strode
through the kitchen doors and confronted the twelve

chefs, busy at their stations, and handed the order slip to the head chef.

"What's this, Alain? Computer not working?"

"I thought it best that I bring this one in person. You'll see what I mean."

The head chef began to read the order: "Table seventeen—eight covers—*risotto* with white truffles. We have no white truffles! Escalope of veal with porcini mushrooms? There were no porcini ordered for today! And what the hell is *this*?"

"*Feijoada,* sir. It's a Brazilian dish."

"I *know* what *feijoada* is," he said with controlled fury. "I was simply wondering what the hell it's doing on your order? Are you hallucinating, Monsieur Dumont?"

"No, sir. And the gentleman asked me to request that the tongue not be overcooked. He likes it undercooked."

"Does he? Maybe he should come in here and supervise it. And this: two chicken Kiev? Easy to make but it needs two fucking hours in the refrigerator or the butter won't spurt out when it's cut at the table. Two hours, Alain—or no spurting butter. And sauerbraten? That's easy. Just tell them to come back in *three days,* after the meat has marinated."

The noisy kitchen had become very quiet, with all eyes on the normally even-tempered boss, who was now seething with rage. What would he do?

"Who are these people?"

Alain looked at his notes and read, in a rather flat tone of voice, "The Baroness Karmanov, la Contessa di Romanesco, Madame Harmon-Cates, and a Madame Barlow—and their escorts."

"I'll be right back."

WITHIN TWO MINUTES the head chef had returned and one could tell that his attitude had completely changed. He looked at his brigade and shouted, "These people are simply four of the richest women in the world! Anybody have any suggestions?"

A long silence was broken by the voice of one of the young potato peelers. "How about takeout?" The youngster's exclamation was like that of the child who said, "The emperor is naked!" He had spoken truth and opened everyone's eyes to the obvious.

"Takeout? TAKEOUT?"

"Why not? You know the chefs in every restaurant in town. Call them and have the food picked up. We'll add some touches here, and *voilà*."

"From the mouthes of babes. You idiot, you're right," the chef said, cuffing the boy affectionately on the side of the head. "I'll call Lino's for the porcini and white truffles, Restaurant de Ipanema for the *feijoada*—I know they have it on the menu. Zarushka's makes excellent chicken Kiev—I'm sure they can spare us a few portions. That leaves the sauerbraten. Damn. There are no German restaurants in the principality."

"How about getting a daube of beef from Le Provençal and we'll fix it up here with a quick red-wine-and-vinegar sauce. They'll never know the difference."

"Son, do you have a car?"

"Yes, sir."

"Then get going while I make the calls. You've got a raise coming. How much are you making?"

"Nothing, sir. I'm an apprentice. My father is paying *you*!"

"Ah, well then, we'll double that," he said, his laugh breaking the tension in the room and allowing the normal kitchen chat and clatter to resume.

The boy seemed very pleased and took off like a shot as the chef cuffed him yet again.

Alain returned to the dining room, trailed by four waiters carrying small plates of *amuses bouches*—which literally meant "amuse your mouth"—little hor d'oeuvres, along with two complimentary bottles of champagne. A delaying tactic. When Maurice asked if everything was in order, he simply replied, "Of, course, *pas de problem*."

The meal was a success. Disaster avoided.

For dessert, Maurice made a suggestion that, while not on the menu, could easily be prepared tableside. "Since we are sitting where *crêpes Suzette* was invented, I suggest we have them."

Alain smiled at this; it was an easy task to whip up the *crêpes* in the kitchen and would afford him the opportunity of working tableside for their final preparation. This always garnered applause (not to mention increasing the tip). A good *maître d'* was rewarded by keeping the service attentive, working close by with a chafing dish, and translating the usually complex menu. (And let it be said here that the French have as much trouble with a French menu at a top restaurant as the Americans do. For example, *partition mentholée* turns out to be chocolate cake decorated with mint-flavored musical ribbons of icing with red berries as the notes!)

"But," said Maurice to Alain, "I would like you to make a few small variations. Instead of the various liqueurs, please use only Poire William and we'll have them with chilled snifters of frozen pear brandy. And, oh yes, bring two fresh pears."

Still no problem for Alain, and he went off to gather the various ingredients. While he was gone Maurice explained the fabled history of *crêpes Suzette*.

"At the turn of the century the Prince of Wales, later to become the King of England, Edward the Seventh, ordered *crêpes* flavored with warm liqueurs—on the menu as *crêpes Princess*—as a dessert for himself and his woman companion. Her first name happened to be Suzette. A young chef, Henri Charpentier, had the flame too high and accidentally set the liqueurs in the dish alight. He thought the *crêpes* were ruined and his job lost, but fortunately he tasted the sauce, found it quite interesting, and sent it off to the table, as there was no time to make another order. The prince proclaimed it excellent—better than the menu version—and asked that it thereafter be named *crêpes Suzette,* after his dining companion. The dish attained worldwide renown and through the years chefs have added their own signatures—as I have added mine. But always, the flaming with a warmed brandy at the end."

Alain had returned with a rolling table containing all of the requested items for the dessert, as well as a silver-lined copper chafing dish set atop an alcohol burner. As he approached, Maurice rose from his seat. "Thank you, Alain. I believe I can handle it from here." Alain was taken aback but had no choice but to retreat with a "very good, Monsieur Gerard." He was becoming a mere factotum, he thought, not the dining-room boss of a three-star restaurant. But one had to bend and not break, as he was taught in hotel school in Lausanne, and had learned the hard way on his way up from busboy in a bistro to the top rung in Monte Carlo.

"I'd sure like to have the recipe," said Darlene.

"I'll explain as I go along and then I'll have my secretary write it out for you."

"Make that four copies," said Eleanor.

"Yes," said Irene, "I'd like to teach it to my chef in Gstaad."

"My pleasure."

As Carla started to speak, Julio whispered to her, "Tomorrow I will make for you *crespelli alla fragola.* The Italians were making *crespelli alla fiamma,* what the French call flaming *crêpes,* since the Renaissance; the French, they stole all of our ideas about cooking and now they deny everything. No matter. Tonight the copy, tomorrow the original."

Reader, do not believe a thing Julio says; they are tales told by a professional Italian!

Maurice continued: "The *crêpes* are made in the kitchen, ahead of time; covered and stacked. For four people you take one cup of flour, one tablespoon sugar, one teaspoon melted butter, one whole egg, and one egg yolk. Mix the dry ingredients together and add the wet slowly and mix. Let it stand for an hour. Now, for my sauce: I melt two tablespoons butter and add one thinly sliced pear and three tablespoons powdered sugar and cook it gently—like so. Then a half cup fresh orange juice. When the pears are soft, put some in each *crêpe* and fold in half twice. When they're all in the pan, spoon some hot sauce over and cook for a minute. Now—a ladleful of pear brandy, heated and set aflame, poured over. *Voilà! C'est fini.* Alain, you may serve."

Eccentric rich ladies or not, Alain could not bring himself to serve and instructed two of his waiters to do so, realizing his tip was probably a distant memory.

Maurice resumed his seat to polite applause—not only from the four women but from all the other tables in the room as well. What aplomb. The sommelier arrived just in time with the frozen pear brandy in frosted snifters.

"Before you taste, breathe in the aroma—it is fantastic," said Jean-Jacques, feeling a bit outclassed, which, of course, he was.

Eleanor noticed that the bottle of pear brandy had a whole pear inside. "How *do* they get that pear in there?" she said to Trevor.

"Ah, the best pear brandy is made in Switzerland. When the first pear buds show on the trees, many are tucked into clear glass bottles and the bottles are wired to the branches, allowing the pear to mature to its full growth within the bottle. Then the distilled pear brandy is added."

"That's amazing," Eleanor said. "I'd like to see that."

"It will be arranged."

After the dessert, the pear brandies, the coffee, and *mignardises,* those marvelous, irresistible *petits fours,* and the chocolates, the men lit cigars and the women went off, together, to the powder room.

THE FOUR WOMEN were bubbling with excitement:

"I feel like Dorothy, in *The Wizard Of Oz.*"

When they all stared at her quizzically, Darlene added,

"Because, I've just met the Tinman. He's a magnate, a tin magnate. It's like winning the lottery the first time you play."

"Even if it ended right now, it would have been worth it."

"It's all happening so fast. It's almost like we wrote the script and now we're the actors playing it out."

"And it's all working."

"Careful, it's only the end of Act One. You know the expression 'a hard act to follow'; we'll have to be super-careful."

"He has a yacht."

"Mine has a jet."

"Julio owns restaurants all over Europe—and that's just his hobby."

"Maurice owns this *hotel,* I'm sure of it. He's invited me to St. Tropez tomorrow, by helicopter."

"Isn't that where all the women go topless?"

"Let's hope not, for her sake."

A little good-natured cattiness.

"We have to be calm."

"Not overly aggressive."

"Not appear too interested."

"I'm so disinterested my panties are wet."

"No fooling around tonight. Remember, it's the first date. Hold back, girls. Hold back."

"Until when?"

"The third date. Never before the third date."

"That's an old-fashioned concept."

"And we're supposed to be old-fashioned girls. Let them work for their conquests."

"If they don't try, I'll kill myself."

"That meal must have set them back a bundle. We're talking a least a thousand."

"Pocket money, to them."

Actually the bill came to $6,258 for the food and wine—including a generous tip for Alain. Maurice asked that the bill be divided among the four women and charged to their suites—$1,564.50 to each. Since Alain had done this dozens of times over the years, he was not surprised and said he would take care of it. Maurice guessed that the women wouldn't see the bill for months, since their hotel bill would no doubt be mailed to them and be passed on to accountants or banks for payment. The bar manager in the bar had agreed, as was not unusual, to add the white-caviar-and-champagne bill to the restaurant bill, so it was hidden in the total amount.

Pocket money, to the ladies, thought Maurice.

"So far so good."

"I'm sure she is in love. It's like taking candy from a baby."

"I think I could be in love. Is that so terrible? If you marry a contessa, do you automatically become a count?"

"Interesting question."

"We must be careful, not appear too anxious."

"And remember, no matter what—no sex tonight."

"*Mama mia,* that may not be possible."

"Well, make it possible. This is a once-in-a-lifetime opportunity. Agreed?"

"*Va bene.* I will make the sacrifice."

Julio whispered something and crossed himself, just as the women returned.

"Ready to try your luck?" said Maurice.

"We are totally in your hands," said Irene, locking onto Maurice's arm.

And so, the four Cinderellas and their Prince Charmings strode off into the night as church bells tolled the hour of ten. Two hours to go until the dream was, as foretold, shattered. Or would they beat the odds?

There'll be time enough for counting when the dealin's done . . .

CURTAIN

ACT TWO
PLAYING THE GAME

12
"Deeper in Debt"

. . . another day older, and deeper in debt . . .
—Merle Travis, "Sixteen Tons"

THE CASINO AT Monte Carlo, a masterpiece of neo-Baroque architecture and decoration, is about as far from Las Vegas or Atlantic City as you can get, both in decor and gambling style. No shorts, sandals, T-shirts, or yokels in sweatsuits holding paper cups filled with quarters here. No "come on, baby needs a new pair of shoes," no tits-and-ass waitresses trying to get you drunk on free cheap booze. Actually, the gambling rooms are rather dull, with attention being paid to the serious players whose expressions are usually blank and morose—true knights of mournful countenances, whether winning or losing fortunes. Nearby, a restaurant offers free dining for gambling patrons. The sign reads AT MANAGEMENT'S DISCRETION. No point in feeding the voyeurs.

Jean-Jacques steered Darlene into the huge Europe Room, where roulette was played. He found two places at the second table and took some chips out of his pocket—ten fifty-franc *jetons*, to be exact, roughly the equivalent of one hundred U.S. dollars. Smiling at Darlene, he casually placed them all on red and waited for the action to begin. The wheel would spin as soon as the biggest bettor had completed his choices, and that might take quite some time. But the croupiers were not in any hurry. Fast or slow, the odds remained heavily in their favor.

Finally the ball skipped and jumped around past potential fortunes, settling on the zero. "I am, as you say, jinxed. I cannot play anymore tonight," said Jean-Jacques.

"What's the matter?" asked Darlene, not wanting the evening to end so suddenly.

"Whenever a zero comes up my luck is broken and I always lose afterward. But I would enjoy watching you play."

Darlene was ready for this and opened her purse. "Well, wouldn't you know, silly me, I walked out without a single franc-y-poo."

"That's not a problem at all," said Jean-Jacques. "*Croupier, s'il vous plaît, des plaques pour Madame Barlow.* How much would you like to start with?"

"Oh, whatever you think," said Darlene.

"*Cinq cent mille francs, pour le compte de Madame Barlow à l'Hotel de Paris.*"

"How much is that in dollars?" Darlene whispered.

"About a hundred K—uh, thousand. Is that enough?"

"Well, we'll just have to see, now, won't we?" Wow, these tin guys are really casual about money, Darlene thought. What a sport.

The croupier nodded to the pit boss, who picked up the phone, got a fast response, and nodded back to the croupier, who began to count out chips. The smallest ones, *jetons,* were round and yellow; they were worth fifty francs—ten bucks. Then up from there, changing colors, one hundred, five hundred, one thousand francs. Then the chip size and shape changed; the five thousand-franc chip ($1,000) and up were called *plaques.* They were oblong, about the size of an index card, and made to look like mother-of-pearl: the ten thousand-franc ($2,000) and the twenty-thousand-franc *plaque* ($4,000). Darlene received a stack of the *plaques* only, so each bet would be a minimum of $1,000 unless she asked for them to be changed into the lesser *jetons*.

But to Darlene, none of this mattered; it was a Monopoly game to her. She never saw that little piece of paper the pit boss stuck in the table slot that read: *Madame Barlow, Hotel de Paris FRS 500,000*. This was not paper play-money. One could truly go to jail, for a long time, for not making good on your credit. Darlene placed her first bet, on her lucky number, twenty-six. The wheel of fortune turned.

MEANWHILE, IN ANOTHER room, at a blackjack table, Carla and Julio stood behind the players. Watchers, for the moment.

"Would you like to play, Contessa?" said Julio.

"That would be fun."

Julio ordered $50,000 in chips from the dealer. A pit boss, who had been watching the heavily jeweled lady Julio was escorting, came over. "Welcome to the casino, Contessa. You are staying with us here in Monte Carlo?"

"Yes, at your wonderful Hotel de Paris."

"I hope you enjoy your evening," he said as he bowed slightly and turned, making eye contact and nodding imperceptibly to the dealer, thereby approving the request for credit.

"Aren't you going to play?" Carla said as a stack of *plaques* was pushed in front of her.

Julio slid into the chair next to her and said he would watch the first hand before deciding how much to wager. Carla put a five-thousand-franc plaque in the betting area in front of her and was dealt her opening two cards, a jack of spades and an ace of spades. Blackjack. An instant winner. "*Dios, l'ace nero*—the black ace, *uno presagio*. It is an omen. I cannot play tonight," Julio whispered, crossing himself.

"What's the matter?"

"If the last card before my chair is a black ace on the first deal, I always lose. Please go on. I enjoy watching you win."

"Grazie."

"Niente. Prego."

MAURICE TOLD IRENE that he would teach her the game of *chemin de fer,* which is exactly the same as baccarat with one exception: in *chemin de fer,* one of the players banks the game instead of the casino. The right to be the banker rotates around the table, with the casino taking a percentage from each banker, thereby assuming no risk. Both *chemin de fer* and baccarat always command the most luxurious of all the casino rooms and many of gambling's heaviest hitters play this game exclusively. Irene thought she had stepped into the James Bond movie *Casino Royale*. She imagined herself as Jacqueline Bisset. She'd always loved the name of Bisset's character in that film: Miss Goodthighs. She recast Maurice as David Niven, who had played the gracefully aging and debonair 007. She had loved the scene they'd filmed at the baccarat table and had always wondered how the game was played. Now here she was, with the reality outdistancing the screen fantasy. She had the smooth *plaques* in one hand and the man of her dreams in the other.

The purpose of the game is to hold cards that add up to nine. It seems simple until one gets into the complex rules as to how that may be accomplished. It is one of the oldest casino games, dating back to medieval times, when it was played with tarot cards. Before one sits down at a baccarat or *chemin de fer* table, one looks at the sign denoting that table's minimum bet. If it's a high-stakes game, watch out; if you're the banker, you could be in for some heavy losses. Not a game for the novice, as Irene definitely was. She said that she would prefer to watch for a while, and Maurice agreed. After requesting

$100,000 in chips of high denomination, he provided a clear and concise explanation of the rules.

"Picture cards—the jack, queen, king—and the tens have no value. They are zero. If the value of the first two cards you are dealt exceeds nine, the left-hand number is dropped. So, a seven and an eight equal not fifteen but five, the one being dropped."

Irene was finding this difficult to follow, especially after so much champagne. "Why don't you play and I'll watch?"

Maurice sat down and her chips were pushed over to his place. "Are you sure?" he asked.

"Absolutely."

And so, Maurice began to play. He was expert in the game, very slick but also very lucky. In a short time he had taken the bank and won over $50,000!

AT THE CRAPS table, a seven on the first roll for Eleanor. All eyes stared in astonishment at the incongruous sight of an obviously wealthy lady screaming like a Las Vegas banshee. Eleanor had never played the game but she'd seen Scorsese's *Casino* and imagined herself as Sharon Stone. "Take me to heaven, roll me a seven." A four and a three. A winner. "House is cold, cold as ice, you gave it to me once, give it to me twice." She was hot. Another seven. The bets on the pass line were piling up and a crowd was gathering. Then a five.

"The number is five, mark the five," the table boss shouted above the din. "Madame needs a five. Place your bets."

"This little lady is stayin' alive, watch her roll a two-three-five." The dice hit the back of the table—a five. Everyone let their bets ride. The table was so heavy with money that you couldn't even see the pass line.

"You've never played this game before?" said an amazed Trevor.

"Beginner's luck," said Eleanor as she doubled her bet

and rattled the dotted red cubes like a pro. An eight.

"The number is eight. Mark the eight," said the table boss.

"Lookin' for a date, with a number named eight," Eleanor chanted. A seven. Crapped out.

"Lady has sevened out. Take the do's, pay the don'ts," said the table boss as all of the pass money that was betting on Eleanor was swept into the casino's coffers.

Eleanor was flushed and hooked on the game. She couldn't wait for her turn with the dice again, and neither could the management; they'd just won the biggest bundle of the evening. Eleanor was a magnet for the normally sedate crowd. Trevor just smiled. What a guy, she thought. Here I am risking all of his money and he just smiles that enigmatic smile of his.

And so the evening progressed. The four women had, between them, $325,000 at stake, since that amount of credit had been charged to their hotel room accounts and would have to be paid before they left the principality. The men had risked nothing. They continued to appear wealthy while the women were being seriously conned into gambling money they didn't have, thinking they were gambling with the men's money. At this point the men had nothing at stake, as they shared neither in the gains nor the losses of the evening. That was the way it had been meticulously planned.

It never occurred to the men that the women were risking anything but pin money, chicken feed, peanuts.

MAURICE WON $38,000 for Irene, but when she played, it turned into a loss of $54,500. Darlene lost $75,000 when black came up ten times in a row while she stubbornly kept doubling up on red. Carla lost all of her stake of $50,000. Eleanor came out ahead by $10,000. So, the total, if it had been made correctly, would have shown a net loss of $169,500.

*   *   *

THE FOLLOWING MORNING the women were having breakfast together on the garden terrace of the hotel, overlooking the yacht harbor. Darlene was the last to arrive.
She looked quite cheerful for a woman who had just lost
so much money.

"So, how'd you girls make out?"

"I never got the hang of it but Maurice won a bundle.
He's very good," said Irene.

"I can't wait to get back to the tables. I tell you, I'm
hooked on craps. Good thing Trevor made me quit while
I was ahead. Ten big ones. Baby's gonna buy a lotta new
shoes today," said Eleanor.

"You mean you kept the money?" asked Irene.

"Damn straight. Why not? Didn't cost him anything."

"I was winning but then I got crazed and kept betting
red. I blew all of Jean-Jacques's money, a ton of it; a ton
of tin of it—but he didn't seem to mind at all," said Darlene. "How'd you do, Carla?"

"Totally tapped out. But Julio acted like it was spare
change to him—which it probably was."

"Come on girls, a shopping spree, my treat," said
Eleanor. "Let's blow it all."

The women finished breakfast and strolled off to shop.
Within the one square mile of Monte Carlo, there are
forty-five jewelry stores and over a hundred and seventy-
five shops selling clothing, lingerie, shoes, and leather
goods. They narrowed the list down to Stéphane Kélian,
Charles Jourdan, Pollini, Valentino, Yves St. Laurent,
Sonia Rykiel, Chanel, Escada, Céline, and Christian Dior.
The ten thousand was gone in the first hour, so the rest
of the morning was spent window-shopping. The women
were having the time of their lives. They all had dates
that afternoon: Darlene was flying to Marseilles in Jean-
Jacques's private jet, Irene was helicoptering to St. Tropez, Carla was to lunch at one of Julio's new restaurants,

and Eleanor had been invited to see Trevor's villa and his yacht. Not bad, for the third day.

The women had sought advice on dressing from the various shop ladies. Suggested were white slacks, or white pleated swirly skirts, big belts, gold sandals, sexy clinging tops or T-shirts, and colorful pastel cotton crew sweaters. Casual chic. Funds courtesy of Eleanor—uh, Greta Harmon-Cates, that is. Dark glasses, big hats, and large straw handbags completed the ensembles. The women would look very à la mode.

THE MEN WERE wearing white trousers, blue silky shirts, with sweaters tied casually around their necks; all except Julio, who wore a white linen suit with the jacket draped across his shoulders (Italian men never put their arms in the sleeves of their jackets on the Riviera), a blue shirt, and a red tie. Gucci shoes and a Borsalino hat completed his outfit.

"So, by my calculations they lost a total of one hundred and sixty-nine thousand five hundred dollars among them," said Jean-Jacques.

"That Harmon-Cates babe—you've got to see her at the craps table. She is something else," said Trevor.

"My beautiful contessa, she knows nothing about gambling. She lost continually after the first hand, but she acted like she was winning. What a woman," said Julio.

"All I know is that *we* didn't make a dime," said Jean-Jacques.

"What are you suggesting?" asked Maurice.

"I had a conversation with the Barlow lady about her jewelry. Said I hoped they kept it all in the hotel safe. I found out that they don't. She said if you were going to worry about jewelry, there was no joy in having it. Anyway, she said, it was all insured. Think about it. Their rooms are all going to be empty this afternoon because they'll be with us. We won't get a better opportunity. We drive to Zurich late tonight, put the jewels in a safe-deposit box in the morning when the banks open, and be back here by afternoon. Don't you see? We'll have the perfect alibi. The women won't suspect us since we'll be with them when the jewels are stolen."

"You know someone who can accomplish this?" said Trevor.

"I have just the man. I've already spoken to him. He'll do it for ten percent. It's a lot, but it's worth it. After the robbery he leaves for Rio de Janeiro, where he's from, and stays there. There'll be nothing to tie us to the crime. Nothing. Nada. Niente."

"Suppose he gets caught?" said Maurice. "Just suppose."

"How does he get into the rooms?" said Julio.

"How do you know we can trust him? Suppose he takes off with the jewels?" said Trevor.

"Too many questions. Too many reasons *not* to do something. And if we don't, we're missing out on the last opportunity we may ever have. I have to make a phone call. Now. My man is waiting. So give me your answers. You'll have to trust me that I've thought this through."

After a long pause, Julio said, "These are very attractive women. I never counted on that. Jean-Jacques is right. I agree. We have to act now before we become emotionally involved and begin to think with our *pecorinos*."

When Jean-Jacques came back, they voted. It was unanimous. The plan was a go. For Maurice a hesitant go, but a go nevertheless. He didn't have too many options left. This one had to work. He couldn't count on a "maybe" marriage to dig him out of his fiscal hole. That was a long shot, and Maurice Gerard did not play long shots.

SOMETIME LATER THAT day Maurice stood chatting with the concierge, Pierre. "What would I do without you, friend? Are you sure it's not an inconvenience?"

"Not at all," said Pierre. "The pilot has a girlfriend in

St. Tropez and was going there anyway while his boss is away. He owes me a favor, so everything is arranged. You won't have any difficulties."

"Merci, Pierre. Merci, mille fois."

AT THAT SAME moment Trevor Weymouth was speaking to an attractive maid in the kitchen at the villa where he worked, trying to cajole her into going along with his subterfuge. "Five hundred francs for you if you play your part. If you don't, you'll be back walking the streets in San Remo."

"You can count on me, as usual. I'll take the money now, please," she said coquettishly, holding out her hand. Trevor grabbed it and pulled her to him. With his other hand he reached under her skirt for her panties and in a second they were ripped off. After a halfhearted moment of obligatory struggle, she bit his lip as they kissed and reached for the zipper on his fly. Suddenly she stopped. "By the way, the price is two thousand francs. Agreed."

"That depends."

Her mouth was on him. She knew exactly what he liked, what all men liked. With her mouth full she managed to repeat, "Agreed?"

"Agreed, you bitch. Agreed. Don't stop."

"The money. Now," she mumbled, feeling his member throb with expectation in her mouth.

"Now? Right *now*?"

"Right now. Of course I can wait if—"

She never got to finish her sentence. The money was out of his pocket and into her hand, and she never missed a stroke with that practiced, professional mouth of hers.

The moment it was over Trevor realized that he could have negotiated a better deal. *Tant pis,* as the French say. *Tant pis and trop tard.* Too bad, and too late.

*   *   *

AT LINO'S RISTORANTE Elegante by the Sea, Julio was pleading with the headwaiter of the restaurant where he worked
as a pasta chef. "Please, Alberto, *prego*—this is the
woman I love, the love of my life. So don't screw up,
okay?"

"You remember our deal, right?" said Alberto, smiling
fiendishly.

Julio sighed. It would cost him a week's wages.
"*Certo. Io concordo.* I agree. You have my word on it."

"I wish you hadn't said that."

"And remember, please, to call me *Signor* Benvenuti,
not Julio."

"I don't remember agreeing to that," said the smug
Alberto as he walked away. "I'll see how it goes."

Julio was a nervous wreck. Could he really count on
that miserable mafioso, Alberto Pasqualini? After all, he
was from *Palermo*! He would hope for the best.

JEAN-JACQUES AND DARLENE stood on the platform of the
railroad station in Monte Carlo, waiting for the train to
Marseilles. "The ride along the sea is so beautiful. Much
better than what you can see from a plane. I hope you
don't mind. I thought it would be amusing. We have first-
class tickets."

"Why, Jean-Jacques, don't be a silly. I just love trains."

"Good. Good." It always helped to remember that very
rich people were eccentric, and knowing their particular
eccentricities could be useful. "I've brought some sandwiches. *Pain bagnat.* Tuna fish, olives, onions, hard-
boiled egg—sort of like a *salade niçoise* sandwich. You'll
love it."

"I'm sure I will," Darlene said, thinking, what a regular
guy her tin man seemed to be. One would never guess he
was a zillionaire.

13

"Four Hearts out on a Limb"

> . . . It's a heart out on a limb,
> When you start to feel forever in a kiss.
> —**Tom Waits,** "Foreign Affair"

MAURICE'S HELICOPTER LIFTED off from Nice airport and headed out over the sea as Inspector George Delarue watched. The pilot followed the coastline past Cap d'Antibes, Juan-les-Pins, Cannes, St. Raphael, and around the bay and over to the seaside beach called Tahiti. The beaches of St. Tropez have been preserved; no high-rises, no new hotels, no glitz and glitter—just two and one half miles of sandy beach dotted with wooden, grass-roofed shacks in the manner of a South Pacific island. One of the best beach clubs is run by that gray eagle, the famous Felix, a fixture in St. Tropez. The helicopter set down in an unused section of the parking lot, within short walking distance of the restaurant. There were four sections to Tahiti: the indoor restaurant (rarely used at lunch in summer), the outdoor terrace facing the sea, and a group of striped, awning-covered booths on a boardwalk at the edge of the sand. Sunning lounges in the sand took up the rest of the beach up to the water's edge.

The first thing that Irene noticed were the young women. It wasn't that some of them were topless, it was that *all* of them were topless, and almost bottomless, and no one seemed to notice—or if they did, they were blasé about it. And many bodies were spectacular, lean and lightly tanned. Few of the women, these days, went in for the Florida look of tanned leather. No jewelry except some fun baubles and a rope of pearls here and there.

Felix and Maurice were old friends and greeted each other warmly. Maurice and Irene were led to one of the best tables, an awning-shaded booth at the edge of the sand. Soft music was being provided by a trio near the open-air bar. Irene watched in awe as a man sent over a bottle of champagne—with a straw in it!—to the cute blond piano player. She took a sip, without missing a note, and looked around for her admirer. What an opening. Anywhere else it would have seemed too much, but not here. Palm trees, gnarled pines, and large striped parasols broke up the sun's rays. It was the sexiest place Irene had ever seen or even imagined. Maurice asked her if she wanted to change into a bathing suit, but Irene demurred, saying, "Maybe later." Irene still had a good body. True, her titties wouldn't pass the pencil test and a quarter wouldn't bounce on her belly, but she still looked fabulous in the right clothes and her Wonderbra. She could still turn a few heads on good hair days.

She noticed one woman alone, lying on her stomach, reading a book. Casually the woman reached around and unhooked the clasp on her bathing-suit top. Irene could almost read the woman's mind. *She wants to see what it feels like to be topless on a crowded beach and is working up the nerve.* She had probably been thinking about this moment ever since she made plans to come to St. Tropez. A clue was the white line the straps left on her back. Moments later she rose up on her elbows as casually as she could and looked around, as if searching for someone; exposing her white, pink-nippled breasts for the *barest* moment before she settled back down. There, she had done it! Irene silently guessed what was coming next: the woman would turn over on her back; then quickly real-

izing that this was not the best position for displaying her
breasts, she would stand and make a dash for the water—
like a flasher. Safe in the arms of Neptune. A few minutes
later she emerged, her nipples hardened from the cold
water. She had completed her initiation. You just couldn't
come to St. Tropez without exposing your nipples. It was
almost obligatory. Probably customs stamped it in your
passport: EXPOSED IN ST. TROPEZ. Now to get rid of those
white lines. She would talk about this moment with her
friends back home for a long time. It was like losing her
virginity, in public. Irene decided she would definitely
skip that rite of passage. The other women would be panting to know if she "did it." They would be sorely disappointed. Or maybe she would lie to them. Yes, she would
definitely lie to them. She couldn't *wait* to lie to them.

The beaches were surrounded with vineyards and Felix
sent over a cold bottle from the best one of them, Château
Minuty, a lovely crisp rosé wine, along with the ubiqui-
tous bottles of Evian and Perrier, a terrine of *pâté,* a sliced
toasted *baguette,* and a dish of *tapenade*. Maurice explained that tapenade was very *provençal*—made from ca-
pers, anchovy fillets, and black Mediterranean olives
mashed together in a mortar with some olive oil and
lemon juice (a bit of fresh garlic was optional) to make a
smooth, loose paste. It was best spread on the toasted
slices of *baguette* or used as a dip for *crudités*—raw vegetables.

Irene was so happy, overwhelmed, and out of her el-
ement that she found it hard to speak. In any event, speech
was unnecessary. A fashion show had just started—beautiful young girls modeling the latest St. Tropez beach and
evening fashions. Irene would have bought all of them.
Maurice ordered a cold lobster salad for two followed by
the famous *tarte Tropezienne* (the recipe was a secret well
kept from the tourists), which was the richest thing that
Irene had ever tasted. There is a saying in the south of
France that it gets dark right after lunch. That's because

one lingers and lazes, and the time drifts without notice. After the food it *was* time to talk.

"Natasha, what a beautiful name. How did you come to be called Natasha?"

"I gave myself that name. I'm glad you like it."

"You changed your name?"

"From Irene."

"You don't look like an Irene."

"I don't feel like an Irene either, anymore. Tell me, why is a rich, attractive man like yourself not married?"

"I'm afraid it's a cliché," said Maurice.

"Worried they're all after you for your money? Haven't found the right woman?"

"Something like that, yes. Those answers are as good as any, I suppose. And I might ask you the same question."

"Ah, too much traveling. Marbella, Corfu, Marrakesh— to the *dacha* in Siberia."

"Siberia? Really?"

"For the skiing," said Irene, recovering quickly.

"I didn't realize they had skiing there."

"They don't. But we had our own little mountain. It was amusing."

"I didn't mean to interrupt you."

"What else is there to say. When the baron died, leaving me a bottomless inheritance"—here Irene paused, threw in a little sniffle, and tried, unsuccessfully, to squeeze out a tear—"I was suddenly alone—with money that meant nothing to me."

"You're a very beautiful woman. If you're alone it must be because you want to be alone. True?"

"No. I would like to find a man who I trusted and loved—and be his last lover. I know that for a man, to be a woman's first lover is very important, but as you grow older that changes, or should change."

"Well put."

"So tell me, Maurice, who are you; what do *you* want?"

"We'll play a game. You tell me who you think I am."

"You look like you don't do much of anything, work-wise that is. You probably spend your days getting ready for your evenings, and your evenings—"

Maurice finished the sentence for her. "Buying beautiful women champagne and white caviar."

"Maybe. Have you ever been married?"

"A long time ago."

"Tell me about her."

"I was twenty-three. She was eighteen. She died two years later—a car accident; she loved fast cars, and—"

"I didn't mean to open old wounds; I'm sorry. Were there any children?"

"One. A daughter. She lives in Los Angeles."

"Do you see her?"

"From time to time, yes."

"And you never married again?"

"No."

"But there must be so many attractive and available women in Monte Carlo?"

"They come for the season, yes. For the balls, the parties, the yachts—anxious women who are divorced or widowed. It's a feeding frenzy. They spend Christmas in St. Moritz, February in Palm Beach, March in Switzerland, visiting their bankers and plastic surgeons, and August in Monte Carlo hunting for rich men. We call them 'headhunters.' "

"Sounds like a description of me. Is that what you think I am? A headhunter?"

"Of course not." Maurice leaned over and took her hand. "It's the last thing I think you are. You're a beautiful, rich, self-assured woman. I could tell you were different from the moment I first saw you."

"Really?"

Maurice took a chance and kissed the palm of her hand, lightly. The Baroness Natasha Karmanov melted.

*   *   *

IN FILM, THE word *montage* is used to describe a series of short scenes edited together, usually without dialogue, and underscored with romantic music, sometimes to denote the blossoming of a relationship. You've seen it in dozens of films. *Breakfast at Tiffany's* comes to mind, the montage in which George Peppard and Audrey Hepburn wander about Manhattan and fall in love—underscored by Henry Mancini's song "Moon River." It is so much easier to use film as a common denominator because so many of our fantasies derive from film. Combine, then, movies and music, and you have the ultimate vicarious experience. Identification of the highest order.

The montage usually ends at the "magic hour," the time of day when the sun has gone from the sky and the blue is deepening, still intense from the refracted rays. Shadows are soft, faces bathed in this favorite light of cinematographers reflect their best complexions. It lasts for less than an hour. It is the perfect time to fall in love, both cinematically and actually. Afterward, foot candles fade and color film photography without artificial light is difficult if not impossible. It is a time that can never be recaptured or recreated or counted upon to exist when you want it to exist. You can't force it or plan it. It becomes an indelible memory, a personal montage that you can replay in your mind, all of your life. It can be that special moment in a relationship when the man knows that the woman is his, and stretches out the moment into a long seduction that ends when the sky finally darkens and the early stars appear. It is the time when a woman decides to give herself to a man, for the first time, and neither rushes toward consummation, both luxuriating in the delay, knowing the final high will be higher.

All four women were in that state of mind. It wasn't a matter of *if* but of *how,* and where and when. Now, reader, you might ask once again, what are the odds of this happening to four women at the same time on the same day? Nothing so logical could have intruded upon the thoughts of our women in their reveries. Have you

seen the British Broadcasting Company's television pro-
duction of *Pennies from Heaven*? In it, the question "Why
can't life be like the lyrics of a song?" is asked. Today,
for the four women, the answer is: It was.

> *. . . a one in a million chance,*
> *You know the moment you cross over the line . . .*

Irene recalled a summer at the Jersey shore when she
and a group went to the beach with a picnic lunch that
included two bottles of wine. Beach police confiscated the
wine and gave them a ticket for disorderly conduct—con-
sumption of alcohol on a public beach, fifty bucks, and
admonished them for their behavior. *Vive la différence*.

Maurice suggested a walk at the water's edge. It was
six o'clock. The beach was deserted. *The robbery had
taken place*. Couples here and there sipping drinks, loung-
ing, listening to music that had suddenly become mellow,
sexy—yes, it was unbelievably sexy. The last rays of the
sun lighting up a sailboat; its spinnaker dancing in the
soft wind. It was no-talking time again. Holding-hands
time. Accidental-touching time. Smiling time. They
reached a small thatched-roof hut on the dunes. Jacques
Brel was singing "Ne Me Quitte Pas" on the sound system, one of the most heartrending love songs ever written.
Irene had never heard the original French version, only
the one with lyrics by Rod McKuen, retitled "If You Go
Away." Maurice suggested they stop. He ordered two
Campari orange drinks—the Campari blazing in the juice
like a radiant sun—and they sat on white-duck-cushioned
lounges and waited for the magic hour. Irene wanted to
tell Maurice everything, the truth. It seemed the right time.
There would never be a better time. But how would he
take it, her admitting to being a headhunter? No, she
wouldn't spoil the day; she'd wait.

*   *   *

JULIO REMINDED CARLA of her late husband, Giovanni di Benedetto. She had always been attracted to Italian men even though she knew the drawbacks. She didn't feel the same about Americanized, assimilated Italians who didn't even speak their ancestral tongue; they were just like all the other guys. She knew what kind of man Julio was, knew instinctively what his needs would be, his likes and dislikes. Knew how he, like all Italian men, viewed women, marriage, divorce, family, love, sex. It was better not to marry them; they would break your heart. How did Marcello M.'s wife feel, knowing he was fooling around with Catherine D. and had fathered a child with her. It was in all the papers. It was no doubt painful, but obviously not painful enough to cause a divorce. Staying married, no matter what, is a talent peculiar to the Italians. Their women accept their men's infidelities, accept their need to constantly validate their manhood. It is in the genes. But family counted, big time. Mama was worshiped, respected. A wife you were indifferent to, privately tolerating and publicly venerating her. Many treated the pope the same way. Carla knew that her husband had had the odd casual extramarital affair, if screwing around can be called casual. Because she was American, her culture made her rebel inwardly against his infidelities. Yet she also knew that he loved her.

One of the most poignant moments in the film *Moonstruck* occurs when Vincent Gardenia says to his wife, played by Olympia Dukakis, *Te amo,* I love you. And she looks at her philandering husband and says *te amo* back to him. They don't caress; tons of unspoken sentences flash past their eyes, and he goes upstairs. She has not accepted, but rather borne his infidelities with unexpressed pain. Now that it has been tacitly acknowledged that the husband will give up his mistress, the subject will be forgotten. A marriage is supposed to be forever, no matter what. So Carla watched Julio strut his stuff and fan his feathers for her, and smiled at his ritualized, shopworn, transparent, seduction technique—and loved him for it.

They were seated on the terrace of the restaurant overlooking the old yacht harbor in Fontvielle. Carla had dressed all in black, in a fitted sleeveless sheath of vintage shantung silk, the V-cut neckline revealing just a tease of cleavage. A small pillbox hat pinned into her hair with a sheer veil edging down from its rim to the tip of her nose completed an outfit perfect for a woman in mourning who was chasing after a man.

Julio had ordered an antipasto that included *pisci a'ovu* (egg fritters), *cappelle di funghi ripiene* (baked stuffed mushroom caps), *sarde in carpione* (fried, marinated sardines), a salad of *treviso* and endive, *canestrelli trifolati* (sautéed scallops with garlic and parsley), and the house specialty: mini-*focaccia* topped with sautéed onions and *gorgonzola dolce*. Following this was a dish that Julio had devised himself: *penne* with oven-dried Roma tomatoes recooked in extra-virgin olive oil from Liguria, pink garlic, and, to make it spicy, a touch of *peperoncino*. Some young, two-year-old, nutty Parmesan, "shaved, not grated," and that was it. Never any basil, it interfered with the intensified sweetness of the tomatoes, which had been baked in a very low-temperature oven for six hours.

The main course was a skinless filet of turbot, pan-grilled and braised in a tomato sauce that had been severely reduced to a jam with fresh gingerroot, garlic, cumin seed, a touch of cinnamon, hot pepper, and some honey. This was served with a circle of fried *polenta*, crunchy with fresh corn. Dessert was peeled sliced oranges topped with their caramelized zest and strewn with wild strawberries. For the wines: a cold, sparkling Lambrusco with the antipasto, a 1985 Marchesi di Antinori red with the *penne,* an Orvieto to accompany the fish, and a sip of sweet and spicy chilled Malvasia di Lippari with the dessert.

Of course he knew that Carla couldn't even come close to eating all of this feast. Julio would be understanding and reassuring: "Just to taste."

Carla's husband had used the same expression. The one time they had visited his family in Rome, her mother-in-law had spent three days cooking every dish she knew—or so it seemed. The morning of the feast Carla had sent a large bouquet of flowers ahead. That afternoon she received a larger bouquet thanking her for sending flowers. Italians! At dinner Carla had foolishly admired a brooch her sister-in-law was wearing. In the car, going back to the hotel, they found it in a small box on the dashboard. One simply could not have the last word. The day they were leaving, her father-in-law pressed a large basket of food on them: Parmesan cheese, a whole *prosciutto di San Danielli,* a large bottle of extra-virgin olive oil, a string of garlic, and a box of *biscotti.* When Carla tried to assure him that they could buy all of this at home in the States, he scoffed at her. "The olive oil you get is from Greece and Spain, with a phony label, the cheese is probably a *grana* made in Calabria," the *prosciutto* he didn't even want to discuss, except to say, "Everyone knows it doesn't travel." Carla had no choice but to buy a large suitcase and lug all of it home. But they discovered that the old man was right; the products were very different from what they could buy in New Jersey. They wrote and told him that. It made his day. *"Americanos!"*

Julio had been known to put six different pastas on the table at the same time—for a table of two! "Just to taste," he would say. Who could resist him? Carla felt warm with Julio; at home with him.

When they arrived at the restaurant the head waiter was effusive: "Ah, Signor Benvenuti, you should have told us you were coming. We would have prepared something special."

"We'll sit by the window," said Julio, brushing past him and sweeping the "Reserved" sign to the floor with a flourish.

"Asti Spumante per il padrone," said the obsequious Alberto, offering the cheapest wine in the house.

"No, no, no—due Campari soda. Pronto."

As the Calabrese went off to get the drinks, Julio apologized for the man's behavior. "Impossible to get good help these days." Lunch was spent talking about the food. Afterward, over the last of the Malvasia di Lipari and an espresso, Julio reached across the table and took Carla's hand—noticing that the ruby ring was missing. If everything went as planned, it would be in his pocket by this evening. "I want to know everything about la Contessa Stephania di Romanesco. Everything," he said.

"I am in mourning. That is why I am wearing black—and this veil."

"When did he die?" whispered Julio.

"Five years ago."

"It is too much. Why do you mourn for such a long time? It is not natural."

"Because I know I can never replace him. He was tall, like you, Italian, like you, charming and rich, like you—and he loved to cook. I don't suppose you cook, do you?"

"A little. For friends. What did your husband do?"

"Do? I don't know. I never asked. It was easier that way. I think it had something to do with cement."

"Ah, cement," said Julio, shaking his head knowingly. *"Cemento."*

"We had an island, near Sardinia. Not very large; a few thousand acres. A small airport for our jet. It was comfortable. I will never go there again. Too many memories."

Julio squeezed her hand in commiseration. "Maybe, one day, we will go there, together," he said, leaning in closer and lifting her veil, "after your period of mourning is over, of course."

"I think it will be over soon. *Very* soon."

Julio took a chance and kissed her ever so lightly on the lips—scarcely touching them. It was as if he were kissing a choir girl, a virgin, a Madonna. She shivered.

"I would like you to leave the veil on," he whispered.

"Of course," she said breathlessly.

*   *   *

TREVOR WAS ON board his employer's yacht, checking on the last details and talking to the boat's captain. He had sent one of the houseboys to fetch Eleanor in the silver Corniche. Another five-hundred-franc tip. This was getting expensive.

"Just remember," said the captain, "this boat doesn't move. You can use the tender, but that's it. The boss watches the fuel like a hawk to see if we're messing around when he's away."

"Don't worry, just do your part."

"You sure that maid won't talk?"

"It's arranged."

"I hear she does incredible things with her mouth."

"I wouldn't know," said Trevor as he took the captain's hat and set it on his own head. "How do I look?"

"You're not my type."

Trevor was just tying up the tender to the villa's dock when the maid announced that Madame Harmon-Cates had arrived. After showing her the villa, he and Eleanor walked out to the pool terrace overlooking the sea, where the maid served them cocktails.

"Is that your yacht out there?"

"Yes. We're going to lunch on board and cruise out to the Isle St. Marguerite off Cannes, if that's agreeable."

"No," said Eleanor facetiously, "I'd rather get a burger, fries, and a Coke at McDonald's."

The maid stood off to the side of the terrace despite Trevor's several signals for her to leave. No way was she going to miss this living soap opera.

"This is a wonderful spot. I've always loved Cap Ferrat," said Eleanor.

"It's rather amusing, yes, for a few weeks a year. But never in August. And how do you spend most of your time?"

"When I'm not slaving nine to five at the office? At

the hairdresser, vacuuming, knitting, gardening, aerobics classes. It's a hellish schedule."

Trevor liked this woman's spunk, her offbeat sense of humor; her I-don't-give-a-damn-what-anyone-thinks point of view. He'd always found the casino to be the dullest place in town, but last night he'd really enjoyed himself.

"How do you really spend your days, Greta?"

Eleanor almost said, "Who?" but caught herself at the last second, reminding herself that *she* was Greta Harmon-Cates. "Selling tanks and rockets."

"Seriously."

"I am being serious. When Harrington died I thought, How can a woman like me operate an armaments business? I managed to learn about it rather quickly. Seems everyone wants to buy a bomb or a tank these days. It's like selling anything else. We put out a catalog—not much different from any of the other catalogs you get in the mail, only we're selling weapons of destruction." Eleanor had her back to the maid or she would have seen her expose her breasts to Trevor and then raise her short skirt; she wasn't wearing any panties. Trevor had seen to that earlier.

Trevor took Eleanor by the arm and steered her out of harm's way, down to the dock. The maid followed. "That will be all, Chantal," said Trevor, rather sternly.

"I thought you would like me to help you get off," she said.

"I'll handle *that*," said Eleanor, under her breath.

"That won't be necessary," he said.

"As you wish. *Bon voyage, monsieur 'dame,*" she said, curtsying so low that her more than ample bosom almost tumbled out of her unbuttoned uniform top. Finally she had no choice but to leave them alone; she'd had her fun.

"Sexy maid," quipped Eleanor. "Have you had her long?"

"Yes. I mean, no. A few months."

"She must be quite a distraction."

"I really don't notice the help that much. They've become sort of invisible to me, as they should be, don't you think?"

As Trevor helped her into the tender, she let go with a zinger: "Don't bullshit me, Trev, one thing a woman can tell is when a man has fucked another woman. It's like a private wavelength that only women are plugged into." Before a stunned Trevor Weymouth could respond, she continued: "Whenever I was at a party with my husband, I could always tell if there was a woman in the room he'd slept with. 'Greta,' he'd say, 'I'd like you to meet Mr. and Mrs. Smith, Harriet and John.' Right away I knew he'd once banged Harriet." As the tender continued toward the yacht, Eleanor continued further: "Men are always amazed that women have this talent because *they* don't. When I confronted my husband, he said, 'Yes, you're right, but that was years ago, before I met you. How did you ever guess?' Truth was I hadn't guessed. I *knew*."

"You're a funny lady," Trevor yelled as he pressed the throttle forward, causing the twin outboards to roar.

"If it's in my head it comes out of my mouth. I don't like bullshit because it's so time-consuming."

Why do I always attract the same schmucks? thought Eleanor. Trevor's just like Harry, a major sport-fucker. Only difference, this one is loaded, the gorgeous bastard. If he doesn't make a pass at me, I'll kill myself.

"Cute boat," she said as the tender's motors cut out. She had to admit she was impressed. But what was the point? What chance did a lawyer from New Jersey have— or want—with a Don Juan like Trevor. Did she have psychic powers? Ha! She'd seen the reflection of that bitch in Trevor's sunglasses, exposing herself and silently laughing. He obviously likes you or you wouldn't be here, thought Eleanor. Sure as hell he's not after your money.

At that moment the hired thief was rifling though her room at the Hotel de Paris, looking for her jewels.

"Make yourself comfortable," said Trevor. "I'll just have a word with the captain before we get moving."

Eleanor walked to the starboard rail and looked out at the fantastic scenery. The hills above the villa were dotted with other Mediterranean-style villas; to her right, the Hotel de La Voile d'Or jutted out into the sea at water level. It was a mini-paradise. She had read in the travel guides that Cap Ferrat was a preserve; you had to have permission to cut down a pine tree and all buildings were limited to a height of twenty-seven feet. She imagined what would happen if the zoning rules were relaxed. The same thing that happened to places like Acapulco: one high-rise luxury hotel after another on the beach. Disaster.

Eleanor walked into the lounge. There was a piano in the corner. A piano on a boat? Why not? Eleanor sat down and quietly started to play the opening measures of Chopin's "Impromptu" in A-flat Major. Trevor stood in the doorway, watching and listening. She played the short piece well. He was impressed. She stopped when she realized he was in the room. "I'm sorry. I was in another place."

"I know what you mean," said Trevor. "The same thing happens to me."

"You play?"

"A bit."

"Classical?"

"For myself. I love Chopin."

"Please," she said, moving to make room on the piano bench.

Trevor sat down and began to play Chopin's "Nocturne" in B Major. It was heartbreaking, perfect for the setting—and it never failed to be the perfect seduction piece.

It made Eleanor cry inwardly for all the things she knew she would never have, all the experiences she would never know, all the time she had wasted. She would find out if Trevor was a Gemini—twins, in the same body. She'd bet on it. She'd seen the two different personas herself. She'd known many men who cultivated a macho veneer to cover their dominant "feminine" characteristics. No man could play like he did, with such emotion, and not have a loving soul somewhere down there. She would just have to dig for it. When he stopped, she pleaded for one more, like a lover begging for tender stroking in the afterglow of lovemaking, and he played one of her favorite nocturnes—the A-flat Major, which was equally heartrending.

Eleanor's "blossoming-of-a-relationship montage" would be scored with Chopin. The sea and Chopin.

WHEN TREVOR FINISHED playing he turned on the hi-fi unit and loaded the disc player with more Chopin. "I'm afraid there's a problem with one of the engines, so it doesn't look like we'll be able to move today. I'll arrange for some lunch. Make yourself comfortable, I'll be right back."

Eleanor couldn't have cared less whether the boat moved or not. While he was gone she thought, Why am I attracted to this guy? Just because he's rich, handsome, and plays the piano? I'll bet he goes through women like me twice a week. Why is it my fate to always be infatuated with narcissistic bastards like him when there are dozens of rich, handsome guys lined up around the block desperate to meet me? Sure. Right. Better go with the flow, babe. Take what you can get. Have a nice day, Eleanor.

They ate from a small buffet that was laid out carefully on the fantail, and sipped cold, gold-flecked Montrachet. Trevor was, unfortunately, the perfect gentleman; Eleanor had to make the first move. She didn't know that this was part of his plan. She asked for a tour of the boat, and when they came to the master stateroom, she lay back on the king-size bed and held out her arms to him. The rest was an afternoon in paradise. The gentle rocking of the boat, the gentle Chopin, the surprisingly gentle man—as sensitive as the last nocturne on the disc, the C Minor. After that there was just the sound of water lapping against the hull of the yacht and the slowly receding tension of their lovemaking, colored by lambent light, as the room glowed softly in the orangegold of a setting sun melting into the horizon. Eleanor was in love, or something like it. As for Trevor, if she could have read his mind, she would have known that far from being in the throes of afterglow, his closed eyes and lazy smile covered scheming thoughts.

I might be able to make this one work, Trevor thought. She sees right through me. She knew about the maid right off, and yet she managed to have a sense of humor about it and still be very attracted to me. Obviously a tough lady—but I think I could handle her. Maybe we each have what the other wants. I know she has what I want. Don't screw this one up like you have the others, Trevor. Take it slow. Business first.

Gemini: witty and charming. The perfect sign for a con man.

A TAXI TOOK Jean-Jacques and Darlene to the soccer stadium in Marseilles on the Boulevard Michelet. It was not a huge stadium by American standards, but 46,000 seats could not be considered small by any means. In 1984, an additional 8,848 people jammed themselves in and stood to see France play Portugal. It was a record-breaking attendance figure. Soccer was a big sport in Marseilles. The biggest, by far. The team that called the stadium home was the Olympi de Marseille, one of the oldest in the league, founded in 1898. Jean-Jacques had played on two championship teams here—in 1972, when they were Champion de France, and in 1976, when the team was the winner of the coveted Coupe de France. Jean-Jacques had scored two goals in each of the games, making him a hometown hero. He was a *buteur*, a striker, par excellence, until the accident in 1977 ended his career. He regaled Darlene with this information, and although she had never seen a soccer game in her life, she was rapt with attention.

"What kind of uniforms did you wear?" she asked.

"They were white, with two blue stripes on each shoulder," he said.

She imagined him as Troy Aikman of the Dallas Cowboys, backpedaling and throwing a touchdown bomb to Michael Irvin.

Darlene thought it seemed oddly quiet as the taxi pulled up to the stadium gate. The vast parking lot was completely empty. Maybe Jean-Jacques had made a mistake about the day? But he didn't seem troubled at all, and after paying the taxi driver, he led her to a door marked PRIVÉ, private. It was the players' entrance and was usually heavily guarded. Players needed serious protection from their adoring fans. Today, the door was unlocked, with only a watchman seated on the other side. He rose instantly and embraced Jean-Jacques as an old friend. They chatted for a minute in French and then the old man led the way toward the gate to the field. After unlocking it, he asked Jean-Jacques to wait. In a moment he was back with a soccer ball and a felt pen. *"Pour mon petit-fils"*—for my grandson. Jean-Jacques signed the ball and the old guy beamed as he walked off with his prize.

Jean-Jacques took Darlene's hand and led her to the center of the field or, as it is called in soccer, the "pitch." This one was covered in real, rather than artificial, turf that seemed to stretch for miles. Like a football field it was surrounded by grandstand seats, with the netted goals at either end. Jean-Jacques asked her to wait as he ran off toward the team locker room.

Standing there had a rather dizzying effect on Darlene. It took her back to another day, another time—when she had ridden into a stadium much like this one, sitting on a huge float, as the homecoming queen. When the float stopped in the center of the field, she stood up and blew kisses to the crowd, which had roared its approval. It was a sound she would never forget. It was the highlight of her life.

Her daydream was shattered by what sounded like a

gunshot. As she turned in the direction of the noise, she saw a black-and-white soccer ball arcing toward her. It landed, bounced, and rolled to her feet. At the end of the field, near one of the netted goals, Jean-Jacques stood, dressed in the white-and-blue regulation team uniform: shorts, kneesocks, and numbered shirt. He laughed and came running toward her. For a moment Darlene didn't realize it was him.

"Kick it to me," he said.

She gave it as hard a whack as she could, sending the ball dribbling in his general direction. Jean-Jacques ran toward it, tapped it from one foot to the other, lofted it with a toe into the air, bounced it on one knee and then the other, up over his head; head-butting it high when it came down. Quickly he tumbled head over heels as he gave the ball a perfect overhead bicycle kick toward the net. Catching up with it, he executed a perfect scissors kick, which sent the ball flying into the net with incredible velocity and force. Falling to his knees, his arms raised in victory, Jean-Jacques turned to Darlene. Her applause reverberated in the empty arena. Jean-Jacques got to his feet and ran around the entire perimeter of the field—like a madman.

Darlene had never seen a soccer game, but now she knew how it must be played, and was anxious to see one. At college, all the jocks had tried unsuccessfully to date her, but she wanted more than any of those machos could ever provide. Not that she wasn't turned on by them; she was. Now here was a jock who not only turned her on but could give her more than she'd ever dreamed of. Would there be enough of the beauty queen left to tempt him? she wondered.

Jean-Jacques ran up to her and dropped to the turf at her feet, exhausted, panting, struggling for breath. "The last time I did that was in 1976," he managed to say. "Do you have any idea why I brought you here today? Obviously, I knew there was no game scheduled."

"I think so," said Darlene. "You wanted to show me

your old house, on a day when the new tenants weren't home."

Jean-Jacques was speechless. This woman, whom he'd taken to be an attractive bubblehead, was more than just a spoiled, rich socialite. She was intelligent and perceptive. At first he'd chosen this ploy because it was a cheap and eccentric way of spending the day. When you chased tips all day as a doorman, you weren't anxious to throw money around casually, especially on rich women. But when he came onto the field, something had happened. He wasn't acting; he was caught up in a wave of nostalgia and pain—and somehow this rich dame understood.

"Can you imagine what it was like? Thousands of people chanting your name over and over: 'Jean-Jacques-Jean-Jacques-Jean-Jacques.' It never leaves you."

"I know," said Darlene. "Believe me, I know."

"It ruined me for a long, long time. After all that action and adulation I had a hard time adjusting to life as a businessman. I must have been impossible to live with. I remember a famous pianist who said he went to discos after his concerts to get the notes out of his head; otherwise he'd be up all night replaying the performance. I lived soccer, I dreamed soccer, replayed the games in my sleep."

"And how did *you* get the notes out of your head?"

"The usual three," he said, smiling sheepishly. "Alcohol, drugs, and—"

"Women," Darlene said, ending the sentence for him. Taking a few steps away from him, she asked, "Were you married?"

"Yes, but there was no room for her—for anyone—in my life. It was too full of 'Jean-Jacques-Jean-Jacques-Jean-Jacques—' "

"And since then?"

"Maybe I'm still replaying my past life instead of living it in the present. When the doctors said I couldn't play again, I refused to believe them. It was like stepping off a cliff and falling, but never hitting the ground."

"What did you do?"

"Part of me wanted to settle down, raise a family. Another part wanted action, so I left France and became a workaholic, in the jungles of Bolivia." Jean-Jacques hadn't planned on saying those last few words, but they sounded great: in the jungles of Bolivia. He was really into it now. The first part of the story had been true, if a bit exaggerated, as stories get with age.

"There were tin mines in the jungles?"

"Yes. Tin—and the danger that goes with it."

"Dog eat dog?"

"Lion eat lion."

"There are *lions* in Bolivia?"

"It's the lion capital of the world."

"Did you ever kill any?"

"Many," he whispered. "Too many."

THEY BEGAN TO walk toward the end of the field; Jean-Jacques listlessly nudging the soccer ball in front of him. "My group used to sit there," he said, pointing to a spot in the stands. "They all wore shirts with my number on it—and got the crowd going, started all the chants. They were like an opera claque—there to start the bravos."

Jean-Jacques suddenly kicked the ball as hard as he could into the net. Then he just stood there and tears came to his eyes as he looked over at his nonexistent claque, waiting for the reaction. He could hear their ghostly voices. He had tried to coach but he'd been too brash as a player, made too many enemies, pissed off too many of the brass with his antics. They put up with him because he was a star, but after his injury he couldn't even get them on the phone.

"Do you have a lot of trophies?" asked Darlene.

"A roomful."

"Me, too. I love to look at them, don't you?"

"Only when I've had too much to drink. Were you in sports?"

"Beauty pageants."

"Which ones?"

"My mother started entering me in local contests when I was five. I won lots of silly titles. When I became a teenager I entered the national events. Pretty soon I was Miss Teenage this, Miss Teenage that. It was more for the mothers than the girls. They really got into it. I must have been in a hundred contests until the Miss Southeast Texas one, which led to my being crowned Miss Texas, and a trip to the 'big show,' the Miss America Pageant. Now it's like it all happened to another person. Even when I look at the trophies and the pictures, I feel like I'm looking at another person. Of course, I *am*. That *was* another person. One day I woke up as an ex–beauty queen. There's nothing worse than an ex-anything."

"Don't I know it."

"I finally understood that I had to spend my time being some*one* and not some*thing*."

"But I'm sure—"

"Don't ask me about other men," she said, anticipating his question. "The good ones are either taken or burned-out."

"Like me."

"I hope that's not true. You seem to have everything."

Shadows were beginning to stretch over the field as they sat at the goal, under the netting.

"Do you still remember what you were thinking about when they put all those crowns on your head?" said Jean-Jacques.

"Probably the same thoughts that went through your mind after you scored goals that won games."

Jean-Jacques reached up and put an imaginary crown on her head. "Sex?"

"Sex."

"And what's going through your mind right now?"

"The same thing that's going through yours," said Darlene.

And right there, under the bower of the goal, the strings

of the netting magically morphed into the branches of a blooming magnolia tree as Darlene and Jean-Jacques dissolved into each other's arms, the golden boy and the golden girl celebrating their past triumphs and considering their possible future alliance. Darlene's montage was scored by the chanting of the adoring crowd. The tendrils of her orgasm started the moment he touched her.

The old watchman looked on and smiled. A former player in his youth, he, too, remembered a time, a game, a girl . . .

14
"To Catch a Thief"

Men should be what they seem.
—Shakespeare, Othello

FIVE DETECTIVES SAT in front of Inspector Delarue's desk at police headquarters. Each had a notebook opened and was ready to report on the day's activities. Darlene and Jean-Jacques had not seen the one spectator high in the stands, behind a pole. Eleanor and Trevor had taken little notice of the nearby fisherman in his small boat. Carla and Julio never even glanced at the other patrons of the restaurant. Even if they had they would have thought little of the small man eating a plate of *ziti siciliana al forno.* Irene and Maurice paid little heed to the topless woman who sat in a lounge near their table at Tahiti Beach. The fifth detective had been dispatched to visit Van Cleef & Arpels, Cartier, Bulgari, and Tiffany to inquire, circumspectly, if any jewels lent to clients of the Hotel de Paris were missing. He had not, as yet, returned.

When the detectives left, Inspector Delarue said to his number two, "I am still suspicious, but sex is not illegal, Bernard." The inspector flipped through his notes. "Jean-Jacques Lacoste right on the soccer field, Trevor Weymouth on his boss's yacht. We don't know about this

Benvenuti character, but our man said he took the contessa into the kitchen for a tour after the chefs had gone for the day and didn't emerge for a half hour. As for the King of Hearts, Maurice Gerard, Ola reports that there was no sex unless it was in the helicopter, which is doubtful. He's clever, that one. Maybe a bit too cool for his own good. I think I'll have another talk with him. By the way, that Ola—she's someone to watch. I like her inventiveness. A topless detective; it may be a first for the department."

THE WORLD'S BEST jewel thieves work the French Riviera during the "season." This is the time and place when they know women are going to show off their booty. But jewelry is rarely stolen while it is being worn; it is taken from guest rooms in private villas and hotel suites. Even the locked safe boxes offered by hotels are no defense against the clever thief, as has been amply demonstrated. The light-fingered gentry are rarely caught because their advance reconnaissance is impeccable. Inside information that tells them who will be where and when comes from their network of informants, who are well paid. Airline, hotel, and limousine reservations are a road map to success and the information is easier to come by than one might imagine. We all tend to think that our comings and goings are private, that we can travel in a safe, invisible bubble. Nothing could be further from the truth. We are all so easy to track.

To a professional, getting into a hotel room is child's play. What he wants to avoid, at all costs, is confrontation. Conveniently empty rooms make his life easy. The police are mostly indifferent to this type of crime because usually no one is injured, no intruder identified, and by the time the thefts are discovered, the culprits are well away and the loot disposed of. Important or identifiable pieces are reset or shipped out of the country. This allows the thieves to strike with relative impunity. The best time is lunchtime—around 1:30 P.M.—when the local gendarmes and municipal police are loath to interrupt their sacred meals unless there is blood in the streets.

Antonio Guzman would have easily gotten away with the theft of jewelry from the suites of the four women had it not been for the unsuspected surveillance of the hotel by Inspector Delarue's men. Hoping to snare bigger fish than Guzman, they followed him in an unmarked delivery van. Followed him, surprisingly, to the apartment house where Maurice Gerard had recently become a reluctant tenant. The inspector had been called immediately and they awaited his imminent arrival. He was in the middle of dinner and would be there as soon as he finished his *lapin à la moutade*—rabbit with mustard sauce. As Guzman, carrying a large briefcase, entered the building elevator, a nondescript woman carrying a bag of groceries stepped in behind him. This time it was not necessary for her to be topless.

Guzman ignored her and stepped off at Maurice's floor as she continued upward. Emerging at the top floor, she began to walk quietly down the stairs.

The men sat around Maurice's small desk as Trevor opened the briefcase. It was jammed full with jewels: strands of diamonds, dozens of earrings, brooches, rings, pearls, emeralds, rubies; a king's ransom, or so it appeared. Trevor looked at the swag suspiciously and put a magnifying loupe in one eye to inspect a few of the items more closely. First he chose what appeared to be a ten-carat diamond ring and, after studying it briefly, tossed it away contemptuously. Next he picked up a ruby choker, followed quickly by a diamond necklace. As he looked up at the men, the loupe fell from his eye and clattered to the floor. "Junk," he said. "Worthless fucking junk. Are you sure you had the right rooms?"

Guzman said that he was sure. In a hurry, he had taken everything there was without studying it closely. The hotel had tight security and he was anxious to get out as quickly as possible. His disguise as a chauffeur had kept security from paying more than cursory attention to him, since they were used to chauffeurs wandering about as they waited endlessly for their clients.

"Merde," said Jean-Jacques.

"Are you sure?" said Julio. *"Da vero?"*

"Look for yourself. It doesn't take an expert to see glass, peeling gold paint, and glued-in rhinestones. Shit, they're not only rhinestones, they're cheap rhinestones."

"MAURICE GERARD'S FIRST adventure in larceny. Serves me right. Nevertheless, it's rather hard to believe. Why would they have this stuff?"

"Who knows? Rich ladies can be nutty," said Jean-Jacques. "I was wrong. They must keep the real stuff in the hotel safe."

Antonio Guzman shrugged. It wasn't his fault. Hell, he'd taken the risk, not them.

"Get this rubbish out of here and toss it, Guzman," said Jean-Jacques. "I'm sorry, I'll make it up to you. It wasn't your fault."

Guzman scooped up all of the "jewels" and snapped the briefcase shut. He had a girlfriend who'd go wild over all this fool's gold.

After he left, there was nothing heard in the room for a minute except the silent hum of dejection. Finally, Julio said, "I'm almost glad it didn't work. I think la contessa and me—*che sacrificio*—it would be a sacrifice, but I would do it."

"I know how you feel," said Jean-Jacques. "Me and the Barlow lady—well, who knows? It might work."

"Marriage is out of the question for me," said Maurice quietly, "especially under these circumstances."

"The end of that sentence—what does it mean?" said Julio. "Are you saying that under different circumstances you could be interested in her—never minding the money?"

"You know as well as I do that I cannot afford to 'not

mind the money' at this point in my life. So the question is moot," Maurice replied.

Julio pressed: "But if it was not this 'moot' as you say?"

"I will admit that she's different from the others I've known. Yes."

"Sounds to me like you're in love," said Jean-Jacques.

Before Maurice could respond, Trevor chimed in. "Look, none of us has the luxury of thinking what could be—only what is. Now we just fucked up rather royally, so I think we should face facts: no matter what we say, when they find out the truth about us—"

"And they will," said Julio,

"When they find out that we're losers, then what?" said Jean-Jacques.

His statement was met with silence.

"Why don't we turn off the love songs and make another plan before they take off."

Nobody had an idea. Except Julio. "We could tell them."

"Tell them *what*?" said Trevor.

"You know—something outrageous. Like the truth."

"Gentlemen," said Maurice, "consider the facts. Everything we are is smothered in subterfuge. Lies upon lies. For me, it's been twenty-five years of telling women what they wanted to hear, doing what they wanted to do, being what they expected me to be. Let's face it: we're all fantasies to them, something they can't get at home. If they find out who we really are, what do you think will happen next?"

"The next time you're together with the baroness, why don't you broach the subject—maybe as a joke—see how she takes it," said Jean-Jacques.

"Look, we're not frogs who are going to change into princes, we're princes who are going to change into frogs before their very eyes. Tiny frogs. *Image,* gentlemen. Image is everything, and we're about to lose ours, and we will never be able to survive in the depths of their disappointment. Don't fool yourselves."

It was a speech made from the heart. It was pure truth. Confession. And they all knew it. Nevertheless, Maurice considered what Jean-Jacques had said. He would think more about it later, when he was alone, and not forced into making speeches.

"He's right," said Trevor. "We all know what wealthy women like them are looking for. Let's face it, I'm a friggin' butler. Julio, you're a pasta chef."

Somehow that was a revelation to Julio, and he almost cried.

"And me, Count Jean-Jacques Lacoste. The only thing I count are the number of times a day I open the door at the Hotel Hermitage."

Everyone turned to Maurice. "Don't spare me," he said.

"We're part-timers," said Jean-Jacques. "At least you've never pretended to be anything other than what you are."

"An aging gigolo," said Maurice.

"But you never lied, like we did," said Trevor. "Women knew what you were—and they not only accepted it but they came back for more. You were discreet elegance they could rent."

"And discard," added Maurice.

"They saw what they wanted to see," said Julio. "You were never other than who you were and everyone gave you respect for that. I have lived a life of pretending, even to myself. I talk lies to the beautiful contessa and I find myself believing them. It is very sad."

"You have so many friends in this town, Maurice," said Jean-Jacques, "which is more than I can say for the rest of us."

"*Da vero,*" said Julio, ending the conversation. "*Da vero.*"

*   *   *

LATER, AT HOME in his depressing apartment, Maurice thought back to the conversation. Could he really even consider being in love with someone like the baroness? Wasn't she just another in the long line of women who would get to wear one of his silk robes? Wouldn't the gold watch be bestowed, as usual, if he let it be? But he *wouldn't* let it be. He was after all the chips on the table this time. But as Julio had said, suppose things were different? Would she be just another easy conquest—or was he actually in love with this woman? It was a question hard for him to even consider let alone admit to. Why was this one different? He'd been with more attractive women, women just as intelligent, just as interesting, so why this one? He didn't know. He left the dreariness of his apartment, which was no place to contemplate the subject of love, and took a long walk down to the port.

Love, he thought. Why does one person love another, fall in love with another? Even the word "fall" was suspicious, denoting a misstep. No one had ever figured that one out.

You're alone with yourself, Maurice. No point in lying. Are you in love—purely, simply, truly—or not? Simple question that needs an unequivocal answer. "Yes," he said aloud, and thought, Now that I've said it, I can forget it and get on with the unpleasant business at hand. What other option is there? None.

ANTONIO GUZMAN WAS arrested by Inspector Delarue's men the moment he stepped out of the apartment building entrance. They took him to police headquarters, where he confessed to everything and gave up all the names of his accomplices: Maurice Gerard, Julio Benvenuti, Trevor Weymouth, and Jean-Jacques Lacoste.

MEANWHILE, THE WOMEN were meeting with the four jewelry salesman, taking delivery of new sets of precious gems with which to decorate themselves.

The men, for their part, had agreed upon a new plan, one they hoped would work better than the embarrassing original one.

The women decided to hold a support group session in the Grill Room, atop the hotel. They would be meeting the men later that evening at Régine's disco, Jimmy Z's. That was Eleanor's idea. None of the women had been to a disco in years and thought it would be fun. The men had reluctantly agreed, adding the caveat that they were lousy dancers. At the time of the Belle Époque, this problem was easily taken care of. The important hotels employed *danceurs mondains*—social dancers, attractive young men who wore tuxedos and had to be good conversationalists—to dance with the wives of men who couldn't (or wouldn't) waltz or fox-trot or tango. They weren't gigolos. For income they depended on tips from the wealthy husbands after they had entertained their wives on the dance floor. In modern French discos, women always danced with each other. This was very common and acceptable in places like Jimmy Z's. If your wife or girlfriend was attractive, and you weren't dancing with her, she might reasonably be asked by a guy coming off the bar, which was also acceptable—maybe.

After ordering salads and grilled fish with no sauce—the amount of food they had eaten on the trip thus far was staggering and they desperately needed to cut down on the calories—Irene asked who wanted to start. All hands went up at once. "Well, that's a change," said Irene. "Let's go clockwise. Eleanor?"

"I'll give it to you short and sweet: the best sport fuck I've had since Harry boffed me in the goalie suit at the ice rink."

"I thought we agreed to no sex until the third date?" said Irene.

"I don't know about you girls, but I wasn't taking a chance that there'd *be* a third date, since I haven't had one in the last five years. Don't tell me *you* held out, Dar? Did you really manage to keep your panties on all day?"

Darlene tried to blush, but couldn't quite pull it off. "I just couldn't help myself. He looked so cute in those little short pants." And she blurted out the whole story of her seduction, leaving nothing to the imagination. When she'd finished, everyone looked to Carla.

"So, is the Madonna still a Euro-virgin?" teased Eleanor.

"It wasn't my fault."

"What the hell does that mean?"

"We were in the kitchen of his restaurant—"

"Did he take you in there to show you his *zabaglioni*? Sorry, I couldn't resist," said Eleanor.

"He was *showing me* the walk-in refrigerator, when suddenly the door closed us in. And to keep warm, we had to do *something!*"

"So you fucked your brains out to keep warm," Eleanor said.

"How did you know?" asked Carla.

"Wild guess."

"Did you know that sex burns calories and that calories create heat?" said Carla.

"So I've heard," said Irene.

"How did you get out?" said Darlene.

"What do you mean? We walked out."

"Wasn't the door locked?" said Irene.

"Did I say that?" said Carla.

"No, but we just assumed," said Eleanor.

"You got laid in a restaurant refrigerator?" said Darlene. "I don't believe it."

"Is that any worse than screwing under a soccer net?" hissed Carla.

"Truce. Let's not start that judgmental shit again," said Irene. "A woman has the right to get laid where and when she wants, without censure."

"How unlike you to say so, Baroness. Is there something you want to tell us about *your* day?" said Eleanor.

They all couldn't wait for the suddenly melting ice princess's confession. Irene closed her eyes, settled her features into a faraway, dreamy look, and began: "It was at sunset. In a secluded cove. The surface of the water was shimmering and golden. He led me into the sea. I had been sunbathing all day—topless, of course. Suddenly I felt him reaching for me under the water—his hands slipping off the remaining G-string of my bathing suit—"

"G-string? *You* were wearing a G-string?" shrieked Eleanor.

"Do you want to hear the rest of the story, or not?" said Irene.

Silence told her to continue. "As I was saying: I felt him grow hard under the water and suddenly he lifted me and I wrapped my legs around his waist and felt him plunge deep inside of me. I don't remember the rest. I must have passed out from the intensity of the you-know-what. I woke up on the beach, feeling him kissing the nape of my neck and whispering my name."

"Wow," said Darlene. "Wow and double wow!"

"So, where do we go from here?" said Carla. "Do we take a chance and tell these guys who we really are and hope they take it as a joke?"

"Not yet. Too big a gamble. Let's not burst the bubble until we have to. Maybe one of us will come up with a brilliant idea," said Eleanor.

"Anyway, we did it. We now smell like money."

"And we've got the aura, no question about it."

"Who had the low-calorie caviar?"

"I had the champagne and grilled turbot."

"That's two hundred and eighty dollars, plus the tip. Call it three hundred even."

"You're the diet Coke and two *biscotti*. Thirty dollars."

The women exploded into laughter. There was no check to pay. It was all magically charged to their rooms. The regular Tuesday-night support-group session had ended, in its new venue: Monte Carlo.

*   *   *

INSPECTOR DELARUE HAD a conundrum on his hands. He had the thief, Guzman, but he wouldn't be able to charge him with more than breaking and entering. The stolen goods were basically worthless, so they wouldn't be able to hold him for very long. He didn't want to ask the women to file a complaint—not yet—and so he decided to keep close watch on the men and see what transpired. Meanwhile, he would meet with the women, return their jewelry, and sniff around—learning what he could learn. One never knew in his business; a clue could often be found most unexpectedly. In any event, it would be an opportunity to meet four of the richest women in the world. Maybe they would tell him why they traveled with enough junk to choke a rhinestone cowboy.

15

"Delay"

Now you must wake up
All dreams must end
Take off your makeup
The party's over, it's all over, my friend.
    —Styne–Comden–Green, "The Party's Over"

THE WOMEN KNEW that the masquerade ball would soon be over and everyone would take off their masks and reveal their true selves. They did not look forward to the revelation. The first night was frivolous, the second date was sexual panic—use-it-or-lose-it time. Tonight, at Jimmy Z's, would be frivolous and *fun*. Tomorrow—tomorrow would be their fourth night; time was growing short.

They met at the disco at ten o'clock. The doors had just opened; no one was there except a handful of tourists who didn't know that the club really got started after midnight. This worked to the men's benefit since the guy in charge of choosing the songs was agreeable to playing some slow stuff in exchange for a decent tip. When the club started to fill up, the decibel level increased to the point where it was impossible to talk. The music was strictly international club tracks, many remixed to augment the drums and bass and to lengthen the time by repeating segments. The women danced with each other and the men checked their watches each time a new round of overpriced drinks was brought to the table. Jimmy Z's was *beaucoup* expensive. There were lots of hard-bodies who never paid for anything, girls let in to decorate the place and to run up the bills of overage yacht owners who were out for a good time and didn't care what it cost.

Irene was watching Eleanor and Darlene dance when she realized that a handsome young man was standing next to her table, staring down at her. *"S'il vous plaît, monsieur,"* he said to Maurice. "Would it be all right if I asked your wife to dance?"

"Well, since she's not my wife, that will be up to her," Maurice answered lightly.

"Madame?" said the young *danceur mondain moderne*.

Irene looked at Maurice; his expression said: "Why not?"

The guy was great. The music was hot, the dance beat very fast. Blinding strobe lights pulsed, making Irene light-headed—so light-headed and disoriented that she never felt her partner slip her diamond necklace off and slide it into his jacket pocket. He danced with the other women, one at a time, performing the same sleight of hand with each. A bracelet, a brooch, a necklace, rings, a set of earrings. As suddenly as he had appeared, he disappeared. In the darkness of the club no one had noticed that anything was wrong. No one except the girl in the shocking green spandex shorts and midriff-baring glittery top dancing with a guy in a French sailor's uniform. She was the infamous Detective Ola, or "O" as she was called by the men behind her back, and he was an insurance investigator employed by the consortium of jewelers in Monte Carlo to look after their precious loaned wares. They saw the thief's every move but waited until he exited the club to arrest him. He confessed—having little choice since all the jewelry was in his pocket—that he had been hired by a man named Benito Cavallo, in San Remo. That's all he was willing to say. Ola checked out Cavallo with the San Remo police and ran his name through the computers at Interpol. They found his file. A jewel thief and fence: Benito "The Horse" Cavallo. He had been dead for five years. The thief, one Gianni Castellini, was from Corsica. He did not implicate any of the four men because he had no knowledge that they were in on the scam.

It wasn't until that evening, when they were undressing back at the hotel, that the women realized pieces of their jewelry were missing. Calls to each other confirmed that they had all been gracefully robbed. The following morning Inspector Delarue called and asked for a group appointment. The women were petrified, thinking that they had been unmasked, but that was not the case. Delarue was very charming, and after telling them that their missing jewelry had been returned to the shops, he showed them the briefcase full of costume jewelry. The women admitted the junk was theirs and said that they wore it when they were traveling or to the beach—never at night. They laughed about the theft—they hadn't even noticed the "jewels" were missing—and promised Delarue to be more careful about their belongings. He suggested they make use of the hotel safe, and carefully broached the subject of the four men: "I hope you are all enjoying your time in the principality?"

"Oh, yes," Darlene said. "We've met some wonderful people. We just love it here—and your security is so good. Imagine I wouldn't want to be a thief around you."

"Please let me know if I can be of any further service," Delarue said, and made his departure. Back at the office, Bernard found him pacing and mumbling.

"Problem, Inspector?"

"Something is not right with those women, Bernard. I can't put my finger on it. But I will, I will."

"Are you going to arrest the men, sir?"

"Not yet, Bernard. Not yet. By the way, how about that O, she's something, eh?"

"Unique," said Bernard. "Unique, to say the least."

"She can teach us all a thing or two."

"I was considering that, Inspector."

"I'll bet you were."

16
"Reflections—The Men"

Maurice Gerard

The Royal in San Remo was, at one time, top-ranked with such great Italian hotels as the Villa d'Este on Lake Como; now it was showing its years. Its elegance had slowly faded due to lack of money for upkeep and a steadily dwindling supply of wealthy visitors to all of the coastal resorts. Maurice Gerard sat on the front terrace facing the sea. He and the other men had taken the seven o'clock morning train from Monte Carlo. It was a trip of about twenty minutes, but that was long enough for him to decide that he was neither a jewel thief nor a con man. Those appellations simply didn't apply.

My whole life has been unplanned. Waiting for the mail; the phone to ring, he thought, with word of my next assignment—or would assignation be a better word? He was reminded of the famous line from *Mission: Impossible:* "Your assignment, should you choose to accept it . . ." Never, to his knowledge, had any of the agents on the show replied, "Are you kidding? Forget about it. Not me." For the past twenty-five years Maurice, too, had always accepted the assignment, no matter what the woman's age, appearance, race, or religion. There was only one hard-and-fast rule: they had to be rich, and they always were.

Maurice had learned the art of social sublimation. If they wanted to talk about fashion or painting or the trouble getting good servants, he gave the appropriate responses. He knew that most people love to hear themselves talk, needed validation for their views on politics, children, other women, other men, whatever. Maurice rarely had to contribute more than the passing interrogative. Of course he did have to tell them his life story, that was *de rigueur*. He had several versions that he alternated so as not to bore himself. Every few years he made major revisions, thereby reinventing himself. It was an amusing game. Even the tour-guide aspect was not difficult. The women usually slept late, needed time for shopping, facials, the spa, hairdresser, and getting dressed. That left no more than two or three hours for show-and-tell.

Maurice looked up at the aged waiter who served him his cappuccino, a drink that bore little resemblance to the one of the same name served outside of Italy. Here it was made with fresh, dark espresso, steamed cream, and dusted with bitter cocoa, served in a demitasse along with superfine sugar. In California, he was once served a large cup of cappuccino and discovered, to his shock, that it had been made with ordinary breakfast coffee and steamed low-fat milk, sprinkled heavily with cinnamon.

The waiter forced a smile, but his eyes remained flat. Did his look of disillusioned dejection come from a life spent waiting upon the rich? Was Maurice in danger of projecting the same look? Did he already have it? Was his studied façade already cracking, revealing slivers of that same disillusionment? He hoped not. He would have to study himself in the mirror for traces when he got back home. Home. Where *was* home?

He looked out to sea, attracted by an ocean liner that was plying its way northeast. It brought back memories of his days as a ship's steward. He probably would have married again had he not been seduced by the goal and the game of wealth. Alas, he mused, we don't always want the things we need, and by the time we figure that out, both our wants and needs have changed. Yes, he had acquired many of the trappings, but real assets eluded him. Today he had hit bottom, hard. He certainly couldn't sink any lower. How had he let himself be talked into this crazy scheme? Part of him wished he hadn't participated, while the other half thought: What other options were there? None. Other than resigning himself to a life as *un retraité.*

It sounded just as bad in French as in English: *retired,* living life on the lowest rung of the economic ladder . . . No matter what, he wouldn't do that.

Inspector Delarue's instincts about Maurice were correct: if a man is trapped, he will do anything to save himself.

Maurice rationalized: Who was being hurt? The jewels were insured. The women would hardly be inconvenienced. Most crimes are committed after successful rationalization: "He deserves to die after what he did." "Society owes me." "The white-collar guys do it all the time in other ways. . . ."

The baroness, if she—make that when she—learns the truth will chalk it up as an adventure, add it to her store of stories about men-the-bastards. And, of course, she'd be right. He was a prick, and any other obscenity she chose to confer upon him. He had knowingly, and with malice aforethought, deceived her.

He had his passport with him. Depending upon the value of his share, he might take the train to Rome and fly Alitalia to California to see his estranged family. Maybe he'd even stay, if they'd have him.

Julio Benvenuti

Julio had set up the robbery with a friend of a friend. Now, ambling in the gardens of the hotel, he had second

thoughts. The whole episode made him feel unclean, like
a criminal. He had never felt that way before. Sure he had
wheedled, lied to, cajoled, conned, duped, and deceived,
women into sharing some small part of their wealth with
him. But he had never outright stolen anything. Ever since
he'd become involved with Maurice and the others, he'd
continually miscalculated, and now he was an accomplice
to grand larceny—by his own hand, to be sure.

Maybe, when this was over and he had some money
he could call his own, he'd tell la contessa everything.
Well, maybe not everything, but many things. He laughed
out loud at the thought. Women want men they can trust.
Repeat after me, Julio. You are a pasta chef at Lino's
Ristorante Elegante by the Sea. There was nothing wrong
with being a pasta chef *except* if you saw yourself as
Marcello Mastroianni coming home at night to Sophia
Loren. He had to come to terms with who he really was.
That's what having high self-esteem meant, didn't it? Julio had very low self-esteem. He had never really accomplished anything worthwhile in his life. A fair chef, a
lousy actor, a bad husband—equals low self-esteem. He
had no dreams left to fulfill. He lived from day to day
hoping that something would happen. What that something was, he didn't know. But now something *had* happened. Where the hell was "The Horse?" He was already
fifteen minutes late.

Suddenly Julio felt a wave of guilt wash over him. He
was fifteen, working at his parents' coffee bar and desperately in love with Anna-Maria Cocienti, who was fourteen.
He needed twenty dollars real bad so he could take her to
the movies and for a pizza afterward. On their last date she
let him feel her left breast when they kissed good night. He
had put his hand under her sweater and was moving it up
under her bra when she stopped him and whispered, "Not
yet." It was the "not yet" that gave him hope, hope that
drove him crazy all week, as only a fifteen-year-old boy
fantasizing about sex he's never had can be crazed. He
asked his mother for the money; his father; his aunt. He had

already borrowed heavily against his meager salary, so the answer was a firm no from everyone.

"Bring her here," his mother had said.

Julio froze at the thought. He had been hard all day thinking about how he might get the "not yet" sign moved to a new, *lower* territory. His mother's words—"Bring her here"—made his member become instantly flaccid. Finally, having no other option, he stole the money from the cash register, convincing himself that he would replace it. He never did and he never confessed, not even at church. The effects of his contravention of God's commandment—thou shalt not steal—had never left him. He never knew when the oceanic swell of guilt would envelop him, just that from time to time it always did. It wasn't too late. His mother was still alive. He would finish with this Cavallo guy and go home to see her. Unburden himself at last. He would go to church, sit in the box, and make it official. Maybe he would stay there—and open a coffee bar with the money.

"Count" Jean-Jacques Lacoste

Jean-Jacques lay on a chaise longue by the hotel pool and thought about how he had acquired his *nom de guerre*. During his playing years his teammates had dubbed him "The Count" because every time he scored a goal, the crowd would yell out his new total number of career goals. The Count. What a laugh. The no-account was more like it. Of the four men in the group, he, like Trevor Weymouth, had tasted money and fame, and he never got the taste out of his mouth. Jean-Jacques was known as a man who was always working on a deal: a hot tip on a stock or a horse, a can't-fail, slam-dunk scheme, a big finder's fee for introducing Mogul A to Mogul B. Somehow they all tanked.

Jean-Jacques had started counting the number of times he opened the front door of the Hotel Hermitage each day and recording the number in a small black book kept for that purpose alone. Again, the *count*. Why was it important? He didn't know. It was compelling. He'd recently bought a small mechanical hand counter to simplify the job.

Working at the hotel kept him near the movers and shakers. They said hello to him, called him by name, and he sat in their cars and breathed in the remembered smell of success. He felt connected; to what he didn't know. Tips were good, especially when it rained. Smart doormen and bellhops never used umbrellas for themselves. Their selfless braving of the elements for the guests usually increased the handout, as did struggling with large pieces of luggage instead of putting them on rolling carts. But no matter if it rained the entire week, and his door-opening count topped his previous personal best, Jean-Jacques barely made ends meet. He always thought of his job as temporary. After five years he realized that it wasn't.

He looked up at the sky and mused about what he would do with his share of the money from the heist. First thing he would do is burn the damn counting book. Images of Lou Ann Barlow (a.k.a. Darlene) mixed with the clouds. She would be just another deal that hadn't panned out. Too bad. She had surprised him. She was somebody he thought he could get used to. He closed his eyes and she was gone. He assumed he'd never see her again. It made him short of breath.

Trevor Weymouth

Trevor paced the long marble-floored hallway of the hotel. Greta Harmon-Cates, the redoubtable Eleanor. Never had he experienced such aggression in a woman. She took what she wanted and wasn't shy about saying *how* she wanted it. He liked that. It made his job easier. The Riviera-Layabout-Ghost-of-Trevor-Past might rise again! He could almost hear the sound of the red Ferrari's twin exhausts; her first gift to him. What the hell, she had everything she needed—except him—assuming that she did need or want him. Trevor gave this last thought more careful consideration. No question. She definitely wanted him. The trick would be to make her want the *real* him and not the man she thought he was. Of the four women, she was the one who might get a laugh out of this quadruple identity dupery. He'd have to take a chance and play it that way, because sooner or later she would find out.

He decided that if he had to tell her the truth, he'd do it in bed. She was most vulnerable there. He'd pretend impotence and she'd ask what was the matter, assuming it was her fault. Then he'd allow her to "force" the truth out of him. He'd bring reality to the surface as slowly as possible—while he stroked both her inner thighs and her ego. He was vaguely sorry that he'd agreed to the scheme to rip her off; maybe he could have succeeded without that. Maybe that would prove his downfall. But he was a fatalist and didn't think his actions changed anything. "What was written was written and couldn't be erased" was his mantra. He would simply say his lines and see how this farcical play ended.

His thoughts turned to the famous lines from *The Rubáiyát of Omar Khayyám*:

The moving finger writes; and, having writ,
Moves on: nor all your Piety nor Wit
Shall lure it back to cancel half a Line,
Nor all your Tears wash out a Word of it.

Was it written that she would be the one?

17
"The Story of 'O' "

. . . wherein the spider goes a-shopping.

ON A HUNCH, **Ola Obolensky,** dressed as a nun, had followed Julio Benvenuti to the Monte Carlo railroad station, where he was soon joined by the other three men. She managed to take a very nice photo of them as they boarded the train. Conveniently, the station name and a large clock showed clearly in the background. Evidence. She sat one seat behind them, quietly reading a Bible. She had decided on the nun's habit so that she would not be harassed by the Italian men on the train and in San Remo—where she assumed they were going. Men never gave a nun a second look. This was important in a country where any man worth his *pasta e fagioli* was an inveterate harasser. It was in the genes. Last year, in Rome, an elevator operator in a first-class hotel had pinched her ass and told her in less than poetic Italian what he had in mind. Ola, fluent in Italian, rewarded the guy by squeezing his balls so hard that he missed her floor.

Unfortunately, the four men didn't speak during the trip, but she did manage another group photo with the San Remo station sign in the background, for her scrapbook.

Knowing that the plan had been busted and Benny the Horse wouldn't show, she decided to do some shopping. Her first stop was the boutique Franco, where she asked to see a La Perla push-up bra, size 36-D. The young, Catholic, shop girl was flustered but brought forth a selection of the requested item.

"We have them in black, red, white, and pink, with or without lace," she managed to say.

"Red with lace, please. And I'd like to try it on."

The girl was so wide-eyed that Ola added, "It's for my sister; we're both the same size. And also that black-and-white teddy you have in the window. Size six."

Ola bought both. She had it in her mind to save them for a "special occasion," Inspector Delarue's upcoming birthday. The shop gave her a *sconto*, a discount of ten percent and the shop girls crossed themselves after she left. This would be gossip fodder for the next week. Ola's next stop was a specialty food store near the old town. There she purchased a tiny bottle of fifty-year-old balsamic vinegar for which she paid the exorbitant sum of 247,500 lire, approximately 150 U.S. dollars. The price was outrageously high because this was a bottle of the Traditional Balsamic Vinegar of Modena, made not from wine, but by cooking and aging the "must" of the white *trebbiano* grape, according to a strict, age-old method. Delarue had mentioned his fond memories of a meal he'd eaten at the famed three-star Ristorante Enoteca Pinchiorri in Florence where he was served pan-seared *foie gras* with porcini mushrooms, sprinkled with a few drops of the precious old balsamic vinegar. He'd told her that it was the best meal he had ever eaten and wished he could afford the vinegar. Throwing caution to the wind, she added a wedge of three-year-old *parmigiano reggiano* to his birthday package. The shopkeeper made her a present of a cheese shaver and told her to try a drop of the balsamic on a thin shaving of the young soft cheese. Ambrosia. The balsamic, the cheese, the bra, and the teddy should work magic, Ola thought. Delarue would be surprised because she had never evinced any interest in him previously, nor he in her. But her instincts told her she would not be making a mistake, or worse, a fool of herself.

Ola had lunch on the port, a simple salad *tricolori* followed by a dish of *trofie* with Genovese pesto sauce and grated Parmesan cheese. She asked the waiter how the excellent pasta and sauce were made.

He said that the *trofie* were tiny inch-long, worm-shaped morsels of rolled pasta, handmade from hard-wheat flour, water, and extra-virgin olive oil. The pesto was a thick sauce made in a mortar from fresh basil leaves, pine nuts, garlic, salt, and olive oil. It was always added cold to the pasta just before serving. She would pass this information on to Delarue; it would make for good foreplay chat. She asked the waiter if she could buy some of the pasta and sauce to take home and he was more than happy to oblige, giving the charming "nun" a neatly wrapped package, at no charge. She promised to mention him in her devotions.

Maybe she'd invite Delarue to dinner at her apartment. Would he think that rather bold of her? Yes. She would tell him that she was trying out a new recipe and needed his expert opinion. The way to a man's heart, her mother always told her, is to endlessly ask his opinion.

But back to business. So far "O" had evidence only of presumptive guilt against the men, but strong circumstantial evidence was building nicely. Ola was a patient woman who usually got what she wanted.

JULIO TELEPHONED A friend, who telephoned a friend, who telephoned Benny the Horse. Word filtered back from the Horse that "the pasta had not been delivered as planned." Nothing more. The four men concluded that they had been ripped off. What else could they think?

"Amateurs," said Maurice. "We should all go around wearing a big red *A* on our chests. *A* for Amateurs."

"Or for Assholes," added Jean-Jacques. The con men had been conned.

"What can I say?" said Julio. "He came well recommended."

"Well recommended by other thieves," added Trevor.

"We have to assume that the police arrested the thief. We're lucky he doesn't know who we are," said Jean-Jacques.

"You *hope* he doesn't know," said Maurice.

"What now?" asked a saddened Julio.

"Truth?" said Jean-Jacques, timidly.

"Who was it that said, 'Truth never hurts the teller'?" said Trevor.

"A man who never told a lie," answered Maurice.

WHILE OLA WAS buying her push-up bra in San Remo, the women were being visited by their respective jewelry pushers. Irene's man, from Cartier, was apologetic about the robbery. "These things rarely happen here, Baroness. Please accept my apologies. You can be assured that it will not occur again. Now, if you will spare me a few moments of your valuable time, I would like to show you a few rare pieces from our newest collection. I'm sure you will find them quite spectacular and original."

Irene sat and stared in amazement as the salesman spread black and gray velour cloths on the table in front of her. "This first item is a sixty-nine-and-a-half-carat pear-shaped diamond. It was bought at auction by Cartier in 1969 and sold to Richard Burton, who renamed it the Taylor-Burton Diamond. It was first seen in public right here in Monaco. Miss Taylor wore it as a pendant. In 1978, she sold it in order to build a hospital in Botswana. It has only recently come back into our hands. Irreplaceable. Would you like to try it on?"

Is the pope Catholic? thought Irene.

*   *   *

SIMILAR CONVERSATIONS AND presentations were being made to Darlene, Eleanor, and Carla in their respective suites. All of the salesmen were in a full-court press to close a sale before week's end. One thing was certain, sale or no sale, the four women would look incredible at the casino that night. Heads would definitely turn. Certain men would be impressed.

Trevor Weymouth suggested that they all keep their dates with the women that evening and pretend ignorance of the theft at Jimmy Z's. They cut a deck of cards to see who would make the first call to the women. Jean-Jacques was high with a king and picked up the phone, with great trepidation. To his amazement Darlene casually mentioned the theft and said that fortunately, the police had returned all of the jewels to them.

"Wasn't that nice of them? We were insured, of course, but it would have been such a bore to fill out all that paperwork. So, are we on for tonight?"

Jean-Jacques was almost speechless but managed to say, "Yes, of course. I'll call you right back."

"Make it around six, because we're all going out for a while."

"Fine. Six it will be."

Jean-Jacques hung up and told the men what he'd just learned. "Do you think Delarue suspects us?"

"If he does I'm sure we'll hear from him very soon," said Maurice.

"What should we do about dinner?" said Julio.

"How about Le Parrot?" said Jean-Jacques.

"Isn't that private?" said Trevor.

"Friend of mine's the manager—and they'll bill the hotel," said Trevor.

"Stick more on their bill?" said Maurice.

"What the hell's the difference?" said Jean-Jacques.

They all nodded in agreement.

18
"The Four Queens"

*What a woman says to her ardent lover
should be written in wind and running water.*
                                        —*Catullus, 50 B.C.*

THE FOUR WOMEN were in the hotel gymnasium trying
to work off some of their indulgences. Irene was ped-
aling, Eleanor was climbing, Carla was treadmilling, and
Darlene was working her thighs on a Cybex. All were
reading books as they did their workouts.

Irene was into *The Great Courtesans,* Eleanor had her
book of astrological signs open to a chapter entitled "How
to Seduce the Gemini Man"—not that she seemed to need
any help in that area—Darlene was reading an old issue
of *National Geographic* (the cover story was on "Tin
Mines of Bolivia"), while Carla did her leg-ups with *Mar-
cella Hazan's Classic Italian Cooking.*

"Listen to this," said Irene. "It's what Maurice told me
at dinner the other night. About this Madame de Pompadour. She visited a fortune-teller who told her that one
day she would become 'almost' a queen. Turned out she
was right. After becoming the mistress of Louis the Fifteenth, she was made a marquise." Irene looked up at the
other women. "In those days, women did whatever they
had to do to get a leg up in society by finding some rich

guy to support them in style. Then there was that other mistress horny King Louis had, Madame du Barry. Hell, she was married and her *husband* helped her get a foot in the castle gate. There are marble heads of both these conniving dames in the hotel restaurant. They both started without a dime and conned their way into fortunes."

"Sounds to me like they were high-priced hookers and that the du Barry babe's husband was a pimp. Anyway, didn't du Barry get her head chopped off?" said Eleanor.

"Do they do that over here anymore?" said Darlene.

"Only to cheats and liars," said Eleanor.

"We *are* getting in pretty deep," said Irene. "No question that these guys are going to evaporate when they find out the truth."

"Damn straight," said Eleanor. "We've been playing our parts too good."

"One thing's for sure, we can't keep this up. If we tell them, they might think it's funny—even pay our hotel bills," said Darlene. "After all, they *are* stinking rich."

"How about this: We tell them we all just happen to be financially challenged," said Carla.

"Yeah," said Eleanor, "since birth."

Irene began to cry. "This is the best time I've ever had in my whole life."

This caused a chain reaction of sniffles and tears. "Me, too," said Darlene.

"But it's not going to last," said Carla.

"They're only comfortable with us because they think we're not after their money," Irene said.

Eleanor summed it up: "Right. You think men like that are really interested in *us*? That they're going to say, 'Oh, it doesn't matter that you lied to us about every detail of your lives, that you're really four bored babes from the 'burbs—we still love you.' "

Irene couldn't stop the tears. "I'd do anything not to have to tell Maurice. Maybe we should check out today. At least we'd have good memories with no ugly endings."

"It's a thought," said Carla. "Let's vote on it. All in favor? Hands?"

No hands were raised. Despite the hopelessness of their collective situation, they remained positive and committed to seeing the charade through to its end.

"Let's vote on telling the truth. All in favor?"

Four hands were reluctantly raised.

THE FORTUNE-TELLER HAD her "office" on an old *barque* tied up to a rickety dock at the local fishermen's harbor. After being assured by Madame Bergaz's thirteen-year-old son that they were in the right place, they somewhat reluctantly allowed him to help them aboard. The boat, all fifteen feet of it, was covered by a tattered, striped canopy.

Madame Bergaz sat amidships at a linoleum-covered table, gutting some small red fish and throwing them into a large dented pot that steamed atop a small portable gas burner. Seeing the women, she wiped her bloodied hands on her already filthy smock and rose to greet them. Her son quickly filled a bucket with seawater and sluiced down the table of its fish scales, bones, and entrails. Another bucketful washed the debris to the stern of the boat. Madame Bergaz covered the table with an old plastic cloth that was imprinted with the signs of the zodiac and produced a pack of large tarot cards from within the folds of her dress. The boy dragged four rickety stools to the table and motioned that the women should sit. Their exchanged glances clearly said, "Let's get out of here." As Irene was about to inform the fortune-teller that there was a mistake and they were leaving, the woman seemed to fall into a trance of some sort. Her eyes floated upward and her lids fluttered and closed. She gasped, began to shake, put one hand over her heart, and collapsed onto the deck—throwing the tarot cards onto the table as she fell. Her son, having seen his mother's act before, did nothing to aid her. As the four women stood, transfixed,

Madame Bergaz raised a hand up high. It held a card. "Death," whispered all of the women, in concert, holding on to each other.

"No," said the fortune-teller. "You will receive rewards. LAVISH REWARDS," she screamed.

"Who?" shouted the four women, at the same time.

"Which one?" said Eleanor, shaking the woman.

Madame Bergaz's eyes opened slowly as she smiled and said, in a hushed tone, "Please, sit and Madame Bergaz will tell all. The cards do not lie."

Eleanor knew this line was from an old film, or many old films. Nevertheless, the women were hooked. They mucked through the fish-murked deck and took seats at the table.

"Five hundred francs each," said Madame Bergaz, suddenly rather businesslike.

"Do you take American Express?" said Darlene.

"Only Visa or MasterCard," the fortune-teller snapped.

Her son quickly produced an imprint machine and ran the cards through expertly. After the women had signed their chits, Madame Bergaz was ready for her performance, which included background music befitting the circumstances. She clicked on a tape that Irene recognized as Kitaro: *Auspicious Omen.* Methodically she shuffled the cards and had each woman cut the deck. Spreading them facedown on the table in a rough circle, she took Irene's hand.

"I want each of you to pass your hands over the cards without touching them—like this," she said, demonstrating with Irene. "Let the cards absorb your aura. Now I want you to choose a card. Don't hurry; your choice determines your fate. Good. Now place it facedown in front of you. Now, all of you, one at a time, do as she did."

They all performed the same hocus-pocus and waited as Madame B. cleared the table of the unchosen cards and lit an incense burner. Incense, Kitaro, and tarot. The first card she turned faceup was Darlene's. It showed a picture of a woman wearing a crown, sitting on a throne holding a large wand. A black cat sat in front of her. "The Queen of Wands," the fortune-teller intoned, most seriously. "It tells me that you were the most popular girl in your class at school and the prettiest. But now your looks will not help, as you are facing a difficult task. You *may* be able to accomplish it if you remain positive."

Darlene found she had been holding her breath. A queen. She would definitely be a queen again, she could feel it.

The next card to be revealed was Carla's. It depicted a woman on a throne holding a large cup. "Another queen. The Queen of Cups. Incredible," said Madame Bergaz.

Darlene was secretly unhappy that she would have to share her throne, but showed nothing.

"I can see that you have been kind to everyone in your life. You have always followed your heart. Trust it now to guide you through this difficult passage. Allow yourself to be sensitive to another's pain and you will prevail."

Eleanor was next. A collective gasp issued from all five of the women and Madame B's son when a *third* queen was revealed. "The Queen of Swords." The fortune-teller crossed herself and placed a hand over her heart as she mumbled some unintelligible words. "The card tells me that you are a forthright person, telling it like it is. You hate lies, tricks, and—if you'll excuse my language— bullshit."

"Damn straight," said Eleanor.

"You also have a good sense of humor. That will help you not to take the events of the next few days too seriously. Whether you get what you wish for depends on your ability to open yourself to the possibilities."

"What the hell does that mean?" said Eleanor.

"The cards tell me no more. And now for the final readng." Irene was biting her nails. Three queens. Her chances for a fourth were almost nil. But almost nil is not nil, as a fourth queen proved. "The Queen of Pentacles. I must ask for a short recess."

"Now?" said Irene.

"A breather, please. Four Queens. I may submit this experience to the *Guinness Book of Records*. I have a form right here, somewhere. You will all be inducted into the Tarot Hall of Fame. You will receive certificates— only one hundred francs each, signed." She held up a hand to forestall any comments, took a few very deep breaths, and finally continued with Irene's prophesy. "The Queen of Pentacles has an icy exterior, although underneath lies a warm and caring woman. If you take a simple and sensible approach to your future and join the other queens, you will find that in numbers there is force." She rose for the next line and spoke it with great solemnity as her son faded the music down: "Let nothing destroy the bond you have with each other."

Then, quite casually, she said, "*Merci beaucoup, mesdames*. And hey, be careful. Four queens! Anything could happen." She then talked them all into buying packs of tarot cards and instruction booklets.

19
"Reflections—The Women"

Money talks, bullshit walks.

Irene, a.k.a. the Baroness Natasha Karmanov

How just a few days can change a person, Irene thought as she sighed languorously in her bath. She had two free hours before it would be time to meet Maurice, time to reflect upon the fortune-teller's advice. She was so god-damned uptight all the time. She had to let the child within her out to play once in a while. Never mind if she fell down and scraped a knee, dirtied her dress, dropped her ice-cream cone. Look what had happened in St. Tropez: she was so cool, reserved, and ladylike that she'd had to lie to the others, make up that story about getting laid so as to compete with them. Funny thing was, she had *wanted* to abandon herself. Why not? The opportunity was there. But what Irene needed far more than sex was to be hugged.

When she was alone in her suite, she had spread out the tarot cards and chosen one. The Hanged Man. She opened her guide-to-the-tarot book to find its meaning. It pictured a man hanging on a cross. The card's main lesson was: "to win one must let go; in effect, surrender, sacrifice in order to emerge the victor. Don't be hasty to act. Wait.

Life's paradoxes are often contradictory but true."

She had to break out or risk making the same mistakes she had made so many times before. Queen of Pentacles: the Ice Queen. Was her skin cold to the touch? Why did orgasms embarrass her? Why did men always have to ask, "Did you come?" She kept it from them and in doing so diminished the pleasure for herself. This game they were playing. They hadn't planned any of the details, the motorcade from the airport, the grand suites at the hotel, the wildly expensive jewelry, the high-stakes gambling, fabulous restaurants, and . . . the perfect new men—man.

What was the perfect man anyway? Irene thought back: three husbands, each far from perfect. If I were to make a list, what would his attributes be, this perfect specimen? Just considering this made Irene realize how silly it was. *That's the problem, I'm always making lists. If I seek perfection, shouldn't I be perfect?* The perfect woman? The perfect woman who had three failed marriages and no children. That says it. If she chose the same path again, she'd end up in the same place.

Irene's first psychiatrist was married to a hairdresser. He had just received his doctorate and wasn't able to afford office space until he built up his clientele, so he shared space with his wife. While she did hair he did heads. Their business card read:

HEADS, INSIDE AND OUT

Why not? Good idea when you think about it. A woman spends at least an hour getting her hair done and can talk to her shrink at the same time. If a few other women were waiting, it sometimes turned into a group-therapy session. The small shop where they worked was next door to a body-piercing shop. Irene always smiled when she saw the sign in their window:

EARS AND BODY PARTS PIERCED:
WITH OR WITHOUT PAIN

It was your choice in life, she thought—with or without pain. The easy way or the hard way. Why did she always choose pain?

Once while she was waiting for her hair color to set, her shrink had said, "We mitigate pain by suppressing its neural pathways. Meaning we sedate the brain to reduce the pain." He continued: "Pain can be oddly seductive. When emotional pain is 'cured' by the use of antidepressants, many times the patient *misses* the pain because it had been comforting, even strangely erotic. That's why when we attenuate mood swings pharmacologically, we have to be careful not to flatten out the creative energy contour of the brain waves. A little neurosis never hurt anyone; indeed, it is one of our more identifying features and if we eliminate it completely, we risk violating the essence of the personality."

"Wow," said Irene. "Are you saying that I'm unhappy *without* my pain? That I'm seeking it again?"

"You tell me."

"I've wasted too much time, too much of my life."

"Then let go of the pain. Don't seek it out. You now know all of the warning signs—mentally and physically. Pay attention to them next time."

"If there is a next time."

"We make our biggest mistakes when we attempt to seek solutions before we understand the problems."

The timer went off. It was time to stop the action of the dye.

Now, as she lay in the huge bathtub, Irene thought this about Maurice: I can either make him run toward me or away from me. What does he want with me, from me? What can I bring to his life that he doesn't already have, can't get from somebody else? And then she considered the lessons she had learned from the Hanged Man card. To make him come toward her, she must move away.

What she had come up with was not the perfect man, but the perfect paradox.

Darlene, a.k.a. Lou Ann Barlow

Darlene stood on the balcony of her suite and looked out to sea. She felt that her normal biorhythms had speeded up, as if she were being lifted up into a whirlwind that might suddenly dissipate and deposit her, like Dorothy, in some strange land.

Margo, the support-group psychologist, had made an analogy between their "foolish" trip and passing through an emotional low point. To have any chance at success, she had said, they would have to maintain hope during the most difficult moments of their "quest." And, as in all quests, there would be barriers to overcome, puzzles to solve, emotions to control, a positive mental state to maintain. Darlene laughed as she recalled a cartoon by that genius writer-cartoonist Shel Silverstein. Was it in *The New Yorker*? Or, possibly *Playboy*? Darlene was one of those women who loved *Playboy* magazine—never missed an issue. She wanted to know how men thought, what their fantasies were (so that she might fulfill them, or was it just an intellectual exercise?). The cartoon depicted two emaciated, bearded men next to each other, shackled hand and foot to a blank concrete wall. A small barred window loomed twenty feet above them. The caption read: *Now here's my plan.* No matter what, Darlene was determined not to give up hope; to keep making plans.

No question that she was still out to please. Still willing to sublimate her personality to a man. No, a *mate*. She looked down at the tarot card she had drawn. The Wheel of Fortune. Round and round she goes, where she stops nobody knows. Interesting that her game of choice at the casino had been roulette. It was an omen. She would try her luck again, tonight.

Darlene needed a chance event to break through the barriers she faced and so to continue the quest. She walked back into her suite, past the desk, where she had written, on hotel stationery, fifty times, *Darlene Lacoste,*

Countess Darlene Lacoste, Madame Jean-Jacques Lacoste . . .

Carla, a.k.a. la Contessa Stephania di Romanesco

Carla still wanted children or, at least, a child. She was
on the cusp of being too old to attempt it. The second
tarot card she had picked was The Empress, symbolic of
the life-giving mother. It shocked her that the seemingly
random act of choosing a card from a deck could be so
on target. The thought of a child, a rich husband who
would cherish her, them, was overwhelming. But she recognized this as a rather immature projection about life
with a man she had only known for a few days.

Carla looked at herself in the mirror. Her complexion
was dark and smooth, her body lush; there was no other
word for it. No matter how she sometimes tried to hide
her sensuality, it spilled forth, made itself known through
layers and folds meant to contain it. Still, she obsessed
about losing her looks. She had always drawn men to her
like a magnet, without trying. But the men who felt her
pull were men who turned out not to want responsibility,
men who were emotionally immature. Nevertheless, they
succeeded in seducing her with words. Julio had dipped
her fingers in the *vino santo* and put them in his mouth;
sucked them gently. She could barely swallow when he
whispered: *Io sono disparato per te—pazzo per te. Io te
bramo, mia contessina.* How could she not succumb to a
man who whispered of his love in the language of love
and told her he was desperate for her, crazy for her,
wanted to kiss her everywhere?

Her late husband, Giovanni, had done the finger-
sucking routine with a *tiramisu.* She never failed to be
touched by these obviously manipulative maneuvers. She
knew that Julio was probably a womanizer in the same
way that other men were golfers, workaholics, or basket-
ball fans. But like any addiction, one exchanged present
gratification for eventual habit-breaking pain. Carla's two

addictions had always been Italian men and Italian food;
preferably together. Giovanni had once made love to her
as they sat nude in the kitchen, feeding each other warm
polenta and porcini mushrooms with their fingers.

If she could have a child with Julio, she would be
happy—even if he eventually left her, or never stayed in
the first place. Of course, she thought, the conception
could have already taken place. She would name him Giovanni. He would be a boy, *certo*. Of course.

Eleanor, a.k.a. Greta Harmon-Cates

Eleanor felt she was immune to falling in love. In her
lexicon, sex was not love, although in the heat of a moment she was prone to confuse the two. Sex was her
shield. If she waited to fall in love, she'd never get laid.
When she was a teenager, conversations with girlfriends
revolved around "if I let him, will he respect me?" What
did that really mean? To Eleanor it was an excuse for
retaining virginity, at all costs, until marriage. All of her
friends had married. Eleanor wondered if their husbands
respected them? Why were they so concerned with respect
at such an early age? What did they think it meant? Did
they imagine that young guys today sat around talking
about what girls they respected? "If you wanna kiss me,
baby, don't dis me, baby . . ." Guys were simply, basically, uncontrollably horny and avoided girls that wanted
respect like the plague.

Trevor. She'd met men like him before. Vain; in love
with the sound of their own voices; legends in their own
minds. Machos who discovered early on that girls like to
"do it" more than boys do. Eleanor could vouch for that.
Were his charms all skin deep? The Brits could be like
that, sometimes. Was it "five easy pieces" or did he really
know the repertoire? It would take more time to find out.
Meanwhile, the sex thing was out of the way.

How about herself? Was *she* all skin-deep? She put on
her self-protective devices like other women put on

makeup to prepare themselves for acceptance: moisturizer, concealer, foundation, powder, blush, eye gunk, until the natural woman was obliterated. Eleanor used almost no makeup but her psyche was layered in defensive devices of brash, bold, funny, aggressive—all of which prepared her for rejection.

"Eleanor takes care of Eleanor" was her unstated motto. She poured herself a cold beer and picked a card from the tarot deck. The Judgment card. What horrors did it portend? Hard choices were on the horizon. To face them successfully, she would have to avoid placing blame on herself and others. But she was a lawyer, and placing blame was her specialty. She searched for truth, and when she found it—or what passed for it—she assigned the blame and came down hard on her adversaries. How would she ever, in her personal life, learn to judge yet not condemn? Could people be reborn, as the evangelists tell us every Sunday on television? What is rebirth? Is one called? Are you freed from your heavy loads, of guilt, depression, anger, pain? Is your past eradicated? Annulled? Do you start your life over, with a blank slate?

When your past is vacuumed away, what do you use in place of experience? she wondered. Do you become a babe-in-the-woods again? Do your friends immediately recognize the "new you" or do they have to be reintroduced? Over time, Eleanor's false bravado had become true bravado. Pretense had evolved into past-tense and Eleanor found herself beginning to like the woman she'd become. Her vulnerability had all but vanished in the process. Since she hid it every day in her work, it was normal to continue to hide it outside of working hours. Her new persona came to be named "bitch"—as in, she's a real bitch; what a bitch; somebody should fuck that bitch; I wouldn't fuck that bitch with somebody's else's cock . . . and dumb bitch, which she certainly was not.

Eleanor was reminded of something her mother had told her about her estranged father: "Deep down he was a really nice guy." And Eleanor, just eleven at the time, had responded, "He was a shit, Mom. He walked out. He must have saved all that deep-down-good-guy stuff for somebody else, 'cause we never got any." Eleanor had taken care of her two younger brothers while her mother went back to work to support them (the deep-down-good-guy having never sent a fucking dime for child support). Eleanor found that she had taken her father's place. When she graduated from college she spent part of a summer trying to find him. She never told her mother or brothers this, and she never found him—mainly because he didn't want to be found. In some ways she had become her father, but that was natural. Her cross to bear. Keep the heart of gold buried, and with time the gold turns to brass.

CURTAIN

ACT THREE
SHEDDING THE MASKS

♡

20

"The Spider and the Fly"

"Will you walk into my parlor?" said the spider to the fly;
" 'Tis the prettiest little parlor that you ever did spy."

OLA, THE SPIDERWOMAN, leaned over the candlelit dining table in her apartment, until the nipple of her left breast dropped into the top of the bottle of balsamic vinegar and was bathed in the rare liquid. (The booklet that had come with the bottle said that when balsamic is fifty years of age, or older—as hers was—it begins to thicken and is wonderful when used as a liquor.) George Delarue, the captivated fly, cupped her breast gently and raised it to his lips, gently sucking and licking every last trace that clung to the darkened pink tip. After this action was repeated with her right breast, Ola leaned back, took a very slow deep breath with her eyes closed, and readjusted her black-and-white teddy to recontain her voluptuousness. Neither one spoke as George dipped a finger into the sweetish nectar, rubbed his wet finger on her lips, kissed and sucked them until she was weak with uncontrolled passion. When he was about to speak, she placed a finger over his lips and slid under the table, taking the magic bottle with her. As her mouth closed around his anointed hardness, he gasped and struggled to delay his satisfaction. Taking her into his arms, he carried Ola into her bedroom, which she had lit with strategically placed candles. Like a surgeon, he poured a tiny drop of the expensive ruby liquid into the valley of her pleasure mound and took his time licking it off—using only the very tip of his tongue. Then he put that same tongue into Ola's eager mouth and entered her. The result was instantaneous and explosive. It was ten o'clock in the evening and Ola had yet to start cooking the *trofie* with pesto sauce. At midnight she asked him if he was hungry and he replied, "Famished." As an hors d'oeuvre, she served a thin slice of Parmesan cheese with a drop of the balsamic on it, which he devoured with obvious gustatory pleasure. "So," she whispered, "which way do you like it best?" She never made the *trofie* with pesto sauce. Not that night. In the morning, after he had left, she looked at the empty bottle of the wildly expensive balsamic vinegar. Well worth the price, she thought. Tonight she would cook the pasta. Maybe.

21
"Benny the Horse"

Oh, give me land, lots of land,
Under starry skies above,
Don't fence me in.
    —Cole Porter, "Don't Fence Me In"

"WHAT ARE WE going to do about Gianni Castelli?" Inspector Delarue asked the detectives assigned to the case. "We caught him with the jewels in his possession, so it's an open-and-shut case. The judge will probably give him three years and he'll be out in one. And what do *we* get out of it? Nothing. We have to find out who is behind this."

"He told us. This Benny the Horse guy," said one of the detectives.

"But do you believe that?" said Bernard.

"Do you think he's lying about not knowing who he was working for, other than Benito Cavallo?" asked Ola.

"That's the problem. I believe him," Delarue answered. "I don't think he knows anything and he's certainly not going to give up Benny the Horse, whoever he is. Forget that."

"I have an idea, but it all hinges on whether I can get him to believe me. That's where you come in, Inspector," said Ola.

"Tell me."

"We offer him a deal if he tells us who was behind the robbery. Three months, something like that." Ola held up her hand to silence the others before they could interject. "All I need is a room and a telephone—and a full day with no interruptions. I want him to telephone this horse guy."

"He'll never do it," said Bernard. "He's too smart for that."

"Don't be too sure."

"You've got a day. What do you want me to do?" said Delarue.

"Just make him an offer. Tell him if he doesn't co-operate with me you'll find a way to put him away for *ten* years," said Ola.

"Will he believe that?" said one of the detectives.

"He's in jail. He wants out. If the inspector says it right, he'll believe it," said Ola.

INSPECTOR DELARUE DID an excellent acting job. "You can say nothing, hire a lawyer. We'll get you for everything we can think of—resisting arrest, grand larceny, posses- sion of drugs with intent to sell—and we'll come up with a few others."

"Hey," said Castelli, "who are you kidding? What drugs? What resisting arrest? And you got all the jewels back, so what's the big deal here?"

"Not all of it, Mr. Castelli. There's still one piece miss- ing. We think you had an accomplice. A ten-carat dia- mond ring," said Delarue with all the cool and confidence he could manage. "And we've got two witnesses to the attempted drug sale. You wanna gamble that we don't? Be smart. Don't bet against the house."

"You're blowing smoke up my ass," said Castelli.

"Then don't inhale," said the inspector. "Take your chances. Here." He continued offering Castelli the tele- phone. "You'll want to call your lawyer, I assume."

"And what's this business about resisting arrest?" said Castelli.

"We've got two witnesses. How many do you have?"

After a long pause, during which Castelli considered his situation, he said warily, "What do you want?"

"Detective Obolensky," Delarue pointed at Ola—"will give you all the details. You do what she asks and we forget about all the other charges except the robbery and get you off with a light sentence. Maybe a couple of months at the most. Or, as I said, if you like the food here so much . . ." The inspector didn't have to elaborate. Castelli got the message. "I'll leave you both. Let me know your decision."

The inspector left Ola and Castelli in the small room, which had no windows and was furnished with only one metal chair, a small table, and a telephone. Ola lifted the phone. "This is a direct line to the outside. It doesn't go through the switchboard. I'm going to leave you here for a while because I feel you may have some personal calls to make. You'll also be able to receive calls. You can tell your contacts to call you back from pay phones if you're nervous about us tracing calls. I don't care how many people you have to call or what you have to say; all I want is a piece of simple information. Who hired Benito Cavallo? Just the name, or names. That's all. I'll leave you a pad and a pencil."

"Suppose I can't get him? Suppose I get him and he won't give me the names? Suppose he doesn't have the names, suppose—"

"Suppose I leave you to work all that out," said Ola as she tossed a pad of paper and a pencil onto the small desk. "It's ten o'clock. You've got until six tonight. Eight hours, Mr. Castelli. Don't waste any of them. I'll check on you every few hours, or you can call me." She wrote her office number on the pad.

"This your home number?" said Castelli, with a grin. "I could give you something better than a name . . ."

Ola put her high-heeled boot up on Castelli's chair, the

sharp heel pressing on his manhood—which was quickly becoming his boyhood.

"Just a joke, a joke," he squeaked through his pain.

"I don't like jokes." She raised her boot and slammed it into his chest, knocking him over the back of the chair.

"Hey. You're not allowed to do that."

"You're right. You want to report it? No problem."

"I'll let you off easy this time," he mumbled.

Castelli got back into the chair and began to doodle nervously on the pad. Ola left, locking and bolting the door behind her and pocketing the key. Delarue was waiting for her in his office, with Bernard.

"You were excellent. Especially the part about the drugs, the resisting arrest, and the ring," said Ola.

"Thank you. It just came to me at the last minute," said Delarue.

Since Bernard was in the room, both Ola and Delarue were scrupulous about conducting themselves in a professional manner. "Let me know, Detective Obolensky, let me know right away if anything breaks."

After Ola left, Bernard said, "Is she your type?"

"I never mix business with pleasure," Delarue replied. In fact, he was telling the truth: he would never have considered making a pass at Ola at the office. Sex was for the bedroom.

BENNY THE HORSE finally called Gianni Castelli at five-thirty that evening. Castelli had made about thirty calls trying to track him down, leaving messages in every conceivable place, with every possible contact.

"Lucky for you there's blood between us," said Benny. "Lucky for you that you're my stepsister's son. Now take down this name. I'm only gonna say it once. I wasted my time, didn't make a fucking dime for all my trouble. Julio Benvenuti."

The phone line went dead. Benny had hung up. But Castelli had the name. He hoped it was the one they were looking for. Castelli stood up and walked around the room. "Damn I'd like to fuck that bitch," he said aloud.

Benito Cavallo had telephoned Gianni Castelli from a phone in the Café de Paris, just opposite the Hotel de Paris. After the call, he sat at a table on the outdoor terrace and ordered the world's most expensive cup of espresso. Fuck it, it's a business expense, he thought. When it came he took a sip and grimaced. Terrible shit the French passed off as espresso. Too cheap to use the best Italian roast coffee. He drank it anyway. Then, from his inside jacket pocket, he brought out photos of four women, the ones that Julio had sent to him through his contact. Benny the Horse never met with anybody directly. That was one of his ironclad rules. They don't see you, don't talk to you, they don't know you. All they got is air. He studied the pictures and memorized the names written below them. It was twenty minutes to six when he asked the waiter to bring him a Fernet Branca on ice. They couldn't screw that up, it came in a bottle. Fifteen minutes later he watched as the women in the photos came to life across the street and walked into the hotel. He paid his bill and left. Twenty bucks for bad coffee and a shot of Fernet plus fifteen percent service and value-added tax. What value did they add? They should have *deducted* the friggin' tax—called it a value-subtracted tax.

The Horse trotted across the street, diagonally, and entered the underground parking area. In the elevator he pressed level four, the lowest in the large complex. It was empty of cars with the exception of one black Mitsubishi passenger van with dark-tinted windows. Every piece of chrome on the van had been recently sprayed black. Cavallo got in and lowered the driver's seat into a reclining position. He had two hours to wait, and set his wrist alarm for seven-fifteen. That would give him plenty of time to change into his tuxedo gear. Benito closed his eyes and was asleep almost immediately. He had lots of experience sleeping in cars.

At seven-thirty he drove out and over to the Hotel de

Paris, where the doorman looked at his vehicle with obvious disdain, until Benny made him smile with a two-hundred-franc note.

"I'll park it myself, if that's okay," Benny said.

The doorman shrugged, pocketed the money, and went back to his post as Benny parked the van just opposite the entrance of the hotel. Twelve steps, at most. Perfect. Then he walked through the lobby and into the men's room, where he washed his face and hands, combed his hair, and checked his appearance in the mirror. Benito Cavallo. He had given himself that name, made it up. Mr. Average. No identifying marks or features. Dark hair, ordinary eyes set above an ordinary mouth and ordinary nose. Add a pair of black-rimmed glasses, as he now did, and you had any tourist businessman. The glasses, along with the tuxedo, the small white button carnation in the lapel, the red silk handkerchief and patent-leather shoes—it all added up to an image of seriousness and trustworthiness, the look of a regular guy. Perfect. From his watch pocket he drew out a calling card printed on white vellum. It read:

Armand Stella
Directeur de Securité
Hotel de Paris

Printed in the upper left corner was the logo of the Hotel de Paris, in dark blue. A very simple forgery; one that any half-assed computer nerd could make in fifteen minutes flat. He had only one copy, but one was all he'd need. It was seven forty-five. In the lobby he picked up the house telephone and made a call—to the Baroness Natasha Karmanov. Perfect. He took the elevator up to the fourth floor, where she was waiting for him at the door of her suite. He explained that the hotel was concerned about the women's security. He assumed that they would be wearing valuable jewels as usual (the baroness confirmed this) and presented his card. She was impressed. He then mentioned that the hotel would provide transportation to wherever they were going that evening. She said that wasn't necessary. He insisted. She agreed. They were meeting some "friends" and would call them to find out where. Yes, she would advise the other three women. He said he was at their complete disposal and they could be assured of his complete discretion.

"You're Italian, aren't you?" said Irene.

"Yes, of course. And if you're wondering why a French hotel would employ an Italian director of security, wonder no further. Who would you rather have attending to your safety—Gérard Depardieu or Sylvester Stallone?"

Irene laughed.

The Horse laughed. He bowed and departed, saying he would be waiting in front of the hotel. "Red handkerchief, white carnation, black-rimmed glasses—you won't be able to miss me."

At the hotel bar he ordered a Negroni, made with chilled Tanqueray gin, Martini & Rossi sweet vermouth, and red Campari, in a stemmed glass. His first sip reminded him that he was still in France. How could they screw up a Negroni? Ah, well, he would be back in Italy soon, where he would have a proper one at his favorite restaurant, Giambelli Casalinga, in Palermo. With *spaghetti alla putanesca* to follow. He could taste it.

Benito Cavallo did not officially exist. He had been abandoned at birth—left by the wayside in the bleak Calabrian hills. He was found by a poor farmer's wife who was barren and believed that Benito had been sent to her by God in answer to her prayers. She convinced her husband to let her keep him without reporting it to the authorities. She called the boy "Bambino," nothing more. The man was an eggplant farmer and kept a few pigs and a mule on his ragged farm. The land was not fertile and the water supply inadequate, but it was good enough to grow *melanzana*—eggplant. In the sixteen years that Benito lived on the farm, he had eaten eggplant in every way imaginable. The worst was his adoptive mother's favorite recipe for Christmas day: slices of eggplant boiled in oil and then cooked in an old sour wine. She added a bit of chocolate, sugar, cinnamon, pine nuts and walnuts (if she had them), raisins, and cedar bark. It was called *Melanzana agrodolce*. Benito always finished his portion and said it was wonderful, when in truth he hated it. From the day he left the farm he was never able to eat eggplant again in any form.

The hills of Calabria were a lonely and harsh place for a boy to grow up. He had no formal schooling but his mother, who could read and write, did her best to tutor him. Her look of gravity and her husband's perpetually troubled visage were inherited by the boy. When he was sixteen, the only mother he had ever known, died, and Benito left home, finding his way across the water to the town of Taormina on the Sicilian coast. There he found work in the hotels and *pensioni,* making himself useful to anyone who would pay him with no questions asked. There were many who wanted cheap labor. In town there was a cinema and a library and it was there that Benito first learned about the world outside of Calabria and Sicily. His at-home schooling had been less than adequate but he remedied that by spending all of his free hours at the local library. Books became his passion, and although he had no friends with whom to share his growing fund of knowledge, he was content to educate himself as a solitary commitment. Taormina was always full of tourists and Benito learned to take full advantage of them, giving the kids donkey-cart rides and taking the adults on tours of the churches and places of antiquity. He also worked the nearby beach of Mazzaro, selling and stealing as opportunities presented themselves. He was clever and soon came to the attention of the local lower-echelon pseudo-Mafia hoods. From them he learned his most important lessons: Always be anonymous. Never appear to be what you really are. Allegiance to family comes first. But Benito had no family and so he adopted one and created an identity for himself from nothing. His second family owned a small restaurant that catered to tourists. Even though it was off the beaten track, Benito dragged his "clients" there, much to the delight of the owners, Maria and Franco Cartoni, who reciprocated by taking Benito in to live with them and their two children.

Because Benito never walked when he could run, everyone began to call him *cavallo*—horse. He added a first name, Benito, after a character in a film he'd seen in the local cinema. He liked the name because it had a sound similar to Bambino, the same cadence of three syllables, and started with a *b*, ending with an *o*. Benito Cavallo or, to his American and English clients, Benny the Horse. When he was twenty he left Taormina and moved to Naples, where he became involved in the cigarette-smuggling trade and other small-time criminal adventures. Benito's forte was his uncanny ability to talk his way in or out of any situation. His biggest fear was being arrested and therefore he planned his nefarious activities with extra care and precision. He had no permanent address, no base, no roots. But he could always be found through his network of far-flung associates, all of whom were indebted to the Horse.

His love life was composed of fleeting affairs, since he feared, most of all, potentially jealous and vengeful women. In any event, he never stayed around long enough to form any lasting relationships. This troubled him vaguely, although not enough for him to do anything about it. That wouldn't be smart. Benny the Horse, Mr. Invisible. As Benito's network grew, so did his bank accounts, which he kept well hidden. Nothing was in his name. Nothing could be traced back to him.

Benito was forty years old when a sudden violent urge to become legal consumed his thoughts. His dream was to be official, a registered citizen. He inquired. It could be done. The price was high—more than he could afford. He needed big money and that meant a big score. Bigger than any he had ever attempted. Recently, an idea for one had fallen into his lap. It was an omen. An answer.

Benito had never killed anyone, had never hurt anyone, and he had no intention of changing that. He had a plan. One that he refined until it seemed foolproof. He would succeed and Benito Cavallo would be legal at last. He would buy a house in Tuscany, marry an Italian girl with big hips and a deep, comforting cleavage and make a lot of babies. And he would change his name so that no one could ever find him.

Benito "Benny the Horse" Cavallo would die.

22

"The Royals and Their Consorts"

What small potatoes we all are,
Compared with what we might be.
—C. D. Warner

THAT NIGHT THE four women looked absolutely regal,
acted regal. Now not only were they pretend rich, they
were pretend royalty—queens—and so with heads held
higher, backs held straighter, bosoms rising to the occasion, smiling confident blue-blooded smiles, they swept
into the marble court of the Hotel de Paris to greet their
awaiting consorts. All that was missing was the pomp and
circumstance and possibly the music of a Strauss waltz or
a Mozart minuet.

Tonight, there were *paparazzi* and television cameras
waiting in the lobby, tipped off by the jewelry-store salesmen that the famous Taylor-Burton Diamond and other
famous stones would be worn tonight by four of the
richest women in the world. Camera lights strobed as the
photogs jockeyed for position. A woman photojournalist
from *Nice Matin,* the Riviera's premier newspaper, took
a close-up of Irene wearing the famous Liz pendant. It
would appear in the Monaco section of the morning edition. Photos of all the women, with attendant stories,
would grace the pages of *Paris-Match, French Gala, Peo-*

ple, and the *International Herald Tribune.* The women would cherish the reportage as irrefutable evidence of their adventure.

Benito watched the goings-on with amused detachment. All those jewels would soon be his. Millions. Many millions. It was so simple.

"Are you going to rename the diamond, Baroness?" shouted one of the reporters.

"Oh, I don't like to talk about that, I hear it's bad luck. Actually, I find the name rather picturesque," said Irene.

Ola wore a press badge and blended in perfectly with the other reporters. Inspector Delarue had asked her to keep an eye on that diamond—just in case. One couldn't be too careful. As she held her camera high and popped off a picture, just to look official, she felt an unmistakable pinch on her left buttock. Wheeling around quickly, she surveyed the space behind her to see who the perpetrator might be. There were just reporters and a nondescript man in a tuxedo, wearing a pair of black-rimmed glasses. He was holding a sheaf of menus; obviously a waiter or employee of the hotel. She ruled him out and searched further for a guilty face. Nothing—no one caught her eye. She decided to forget it. She'd been pinched before and she would no doubt be pinched again; Italian men were everywhere in Monte Carlo.

When the ravenous media vultures had picked the bones of the story clean, Irene led the women out of the hotel and down the short flight of stairs. It all happened so fast that Ola barely had a chance to take a photo of the departing black Mitsubishi van with the dark-tinted windows. Why were four of the richest women in the world traveling in a van? she wondered. Something felt wrong. Every instinct told her to follow it, and Ola always obeyed her instincts; they had rarely let her down.

Running to her car, where her partner was sitting in the driver's seat reading a comic book, she screamed, "*Go, go, go!* The black van. He'll take the fastest way out of town—probably to the autoroute." But Ola's blue

Renault-5 was hemmed in by two double-parked press cars, and by the time her driver managed to get clear, the Mitsubishi was nowhere in sight.

"He took the turn toward the autoroute—up on the *grande corniche.* Go, go, go—and no siren," she said. "We don't want to put those women in any more danger than they may be in already. Just try to keep him in sight."

The four women had no idea they were being kidnapped. They had told Armand Stella, head of security for the hotel, that they were to meet the men at Le Parrot—did he know it? "Yes, of course. A very nice place. Up on the *grande corniche* above the village of Roquebrune. Should take no more than fifteen minutes."

Benito steered the van into a long tunnel and up through the narrow winding streets that led to the upper roads. He assumed he was being followed, although he had no evidence of this. It was simply part of his careful philosophy: if something wrong can possibly happen, assume that it will. His rearview mirror showed him nothing unusual, but he drove at top speed while the women chatted casually, looking forward to the evening ahead.

Just before the turn to the upper roadway, Benito pulled off to the side of the road and into a cul-de-sac. The overhead streetlights had been purposefully broken earlier that day and so the totally black Mitsubishi van, with its lights extinguished, blended completely into the dark shadows. No one driving by would even notice it.

"What's going on?" said Eleanor. "Why are we stopped?"

"I think we're being followed. Can't be too careful these days."

And he was right. Within two minutes a blue Renault-5 went screaming by at top speed. Benito merely nodded at the women and they nodded back their appreciation for his obvious intelligence in these matters. Whether the blue Renault was actually following them seemed somewhat irrelevant. He waited another fifteen seconds before steering the van back onto the road, turning almost immediately up a narrow winding road that led to the Monte Carlo golf course. Pulling out a cellular phone, he punched some numbers and, after speaking a few words in rapid Italian, pulled over in front of a darkened restaurant. "This is it, ladies."

"It looks closed," said Eleanor. "You sure this is the right place?"

Benito pulled out a revolver and pointed it at Irene, who was sitting next to him in the passenger seat. With his other hand he pressed a button that locked all of the van's doors and another that closed all the windows. "No one will get hurt, I promise you. All I want is the jewelry. It's all insured by Lloyd's of London, so there's no point in your risking your lives for it."

The women were speechless but did as they were asked, removing all of their jewelry and placing it in a cloth sack that Benito held out. When he had collected everything, he asked Irene, "You think you can drive this?"

"Yes," was all she managed to say.

"Good. When I get out, you slide over and drive out of here. And don't try any hero shit."

"Make that *heroine* shit," Eleanor said.

He ignored the gibe. "Just drive—back the way we came." Benito got out of the car, keeping his gun aimed at them until Irene put the van in gear and drove off. Walking to the parking area, he pulled a cover from a green Peugeot, revealing a man sitting in the driver's seat. The minute Benito got into the car, it pulled away, continuing up the hill. No other cars were anywhere in sight. Benito snapped off the tight skin-colored gloves he'd been wearing and stuffed them into a pocket. The van had been wiped clean and there would be no prints other than those belonging to the women. Benito had stolen the van that afternoon, from a supermarket lot in Nice, and driven it to the parking complex in Monte Carlo. The Peugeot they were riding in had been stolen by the driver, a friend from Torino, who would be well paid for the trip.

Irene drove the van cautiously, for two reasons. First, she didn't know where she was going, and second, she was frightened out of her mind and trembling. The other women held their breath and looked for road signs to Monte Carlo. They had not driven more than a quarter of a mile when Irene was blinded by bright headlights coming straight at the van. She jammed on the brakes and swerved just in time to avoid colliding with a Renault-5 that was barreling up the narrow road. All Irene could see were two dark figures leaping out of the R-5, with guns drawn, rushing toward her.

Ola flung open the driver's side door and panned her flashlight around the interior of the van while her partner kept his gun at the ready, covering her. Irene screamed; Ola ignored her until she was satisfied that the four women were alone. Then she flashed her badge.

"Police. I'm sorry to have frightened you. Is everyone all right?"

Irene was breathless. "No, we're not," she said, relieved that Ola was on their side. "We've been conned and robbed."

"All of our jewelry," said Darlene.

"Again," said Carla. "I thought Monte Carlo was supposed to be safe."

"It seems you four have changed things. Do you know who it was?" said Ola. "And what happened to him? I assume it was a him?"

"He said he was head of security for the Hotel de Paris. I have his card right here," said a nerve-shattered Irene.

Ola looked at the calling card: Armand Stella. Ha. Whoever it was had planned this carefully. "Is there anything you can tell us about him? What he looked like? Identifying marks? Something?"

"He was sort of ordinary looking—like a regular guy, nothing special. He was wearing a tuxedo. Black-rimmed glasses. He seemed nice," said Darlene.

"Bastard," Ola said almost to herself. "He was the one who pinched my ass. I should have known. Damn!"

"What?" said Darlene. "You know this guy?"

"No. But I'm going to get to know him very well."

"There is *one* thing," said Carla. "Before he robbed us, he made a call. He spoke in Italian, so I understood some of it. Something about a place called Vintimiglia, to-night."

"Then he must have had another car waiting for him," said Ola.

"I didn't see any, but I really wasn't looking," said Irene.

"I'll have our office contact the Italian border cross-ings, especially the one at Vintimiglia," said Ola's partner as he headed for the two-way radio in the Renault.

"It's a waste of time. What can we tell them? Look for a *car*—we don't know what kind—and a man, whom we can't describe? But what the hell, do it anyway. You never know." Ola returned her attention to the women. "Could you take us back to the spot where the robbery took place?"

"That's easy; it's just up the road. There's a restau-rant," said Irene.

Of course they found nothing at the restaurant. "He could have walked, but I doubt it. He *must* have had someone waiting for him," said Ola. "Ten to one Benny the Horse is involved in this one, too," she said to her partner.

IN THE PEUGEOT, Benito slid out of his tuxedo and put on slacks and a shirt.

"Where are we headed?" said his driver.

"To the one place they'll never think of looking. Take the next turn to the right."

Benito threw the gun out of the car window. It was worthless. No bullets. Wouldn't shoot even if it was loaded. No firing pin. It was a fake. Then he tossed away his latex gloves.

*   *   *

OLA WENT BACK to her office where Inspector Delarue was waiting. After giving him the details of the robbery, she began to pace. "If this was pulled off by this Horse character, then he's a very clever guy. Not a fingerprint on the van, which was stolen from Nice just this morning. He obviously had someone waiting, hidden near the restaurant. Smart of him to give the women the van so that he couldn't be tracked in it. He had them out of the hotel, into the van, and away in ten seconds. Even I was fooled."

"So, put yourself in his shoes. What would *you* do next?" said Delarue, challenging her. "Or, what *wouldn't* you do?"

"I think the phone call he made was probably a phony, to throw us off. He's too smart to try something like that. So, I don't think they crossed the border at Vintimiglia or at any other French/Italian border point."

"Good supposition."

"In fact, if I were he, I probably wouldn't chance crossing any border at all, at least not so soon after the robbery. I think he would assume we'd cover them and he'd be concerned with taking a chance on even a spot check since he has the jewels with him."

"So, he gets rid of the tuxedo, changes clothes, throws away the glasses, the gun, combs his hair a different way, and the women probably wouldn't be able to identify him if he walked right past them."

"Right," Ola agreed.

"So, where would the safest place be?"

"Right here in Monte Carlo. He'd most likely think it would be the last place we'd look."

"Then we should photograph all the cars coming in, see what we get. Check all the license plates in the computer for stolen vehicles," said Delarue.

"I've already asked for that. It's being done as we speak," said Ola.

Delarue smiled. This one was smart *and* sexy. Really smart; really sexy.

MONTE CARLO WAS an easy place to surveil since there were very few roads leading in. The same system was used to identify traffic offenders—speeders, red-light runners, stop-sign ignorers, etc. The cameras were aimed at strategic, well-lit spots and usually delivered an excellent picture of driver, passenger, license number, and documentation of the offense. Each camera shutter was tripped by a chip embedded in the roadway.

Benito Cavallo, who never made mistakes, made one small one this time. He'd done everything perfectly but had forgotten to take off his black-rimmed glasses until he had crossed the Monte Carlo border with France. A photo of Benny and his driver, along with the front of the Peugeot and its plate number, was immediately checked. Records showed the Peugeot had been stolen that afternoon from the hilltop town of La Turbie, in France. By 10:30 P.M., Detective Ola Obolensky knew that the robber and kidnapper were driving a dark green 1995 Peugeot 206, license-plate number 217XS986. A street and parking-lot sweep began at eleven P.M. At 12:15 A.M., the car was found in an underground parking lot opposite the casino.

Ola and a squad of police opened the car and, to Ola's surprise and delight, found the cloth bag of jewels in full view—in the car's trunk. No doubt the thief thought he was undetected and that the jewels would be safe while he went about other business. One thing Ola knew for sure was that sooner or later he'd be back. She only had to be patient. At two A.M., Detective Obolensky easily arrested a man who matched the photo of the passenger in the car. He was the one *with* the black-rimmed glasses. He had no identity papers, no wallet, no passport, no credits cards—in short, nothing to identify himself. She guessed he was the notorious Benny the Horse, but he refused to confirm or deny this, saying only that he wanted a lawyer. He did, however, deny having played any part in the robbery or kidnapping, although he admitted to stealing the car only hours before.

Ola stared hard at him, trying to connect him with the man in the tuxedo who may or may not have pinched her bottom. She couldn't swear to it.

HIS TYPED STATEMENT said that if there were jewels in the trunk of the car he was unaware of them. He swore that he had stolen the Peugeot from the parking lot of the Hotel Metropole and driven it here while he went to get something to eat. He produced a copy of the bill from the restaurant. He said he'd been held up by thieves earlier in the day and his own car and papers had been stolen. He'd "borrowed" the Peugeot because he needed transportation back to his home, in Naples. He was no thief, and said that he fully intended to return the car to its rightful owner. When contacted, the car's owner, after hearing Benny's story, refused to press charges. He just wanted his car back.

The next morning, Benito was put in a lineup with four other nondescript-looking men. The four women could not agree upon which one was the robber. Each picked a different man. Only Eleanor properly identified Benito.

Ola and Delarue mulled over what they had: the women were uninjured, the jewels recovered. Ola's photo of him getting into the black van showed only his back.

PROSECUTING THIS GUY would mean a lot of pain-in-the-ass paperwork and they doubted that a judge would indict on such circumstantial evidence. So they reluctantly (happily) let him go. He would have no record. A bit of Gallic pragmatism. Why trouble with small potatoes?

Ola, dressed as a gypsy beggar, decided to tail him, to see if the "small potato" might be part of a bigger stew, while Delarue went to the Café de Paris to look for Maurice Gerard.

The inspector found Maurice at the café, sipping a *café au lait* and reading his usual array of newspapers.

"Mind if I join you, *mon ami*?"

"Please," said Maurice.

"So, how goes the quest, the search for the perfect rich woman?"

"I am so used to being alone that I don't know if I could marry again even if I found her. I'd have to be in love as well, so that makes it even more complicated."

"In love? The King of Hearts in love? Maurice, think of your reputation."

"The days when I had a reputation are long gone, Georges."

"And the tall one? Not rich enough?"

"You don't miss a thing, do you?"

"One tries one's best. Monte Carlo is a tiny village." Delarue paused and ordered a *café crème*. "I see you have your 'boys' in action."

"Just trying to keep the guests of the principality happy. There's nothing for you to be interested in, Inspector. Just business as usual."

"Let's hope so," said Delarue enigmatically.

It was then that Sophie announced that Maurice was wanted on the telephone. The call was from Julio. Trouble. As Maurice walked off, Sophie sighed. "I'm worried about him, Georges."

"So am I. He's changed in the last week. Seems very down on himself. Have you seen his latest?"

"Yes," said Sophie, "but I can never tell if Maurice is serious; he's such a good actor."

"Sit down, please," said Delarue, motioning to a chair opposite his.

Sophie sat down at the table and for a moment neither spoke. They had known each other for more years than either wanted to admit. Funny with people one sees day after day in the same place. You pass them in the street, a restaurant, at the market, and there's no instant recognition because they're not *in situ.* You don't know whether or not to say hello. Then—flash!—you realize who they are and you're embarrassed and make some remark like, "I'm sorry, I was so wrapped up in my thoughts that I almost walked right past you." But the other person always knows. It's like being introduced to someone you've met before but who, for some reason, has forgotten you.

Delarue realized that he didn't even know Sophie's last name, or anything about her background. She was simply Sophie from the Café de Paris. She was a handsome woman, a few years younger than the inspector. He would make it his business to learn more about her. After all, knowing about people was part of his job.

Sophie, on the other hand, knew everything about him—that he was French and not *Monégasque* (it was required by law that the chief of police be French), that he'd never married; that if he conducted affairs, which surely he did, they were not observed in Monte Carlo.

Sophie, herself, had been married twice—to a blackjack dealer and a wine salesman. The first left her; she dumped the second. Both had one trait in common: they were always short of money and borrowing from the hardworking waitress.

She liked her current job managing the café because she was a people person, but in the confines of her small apartment her normally cheerful countenance disappeared, replaced by a mask of abject loneliness. The café had become her whole life, and as she grew older, her longing for someone to share her life with grew exponentially.

Over the years she'd seen Delarue in Nice or dining on the harbor at Villefranche. Once he walked right by her. It was apparent to Sophie that he liked younger women. Every man, it seemed, liked younger women. Sophie was not a younger woman. So be it.

"I hope he holds up until . . ." Delarue had started a sentence he couldn't finish.

"Maurice is a good man, Inspector."

"I hope so, Sophie. I really hope so."

BENITO MADE A few phone calls at two public booths and then went into the movie theater off the main square. Ola waited patiently outside, earning forty francs begging, before he emerged. After he gave her a handout of five francs, she followed him at a distance, to Lino's Ristorante Elegante by the Sea. Benito had called Julio to arrange a meeting, demanding that Julio come up with some money for the bungled robbery at Jimmy Z's. Benito had done his part, it wasn't his fault the robbery had failed. He claimed that he'd had to pay Castellini half his fee in advance (not true) and told Julio that he wanted twenty-five thousand francs today or he'd let the police know who was behind the attempted robbery.

The four men sat at a table, looking distraught. It had not been easy to come up with the money on such short notice, but somehow they had managed. It was better than the alternative—jail.

"This is all going the wrong way," said Jean-Jacques. "We're supposed to be conning these women out of their money and it's been costing us a fortune."

"No way we're ever going to get our hands on their jewels now—not after what happened last night," said Trevor.

"Obviously there are others who have them in their sights. I'm sure the women will be wearing the rhinestones from now on," said Jean-Jacques.

"Our only hope is that love, the ultimate con, will conquer all. They have no idea we're involved, so if Cavallo keeps his mouth shut, we should be in the clear," said Julio.

"*If* he keeps his mouth shut," said Jean-Jacques.

"What's he got to gain by telling the police about us?" said Trevor.

"Nothing, we hope," said Maurice. "Let's get this over

with as quickly as we can. No food, Julio, please."

"*Sì, sì.*"

OLA LOOKED IN the window of the restaurant and took a perfect shot of the four men and Benito with her tiny Minox camera. Another scrapbook item; exhibit 27. The evidence was growing nicely. While she waited outside she held her hand out and begged another few francs from a passerby, a continuing test of the authenticity of her disguise. She turned, just in time to get a second photo of Julio handing Benito a large envelope. *Bingo!*

OLA THE GYPSY trailed Benny the Horse to the Monte Carlo railroad station, after calling for backup. She found him standing at the bar of the café in the station, drinking an espresso. She carefully moved in next to him and ordered an espresso as well, being sure to put some money on the bar first; gypsies were not trusted in this part of the country. As she took her first sip, momentarily distracted, she felt a pinch on her bottom. She recognized the pinch instantly and whirled as he passed and karate-chopped him to the floor, flipping him and handcuffing him in one fluid movement. Her backup arrived to haul him away.

They impounded the money and put Benito in a cell next to Antonio Guzman and Gianni Castellini. Benito said nothing, waiting to see which way the wind was blowing before making his deal. The Horse was very good at making deals.

Ola wanted as much evidence as she could get before they arrested the four men.

Delarue insisted upon it since he considered Maurice Gerard a friend and didn't want to be embarrassed.

Rhinestone Cowboy Guzman had been through the system before and knew that he wouldn't get a long sentence for stealing some worthless junk posing as jewelry. When Ola told him that he'd made a mistake, that one of the rings was real (a five-carat bauble), he was suddenly amenable to giving up Jean-Jacques Lacoste as the man who had hired him. The circle was complete. A picture had formed that made the men's guilt seem irrefutable. Inspector Delarue requested that he be the one to bring in Maurice, and Ola reluctantly agreed. But it could wait until tomorrow, since tonight he and Ola had plans that, while they may have included handcuffs, did not qualify as official police work. Yes, Ola agreed, tomorrow would be fine. Tonight she would see what mischief they could get into with a bottle of honey and a magnum of vintage Krug.

23
"Revelations"

'Tis better to have loved and lost,
Than never to have loved at all.
—Tennyson

Low points

The women had been robbed three times and were concerned and surprised that this rich routine had some serious pitfalls. They also questioned why Monte Carlo had a reputation as one of the safest places on earth. Back to the rhinestones tonight. They hoped the men wouldn't notice.

Of course they would.

THE MEN'S FINANCES were close to touching bottom. They considered throwing themselves at the mercy of the women and letting the chips fall where they might, but optimists that they were, they decided to wait at least one more day. They would all be with their dates today and then meet up as a group for gambling at the casino and dinner afterward.

High points

Benito Cavallo was out of his mind crazy in love with Ola Obolensky. Her full hips, her bountiful bosom, her withheld sexuality. She was everything he had been look-ing for in a wife. The fact that he was in jail and she was the jailer did nothing to cool his ardor; if anything, it increased it.

OLA OBOLENSKY HAD never been in love and had had few lovers, certainly none as appreciative as Inspector Georges Delarue. Part of his charm was that he was always sur-prised at her boldness and sexual ingenuity and seemed to enjoy it as a game rather than as a commitment. She wasn't sure whether she liked it that way or not. At the moment she was thinking of other things, like warming the honey and chilling the bubbly.

INSPECTOR GEORGES DELARUE had never had honey and champagne in such an interesting fashion. He wondered if he was in love with Ola Obolensky or just becoming addicted to her sexuality. At the moment it didn't matter.

24
"The Love Song Duets"

She: *Would you love me, if I weren't me?*
         Not a princess, born of royalty.
He: *Could a princess love a prince who's just pretending?*
Both: *Couldn't I be me,*
         Couldn't you be you . . . ?

IRENE AND MAURICE sat at a table on the outdoor terrace of the Château Eza, high atop the picture-postcard-pretty-perched village of Eze, a ten-minute drive from Monte Carlo along the *moyenne corniche*. The last gusts of a mistral wind were turning into breezy sighs, leaving the intense blue sky cloudless and the sea varying shades of turquoise, depending upon the water's depth. An ocean liner slid into view, heading in the direction of Italy. From their vantage point it looked like a toy model, so dwarfed was it by the immense expanse of the Mediterranean. With binoculars they would have been able to see the shadow of Corsica straight ahead of them, due east. A few sailboats, their ballooning spinnakers driving them forcefully through the light chop, made the seascape heartbreakingly unblemished.

Irene thought of all the things she wanted to say, all of the things she would have said were she not hindered by the existence of her rival self, the Baroness Natasha Karmanov. It was becoming more and more like acting in a play, one in which the actors had not yet been given their lines for the last act. What would Act IV bring? she wondered. There were only a few possibilities to be considered, and she liked none of them. She longed to play the prima donna and ask for a rewrite. Her ending would have her and Maurice sailing on the liner that was just slipping from view, off together on an endless adventure around the world, as opposed to the denouement she was now heading for—the one without the happy finale. She felt that whatever move she made, whatever sentence she spoke, question she asked, answer she gave—would be wrong.

"Do you believe in horoscopes, fortune-tellers, tarot cards?" she said.

"I guess there is something to be said for those things, although I've never tried them. I suppose it all depends on just how much you want to believe. Self-fulfilling prophecies, and all that."

Irene took out her tarot cards and spread them on the table. "Will you indulge me, and play a little game?"

"Of course, as long as you don't take it too seriously. As long as it remains a game, as you said."

Irene showed Maurice how to choose a card, which he did. It pictured a tower. Irene opened her little tarot guide and began to read. "Maybe this is a mistake," she said, closing the book.

"Don't be silly. Read it. Remember you said we'd treat it as a game. Here, let me." Before she could react, he took the book and began to recite the written interpretation of the card. " 'An unsettling card. Fire, lightning, falling on jagged rocks. Definitely trouble. This card will not be welcomed by people who dislike change.' It says that I will shortly undergo a sudden, dramatic upheaval or reversal of fortune. How I respond to the changes will make all the difference in how painful the experience will be. It may cause me to have a burst of insight about my situation and reach a new level of understanding about it. To keep from harm's way, it says I must break through pretense." Maurice closed the book. For a moment neither spoke. "Maybe it's less of a game than I thought?" he said.

"Do you feel your life is about to change?" said Irene.

"As a matter of fact I do. It has already begun to change. It started the moment I met you."

"Maybe I'm not who you think I am," said Irene.

"Maybe I'm not either?"

"Would it matter?" they both said at the same time, and laughed.

"You first," said Irene. "I can't imagine what I could find out about you that would make any difference."

"Suppose, just suppose, that I was pretending to be someone I'm not," said Maurice. "Say that I was a penniless writer who had not been published in years?"

"You would still be the man I've been with these past few days, wouldn't you?"

"I'm not sure."

Irene changed the subject, which was hitting too close to home. She complimented him on his choice of the food, the wine, the restaurant, which were impeccable, as usual.

Maurice had planned the seduction meticulously. A light lunch of cold salmon trout with a crisp Montrachet. He held up his stemmed glass of the golden wine, which reflected the purple bougainvillea that grew on the restaurant walls and balustrades, and made the glittering sea look like tiny bubbles in the wine. They toasted each other, silently. It was all so perfect and serene that words seemed superfluous. They finished the last of the wine with bowls of tiny wild strawberries and sinfully luxurious triple cream from Isigny.

"This is magic," said Irene, "simply magic."

Maurice took her hand gently. "Come," was all he said, all he needed to say. He led her out of the restaurant and down a stone stair-walk that led to the individual cottage rooms, set in a garden of the hotel La Chèvre d'Or, overlooking the sea and the mountains beyond. When he produced a key she smiled and squeezed his hand in answer to the unspoken question. The very private room was decorated in light *provençal* fabrics that perfectly complemented the setting.

Maurice tried to remember that all this was part of the plan or, as Jean-Jacques had called it, "love, the ultimate con." But here, today, there was more to it than that. It was altogether possible that Maurice was, could be, in love with this woman. In his mind, the two missions clashed.

Maurice closed the heavy wooden shutters so that only soft strips of amber light carpeted the love nest. When he turned, he found himself in her arms, kissing her. The undressing that followed seemed the most natural thing in the world, as his trepidation vanished. He brought her slowly to climax with his hands and mouth, before he entered her.

If it must end, Irene thought, let it be here and now. Let me walk away and spare him the conclusion, the revelation, the unmasking. Let us both keep this as an unsullied memory. Her thoughts were drowned in the undertow of her second orgasm, after which she lay in his arms, both remaining in that floating, sensuous state between sleep and wakefulness. Books called it afterglow. To Irene it wasn't *after*—it was still during. They never made it to the casino that night. Irene would learn the awful truth of what had happened there secondhand.

Byron, in *Don Juan,* defined a lie best when he wrote, "And, after all, what is a lie? 'Tis but the truth in masquerade."

JEAN-JACQUES HAD TAKEN Darlene to the seaside club at the Monte Carlo Beach Hotel, where he'd arranged for lunch, swimming, and sunning, with their own private cabana. Everything, of course, would be charged to her account at the hotel.

After Jean-Jacques closed the white canvas door of the cabana and tied it, he slipped out of his clothes and into the skimpiest bikini Darlene had ever seen. He was surprised when she asked him to leave so that she could change, but he did so with good-natured amusement. When she reappeared, wearing a bathing suit that hid most of her physical attributes, he chided her.

"Take your top off, or you'll get strap lines."

"I'm not going to sit in the sun, so it doesn't matter."

As Jean-Jacques moved to kiss her—the bulge in his bikini telegraphing his further intentions—Darlene held a finger between their lips and removed his hand from her breast. "Not here. Not now," she whispered.

Darlene had decided that she would not have sex again with Jean-Jacques. She would not revert again to her youth, when potential sex was both her lure and her allure. "Don't give it away," her mother had said. "Men don't buy what they can get for free." What she didn't tell Darlene was that all men were not buyers, and that even if they were, a lot of buyers were also losers. And she remembered her first tarot card, the Queen of Wands, and its message: "Your looks will not help you . . . remain positive."

"No one can see us. It's very private here."

"I'm a born-again virgin, and I intend to stay that way."

He laughed, thinking this was her idea of a sex game. "Are you saying that our wonderful lovemaking the other day never happened?"

"Think of it as sex-annulled."

"What does that mean?"

"It's like marriage annulment. It means that you never did it, as opposed to divorce, which means that you made a mistake."

"You're saying our lovemaking never happened?"

"Right. So we have a clean slate to work with. Or, to put it rather crudely but precisely, I'm no longer an easy fuck."

"Hey," said Jean-Jacques, with a leer, "I'm willing to work hard for it."

"That's not funny. You're not taking me seriously."

"I am. Whatever you want, just ask."

Darlene walked away from him and down to the edge of the beach where the rocks met the water. She looked up at the sun until her eyes began to tear. Then, quite theatrically, she turned, holding her head high, and let him see her tear-streaked cheeks as she slowly closed her eyes. If it all appeared rather dramatic to Jean-Jacques, that was just the effect she was striving for. In almost a whisper she said, "I'm looking for permanence"—a pause—"roots"—a longer pause—"substance. That's who I am now."

Then she turned her back on him and said, in a whispery voice, "The woman you fucked in the soccer stadium no longer exists."

Darlene had memorized her speech perfectly and was content with her performance.

"I liked that person in the soccer stadium," said Jean-Jacques. "And I like the person who's standing in front of me now. I'll take either one."

"You've ignored everything I've said."

"Maybe it's because I'm not sure what you're getting at. We've only known each other for a few days. Are you looking for commitment that fast?"

"That's where men get it all wrong. Women aren't looking for *instant* commitment, just the *possibility* of commitment. We know right away if there's no possibility, even if we sometimes delude ourselves for a while."

"Do you want there to be that possibility with me?" Jean-Jacques said. "Is that what you're getting at?"

"Two people have to want that," Darlene answered as Jean-Jacques pulled her close and whispered, "I've never had a virgin before."

"Will you be gentle?"

"I don't know."

"Will you make me come so hard that I won't be able to make a fist for a week?"

"Two weeks." Jean-Jacques didn't remember being so horny since he was in his teens.

Afterward they swam naked in the sea and were purified.

CARLA WANTED TO visit an Italian church and so Julio drove her an hour and a half down the coast to Genoa, where they walked through the old city, in the intricate web of tightly packed streets that tumbled down to the waterfront. It was here that Julio showed her the beautiful Cathedral of San Lorenzo and, afterward, the church of San Giovanni di Pre, where she chose to linger.

Julio watched anxiously as Carla lit a candle and knelt in silent prayer in front of a statue of the Virgin Mary. He had not been to church since the day of his marriage and was suddenly overwhelmed by pangs of guilt. Kneeling beside Carla, he, too, lit a candle and asked forgiveness for stealing money from his mother and father's coffee bar when he was a teenager. So many years had passed, but the guilt had never diminished.

Julio dropped some coins in the donation box as Carla rose to speak to a lay churchman. He could hear her questioning him about the possibility of a confession. She was directed to an ornate wooden booth and told that a priest would be with her shortly. When the priest arrived and had seated himself behind his screen, she spoke for ten minutes. Whether the father confessor understood a word of what was said was both questionable and immaterial, for when she concluded her testimony he said his obligatory *ego te absolvo* and she was duly and officially absolved of her sins.

At lunch, in a small *trattoria* in the port, she told Julio what she had done. How she had confessed their affair. Julio was horrified but remained placid on the surface.

"It was too soon," she said. "I felt that my dear departed husband, Giovanni, was looking down at us. It was a sign that the church you took me to was named San

Giovanni—because he was a saint, my Giovanni." Carla began to weep silently.

Gently, Julio said, "Five years is not too soon. You had nothing to confess. You are an angel."

"Sex out of wedlock is a sin," Carla countered.

"If you are a sinner, the whole world is made up of sinners."

"I must not allow myself to go astray again," Carla whispered, like a spy in a B movie.

"Never?" said Julio incredulously.

It was then that Carla dropped the bombshell, went for broke with the line she had prepared: "I've been thinking about becoming a nun."

It had the effect she'd expected.

"Mama mia," Julio said, unconsciously crossing himself, as if to ward off an unseen evil spirit. "A nun? *Una suora?"*

Carla had looked up the Italian words for a "nursing nun" and now she used them to great effect: *"Una suora infermiera,"* she said, with great passion.

"A nursing nun? *Mia bella Madonna."* Julio wrung his hands in anguish. Then suddenly his composure dropped away and he almost shouted, "It would be bigamy!"

"Why do you say that?"

Julio launched his lightning bolt, his bombshell, one he had not rehearsed, as he stood, knocking over his chair in the process: "You cannot be married to me and to God at the same time."

It was as if God himself had spoken through Julio and issued an eleventh commandment.

Every head in the restaurant turned toward Julio and Carla to see what would come next. It was a living soap opera and they loved it.

They were not disappointed, because Julio's next line was: ". . . and what about children?"

The crowd leaned in and nodded in agreement when they heard Carla's response.

"All children in the world would be mine."

The chorus of onlookers smiled and waited for the riposte. Two waiters held their breath while four plates of *frito misto mare* cooled in their hands.

Julio sat down slowly and took her hands in his as a woman at a back table sobbed and was shushed by her husband.

"It wouldn't be the same," Julio said. "They wouldn't be mine."

Applause thundered in the restaurant and Julio nodded to the diners like an emperor to his subjects.

Carla drew him in close to her and whispered quietly, "What are you saying?" But the line was heard by a woman at the next table and repeated, *sotto voce*, to her neighbor. It quickly made the rounds of the restaurant.

"I don't know, but I'm *saying* it. Let us go back to the church and I will say it before God," Julio pleaded—as the chorus of diners gasped as one, in response.

"God can hear you from here," Carla answered.

A shout of *e vero*—that's true—escaped from the mouth of a woman at table 27.

The room hushed. Chefs crept out of the kitchen to watch and listen as Julio choked out the words, "Then—*Dio!*—then—" He began to perspire. Everyone began to perspire. "Then—yes—YES."

And her answer, in the form of a question: "Yes?"

"I mean, maybe—it's possible—after we know each other a little longer."

Hisses were heard.

"I would like to know you a little longer right now. But not here. Come," he begged.

As they rose, Carla's face was positively beatific and Julio glowed with pride at having her on his arm. When he asked for the bill, the manager said there would be no charge.

Shouts of "brava" and "bravo" filled the air as flowers were taken from vases and showered upon the lovers. Stage lights, had there been any, would have slowly dimmed.

* * *

"THERE IS A hotel, right next to the church," Julio said, once they were outside.

Carla stopped and crossed herself. "I would have to confess again."

"But think," said clever Julio, "this time it would be easy since we will be right next door to the church."

"Don't rush me. I need time to think," she said.

"How much time?" he ventured meekly.

"Seconds, minutes, hours, days, weeks, months . . ."

"STOP," he shouted.

"I will sleep on it."

"Let's sleep on it together," he said quickly.

And so, Julio and the Madonna entered the Hotel Paradiso, next to the church, and under the ever-watchful eye of the Almighty, they slept on it—and reached no conclusion except to agree that they would sleep on it again until the answer came to them in a vision.

LESS THAN AN hour's drive from Monte Carlo there is a wild and mountainous countryside, an undeveloped national preserve, called the Mercantor. There are no guns, dogs, radios, camping, cars, or campfires allowed. It is pure nature, home to the chamois, ibex, wild sheep, marmot, partridge, and white hare. Here, in the lower Maritime Alps, the varied flora is rich in color, and pure spring-fed lakes interrupt the woodlands. Trevor drove as far as was allowed and then they began to hike along marked trails. Eleanor had asked if there was a place like this and Trevor had been very happy to show her this spot, which he hadn't visited since he was a boy.

As they walked, not allowing their voices to pollute the pristine environment, Eleanor looked at Trevor and tried to read what was in his mind—as she did with juries. Sometimes, just as she was prepared to make her summation, if she read in their faces that they had decided to convict, to find her client guilty as charged, she would change her strategy on the spot and cross the line, joining them, as a tactic.

"If I were in your shoes," she would say, "I, too, might be tempted to cast a guilty vote. Hopefully I would be able to suppress that emotional—or let's call it an instinctive urge—and try once more to review all of the evidence in order to give the accused the full benefit of the doubt. And then, after being as impartial as I possibly could, I would look to the law before making my final determination." Here she would pause, dramatically. "We have a life in our hands. We must be diligent and not exercise our prejudices." Always the "we."

The trail had narrowed and Trevor led the way. He will find me guilty when he discovers the truth, she concluded. What could be said in my defense that would sway him?

"Trevor Weymouth, you sit as judge and jury in the case of this woman who stands before you, and from your look, I surmise that you find her guilty as charged of the crime of premeditated impersonation for the sole purpose of toying with your emotions and inducing you to form a relationship. Ergo: fraud. But before you rush to judgment, let us examine the facts in the case one last time. One: Is it not true that you, without inducement, and of your own volition, picked up this woman in the bar of the Hotel de Paris? Two: Is it not a fact that, with malice aforethought, and for the sole purpose of attempting to seduce, you invited her onto your private yacht and plied her with wine and music? Three: Would you not agree that, after all, what is a lie but truth in masquerade? Four: Is it not also true that while you contend that this woman's initial motivation to form a relationship with you was based upon your wealth and power, there came a time when it could have deepened from interest, to affection, to love? In summation, then, let me say: What can you accuse this woman of that all women have been not been accused of since the beginning of time? Is there not a moment in every woman's life when she masquerades in order to intensify her desirability? Are there not whole industries that have come to be and have prospered by catering to the basic female instinct to create mystery and allure? And will not a man, given the opportunity, offer pretense in place of honesty at every turn when he wishes to attract the female into his lair? I say this to you, Trevor Weymouth: Judge not lest you be judged. All this woman asks is that you evaluate her pure essence, stripped of the trappings of affectation and wealth. For is it not a fact that if man builds a city in a natural paradise, such as that where we now trespass, he destroys its essence? Consider, then: If you strip this woman of her wealth, do you not then recreate her wondrous basic essence? I rest my case and leave my client's fate at your mercy. Will you destroy a relationship or create one? The choice, Trevor Weymouth, is yours."

If I actually said any of that, Eleanor thought, he'd probably think that I was a clever bitch and he'd be smoke.

Eleanor was determined to suppress her aggressiveness today. If anything happened, sexually or otherwise, it would be as a result of *his* actions, not hers. She would not play the temptress, as she had done on the boat.

As these conclusions slowly drained from her psyche, Trevor stopped in a field of wildflowers next to a stream, and took a blanket from his backpack, spreading it out on the ground so that they could rest. They had been walking for two hours. He filled a water bottle from the stream and they both drank greedily. Making a cradle of his arms, he beckoned her into it, and as they lay there, watching butterflies hovering under a canopy of pine-tree boughs, Trevor thought, There will never be a better time to tell her. The setting is perfect, and I may never have another opportunity if I let this go any further.

Fluttering butterflies watched two souls in their undeveloped state about to undergo their metamorphosis. The transition was either going to be very easy or extremely difficult. Trevor, for the first time he could remember, was nervous as a teenager on a first date. *I won't even have to pretend that I'm suddenly impotent—I already am!* He began, as planned, stroking her thighs and kissing her lightly on her closed eyelids.

Eleanor tried to hold back her tears. *Funny thing,* she thought, *after all the planning, the one thing I wasn't prepared for was success. I should tell him now. There will never be a better time.*

Fear of losing kept Eleanor from speaking.

Trevor had the same fear. He suddenly realized that if his plan didn't work, he would stay as he was. He would lose her as he had lost so many others—and it would be back to being a butler again and hoping that Maurice Gerard would send another potential mark his way. Suddenly Trevor had a premonition that his plan was about to backfire. *Mayday! Mayday! Abort mission!* He'd have to do this another way. He needed more time to think this through.

What Trevor and Eleanor didn't know, as they cuddled together watching butterflies in the forest of the Mercantor, was that time had already run out—for both of them.

25
"The Death of Benito Cavallo"

*A good name is rather to be chosen
than great riches.*

—Proverbs XXII

BENITO HAD SENT word to Ola that he was ready to make a statement, on condition that Detective Obolensky would be the only one present and that it would be recorded on tape—to be typed and signed thereafter.

Ola marveled at Benito's chameleonlike ability to blend into his surroundings. No wonder the four women couldn't agree on an identification; even Ola would have had difficulty coming up with a description. As she set up the tape, keeping a careful eye on him and her *derrière* out of his reach, she wondered what he would have to say; why he wanted it recorded in this fashion.

"You can start now," said Ola as she pushed the red button and the recorder slipped into the record mode.

Benito picked up the microphone and began: "I, Benito Cavallo, being of sound mind and body, declare this to be my last will and testament, dated—"

Ola hit the off button. "I thought you wanted to record a statement about the robbery? I don't have time for bullshit."

"It's all part of it," Benito said. "Look, I'm about to

kill myself, and before I do, I'd like you to witness my last words."

"Why me?"

"If I told you, you'd think I was crazy."

"I already think you're crazy."

"Indulge me. A few minutes."

Ola realized that he was serious about this, and she was intrigued. What the hell, maybe she'd learn something. "You've got fifteen minutes, that's it—and there'd better be something about the robbery. I might also mention that if you're stupid enough to want to kill yourself, you'll have to wait until you're out of here," she said as she hit the record button again.

Benito picked up the microphone and continued where he had left off, reciting the date, time, place and naming Ola as witness. "My name was not given to me, as it should have been, as a name is supposed to be given to every new life brought into this world. I chose it myself when I was old enough to need one. That name no longer suffices, for reasons I shall soon detail, and so I now choose a new name: Luigi di Capodanno." He paused for effect and then said in a most grave and reverent tone of voice, as if he were performing his own baptism, "Luigi di Capodanno, today is the first day of the rest of your life and the last day in the life of Benito Cavallo."

He proceeded to record a brief history of his life to date, starting with his abandonment as a newborn infant.

"You are supposed to be wanted, loved, and nourished on the first day of your life, not disposed of like garbage. Luck, or fate, choose what you will; before today I thought it was fate, but now I realize it was luck that has brought me this far, and I cannot go any further. A child only knows his history after he is no longer a child. From that time onward, until his adulthood, there is a space— the most important space in his life—a time when his character and identity are established. To navigate this vast and forbidding void, one has need of a guide, a mentor. Without such an influencing pilot, the possibility of losing your way and crashing is high. I did not know that then; I know it now. At first, for me, surviving without an identity was a game, but then the game became life and life became an endless game in which there was no winning or losing; there was just the playing. Unfortunately, I was a man when I discovered this. A year ago I realized that there was no choice but for Benito Cavallo to die because only in this way could the repetitious cycle be broken. I would come out of the jungle, like a wild boy suckled and raised by wolves, and learn how to properly navigate the world—with a job and a wife and a family. But, most importantly, with an *identity,* so I could pass on my name." Benito stopped and took a sip of water.

The fifteen minutes had long since passed and the tape was nearing its end, but Ola made no attempt to stop the bizarre proceedings because she was fascinated and touched by both the sincerity and the intelligence of this man, who, only minutes before, had seemed a common criminal.

As if reading her mind, he continued: "I have never seen myself as a criminal. I have never injured anyone physically. True, I stole and lied and cheated, but no more so than most successful businessmen I have read about or come in contact with. That is not meant to be an excuse, a rationalization for my actions—just what I have observed to be a simple fact. I know that many men fear commitment; I *ache* for commitment. That is my statement. To conclude, I hereby will my body, my soul, and all of my worldly goods, such as they are, to the man who will emerge, the man previously known as Benito Cavallo." Benny reached over, clicked off the recorder, and said, simply, "Thank you."

"Why have you chosen me to tell this story to?" said Ola.

Benito answered obliquely: "You will come to know the answer. That is all I can say at the moment."

Ola took the tape and went to her office. Moments

later, when Inspector Delarue came in, she told him that
Cavallo had had nothing to say, that it had been a waste
of time. It appeared they would gain nothing by detaining
him any longer. Why waste the taxpayers' money? Delarue agreed.

Luigi di Capodanno was released into the world, and
his life changed, all because four women from New Jersey
had decided to come to Monte Carlo. They didn't know
this, but they would.

THAT EVENING, OLA found a large bouquet of flowers on
her doorstep, with a card that read:

> *Pillowed upon my fair love's ripening breast,*
> *To feel for ever its soft fall and swell,*
> *Awake for ever in a sweet unrest,*
> *Still, still to hear her tender-taken breath,*
> *And so live ever—or else swoon to death.*

It was signed: *Written by Keats, borrowed by Luigi di
Capodanno.*

She played the tape over and over, wondering about
this strange man—and why she had lied to Delarue? Ola
was an adopted child. She never knew her mother or father or the circumstances that brought her to Mr. and Mrs.
Obolensky. For this reason Benito's statement hit an exposed nerve or, we should say, a sympathetic nerve. For
some unexplained reason, Ola always felt she was Italian.
In Italy everyone thought she was. The language came
easily, and she spoke it like a native. Despite her many
pleas, her adoptive mother refused to help her identify her
ethnic background. Ola had always hated her name and
would have changed it had it not been for the distress she
knew such an action would cause to her adoptive parents.
Secretly, she toyed with names: Benedetta, Claudia, Sophia, Maria, Carlotta. Her favorite was Claudia Corsini.
She knew how Benito felt. At least *she* was official. She

tried to imagine what it would be like not to have a registered identity. It didn't compute. When she'd started in police work, she had access to the administration's computers and to the files of public agencies. After an exhaustive search, on her own time, she found her mother: Ottavia Maselli. So she was right; she did have an Italian heritage. Unfortunately, she discovered that her mother had died five years previous. There was no mention of a father. Ola cried for hours.

An hour after the flowers arrived, her doorbell rang. It was a messenger with another bouquet, and another poem. This time it was an original:

> *You are my first love*
> *You are my last*
> *You are my future*
> *I have no more past*
>   *L. di C.*

Ola never dated Italian men. They had reputations, whether earned or not, of wanting to marry their mothers and then fool around with other women, with self-declared impunity. Under those circumstances, Ola would have much preferred being the mistress than the wife. Admittedly, she had always been a free spirit where sex was concerned. She liked to play, to experiment; commitment always stopped her. Maybe it was because she saw so much of the underside of life in her work. Such average people committed such heinous crimes. That was the problem with profiles; they didn't apply to one-timers, only to the career criminals. Benito had a profile that fit into this later group. What did he want with her? He was probably a nutcase. She'd run into plenty of those.

Normally, Ola unloaded her gun and placed it on the shelf in the hall closet. Now she loaded it and kept it next to her. One could never be too cautious under these conditions. Many, before Benny the Horse or Luigi di Capodanno, as he now called himself, had killed because of unrequited love.

One hour later the third delivery was made.

> *I am not*
> *Who you think I am*
> *For I can be no one*
> *Until you think I am*
> > > *Luigi*

Five minutes later her phone rang. She considered not answering it, but curiosity got the better of her.

INSPECTOR DELARUE DIDN'T look forward to confronting Maurice Gerard with evidence of his suspected crimes and, necessarily, arresting him. Sometimes he hated his job, but being a civil servant in the higher ranks brought with it certain benefits: he could look forward to a decent pension and time to pursue interests other than law and order. He had his eye on a small country inn near the village of Gordes, in Provence. It had once been a hotel/ restaurant but was now closed and in a state of disrepair. Delarue had made inquiries; it could be had for a very low price. There were olive trees, a small vineyard, and nice views. He liked to cook; he'd even written some sample menus he thought he could handle without too much trouble. He would offer one set meal each day, served family style. There were ladies from the village available to do the rooms, help in the kitchen and dining room. He wouldn't need many—maybe two, to start.

Of course there was the downside to retirement, even though he'd still be relatively young: being alone. Not so bad in a city like Monte Carlo but problematic out in the sticks. He couldn't, for instance, imagine someone like Ola wanting to share such a life. She was too young for that and probably more interested in procreating than veg-etating. True, they were enjoying a hedonistic moment in time, but that would pass as the road ahead divided and took them in different natural directions. As it should be, he thought.

Delarue had known many women, but his permanent mistress was the law: his job. It didn't leave much time for dedicated romance. Ola was a hot one. He'd be sorry when it ended. In his mind he rummaged through all the women he knew—and rejected them all as one would reject untalented job applicants. He needed someone like, for instance, Sophie. He wondered what she was like away from her job at the café? He decided that it was time to find out.

Yes, she knew the restaurant, La Salière, on the port in Fontvielle. Yes, nine o'clock would be fine. Yes, she would meet him there. Delarue put the phone down. Done. Meeting at a restaurant had been a ploy Delarue had used before. It meant that both would have cars and the evening would end naturally at the parking lot.

The restaurant was on the quai, opposite a line of sailing boats and huge yachts, with the cliffs of Monaco serving as background, across the bay. It was a warm evening and Delarue chose a corner table on the outdoor terrace. Sophie wore regulation boating attire, perfect for the surroundings: white slacks, a blue-and-white-striped cotton shirtwaist, and a lightweight blue blazer. Her blond hair had been combed back, girlishly, into a ponytail, tied with a red-and-white ribbon. As Delarue rose to greet her he thought, How chic. What a very handsome woman. They exchanged French-style kisses on both cheeks, and Delarue, with her consent, ordered two vermouth cassis on ice.

Afterward, they shared the house antipasto, followed by *vitello alla Milanese* for him and *gnocchi* with artichokes for her, with a bottle of chilled Valpolicella. Conversation was easy, relaxed, unforced. They spoke of their lives, their hopes, their dreams—everything except their work. It was as different from an evening with Ola as could possibly be imagined—but at its end, Delarue would have been hard-pressed to say which he enjoyed more. In fact, it was unfair even to consider comparing them. Delarue was sorry they had taken two cars. Next time he would pick her up.

SHE AGREED TO meet in the lobby of the Grand Hotel and have a drink with him at the rooftop terrace bar. If he intended to continually harass her or play stalking games, she would get it over with tonight—and show him that he'd made a bad choice. Had he not walked up to her and called her by name, she would not have recognized him at first glance. Everything about him was different: the way he combed his hair, his walk, his way of dressing. Tonight he looked quite handsome in a cream-colored Armani suit, medium blue shirt, dark blue tie, and shoes that Ola recognized as Ferragamo. If nothing else, she had to admit, he had balls—hitting on his arresting officer.

Ola had dressed down—a loose cotton sweater, dark full slacks, her hair in an unflattering bun. Everything hidden, including the 9mm Walther in her innocuous-looking straw handbag. "Let's go," she said. "I can't wait to hear your pitch."

Benito/Luigi grinned. Her attitude was just what he had expected.

They were alone in the elevator when Ola hit the emergency stop button, bringing the car to a sudden halt between floors. Her revolver was out at the same moment she shoved him up against the elevator wall. "Spread-eagle—*now*," she said, kicking his feet into position. She frisked him expertly; he was clean. He was also, Ola couldn't help noticing when she brushed his crotch with a searching hand, extremely well hung.

"You're a very aggressive lady. Reminds me of a line from an old Mae West movie. She says—"

"Never mind. This is what you get for hassling a police officer. What did you expect, pink angora and giggles?"

"You're here. That's more than I expected."

The bar was the kind you look for but rarely find—softly lit, not crowded, view of the sea, Sinatra on the sound system, two empty stools on the corner end, a friendly, but not too friendly, bartender. He ordered an *americano* for her and an Averna on ice for himself; no sense taking a chance on another Gallic Negroni.

"You like movies?" he said.

"I don't have time for them."

"I love 'em. Especially the oldies, the black-and-whites. Bogart, Bacall, Tracy, Hepburn, Rita Hayworth, Ava Gardner. I was in love with Ava Gardner; me and a million other guys. No question she was one of the most beautiful women in the world. Imagine her marrying Mickey Rooney when she could have had anybody. That's the way it goes. Either it was chemistry or he asked her and nobody else had. Maybe every other guy thought she was unapproachable because of her beauty? Who knows? There are so many elements that go into making a relationship happen. Take us, for example—"

Ola cut in. "There's no *us*."

"Then take you and me separately, for example. Now, normally, I'm probably not your type. I'm sure you don't see yourself as someone who dates criminals. But, like I said, that was the other guy, Cavallo. Now, I wouldn't blame you for not wanting to give *him* a shot—"

"The only one who's going to get any shots is you—whatever you call yourself—right where it hurts the most, if you try anything stupid. I only agreed to this meeting so we could put an end to this crap. You wanted to see me? I came. So if you've said what you came to say, I suggest you walk out of here and out of my life—permanently—unless you want to book yourself back into that cell again."

"One more drink," said Luigi, "and I'm out of here. I promise."

"Ten minutes."

"Deal." Luigi ordered two more drinks and continued his pitch like an elephant-hided insurance salesman.

Ola began to laugh, in spite of herself. "You're persistent, I'll give you that. You plan on getting a job?"

"I've saved everything I could—enough to get my papers straight—but you don't want to know about that. I'll take my time looking around. I was never one to rush into things."

"Could have fooled me."

"How about you? You like this police business?"

"Yes, I do, and I'm good at it."

"Then what? One day you wake up and the alarm on your bioclock is ringing. Men, by the way, have the same clock, only ours doesn't ring, it just runs down and stops. After that there's no way to get it going again."

"Thanks for the update," Ola said. "Where's all this taking us?"

"Ah, *us*. I was hoping you'd come around to *us*. It's only a first date. Hopefully, it's taking us to the second date."

"You're a real dreamer, aren't you?"

"Always have been. You spend your life like I've spent mine and dreams are all that keep you going. Dreams of the future are the poor man's aphrodisiac."

"So, what's your big dream?"

"I've been fixing up a little house near Grosetto, in Tuscany. Work on it every chance I get. About a year more to go. It's been livable for a while, but I didn't want that jerk Cavallo staying there."

"You're doing it all yourself?"

"Except for the plumbing. You don't want to mess around with plumbing. I've got some pictures here. Look," he said, pulling out a stack of photos from his jacket pocket.

They surprised her. The house was beautiful, romantic; set in an orange grove, it was a Tuscan gem, built in the old style. Literally, a dream house. Oddly, it spoke to her.

Luigi began to speak in Italian, assuming she spoke the language. His persona changed radically when he spoke his native tongue, lovingly describing each detail of the

house, putting special emphasis on the four bedrooms reserved for children yet unborn.

"Four is just right; two boys and two girls. The two
boys first, then the girls. That way the boys can look out
for their sisters."

"You think it's going to happen, just like that?"

"Why not?" Like most people, Luigi sounded more
intelligent in his own language—no longer the sly fox;
more the educated gentle man; less a caricature; more of
a person. The ten minutes and two drinks stretched into
a late dinner, at the end of which Ola found herself agreeing to a second date. She would leave the gun home.

*On the second date they would drive to the town near
Grosetto.*

26
"The IOUs"

. . . and forgive us our debts . . .

DARLENE WAS STANDING alone at the roulette table, watching the wheel and waiting for Jean-Jacques. It had been a perfect day; her shoulders were lightly tanned with no bathing-suit-strap lines. A waiter offered her a glass of champagne and she sipped it slowly. She didn't want this trip to end; it had been perfect, beyond her wildest expectations.

The casino manager had been very courteous and attentive and now he walked up to her. "Would Madame like some chips to play while you wait for the monsieur? If it is convenient I can charge them to your hotel account, as before."

"As before?" Darlene said.

"Yes. There is no problem, Madame Barlow."

"Can you tell me where my account stands at the moment?"

"Certainly. I will be right back, madame."

As the manager walked off, Darlene knew what the answer would be and dreaded having it confirmed. There must have been some mistake. It was surely Jean-

Jacques's money. She was positive of it. She held on to the edge of the table, trying not to faint, as the manager came back holding a slip of paper, which he handed to her. It was a copy of her request for funds; her IOU, so to speak. It said, simply: *To the account of Madame Barlow, Hotel de Paris FRS 350,000*. Signed by the manager along with the date. Darlene made the amount to be in the neighborhood of $60,000. She managed a smile and a thank you before tottering off unsteadily to the ladies' powder room, her rhinestones weighing heavily against her heaving bosom. She barely made it to a stall before losing her dinner. If life were like a film, there would be a "hard cut" to a scene where all of the women were looking at their humongous hotel bills. But this was real life and Darlene had fifteen hours to get through until she would see her sisters-in-crime.

JEAN-JACQUES WAS LATE because he was working the early-evening doorman shift at the Hermitage Hotel, where he'd just received a heart-stopping shock. It was 9:15 P.M. when a huge chauffeured black-and-burgundy 1979 Daimler limousine pulled up in front. As Jean-Jacques rushed to open the car door, four pure-white Russian wolfhounds bounded out followed by a heavily jeweled woman who swept by quickly, barely giving him time to open the hotel door for her. As he tipped his hat she gave him an imperious grunt and was met by the hotel manager, who greeted her effusively. "So nice to have you back with us again, Baroness."

Jean-Jacques looked at the pile of mounting luggage being taken from the car by the chauffeur and two bellmen. All of the pieces were marked with a Russian seal and a large gold letter *K*. It was then that he heard two high-pitched women's voices.

"Natasha, you are here. The season can begin."

"Masha, you look wonderful."

Baroness? Natasha? The letter *K*? It must be a coin-

cidence. The manager's next words, spoken to the bellmen, made the hair on his toes rise and tingle: "Take the
luggage up to Baroness Karmanov's suite, number five
hundred—quickly, quickly. And don't hang around waiting for a tip. She never carries any money." Jean-Jacques
took the manager's arm and pulled him aside.

"Was that the Baroness Natasha Karmanov?"

"Yes," the manager whispered, "some say she is the
richest woman in the world."

As the manager walked off, the color drained from
Jean-Jacques's face and he began to perspire. *Merde!* He
had to make some phone calls—fast.

He couldn't locate any of them; Maurice was still in
Eze, Julio in Genoa, and Trevor in the Mercantor. He
decided that his best approach would be to keep his date
at the casino with Lou Ann Barlow, a.k.a. Darlene, and
see what he could learn about the *two* Karmanov ladies.
Before leaving, he had another, more important call to
make.

A SHAKY DARLENE, makeup repaired, gulped another glass
of champagne to try to steady her nerves as she prepared
to give the performance of her life for Jean-Jacques.

"Sorry I am late, *chérie.* Some minor complications in
Bolivia. Is everything all right? Have they been taking
care of you here?"

"Everything is wonderful. I just adore gambling. I
mean, what else can you do with money that brings such
instant fun?"

"Shall I arrange for some chips?"

"No, no, I've already played a few numbers—lost
every time. How about taking a walk; it's very stuffy in
here and tonight's just not my lucky night."

"We'll walk on the promenade behind the opera
house."

For several minutes they didn't speak, Darlene trying

to calm down and Jean-Jacques phrasing questions in his mind—none of which seemed appropriate. After the experience with the second baroness, he'd telephoned a friend who worked at Cartier to inquire about the widely reported purchase of the Taylor-Burton diamond pendant. The man said that unfortunately, the baroness had returned it—just as she'd returned all of the other jewelry they had lent her, hoping for a sale. "Tight with her money, that one, but then aren't all the super-rich?"

So, the jewels weren't hers after all. The big Aha! He wondered about the other women. About Lou Ann Barlow. He had immediately noticed the cheap costume jewelry Darlene was wearing. Something was very wrong. Where the hell were the other guys? Damn.

He'd float a question and see if he got a nibble or a bite. "By the way," he said casually, "does the baroness have a sister?"

Darlene was immediately on guard, suspicious of the question, not knowing why she felt that way. "I don't think so, but then again we're not that close. Why do you ask?"

"Oh, nothing important. I saw a woman today that could have been her double."

After they walked a bit more, Darlene said, rather absently, "There must be a lot of suicides here, people who lose all their money and can't go on?"

"If there are, we never hear about them. My guess is that publicity would be bad for business."

"Did you see the movie *Thelma and Louise*?" she asked.

"No, I don't have much time for films."

"Well, at the end, these two women are in a car; they're really in bad trouble, surrounded by the police, and so they drive right off a high cliff. Bang. Problems over."

"If you consider suicide as a method of problem solving."

"Sometimes there's no other way," Darlene said as she

looked up at the mountain behind Monte Carlo—at the top road, the *grande corniche*, a narrow serpentine sliver, poorly protected; easy to crash through the flimsy guard rails, and *bang*. Problems over.

CURTAIN

ACT FOUR

Coping with the Results

♡

27

"Who Will Pay the Piper?"

> *It's time to wind up,*
> *The masquerade,*
> *Just make your mind up,*
> *The piper must be paid.*
>   —*Styne-Comden-Green, "The Party's Over"*

*T*HE TOP-STAIR LANDING *of the casino held an eighteenth-century guillotine. In the square in front, a huge crowd had gathered to watch the beheading. At the sound of trumpets the King and Queen of Monaco (looking very much like Inspector Georges Delarue and Detective Ola Obolensky) arrived and took their places on thrones in an elaborately draped royal box that had been placed on the terrace of the Hotel de Paris. A herald stepped forward and announced: "Let the trial begin."*

A woman (the spitting image of Darlene) was brought into the square, bound in chains. On the breast of her tattered gown, in red cloth, surrounded with elaborate embroidery and fantastic flourishes of gold thread appeared the letter H. *She was forced to kneel before their royal highnesses as the Lord High Magistrate unrolled a parchment and read: "This woman is charged with impersonating royalty, stealing funds from the imperial treasury, nonpayment of her lodging bill at His Majesty's hotel, and"—theatrical pause here—"the crime of head-*

hunting the rare nobleman—which, if she is found guilty, is punishable by death."

The King looked at the Queen, who said simply: "She looks guilty to me." "Off with her head," said the King, in an equally bored voice, as the queen smiled in agreement.

The crowd, hungry for blood, roared its approval and chanted: "Off with her head." The accused had no chance to defend herself as she was dragged through the square and pelted with all of the ingredients of a rotten salad niçoise *by the angry crowd. At the guillotine, she was forced to kneel as her head was securely locked into the wooden slot below the fearsome blade. "Let the Lord High Executioner perform his duty," bellowed the herald, over the cries of the unruly multitude.*

A huge, hooded man stepped forward and bowed to the applause of the assemblage. The woman's cries and pleadings were to no avail as a lone drummer rolled his sticks. The executioner reached for the rope—and slowly raised the killing blade.

The crowd grew so silent you could hear a soufflé rise. The King took a lace-embroidered handkerchief from his sleeve and dropped it over the balustrade, where it fluttered to the ground. The beheader-person let loose the rope and the giant blade of the guillotine screeched downward, on its unerring rusted pathway of rails, toward the woman's neck. She had barely enough time to scream her final awakening scream.

Darlene's head fell over the edge of the bed and into the present. Even beyond the realm of the dream she still could not shake off its reality. Was it a harbinger of events to come? Understanding its symbolism was child's play. One thing stood out in her mind: no white knight had come to the rescue in her moment of terminal distress. Would Jean-Jacques be there in real life? She looked at her bedside clock; it was noon. Hopefully, the other women had returned. She reached for the phone.

* * *

THEY MET IN Irene's suite, where Darlene told them what she had learned the previous evening at the casino. When she concluded, no one spoke. It was so quiet you could hear their hearts breaking. How could they have been so gullible? Eleanor telephoned the hotel cashier and asked that their respective bills to date be delivered to them, posthaste. An hour later she had calculated the damage.

Gambling at the casino:	$169,500.
Restaurant bills:	$6,800.
Hotel suites & room service:	$86,300.

"I make the total to be a little more than a quarter of a million bucks: $262,600, give or take a few thousand in currency fluctuation. Divided by four, that comes to $65,650 each."

Carla crossed herself. "Julio will pay my share. What's it to him? Pocket money!"

"What about the others?" said Eleanor. "I hate to ask Trevor, but what choice do we have?"

"We have to look at this positively," said Irene. "Maurice is a real gentleman. I know he wouldn't let me down."

Then Darlene told them about her dream. She wasn't so sure about Jean-Jacques. "Suppose they all get really pissed off that we lied to them about who we are? Let's not fool ourselves, girls, if they get the message they've been conned by headhunters, we're dead meat. A week's summer romance isn't worth what we're asking them to come up with."

"Depends how we put it," said Eleanor. "We have to work on the pitch. Let's get out of here in case they call."

As the four women were leaving the hotel, Masha and the true Baroness Natasha Karmanov arrived with their menagerie of Russian wolfhounds and assorted French poodles. Irene and the real baroness traded quick eye-

ballings as they came within a wolfhound's breath of each
other.

"I know they allow dogs, but *that* is ridiculous," said
Irene.

The real baroness and her friend Masha strolled to the
terrace restaurant overlooking the sea, in the rear of the
hotel, where both they and their dogs would be regally
feted. "So, Natasha, will you be going to the prince's ball
on Saturday?"

"Possibly. You're going, no doubt? With Ramon?"

"Of course—to both questions. Do you have an escort?"

"No, what a bore."

Seemed the real baroness had just as much trouble getting a date as the fake one.

"Who's around this year?"

"Do you know Maurice? Maurice Gerard? Very elegant. Katcha used him last season and said she was very
satisfied."

"That bitch. I wouldn't trust her taste."

"Then trust mine. I assure you he'll do perfectly."

"Oh well, if I must, I must. Be an angel and call him
for me?"

"Of course."

That settled, they added dollops of caviar and *crème
fraîche* to their warm blinis and began to gossip about
who did what to whom and when and why . . .

JEAN-JACQUES CALLED THE other men and told them it was
urgent that they meet. He chose the outdoor Bar de Soleil
café behind the casino. Only the tourists ever went there,
so they'd be away from prying eyes and ears. The small
outdoor café was almost deserted when they arrived. After
choosing a table out of sight of any passersby, Jean-
Jacques told them what he had learned, and of his sus-
picions. Maurice said that he had received a call from a
Masha Pavlovna asking if he would escort the Baroness

Natasha Karmanov to the prince's ball on Saturday. He had agreed, of course. He was to pick her up at 8:30 P.M. at the Hermitage Hotel. A not-so-pretty picture puzzle was beginning to form.

"If our baroness is not the real one, then who the hell is she? And what about the others? We may have all been set up," said Trevor.

"I've saved the best—or the worst—for last," Jean-Jacques replied. "Those jewels they were all wearing? They didn't belong to them. They were on loan from Cartier, Tiffany, Van Cleef and Arpels, and Bulgari."

Another piece fitted into a picture, which was getting uglier by the moment.

"I'll call Pierre at the hotel and see what he can find out," said Maurice. "I can't believe he'd make a mistake like this."

"I've got to get back to work," said Julio. "Call and let me know what you find out. Your baroness may be a fake, Maurice, but my little Madonna is a real contessa; of that I am sure."

Although Maurice knew in his heart of hearts that the King of Hearts was about to be aced, he had no choice but to play out the hand.

THE WOMEN ENDED up at the aquarium. As they stared at a huge walleyed fish, Darlene said, "I knew I should have saved it. My mother always told me, Darlene, save it."

"You were probably sixteen when she told you that," said Eleanor.

"That may be, but good advice is good advice. If I *had* saved it I could probably get Jean-Jacques to do anything."

"It's over, isn't it?" said Carla, her nose pressed up against the damp wall of thick glass.

"How could they have done this to us?" said Irene.

"They didn't," said Eleanor. "We did it to ourselves. Those jewels were the capper. What were they supposed to think? They assumed we were richer than they were."

"How about all the things they charged to us when we thought they were taking us out?" said Carla.

"Look, when you have that much money, it doesn't matter who pays the check. It's a detail," said Irene.

"I'm not so sure," Eleanor said. "Something's not right here. We don't know that much about these guys. They could be con artists."

"Maurice Gerard, a con artist? Come on, get real."

"I guess you're right. How about this: We pick one and try it out on him," said Eleanor.

"You mean expose ourselves?" said Carla.

"Sure. Why not. We can't be worse off than we already are. Failing that, we just work for the rest of our lives to pay off these bills. Or—"

"I hear French jails are the worst," said Darlene.

"Croissants and water," said Carla.

"Who's the best fish?" said Eleanor.

They all agreed upon Maurice.

HIS CONVERSATIONS WITH the concierge had confirmed his worst fears. Pierre had quietly investigated the matter, using all of his sources, and concluded that yes, unfortunately, the baroness at the Hotel Hermitage was the genuine article. It was more than likely that the other women were frauds as well.

"I will report this to management and the police immediately," said Pierre as he reached for the telephone.

Maurice stayed his hand. "And what will you tell them? That four women checked into the hotel and you *assumed* that their identities were correct? That no passports or credit cards were requested? Have you looked at their bills?"

"Regrettably, yes. They amount to over a half-million francs."

"And suppose, just suppose they can't pay?"

"Unacceptable."

"Pierre, play the game with me. Just suppose . . ."

"You think they are defrauders? Con *artistes*?"

"Where is it written that only men can be con *artistes*?" said Maurice.

Pierre rose to his full height and, in an impassioned voice full of French incredulity, said, "Maurice, you haven't done anything foolish with these women, have you?"

"Foolish?"

"Illegal."

"Yes, old friend, I'm afraid I have." He then told Pierre everything.

"It looks like we are both *dans la merde,* or as you say, in the deep shit."

"I'm meeting the false baroness in an hour."

"Let me know what I can do," said Pierre.

"Think, Pierre. Think hard."

MAURICE, DRESSED ELEGANTLY in formal evening clothes, sat at a small table in the bar at the Hotel de Paris waiting for Irene. He couldn't imagine what her story would be.

"Mind if I join you, Maurice," said Inspector Delarue.

"Of course, Georges. I didn't see you come in."

Delarue was also in evening attire. The arrest would be in keeping with the surroundings.

"Champagne?"

"No, just Perrier," said Delarue.

"Georges, you can't drink Perrier at the Hotel de Paris dressed in a tuxedo, now can you?"

The inspector took a seat opposite Maurice. "I'm a man of simple tastes, as opposed to yourself. Frankly, I'm surprised. I never thought of you as a jewel thief."

Maurice fought to maintain his composure.

"We have several statements, witnesses. I wouldn't be here unless we had all the facts. I'm sorry, *mon ami,* I'm afraid I'm going to have to ask you to come along with me to the *préfecture de police*."

"Shall we have our drinks first?"

"Of course."

Maurice signaled the waiter. *"Deux Perrier, s'il vous plait."*

At that moment Irene entered the bar and walked over to the table. Both men rose. "Baroness Karmanov, I'd like to introduce you to a friend, Inspector Georges Delarue of the Monaco police."

Delarue, ever the gentleman, pretended not to have met her before. *"Un plaisir,* Madame Baroness." Then, to Maurice: "I don't want to disturb you, Shall we meet in my office in, say, one hour, if that is convenient?"

"Most convenient," said Maurice. "I'll be there."

"I hope you will, Maurice. Madame Baroness, *bon soir.*"

When he had taken his leave, Irene said, "Charming man."

Maurice had no more time left. Whatever the questions, however difficult the answers, the discussion would have to be concluded in the next hour.

"Maurice, I have something to tell you."

"You're not the Baroness Natasha Karmanov."

Irene was shocked. "How did you know?"

"It's not important, what's important is that you may have a problem and I am unable to help you. You see, I've been arrested. That's why Inspector Delarue was here. He was about to take me into custody when you arrived. I gave him my word I would give myself up in an hour."

"What have you done?"

"Betrayed your trust in me."

"I've done the same to you. And I'm frightened that it may have the same result."

Maurice and Irene spoke for the rest of the hour, following which Maurice went to police headquarters, as promised.

*   *   *

TREVOR'S INSTINCTS TOLD him to run. He was stopped at the entrance to the autoroute above Monte Carlo. Jean-Jacques was about to board a flight to London, where he had friends, when he was detained by airport police. Only Julio had not panicked. He was arrested by Ola as he was putting the finishing touches on a *vitello tonnato* that he insisted she taste. She had to admit it wasn't bad. "You should have stuck to cooking," she said as she snapped on the cuffs.

28

"Conduct Unbecoming"

For de little stealin' dey gits you in jail,
soon or late. For de big stealin' dey
makes you emperor and puts you
in de hall o' fame when you croaks.
    —*Eugene O'Neill*, **Anna Christie**

THE MEN HAD nothing to show for their folly. "Folly is
an ill-chosen word to describe their duplicity and
thievery," you may say. But within the context of their
story, it seems best to describe their botched attempts as
infamous conduct. The women's folly had yet to be revealed. What had started for them as a silly escapade had
turned from lark to larceny. Inspector Delarue, as yet unaware of the women's equally duplicitous acts, had allowed them to visit the men the day following their arrest.

Gray metal chairs lined both sides of the wire-mesh
screen that separated visitors from prisoners. The
women's eyes were red from crying. The men were obviously embarrassed at their predicament. No one had
wanted it to end this way. Julio's chin touched his chest;
he had difficulty meeting Carla's eyes. "Contessa. *Madonna mia, mi dispiace*. I'm sorry."

"No more pretending, Julio. I am not a contessa or a
movie star; I'm not even a little bit rich. Just Carla di
Benedetto, a nice Italian girl from New Jersey. *Va bene?*
It was a game that got out of hand. And now this ending;

it's just a surprise to all of us, you know what I mean? I want to say good-bye to you with this thought: I don't regret a minute of what we had. I will always remember you, darling. Always. I will wear a veil for you for a year, and pray for you," she said as she leaned forward and kissed him through the screen.

Julio tried to smile through his tears but did not succeed. "*Cara mia,* a man finds a woman like you only once in a lifetime. What can I say? Whoever you really are, whoever you pretended to be, I only wish I could have been the man to share the rest of your life with you."

ELEANOR LOOKED AT Trevor, who had lost his ability to communicate. He seemed more annoyed than contrite. The truth was that he was embarrassed to be facing Eleanor from his weakened position; couldn't come to terms with it.

"I think you're a dumb asshole," Eleanor said. "And if it's any consolation, I'm just as bad. Not only that, if I can't think of a way to raise a lot of cash fast, I'll be right in there with you."

Then she softened. "On the other hand, if we hadn't done what we did, I would never have met you. Somehow, despite everything, I think we could have made it work. No, I'm saying that wrong; I'm putting words in your mouth. Let me put it another way: I think I could have dealt with who you really were if you had told me before all this blew up. If you had given me half a chance to know the real you—assuming there is one. I don't know how far our relationship would have gone. One is never sure about that, no matter how well you know the other person. The real question is: Were you ever interested in me—aside from my money? Just me. I've asked myself that question a lot of times . . . never came up with a good answer. I'm not young, I'm not sexy-gorgeous, and you seem to be a man who can still attract that kind of woman. You're one of those men who get more attractive as they get older. But now I'm telling you things you already know. So, why me? The answer always comes up wrapped in dollar signs.

"If there was ever a time to be honest with each other, it's here and now. On the other hand, maybe you have nothing to add. You were after a rich woman—like I was after a rich man—and maybe that wraps it up for you. Do me a favor, don't just sit there letting me make a fool of myself. Just tell me something that resembles the truth and we can close the book on this case. Or at least tell me something I don't know."

In the long moment of silence that followed, Trevor wanted to tell her a lot she didn't know. The truth: that young gorgeous-sexy ladies are not attracted to butlers. But he couldn't bring himself to say the words. That part of my life is over, he mused. Dead and done. But how could he admit that to her when he had only just admitted it to himself—and hated the sound of the words—true as they might be?

What Trevor needed was someone he could be honest with. Someone who accepted him for what he was. But was he ready for that? Was he ready for an Eleanor in his life instead of a Greta Harmon-Cates? By the time he'd decided to share these thoughts with her, it was too late. The door had already closed behind her.

"YOU KNOW SOMETHING," Jean-Jacques said, "I like you more now that I know who you really are. I was intimidated by you. You looked like you had everything, so what could I do for you? I don't blame you for what you did; women do that every day. You just played the game harder—and I know about playing the game as hard as you can; at least that part about me was true. I was somebody, once. Darlene, I'm a doorman. How could I have ever thought that you could love a doorman? Love conquers all? I don't think so. From billionaire tin magnate to doorman? It's a hell of a fall. I couldn't even support you. We'd both have to work. Great, huh? I'm nothing, Darlene. I was something and now I'm nothing and I'll always be nothing because I can never get back what I had."

"You can say all of those words about me, too, Jean-Jacques. I know I'm not trophy-wife material anymore. That was yesterday. A lot of yesterdays ago. I depended on that and where has it taken me? Here. Still pretending to be something I'm not. Why couldn't it all have been different? We're still the same people we were under that soccer net. Nothing changes that, does it?"

"Unfortunately, a lot changes that. I wish it weren't true—but you were making love to some other guy."

MAURICE HELD HIS hand flat on the screen that separated him from Irene, and she pressed it with hers. "Don't say anything, Maurice. I understand."

"Do you? Do you really? I'm sure that whatever there was or could have been between us has died, as far as you're concerned. When Oscar Wilde was in jail, he wrote, 'Each man kills the thing he loves. Some do it with a bitter look, some with a flattering word; the coward does it with a kiss . . .' I'm a coward, Irene, but that doesn't change the fact that I meant every kiss. I hope you can believe that."

"You're not a coward, Maurice. You just gave in to temptation, like we all did. Now we're rid of it and we can be ourselves."

"It's too late, Irene. You know that as well as I do. I'll be in here for at least a year. Rich or poor, you're a wonderful woman and I did not deserve you—even for the brief time we had." Maurice rose and walked away, truly a beaten man. Irene was too choked up with emotion to call after him.

Irene, good night, Irene,
Irene, good night,
Good night, Irene, good night, Irene,
I'll see you in my dreams . . .

29

"Prisoners of Hope"

If a man is wise, he gets rich,
An' if he gets rich, he gets foolish.
                    —**"Mr. Dooley"**

THEIR CLOTHES HAD turned into tattered rags; the horses into mice, the footmen into lizards, the coachman back into a fat rat, and the carriage became, once more, a pumpkin.

They were between a rock and a hard place. Impenetrable barriers loomed in all directions. Impossible to go back; seemingly impossible to move forward. Was there a way they had not contemplated? Was there a riddle that needed solving before the door in the mountain would magically open? Were they victims or the ones who had victimized? Confusion rained down upon them, clouding their minds and frizzing their hair. What would it take to produce a happy ending to their ill-conceived fairy tale of a quest? They were prisoners of hope, and that hope was focused, for the moment, upon the concierge, Pierre Goujon.

"The way I look at it," said Eleanor, "if we want to sell, we have to be in the marketplace. That means we have to find out where the marketplace is, who the buyers are, what they're looking for, and what they're willing to pay."

"You think this Goujon guy has that kind of information?" said Carla.

Maurice had told Irene to take Pierre into her confidence, that he would help. For his part, the concierge had come up with a rather bizarre scheme. If it worked, then maybe the women could undo the Gordian knot of their dilemma, and he could keep his job. What the women needed was money—lots of it—and fast.

"Why would anyone in their right mind want to give us over a quarter of a million dollars?" said Darlene. She was right about one thing: no one in their right mind would give the four women so much money. That left only one group: *stinking rich fools*.

PIERRE TOOK THE women up to the exclusive Monte Carlo golf club, located on the lower slopes of Mont Angel, not far from where they had been robbed of their jewels by Benny the Horse. It affords a beautiful view of the principality, the Côte d'Azur, and the Italian Riviera and has been host to many top professional tournaments. Close to the putting green of the eighteenth hole is the clubhouse terrace, where one can sit, have a drink, and watch the players as they complete this final hole of the course. As Pierre and the women watched, two motorized golf carts pulled up to the side of the putting surface. Each carried two doddering old men dressed in old-fashioned golfing knickers, high socks and white caps with pom-poms.

With great difficulty they managed to extricate themselves from their carts, sourly refusing offered help from their caddies. The first man to putt was Niko Karras. His ball was less than a foot from the cup. He studied the terrain meticulously, lining up the best route to the hole. To check his lie precisely, he stretched out prone on the grass, his eye inches from the ball—and promptly dozed off, only to be quickly prodded awake by his caddie. Finally satisfied with his angle projections, and after much discussion, he approached the ball. For a full minute he stood over it and almost nodded off again before resetting his feet, yelling "fore," and hitting the ball with such a powerful stroke that it soared a hundred yards, barely missing the clubhouse windows. Throwing his putter at his caddie, he snarled, "I told you I should have used a two wood."

The second man to putt was Theo Papadopoulos. Although his ball was about twenty feet from the cup, he barely managed a weak stroke that nudged it a mere six inches. Not dismayed with the result, he continued to putt—for a course-record forty times, in six-inch increments, until the ball dribbled into the hole. His caddie pumped his hand and patted him on the back, as if he had just made a hole-in-one.

The third player, Costas Vernikos, was in a sand trap at the edge of the green. After four quick hacks—which caused a minor sandstorm—he stared down at his feet, prodding the sand for the elusive ball, which was nowhere to be seen. Getting down on his knees, he scooped up sand furiously, like a dog digging for a bone. Finally, he succeeded in locating it, and making sure the others weren't looking, he blithely tossed it onto the green, where it rolled unerringly into the hole. "Birdie," he shouted.

The fourth old man, Spyros Pateraki, had fallen asleep in his golf cart.

Ready to field what he knew would be a barrage of questions from the women, Pierre said, "Those are your boys."

"Are you kidding? They're barely alive."

"They happen to be the four wealthiest men in the principality. They're known as the Four Rich Greeks."

"Which one is the richest?"

"The one asleep in the golf cart."

"He must be a hundred and ten."

"Actually, he's only ninety-one."

"Oh, well, that changes everything."

"What do they do besides golf, if you can call that playing golf?"

"Talk about their money," said Pierre. "Who has what, who has more . . ."

"At their age they still care about that?"

"It's *all* they care about. It's like a game to them."

"Whoever dies with the most money wins, right?"

"Exactly."

"Have they ever been married?"

"That's how they made their money. Among them they've outlived fifteen wives. They've never worked a day in their lives."

"All of them are disgustingly rich, no doubt?"

"Billions. They're inheritors fifteen times over."

"You're absolutely sure about that?"

"Positively."

"And they're all single now?"

The women all leaned in to to hear the answer to this most important query as Pierre nodded his head slowly. "Yes."

"So," Darlene asked, "if one of these cute little old guys was to meet up with somebody he thought was really rich, like one of us . . . ?"

"And if he thought he could do it one more time . . ." Carla continued.

"Just to show the other guys . . ." Irene added.

"As they say in your country, 'You got it,' " said Pierre.

"Now that we've *got* it," Eleanor said, "how do we *get* it?"

"Here is my thinking," Pierre whispered as the women huddled closely around him, hanging on his every word.

BACK AT THE hotel the women met to discuss their plight.

"Bastards. How could they have done this to us?"

"What's the difference between what they did and what we did?"

"We got stuck with the *bill*—that's a big fucking difference."

"We didn't cost them a dime."

"You have a point there."

"What now? We don't have a lot of choices."

"We have to make a killing—a legal killing."

"You think this plan of Pierre's can work?"

"I don't trust him."

"I agree. His palms are so greased he must have to powder them ten times a day."

"It's not like we have a lot of choices."

"If it doesn't work, we'll take the French fucker hostage."

"It's up to you, Darlene. You've got to make it happen."

"How come it's me?"

"We think he'll see you as a trophy."

"He's ninety-one; you'll look like jailbait to him."

"I promise you it's legal."

"Think of yourself as Lady Robin Hood."

"Suppose he wants to get in my pants?"

"Then think of yourself as Julia Roberts in *Pretty Woman*. She didn't do so badly."

"This guy is no Richard Gere."

"Anyway it's a moot point."

"What's that mean?"

"Deprived of practical significance. Meaning he probably hasn't gotten it up since Eisenhower was president."

"He'll try for a little touchy-feely, that's all."

"Suppose he wants more?"

"Then give him a quarter of a million bucks' worth."

"Very funny. It's my virtue we're talking about here."

"You thinking about getting born-again?"

"Isn't there some limit on how many times you can do that?"

"Anyway, the odds are a thousand to one that he's a limp-o."

"There's still that one chance in a thousand. You never know with Greek men. Remember that movie with Anthony Quinn?"

"Think of yourself as Deborah Kerr in *Tea and Sympathy*. Remember the scene under the tree where she makes a personal sacrifice and seduces her young student, and she says something like: 'Years from today, when you speak of this, you will . . . be kind.' "

"You really think I'm worth a quarter mil?"

"No question about it."

"Hey, there could be a business here?"

"Yeah, we could give her a pseudonym: Madame Ovary."

Lots of laughter, at Darlene's expense.

30
"Going for Broke"

When famous bank robber Willie Sutton
was asked why he robbed banks, he replied:
"Because that's where the money is."

SHE HAD TO be the aggressor, yet make the nonagenarian mark feel that he was the one doing the pursuing. She had to appear calm, look straight into his eyes, with a steady, unwavering gaze, coupled with a *Mona Lisa* smile. She had to appear unavailable, untouchable, virtuous, and most of all, she had to radiate wealth from every pore.

Darlene spent all of the next day in the beauty salon of the hotel, where every inch of her that showed was beautified. Her blond hair was made blonder and piled upon her head with romantic tendrils escaping here and there. Her brows were gently arched, her lips scrubbed with a firm toothbrush and toothpaste—a trick of movie and model makeup artists that has the temporary effect of making the lips look fashionably bee-stung—after which they were painted a deep red with a small squirrel-hair brush and then highly glossed. Her cheeks were lightly blushed, her eyelashes lengthened, and her eyes made to appear larger, with dusky shadowing. Her bosom was el-

evated, with an underwired brassiere, and her waist pain-
fully cinched in a corset that Madame du Barry might
have worn to seduce the king. To offset her extreme
blondness, her low-cut, floor-length dress was of silver-
embroidered latex material that emphasized and exaggerated her every curve. Her fingernails were painted black
and showered with sparkling silver dust. The jewelry
salesmen were so very happy about the publicity their
shops had received in the press as a result of the women's
misadventures, they couldn't wait to lend them whatever
they wanted. Darlene had seduced the young salesman at
Cartier with promises she would never keep and he had
lent her, against his better judgment, a two-foot rope of
diamonds that were woven into her coiffure, with earrings
and a ring to match. She wore jewelry from all four stores;
rings on every finger, dozens of bracelets on her wrists, a
necklace worth a king's ransom. She looked like an over-
decorated Christmas tree; a woman who was going out
for good. Pierre borrowed two dogs for her, both poodles,
one black, one white, to complete the effect.

They had decided that Darlene would try to attract the
richest man, Spyros Pateraki. "You don't think all this is
too much, do you, girls?"

"It's perfect. I'm jealous," said Carla.

"They did a great job with your hair," said Irene.

"You're looking at a million dollar hairdo. It took them
three hours to weave the diamonds in."

"It was worth it. You're dynamite," said Eleanor.

"You don't think I'm showing too much boobs?" said
Darlene.

"Not for *that* guy? I just hope it's enough to keep him
awake," said Eleanor.

"I can't wait to see this," said Irene.

"We're counting on you, Darlene," said Carla.

"You're our last hope," said Eleanor.

Darlene strutted around the hotel suite, admiring herself in every mirror. "First, I'll do my little-girl stuff and

then I'll give him a little of my Texas hospitality." She hugged herself, enhancing her cleavage.

"The man doesn't stand a chance," said Eleanor.

THE MEN SPENT most of their time at La Mer Privée, a very expensive and staid men's club. Membership was by invitation only and no new members had been admitted in the past five years. This may have been due to the fact that there was no waiting list. Most of the members were over eighty. The club was so quiet you could hear blood pulsing through clogged arteries and the wheeze of exhaled Monte Cristos.

The four doddering old Greeks, wearing tuxedos, sat in wing chairs near a blazing fire. The fact that it was August did not seem to concern them as they sipped white claret and stared at the burning embers. They spoke in cryptic Greek, which translated, as follows:

Nikos: "Bridge?"

Theo: "Hmmmph."

Costas: "Right."

Spyros: "Can't."

The three looked at Spyros, rather surprised that he had declined their ritual game.

Nikos: "Why?"

Spyros: "Date."

All: "Date?"

Spyros: "Yes."

Niko: "Who?"

Theo: "How?"

Costas: "Rich?"

Spyros: "Very."

All: "*How* very?"

Spyros smiled, as the ashes of his Cohiba cigar tumbled down over his studded shirt, into the folds of his
cummerbund and the cuffs of his trousers. After a lei-
surely sip of his wine he said: "Extremely very." Following which he cackled some obscenities in Greek at the
other three men, who exchanged frowning, jealous looks
with each other.

Let the games begin.

PIERRE HAD MET with old Spyros Pateraki and mentioned,
in strict confidence, that an attractive, very wealthy
woman, recently widowed, would be having dinner alone
at the hotel that evening. Would he care to make her ac-
quaintance? It *might* possibly be arranged. Spyros said to
arrange it, at all costs. Money changed hands and it *was*
arranged. Spyros trusted Pierre; he had been responsible
for introducing him to his third wife, a plain, sickly
woman, the sole heiress to a shipping fortune. Spyros had
the biggest yacht in the harbor, which he rarely visited
and which hadn't left port in ten years, although it was
fully crewed, provisioned, and ready to sail at a moment's
notice. He owned a fleet of oil tankers, houses on all con-
tinents, a large share of S.B.M., mounds of gold bars reposing in several Swiss banks, office buildings, a satellite
network, and a tiny Greek olive farm, where he was born.
Despite his enormous wealth, he lived in a single room
at a small hotel in Monte Carlo and was chauffeured about
in a Volkswagen hatchback. Keeping a low profile and
preserving capital were his main concerns. Anything that
did not appreciate in value he disposed of dispassionately.

*   *   *

PIERRE ARRANGED FOR Spyros and Darlene to have dinner in the candlelit Empire Room. He also slipped word to the other Greeks (in exchange for a modest honorarium) and reserved a nearby table from where they could monitor the proceedings. He knew that Spyros Pateraki would enjoy entertaining Darlene with his jealous cronies as audience.

Pierre's last words to Darlene had been: "Remember, he loves to gamble but he hates to lose."

"Don't we all," she answered.

ALL EYES WERE on Darlene as she stood in the doorway of the dining room, waiting for the *maître d'* to escort her to Spyros's table. The three Greeks inspected her carefully through opera glasses.

Niko:	"Cartier."
Theo:	"Bulgari."
Costas:	"Van Cleef."
Niko:	"Two-million-five."
Theo:	"Three."
Costas:	"Son of a bitch."

Three heads turned to watch as she took her seat across from Spyros—purposefully leaning forward to treat him (and the other three Greeks) to a faceful of recently chilled cleavage, just shy of her nipples. Nikos popped a nitro under his tongue; Costas poured himself another glass of champagne and downed it in a swallow; Theo's face was reddened by twenty points of increased blood pressure. Spyros said, "Lovely," and tore his glance away from the offered *belle poitrine* long enough to cackle in Greek at the three men. For a nanosecond he forgot where he was but quickly regrouped his neurons and managed the word: "Champagne?"

Spyros listed from one side to the other. Not only was it making Darlene a bit seasick, but she was afraid he would fall over at any moment; but he always managed to regain his balance at the last second. "Thank you," she said, "champagne would be lovely."

Spyros lifted the bony index finger of his right hand, which rested on the table's edge, and waggled it. This was sufficient to attract the attention of several waiters, who rushed over. As Spyros was in his nodding-off phase, Darlene ordered for him: "We'll have a magnum of that nice Krug eighty-six."

This brought Spyros to life. "Magnum?" he belched.

"This dinner is on *me,* Spyros. I hope y'all won't deny me the opportunity of offerin' you a bit of old-fashioned Texas hospitality?" Darlene had acquired a very strong, sexy, Texas accent, which added to her allure.

Spyros forced an evil smile and cut his eyes to the three Greeks to make sure they had heard. They had—and were seriously concerned at this turn of events.

"So, Spyros, darlin', I hear you're a gamblin' man."

"I've been known to make a wager now and then," he said, breathing heavily from the exertion of having managed a complete sentence.

"Do you like to play craps?"

"I'd rather put my nose between your titties and take a nap."

"You don't waste any time, do you?"

"Don't have time to waste."

"Well, after dinner why don't we just try our luck at the tables and maybe afterward we'll see about that nap of yours."

"Mergers and acquisitions. Mergers and acquisitions," he mumbled as he nodded off.

Darlene quickly ordered dessert, assuming that he wouldn't remember that he hadn't eaten the first and main courses. In any event, she was too nervous to eat and too strapped into her corset. She was anxious to get to the casino, and the next step of the scheme. Spyros blinked awake just as she was finishing a *mousse au chocolat.* "Excellent meal, didn't you think?" she said.

"—then I'd like to put my tongue in a little Calvados brandy and lick—"

"Shall we?" she said, standing up—and wondering how she was going to get him across the street to the casino.

"A peach half."

"A peach half?" said Darlene.

"You rub it on—"

"Afterward, Spyros—afterward." This guy was not just a rich old man, he was a dirty rich old man—although she did have to admit that some of his ideas sounded interesting. He drifted, he listed, he hesitated, but little by little he managed to make the trip—spurred on by the thought of the potential nap and the possible merger and acquisition of this lovely, rich, lady. The three Greek men followed. The three American women followed. Pierre Goujon followed. Ola Obolensky, dressed as a cigarette girl in net stockings and a frilly bustier, followed—and was followed in turn by Inspector Delarue. Bringing up the rear were the four jewelry salesmen, who had been sitting in the hotel lobby as the entourage passed, and were shocked to see Darlene wearing *all* of their jewelry. Eleanor, Carla, and Irene had already taken their places on the mezzanine of the casino, where they had a perfect view of the craps table.

31

"Stayin' Alive"

Come on seven, don't you fail,
A seven keeps baby out of jail.

DARLENE HAD SPENT two hours that afternoon with Eleanor, learning the game of craps. She had never touched a pair of dice, but she was really pumped. "It's not over till it's over," she kept repeating to herself. It was all riding on her ability to pull this off. But she knew that the odds were poor because she was playing against the house and they already owed the house a mini-fortune.

Eleanor had bought a small craps game in a local toy store, along with a booklet of instructions on how to play. "You'll see four house personnel working the table. Two *dealers,* who do the placing and paying off of bets, and a *stickman,* who handles the dice and controls the speed of the game. The fourth person is the *boxman,* who sits opposite the stickman and makes sure the big payoffs and the chip-buying transactions are accurate. He's the boss. So, when it's your turn to be the *shooter,* you place your bet with a dealer and the stickman will push five dice at you with his long stick. You choose two and roll them. The dice must hit the back padded wall of the table or the roll is nullified.

"Let's say, on your first roll, called the *come-out roll,* you roll a six. You will notice that one of the dealers puts a round disk called a *puck* on the number six with the word *on* printed on the top. This is to let all bettors know that the number is six. He'll say: 'Six, mark the six.' If you roll another six before you roll a seven, you win. Roll a seven before, and you lose—that's called *crapping out.* If you win, the dealer will say: 'Pay the do's, take the don'ts.' If you're betting when someone else is the shooter, you can bet with him, on the *pass line,* or against him, on the *don't-pass line.* The don't-pass line will pay you half your bet if you win. So, if you bet a hundred francs on don't pass and the shooter craps out, you win fifty francs. There's a lot more to the game, but for tonight you just memorize this much and stay with what you've learned."

Darlene's mind was whirling. For someone who had never touched a pair of dice, the thought of what she had to do was stomach churning. For the first hour of practice she continually lost. "What are all those other numbers and words on the table?"

"Don't worry about them. Keep it simple. If you win on the pass bet, you get paid even money. Let's go over a few things again. Remember, to bet on yourself you place your bet on the pass line. That means, on your first roll, the come-out roll, you establish your number. Say you roll a five. On your next roll you must roll another five before rolling a seven. If you roll a five, you win even money; if you roll a seven, you lose your bet. Another important thing to remember: If, on the come-out roll, you roll a two, three, or twelve, you lose your bet. If you roll a seven on the come-out roll, you win. Other people around the table may be betting with you, on the pass line, or against you, on the don't-pass line."

"The book says something about side bets. What are they?"

"Forget them. The odds are terrible."

"But just so I'll know," said Darlene.

"They're called sucker bets. For example, at any time you can bet that on the next roll the shooter will roll, for instance, a two or a twelve. If that happens and you've bet the two/twelve, you win thirty to one."

"Wow. How come they pay so high?"

"Because there's only one way to roll a two—two ones—and one way to roll a twelve—two sixes. For other numbers there are two ways, so the odds go down."

"So making a high-odds side bet is like betting on a longshot at the racetrack or on one number in roulette?"

"Exactly. The house loves those bets because they have a big advantage."

SPYROS HELD ON to the edge of the craps table with both hands. Darlene stood next to him. A game of chance with the odds of winning favoring the house would soon determine her fate and that of her friends. Nikos, Costas, and Theo stood on the opposite side of the table where Ola had just sold them some expensive Churchill Havanas. Inspector Delarue loitered in the background and the four jewelry salesmen huddled behind the three Greeks. Spyros nodded at the boxman and waggled his index finger four times. The boxman whispered to one of the dealers and four stacks of ten-thousand-franc chips were pushed in front of Spyros—the equivalent of $400,000. The shooter to Spyros's right was trying to roll a five and rolled a seven, crapping out. The stickman moved five new dice in front of Spyros, who lost his balance reaching for them. Darlene managed to get him upright before he fell.

"Let me, Spyros. I feel lucky tonight."

He nodded, and Darlene chose two dice, as Spyros flicked a ten-thousand-franc chip onto the playing surface and said, "Pass." Darlene took a deep breath and held it, shook the dice, and threw them at the back wall of the table. A twelve.

"Pay the don'ts, take the do's," said the dealer. Darlene

had crapped out on her first come-out roll, losing ten-thousand francs—about $2,000. The dice moved to Nikos, who rolled a seven and won. Spyros had bet against him and lost another $2,000. Nikos rolled again. A five. Then a six, a four, and a five. He won, Spyros lost. Nikos was, as they say, on a roll, and made four more passes before crapping out—costing Spyros $10,000. Spyros began to double his bets. Costas and Theo each made three successful passes before the dice were pushed back to the man next to Spyros. He rolled a seven and then an eleven. Then a five and a seven. More losses for Spyros, who always bet don't pass, hoping the shooter wouldn't make his number.

By the time the dice were back in Darlene's hand, they had lost $54,000. Spyros was grumbling. He waggled his finger five times and the dealer took five of the ten thousand *plaques* and put them on the pass line. He nodded at Darlene, who looked up at Eleanor for support, and rolled the dice. A six. Spyros nodded. Darlene rolled again. A seven. Crapped out again: $104,000 down. By the time the dice rotated back to Darlene, they had lost $300,000.

"Maybe we should quit," she said nervously.

"Never lose. Never."

The three Greeks chortled with glee. Spyros took half of the remaining *plaques* and shoved them onto the table. Then, with a shaking hand, he took up the dice and threw them weakly. They did not make it to the back wall of the table and so the roll was disqualified. He nodded at Darlene and she began to pray as she had never prayed before. Eleanor held her breath and prayed with her—but to no avail. She threw a three—crap out again. They had $50,000 left of their original $400,000 stake. The dice went to Nikos, who was smiling so broadly that the skin on his old lips was cracking. Spyros closed his eyes and seemed to nod off. Darlene realized that he was losing interest. Men his age had very short attention spans. Panic time. Longshot time. She shoved all the remaining *plaques* at the dealer and said, "Twelve."

"Two hundred and fifty thousand francs on twelve?" said the dealer, looking to the boxman for an okay on this large bet. The boxman nodded his approval. The house loved big sucker bets. Nikos knitted his bushy brows. Eleanor almost fainted.

"What the hell does she think this is, Monopoly?" Eleanor said, and started down the stairs, hoping to reach Darlene and have her take the dumb bet off the table before it was too late. Just as she reached her, the dice were tumbling toward the back wall. The crowd gasped. Nikos had rolled two sixes—a twelve. A thirty-to-one shot had come in. Darlene tried to do the arithmetic in her head— thirty times 250,000 francs? She came up blank. Eleanor grabbed her and shouted, "Seven million five hundred thousand francs—a million and a half bucks."

"Spyros, wake up. We won. We won."

Those were magic words to Spyros Pateraki, who opened his eyes, looked at Darlene, gave *the finger* to the three Greeks, and said, "I love you. Will you marry me?"

"No, but I'll split the winnings with you."

Eleanor immediately stepped in to do the arithmetic. "That's $1,500,000—less your stake of $400,000. I make it $1,100,000 divided by two—which comes to $550,000 each."

As the dealers began to count out the winnings—no small task—another drama was taking place in the next room, at a roulette table. The real Baroness Natasha Karmanov and her friend had just been seated at Natasha's favorite spot, close to the wheel. They were immediately offered champagne and asked if they would like to play.

"Do we look like tourists?" Natasha replied, in her most imperious tone. Turning to Masha, she said, "New people. Of course I haven't been in here for twenty years, but things shouldn't change. It's so annoying. I wonder if the old casino director is still here? Probably not. Ah, I hate new people, don't you, Masha Pavlovna?"

"Detest them, Natasha Feodorovna, darling. Shall we play or leave?"

"Oh, let's play—or I should say, let's dabble. I'm not in the mood for serious gambling; say two hundred and fifty thousand francs?"

Masha nodded and looked at the man in charge and said: "*Deux cent cinquante mille francs pour la Baronne Karmanov.* We're at the Hermitage this year."

The head croupier wrote something down on a small piece of paper and walked off. A hurried conversation with lots of shrugging and eyebrow lifting then took place between the croupier and the pit boss. The only word that could be heard was the last one: "Impossible!"

As they both walked back toward the real baroness, the pit boss spread his hands and said quietly, "I'm terribly sorry, Baroness, but there's a slight problem. We do have an account for a Baroness Karmanov—and please try to understand my position. We are not asking for payment, of course, but . . ." He was too flustered to go on.

"What in the world are you babbling about, you fool?" Natasha hissed under her breath. They were holding up the game, and people at the table were beginning to stare.

"The baroness . . . uh, the other baroness . . . she . . . you. What I mean to say is—she is in the *salle* just next door. I'm sure there is some simple explanation. Your sister perhaps?" he said hopefully.

The baroness was no longer in the mood to whisper. "*NYET!* I HAVE NO SISTER. Show her to me—at once. Can you *imagine,* Masha Pavlovna?"

"Obviously an imposter," said Masha. "Monte Carlo is full of them."

The baroness rose up from her chair and addressed the pit boss, in a tired voice, as if she were speaking to a misbehaving child: "Is Monsieur Carrier still the casino director here?"

"Yes, Madame—uh, Baroness."

"Good. Find him."

"He is quite busy tonight—I don't think—"

"It's true, you don't. Now."

"But—"

"NOW, or I shall make a scene you will not soon forget," she hissed.

"Of course, of course. We will try."

The pit boss nodded to his assistant, who immediately walked off.

"In the meanwhile, if you will please follow me," he said, trying to defuse the situation.

THEY ARRIVED IN the next salon just as a big stack of chips was being pushed across the felt of the craps table toward Darlene and her benefactor, Spyros Pateraki.

"Let's buy some peaches and Calvados and go back to my place," Spyros said as he collapsed onto Darlene, his nose falling directly into her warm cleavage. He was asleep instantly. Darlene let him stay there for a few moments; after all, the dirty old man deserved at least that for saving their lives.

Ola looked at Inspector Delarue and shrugged. Nothing illegal here.

Just as Darlene started to sweep all of her winnings into her rather large handbag (she had come prepared to win!), the silence was shattered by a commotion: Natasha, Masha, two casino security men, and the pit boss hurried into the room. "Where is this shammer, this masquerader, this carpetbagger, this pretender to royal Russian blood," thundered the baroness. "Show her to me." Inspector Delarue and Ola turned as the red-faced pit boss reluctantly pointed up at the mezzanine—clearly in Irene's direction.

"Her?" the baroness shouted. "HER? Surely you are joking." The baroness turned on her heel just as the manager of the casino entered the room. "Ah, Philippe, will you be so kind as to tell these idiots who I am."

The manager was nonplussed, to say the least. "What is the problem, Baroness Karmanov?"

At this, all hell broke loose. Irene ran for an exit, followed by Eleanor and Carla, as Darlene snapped her handbag shut and slipped into the crowd, most of whom were distracted by the activity on the mezzanine. Spyros Pateraki, having lost his leaning post, fell to the ground, creating yet another distraction. Only Ola saw Darlene slip into the ladies' powder room. But what she didn't see was a nondescript man wearing a blue suit as he expertly hooked and stole the handbag from Darlene's arm and slipped away unnoticed, through a side door. This took place so quickly that Darlene had no opportunity to react. In fact, she hadn't even seen him!

Inspector Delarue kept an eye on Ola and quickly followed her. Ola stationed herself outside of the ladies' room, considering her next move. She was happy to see Delarue approach. It certainly wouldn't look right for a casino cigarette girl to arrest someone . . . if indeed that someone required arresting! They still had no idea exactly what was going on. The security men had taken off after Irene, Eleanor, and Carla—so that left just Darlene, and her winnings . . . or so they thought. They had not seen the slick theft of her handbag.

"What do you think, Detective Obolensky?" Delarue was being formal now that they were no longer having an affair.

"I don't know, Inspector, but my instincts tell me that we should think of a reason to detain Madame Barlow—if that's who she really is."

"We could be sued for false arrest."

"You stay here. I'll go in and just talk to her. It may take some time, but whatever you do, don't come in and don't leave."

The inspector agreed.

Ola went in, and for the next half hour, woman to woman, Darlene cried and poured her heart out to "the cigarette girl." She told Ola the whole story. In a way she was happy to finally have it all come out, no matter what the consequences.

When she had calmed down a bit, Ola asked her where the money was.

"I don't know. Somehow I lost it on the way in here."

When the two women finally exited the ladies' room, they found the inspector and the casino manager having what appeared to be a rather serious conversation. As the inspector turned to face Darlene, she knew from his expression what was coming.

"You caught my friends, right?"

The inspector nodded.

"And they confessed, right?"

The inspector nodded.

"And now you're going to arrest me, right?"

Once more, the inspector nodded affirmatively.

"Shit!"

THE JEWELRY SALESMEN had no idea what had happened. All they knew for sure was that one of their clients had walked off with a ton of winnings.

"Rich people are nuts," said the man from Cartier's.

"Maybe we'll make some sales," said the Tiffany guy.

"I've got a good feeling about that," said the Van Cleef rep.

"I agree," said the Bulgari salesman. "I think we'll be taking home some hefty commissions come tomorrow."

"Let's drink on it. Champagne and cigars on me," said the Cartier man, just as Ola was passing with Darlene in tow.

Ola, still dressed as a cigarette girl, sold four more cigars.

The ladies' room was carefully searched; no money or handbag was found.

32

"C'est la Vie"

Hold me close and hold me fast,
The magic spell you cast,
This is la vie en rose . . .
—*David–Louiguy–Piaf, "La Vie en Rose"*

IRENE HAD A triple-layered dream that night that seemed to last until morning. She dreamed she was in bed with Maurice and longing for him to wake and take her into his arms. Moments later he did and she sensed she was dreaming and awoke. Shockingly, she found herself in his arms. They began to make love when she awoke for a second time and realized that the first awakening had still been part of the dream. She was alone in her jail-room bed.

Irene soon fell back asleep and, as sometimes happens, was back in the same dream. She reached down and felt her wetness, and touched his shoulder with damp fingers, all the while experiencing an intense longing for him to awaken. She knew she would come the moment he entered her. Suddenly she felt strongly that she was dreaming and forced herself awake. He was there. He kissed her gently, felt her desire, and entered her. Her orgasm shook her. Once again she was alone in bed. She had never experienced awakening from a dream and into a second layer of the same dream. What did it mean? We have all

probably had the experience of wondering, within a
dream, *if* we are dreaming; that is the intrusion of the
conscious into the subconscious. But Irene had never
heard of the subconscious trying to block the conscious.
She analyzed it. To her it meant that she so much wanted
the dream to be true that her subconscious self kept her
conscious mind from prevailing as long as possible.

Was Maurice that important to her? Since she would
never see him again, she hoped he would not be; that she
could treat all that had happened as a summer romance;
file it away in her store of memories and bring it out from
time to time to recall her part in the fairy-tale quest.

All the women discovered that they had had similar
dreams. Was it simply the triumph of hope over experience? They all knew that if they somehow managed to
get out of the mess they were in, they would be going
home without their holy grails. All the hoping in the world
wasn't going to change that. Even if they each still had
their huge profits, they would have gladly traded them for
a different outcome. *C'est la vie*—that's life.

SPYROS PATERAKI TRIED to call Darlene at the jail every fifteen minutes and sent flowers every hour, but despite his
determined attempts, and her gratitude for his help, she
told him—the one time her jailers allowed the call—that
he was nosing around in vain. Nevertheless, he persisted.

"IT'LL BE JUST a judge—no jury," said Eleanor as she paced
their cell. "It's not really a trial. It's like what we call in
America—"

"An inquisition?" Irene interjected.

"An arraignment," Eleanor said as she continued.
"We'll probably be brought before this guy who's a com-
bination DA and grand jury wrapped into one—and told
specifically what we're being accused of. Then we plead
not guilty."

"How come we plead not guilty when we're guilty?" said Darlene.

"Because that's the way you do it. Then we rot in jail for around six months until the trial—which will give me lots of time to prepare our case."

"An insanity defense?" said Irene.

"It's a thought," said Eleanor.

"Matter of fact it's pretty close to the truth," said Darlene. "You'd have to be crazy to try what we tried."

"I read somewhere that they feed prisoners waiting for trial pretty good in France—and if you want something special you just order from the local bistro or pizzeria and they deliver it," said Carla.

Irene looked at Carla like she had lost her mind. "Or maybe we could get stuff sent FedEx from New Jersey. We're flat broke, in case that little fact has escaped your attention."

THE NEXT AFTERNOON the four women were led into the judge's chambers. Darlene had slept in her evening gown and over a million dollars in borrowed jewelry and was struggling to look pure and innocent. Needless to say, she wasn't succeeding.

Also present were Inspector Delarue, Ola, and a man from the American embassy. The judge's clerk began to read the charges against the women. He read slowly and with great emphasis—in flowery old formal French—his words of foreboding echoing through the mostly empty chamber. Darlene recalled her dream, the sound of the lone drummer, and the order for her beheading. She almost fainted but was steadied by Irene. Throughout all of this the judge never looked at the women. Even detailed in French, of which the women understood nothing, the case against them sounded fearsome.

At each pause the embassy man whispered a terse interpretation to Eleanor, occasionally consulting a tiny computer that held a French/English dictionary translating program.

"Falsifying your identities . . ."

"Theft . . ."

"Nonpayment of obligations . . ."

"Resisting arrest . . ."

"Felonious assault . . ." (Eleanor had bopped a security man pretty good.)

"Entering France under false pretenses . . ."

"Conspiring to defraud . . ."

"Committing dupery, chicanery, fiddle-faddle, pettifoggery, and indulging in confidence tricks . . . and—" Before his intense delivery of the next word, the judge's clerk looked directly at Eleanor and spat out the offensive polysyllable as if it were a piece of rotten fish: "PROSTITUTION!"

There was no need to translate this word since it is the same in French as in English.

Eleanor automatically screamed out: "OBJECTION."

"Quiet," urged the embassy man, "or they'll add contempt of court to the list, which is long enough as it is."

The reading of the indictment was now complete. The clerk folded his paper neatly and handed it up to the judge, who called for absolute silence while he perused the document for several long minutes.

It was so quiet you could hear a plea bargain in Eleanor's head.

She knew that if she didn't say something, do something right now, they would end up in a dire predicament from which there would be no easy exit. Spending time in a French jail was not an option she could live with. She thought back to what their group psychologist had said when first told of their insane plan. *There will be barriers to overcome, puzzles to solve, emotions to control, and a positive mental state to maintain.*

Eleanor knew she was at the first barrier, facing a complex legal puzzle. The other women depended on her. This was not the moment to allow a fog of negativity or any internal emotional babble to cloud her trained legal mind. Focus, Eleanor, she thought. Focus and act! You've faced much worse than this in your career and won the case. Get with the program, Eleanor. Shift into high and pump up those brain cells. Flashdance, baby—show 'em your stuff!

Eleanor turned quickly to the man from the American embassy. "Tell the judge we need a continuance."

"I'm not sure what the word for that is in French."

"Look it the fuck up!" Eleanor hissed, in her old court-room voice. "What the hell do you think we pay taxes for?"

The embassy man turned pinkish, blinked, and shook his head, mumbling to himself, as he consulted his tiny computer translator. "Shit, it's not in here . . ." he said just as the judge cleared his throat, obviously ready to throw the book at them.

The embassy man was still scanning.

Eleanor was about to explode as the judge removed his glasses, sniffed three times, and directing his studied ju-ristic voice to a spot in the back of the room, intoned: "It is the decision of this court that—"

"CONTINUATION," shouted the embassy man, having found what he thought was the correct, legal word at long last. It was the same in French as in English, with the exception of the accent.

The judge pounded his desk with a paperweight. "What in the world are you trying to say, young man?" he shouted in French. "Are you asking for an adjournment?"

"Yes we, they—the women—respectfully beg the court for a delay—to—to—"

He was lost.

"To prepare our case," said Eleanor forcefully.

"To consult with our attorney," said Irene, immediately realizing what Eleanor had in mind.

At this, Darlene went limp and slipped to the floor in a dramatic faint. "And our doctor," pleaded Carla, with hands clenched under her chin, in prayer.

The embassy man translated frantically.

The judge looked at his clerk, who shook his head negatively, as if to say "crazy Americans."

A millisecond before the judge opened his mouth to deny their request, the embassy man had a revelation. Rising up to his full height, he said, in the most stentorian tones he could muster: "The United States of America would appreciate your consideration in this matter, Your Judgeship."

The judge put his glasses back on and nosed toward the embassy man. Today, he rationalized—for the French are world champions at rationalization—today was not a day to confront the United States of America. Not when he was late for his *cinq-à-sept* rendezvous with his demanding, but delicious mistress.

"In memory of the landing of American forces near my grandmother's home in Calais, I grant you one day. We will reconvene tomorrow at eleven o'clock in the morning. This court is ad—"

"Wait," Eleanor shouted.

The judge heaved a big sigh. These women were getting to be tiresome.

"What is it now?"

Eleanor nudged the embassy man and whispered, "Tell him we would like to be freed on our own recognizance until tomorrow morning."

"Are you kidding? There's no way."

"Tell him the United States of America guarantees our return. I'm a lawyer and I can't prepare my case in jail," Eleanor hissed.

"But the others?"

"They come with me. I'll need to take their depositions."

"He's not going to buy it," the embassy man said.

The judge looked up at the clock on the wall. It was already five minutes before five o'clock. He was never late for his *cinq-à-sept*—his five-to-seven with his mistress. Never. Every minute was precious to him, not to mention expensive on the salary of a judge. He'd had enough. "This court is adjourned. Good evening, ladies."

Eleanor shoved the embassy man toward the judge as he was about to enter the door to his private chambers.

"Go after him."

"I can't do that!"

"Then we'll have to tell your superior what you did to Darlene."

Darlene got it right away.

"And don't touch me again, sir," she moaned.

"You wouldn't make a tired claim like that," he said.

"Try me," Eleanor said in her most charming, sinister voice.

He knew she was desperate. He wanted out of this dumb case that now stood a chance of ruining his career, and so he headed for the judge's chambers, with the judge's clerk tight on his heels

They were both back out in what seemed like seconds.

The women converged upon him, trapping him in a corner. He had no chance of escape without causing injury to one or more of these conniving creatures.

"You're all going to step aside and let me leave," he said firmly. "And then *you* can leave—and if you are all not back here tomorrow morning at eleven A.M. *sharp,* I will send the entire embassy marine fucking guard after you." Having finally vented his spleen, he felt much better.

"You will all leave your passports and return tickets, and all of that jewelry, with me, please," the judge's clerk said.

Darlene leaped toward the embassy man, who instinctively put both hands over his crotch, fearing for his manhood—but she only grabbed him by his ears and planted a big wet kiss firmly on his mouth while Carla kissed him on one cheek and Irene on his other.

"How did you do that, if you don't mind my asking?" Eleanor said as he broke away and flattened himself against the wall, still hemmed in by the four women.

"I don't know. The judge seemed so panicked to leave that he told his clerk to give me anything I wanted, saying he didn't care."

Eleanor smiled and stuck out her hand. "Thanks. Much appreciated."

The embassy man tentatively removed one set of fingers from his gonads and shook her hand limply. Then he ran for his life.

WHERE COULD THEY go? They had no money. Where would they sleep that night? True, they were out of jail, but what next? They had only eighteen hours before they were due back in court.

They trudged back to the Hotel de Paris. Maybe the concierge, Pierre, would feel sorry for them. In any event, it was a place to start—and the only one they could think of.

PIERRE DID INDEED sympathize with their plight—but not to the extent of offering to house them for the night in their former expensive suites or even give them a room or two.

"The best I can do is one *chambre de courrier,* a room we use from time to time for the maids and chauffeurs of our clients. There is *one* empty. I'll have an extra bed moved in." Pierre smiled the smile of a French concierge who has not been tipped, bowed slightly toward the women, and departed.

"Well, it's better than the street," said Irene, trying to be positive.

"Sleeping's the least of our problems," said Darlene.

"Where do we start?" said Carla.

"We don't have much time, so we'll split up. Irene, you try to talk to that baroness; Carla, you sweet-talk your cute ass off to the hotel manager; Darlene, you take the head man at the casino—and I'll see what I can do about making sure the men don't decide to testify against us.

We meet back here, in the lobby, at eight."

"What do we say to them?" asked Darlene.

"I've worked that out. Now, here's the way I see it working . . ."

The four women sat in a corner of the lobby for the next half hour while Eleanor outlined her scheme to confront the accusers . . . the witnesses for the prosecution.

At the casino . . . Darlene

"If I still had it, I would give back all the money I won. I was intending to use it to pay you everything we owed. Everything. I swear. But it was stolen from me before I could do that."

The casino manager just stared at Darlene silently. He'd been through this routine so many times before. They always had excuses, some of them quite creative.

"I don't doubt your intentions, madame, but the fact is we are owed a substantial sum, and if word got out that we were forgiving our debtors, well—you can imagine what would happen."

Darlene considered crying—not an option. She was desperate. Offer sex in exchange for . . . ? Forget it! Not with the numbers they were talking about. What did Eleanor say? she thought. A brain spark fired; her eyes lit up and widened. Right!

"Well, I didn't want to have to do this, but I'm afraid you give me no choice. I will have to turn this over to my attorney and bring suit against the casino."

"Bring a lawsuit? Surely you are joking," said the casino man.

"Not at all. I won that money fair and square, true?"

"True."

"And it was stolen from me in your casino."

"Yes?"

"I assume you are insured?"

The casino man carefully considered what she had just said, realizing he was in over his head in this situation.

These women were obviously unscrupulous and would stoop to anything to avoid jail. He would end this conversation and turn the problem over to the casino's law firm immediately.

The hotel manager ... Carla

Carla walked across the square from the hotel and looked out to sea. It was a beautiful day, the sun glinting off the incredibly intense blue water; the sailboats gliding effortlessly toward a horizon they would never meet. Carla thought of her own horizons; were they, too, out of reach, moving forever away as she got closer? It did seem that way. Just when she thought she had her goals in sight, they shifted out of reach. Her man was in jail and she was headed there, too, unless she and the others were very, very smart. And what were the chances of them all succeeding? Would New Jersey street smarts help them here? She doubted it. She looked back at the hotel and up to where their suites had been only hours ago. It seemed like it had all never happened and Carla struggled to keep the memories fresh, for they might have to sustain her for a long time. If only they hadn't met the men in the first place. If only . . . wait, she thought . . . that's it. Eleanor was right. That could be the mitigating circumstance. At least it was worth a try. Words. Straws in the wind.

The hotel manager had refused to see her, at first. It was only after she had sent him a note threatening to cause a commotion in the lobby that he deigned to appear.

A supercilious bastard, was her first impression. This wasn't going to be easy. But maybe she could use that against him. The first thing she did was speak at the top of her voice—adding as much New Joy-see accent as she could. He immediately ushered her into his office, which was where she wanted to be.

He refused all of her entreaties to pay off the hotel bill over time.

"I'd be long dead by the time you managed that," he said, not even trying to hide a smirk.

"Putting us in jail isn't going to get your bill paid," Carla said.

"That, madame, is not my problem. I am an employee of the hotel—not an owner. It will not affect my salary a sou."

Carla asked for a glass of water, which the manager poured reluctantly. "Two minutes. I have another engagement. I can give you two more minutes and then I'm afraid I'll have to insist that you leave. If you refuse, which I find likely, I will let you deal with my security men. Now, is there anything else you'd like to say?"

Carla hated to nail Pierre Goujon, especially after he had helped them, but she realized that throwing him to the wolves was her only hope at getting the manager to react. So, she went for it—claws bared!

"Just this, asshole: Your concierge, also an employee and representative of this hotel, induced us to—introduced us to—this gigolo and known con man, Maurice Gerard, who I understand also lived in this hotel—made it his 'base of operations,' so to speak. In my mind that makes the hotel and certain of its staff guilty of complicity to commit a crime. In other words, had we not been *solicited* by your concierge, we would not have met the four M-E-N and, ergo, we would not now be in the predicament in which we find ourselves. Am I making myself clear? Or would you rather hear it from my attorney?"

The hotel manager shot his cuffs and walked over to a sideboard, where he procured a cold bottle of champagne and two glasses. "Let me make a call," he said, "so that we don't have to hurry this discussion."

"I might also mention that I think I'm pregnant," Carla added for good measure.

The prisoners . . . Eleanor

Eleanor was refused admittance to the jail and so she had to come up with plan B.

Maurice, Julio, Jean-Jacques, and Trevor had all been put in separate cells so they could not communicate with each other. Each was given a statement to sign that, in effect, was their damning testimony against the four women. Each was told that their sentences would be reduced if they complied and signed—*but only if they all signed*.

Maurice, Jean-Jacques, and Julio had refused immediately; Trevor still had his copy and was reading it for the third time when he was called to the phone.

Eleanor had convinced Pierre to make the call, which he considered his final act of futile kindness. At her urging, he told the jail superintendent that he had been retained by Trevor Weymouth and insisted upon speaking to him. He then passed the phone to Eleanor when Trevor came on the line.

Eleanor had no idea that Trevor held her destiny in his hands. But if she had a chance with anyone, it was with him.

Upon reflection, and endless argument with his inner voices, Trevor had decided to spare Eleanor his emotional ramblings. The truth was too ugly for him to contemplate, let alone impart. Bottom line was: She would be better off without him. He had absolutely nothing to offer her. Less than nothing. Best to let her down fast and hard and assume all of the blame. Close the book, as she had said. Slam it closed! He would be the prick she always thought he was. And so he came right out with his prepared lines the moment he heard her voice.

"They're asking me to sign a statement against you. I assume the others have been given the same document."

"And what are you going to do?" Eleanor asked, in a matter-of-fact tone of voice.

"They've offered to cut my sentence in half if I sign."

"That wasn't my question. Are you considering signing it?"

"I'm wavering."

"You prick."

"Why don't you say what you really mean?"

"I wouldn't sign it if our positions were reversed," said Eleanor bitterly. "I hope you know that?"

Then Trevor said the line that finished it: "Sounds like bullshit lawyer talk."

"It isn't."

"You'll probably all get off with a light sentence anyway, being Americans."

"Is that all you have to say?"

There was silence on the line.

This wasn't working the way she'd planned. She was being overly aggressive. It came naturally to her. But this wasn't a courtroom—it was her life—and she couldn't afford to lose this one. She was doing the very thing she had promised herself not to do: placing blame.

"Well, maybe you're right. Maybe if I were in your shoes I'd sign it, too. Guess I can't really blame you . . . after all, what was I to you? The other day when I visited you in jail you didn't even say anything. That could have been my fault for not giving you a chance and doing my usual 'summing-up' act. Probably everything's been my fault. Any last words?"

There was silence on the line.

"Good-bye, Trevor."

She hung up. Tears in her eyes. It had started out as an act but it hadn't ended up that way.

Trevor stared at the phone in his hand. He'd never felt conflicted before. It was an unsettling emotion. He looked up. There was no sky, no butterflies—just the cold harsh glaring light of flickering fluorescent bulbs hanging from the cement ceiling. He'd probably be here for a long time. He'd have no job when he got out. He had nothing before but his freedom and a bighearted lady from New Jersey who said she could love him. Now he'd lost everything.

He looked at the document that he'd been asked to sign . . . and slowly tore it to shreds.

The real baroness... Irene

The "real" baroness had reluctantly agreed to see Irene in her hotel suite at the Hermitage. When Irene entered she was surprised to see that it was just a large room with a sitting area. Nothing like the extravagant suites the four women had had at the Hotel de Paris. Her second surprise was the baroness herself. Without her gown and jewels, she looked like a rather ordinary woman, nothing special about her at all. Outside of this room she wouldn't warrant a second glance.

"Why are you here? Irene, is it?"

Irene nodded. "I'm here to ask you what it's like to be you?"

Most people like to talk about themselves, given the opportunity; the baroness was no exception. "Do you mean, what is it like to be old and rich?"

"I wouldn't have put it that way," said Irene.

"Well, that's what I am. Very old and very rich. I imagine you've had more fun being me than I have."

Irene looked at the baroness and knew that she was speaking the truth.

"Not that that's any excuse for your impersonating me—stealing my identity, running up debts in my name. That's grand larceny. And I'm afraid you'll pay dearly for it. Why did you do it, if I may ask?"

"My skin wasn't working, so I thought I'd try on another's; you happened to be the one. It could have been anyone. I saw your picture in a magazine. You seemed to have everything. The world at your feet."

"In the magazine pictures, I do," said the baroness. "If only life continued to be that way once the party was over and the photographers gone. Have you ever considered why you chose me? I'll tell you why: because it's easy to impersonate someone older—but impossible to pretend to be younger. If it *were* possible I'd pay anything to achieve it. Not to have to demean myself with paid escorts ... to wear a bathing suit at the beach. To meet people who talk about more than the price of their cars and yachts and airplanes. Not to have to attend another formal dinner party in my life. What did Tom Wolfe call us? Social X-rays? He was right. We worry about our weight, as if it made any difference, as if it would gain us entry into some new and exclusive club. Well, I'm here to tell you that thin and rich doesn't do it. There's a helluva lot more. Money has only one real value: it keeps you in control. No one can fire me, throw me out of my homes. But I have to keep moving. Most people like me do. We convince ourselves that around the next mountain is a new and exciting adventure that will change our lives. Truth is that for me, and for all like me, around the next mountain is just another mountain. So, we make our days as full as possible—taking care of many homes, buying new wardrobes, planning parties, et cetera, et cetera, et cetera. Why? Simple. What's the alternative? I was born to be someone's wife. I trained for that until I achieved it. Twice. That's all I know. I speak four languages—but so do many headwaiters. And you wanted to be me? Ha! What did you have to gain in the long run being me?"

"I met a man, being you. Would you like to hear about him?"

The baroness was, of course, hooked. What woman would answer no to that question?

THE MAID'S ROOM the women were to share at the Hotel de Paris was approximately eight feet long by seven feet wide. Barely enough room to contain the two beds and allow the door to open. The women had to enter one at a time to undress and get into bed; only then was there standing room for the next woman.

It took almost twenty minutes for all four of them to squeeze into the room. They lay on the bed sideways, looking like sardines packed into a can.

"Reminds me of the pajama parties we had as kids."

"Only we were half the size we are now."

"Okay, who wants to start?"

"Aren't we going to order anything to eat? We always have something during the sessions."

"How do we call? There's no phone."

"Where's the bathroom?"

"Down at the end of the hall."

"I wonder what they usually charge for this room?"

"They probably give it away."

"It's hot in here. Can we open the window?"

"There isn't any window."

"Does anyone have to pee except me?"

"I'll go with you."

"Hurry up. We've got to get started."

BY TEN O'CLOCK that evening the women had exchanged information about their individual meetings with their accusers.

"Sounds like none of them actually committed to anything," said Darlene.

"We did our best," said Carla.

"I think Trevor's the weak link," said Eleanor. "You think the baroness will change her mind?"

"We never actually discussed her not testifying," said Irene.

"What were you doing in there for three hours?"

Irene was silent. What had they talked about all evening? Why hadn't she tried to convince the baroness not to press charges? Irene had let go, had admitted guilt, had bared her soul. She had left it to the baroness to come to her own conclusion. Maybe that was a mistake, but that's what felt right at the moment.

"Did you get a definite answer from Trevor? Did you even ask for one?" Irene countered.

"No," Eleanor answered. "I was afraid that if I pressed him I would get a no—and I didn't want a definite no. I understand that the complaints have to be in and signed by tomorrow morning. There's not much more we can do."

The four women lay there studying a tiny spider crawling across the ceiling. Then Eleanor turned out the light, and each of the women imagined where the many-legged bug was headed. It was obviously looking for a victim.

The room was so silent you could hear the spider laughing.

Eleanor snapped the bare-bulb ceiling light back on. The suspense was too much to bear. She would kill it. But the spider had disappeared. Four pairs of eyes scanned the room, felt their faces, scratched imaginary bites. No one slept that night.

THE NEXT MORNING the exhausted women presented themselves at the courtroom. The embassy man heaved a sigh of relief when he saw them. The marines could be taken off combat alert. His job seemed safe.

Inspector Delarue and Ola stood at the back of the room. Delarue saluted the women as they entered—much as the *gendarmes* salute you in France just before they issue you a ticket for a traffic violation. It's all part of the French style.

When the judge entered, preceded by his clerk, Eleanor rose and tried to look confident . . . as if merely having returned as promised would make a difference in the verdict.

For ten long minutes the judge perused the many pieces of paper handed to him by his clerk. He nodded, grunted, sniffed, sighed, and dithered as the women sweated.

Finally he looked at Eleanor, cleared his magisterial throat, and rasped, "You are all unquestionably guilty." The embassy man translated, but since the word for "guilty" in French is *coupable,* very close to the word "culpable" in English, Eleanor knew what the translation would be.

Darlene thought she would faint for real when she heard the dreaded word, but breathed deeply and managed to stay upright.

The words seemed to echo around the room, taunting the women: *Guilty, guilty, guilty . . .*

The judge let his words sink in for a longer moment than necessary, before continuing. "Nothing would give me greater pleasure than to see all of you pay for your crimes with the long jail sentences you deserve. You are all guilty of deception, deceit, and fraud."

He paused for a moment, wondering if *he* was not guilty of similar charges by having, unbeknownest to his wife and five children, a mistress. He decided in his own favor and put it from his mind. After all even the presidents of the Republic had had mistresses. It was *de rigueur.* Normal.

Continuing, he said, "But, unfortunately for the State, and for all law-abiding *Monégasques,* this case is being dismissed for lack of evidence."

The women tightened the muscles of their collective abs as he went on.

"The hotel has tendered a statement affirming that it has been paid; the casino has done the same. The *real* Baroness Karmanov has refused to testify or make a complaint and, in any event, has left for St. Petersburg. The jailed men who are the subject of the attempted confidence game are themselves confidence men and their trial will commence one week from today. I find whatever statements they have made to be inadmissible." He looked up. "As for the charge of prostitution . . . *pooof.*"

The embassy man was translating as fast as he could. Eleanor couldn't believe what she was hearing. After the judge announced, "Case dismissed, the women are free to go," he added, "Inspector Delarue, you will see that these women leave the principality no later than five P.M. today." As he reached the door he turned, directing his glare at Darlene: "And you will, of course, return all of those *baubles* before you leave."

The women cried and embraced each other.

Delarue looked at Ola, shrugged, and said, *"Pooof?"*

And Ola nodded, and *pooooffed* back at him.

A CONFUSED INSPECTOR Delarue stood in the lobby of the Hotel de Paris, at the concierge's desk, interrogating Pierre Goujon. "How was their bill paid?"

"A man appeared at the cashier's desk very early this morning and said that he wanted to pay the hotel bills and casino debts of the four women—which came to a bit over a quarter of a million dollars."

"What did he look like, this man?" said Delarue.

The concierge thought for a moment and then said, "Funny, I'm not sure I could describe him to you. He was rather ordinary—nondescript, you might say. He paid in cash. Incredible."

"And the hotel simply accepted that—with no questions asked?"

"My dear inspector, must I remind you that this is Monte Carlo, the gambling capital of Europe. When someone wants to pay a debt—when *anyone* wants to pay a debt—we do not ask questions. In any event, it is not illegal, correct?"

The inspector nodded. In any event, it was too late to do anything about it. Done is done. All that was left now was to be sure that the women were gone by the appointed time. Today was checkout day.

FOUR NICELY DRESSED women from New Jersey, who had recently broken the bank at Monte Carlo but had nothing to show for it, descended the marble staircase into the rococo entrance hall of the Hotel de Paris.

As they passed the concierge's desk, struggling with their own luggage so as to avoid having to tip the bellmen, Inspector Delarue nodded and tipped his hat to them. *"Bon voyage, mesdames."*

They responded with the thinnest of smiles and continued on their way out.

"I'll bet that we're the first ones ever to take a bus from this hotel to the airport. I don't know if they even have one," said Irene.

Just as Irene was about to ask the doorman that question, a beeping horn caused them to turn. A black Mitsubishi van with dark-tinted windows was at the curb, its motor idling. The driver's-side window slowly slid down, revealing a nondescript man who was smiling, beckoning them to come closer, and holding up a handbag—Darlene's handbag—which she recognized immediately. They all remembered the van as identical to the one in which they had been kidnapped; only Eleanor recognized the face.

"Darlene, careful of those jewels."

Darlene quickly moved the velvet bag of borrowed jewelry behind her back and clutched it tightly. The last thing they needed was a repetition of their last meeting with Benny the Horse.

"Let me deal with this creep."

The guy has balls, Eleanor thought, trying the same thing in the same place in broad daylight. "Forget it, Charlie-Horse, we're not that stupid. Anyway we're tapped out—unless you're interested in some rented rhinestones."

Luigi, a.k.a. Benny the Horse, smiled and handed Eleanor the handbag through the van's open window.

"Check it out for yourselves."

Eleanor opened the bag. It was stuffed with money. She quickly snapped it shut and looked around to see if anyone was watching. No one was.

"Ride to the airport, ladies?" Luigi said, beaming. When they still hesitated, he continued, "What have you got to lose?"

The women looked at each other. Darlene was the first to speak. "Can you wait here for a few minutes?"

"Sure," said Luigi. "I'll load the luggage. Take your time."

"Where are we going?" said Carla.

"To return these jewels and do a little last-minute shopping."

"Lead the way," said Irene.

"And guard that handbag with your life," Eleanor whispered. "We're walking around with *millions*!"

Once out of sight, the women divided up the jewelry and headed for their respective lender shops.

Darlene walked up to the counter at Cartier, where Armand greeted her. "Don't tell me; let me guess," he said. "You've decided on the emeralds. Am I right?"

"I just can't make up my silly little mind. In the meanwhile, I'm returning everything you lent me the other evening. They were *very* successful. I had lots of comments."

"I assure you the emeralds would be your best choice."

"No, no. Maybe next time. What I'd like today is a key ring—you know, as a memento?"

"A *key ring,* madame?" said Armand, in a haughty voice usually reserved for window-shopping tourists who were carrying McDonald's balloons.

"Yes," said Darlene, in an equally haughty voice.

"In *gold,* Madame?"

"Silver plate, if you have it."

Armand rummaged in a drawer and finally held up a silver key ring as if it were a dead smelly fish. "Something like this?"

"Perfect. How much will that be?"

"There'll be no charge, madame. My pleasure."

"Well, isn't that nice and aren't you nice and, honey, you never know—I just might be back next year for those emeralds. In the meanwhile, if you have one of those nice little padded boxes and some red ribbon . . . ?"

Armand produced the box, the ribbon, and a Cartier shopping bag and held the door open for her. One never knew with these rich eccentric women; she might indeed return for the emeralds. After all, he did see her win seven

and a half million francs at the casino the previous evening—causing the craps table to be closed and draped in
black for the rest of the night.

IN THE BLACK Mitsubishi van taking the women to Nice
airport the former kidnapper and thief, Benny the Horse,
told his story.

"Why did I do it? Simple. The man who kidnapped
you has died. He was my twin brother and I am very
ashamed of him and his actions. I did what I did to make
amends, restitution. I hope you will accept my apology."

"Honey," said Darlene, "we not only accept your apology, we thank you from the bottom of our conniving
hearts." So saying, she leaned over and planted a wet kiss
on the cheek of Luigi di Cappodano.

Funny, thought Eleanor, twin brothers with different
last names. But she said nothing. Never look a gift Benny
the Horse in the mouth.

A MAGNIFICENT 1936 burgundy-and-black Lancia Astura
Pinin Farina cabriolet followed them all the way to the
airport. When they arrived, the driver presented Darlene
with a huge bouquet of rare orchids, a small silver basket
of peaches, and a bottle of very old Calvados, along with
a note that was so filthy that Darlene didn't even finish
reading it.

On the plane the women compared the gifts they had
bought at the jewelry stores. Irene had a lucky charm in
the shape of a dollar sign; Carla, a tiny gold-plated flashlight; and Eleanor, a big box from Bulgari. "Don't worry,"
she said, "it's empty. It's to keep my rhinestones in."
They all laughed; they all cried. It was that way for the
entire trip.

33
"One Year Later"

The men

Four elegantly attired and immaculately barbered men, having paid their debt to society, walked into the new restaurant where they all now worked, and set about their individual tasks.

Trofie alla Genovese had recently been introduced to America here.

The men had used their combined experience to open one of the most successful and unique new restaurants in New York. Here's how one reviewer described it:

Hate first dates, even if you knew where to find one? Given up on dating services, singles' bars, Internet chats, and magazine ads? Here's the latest twist on meeting cute, not as cute as Tom Hanks and Meg Ryan in *Sleepless in Seattle*, which I'd give four stars, but if you're willing to settle for three-star cute in Manhattan, here's a new restaurant-cum-meeting-spot that gets my vote. Its first unique feature is that it only accepts reservations for *one*—provided you've already registered by filling out a three-page résumé, which includes, among other things, your name, age, job, hobbies, special interests, sports activities, food preferences, marital history, attributes you'd like to find in a mate (read: date), and a list of detailed predilections, inclinations, and peculiar partialities. I was told that I had to submit the form two weeks ahead of my request for a reservation (and even then there was a two-week waiting list for a table! Who do they think they are, Le Cirque?). All of this can be accomplished by mail, a visit to their Internet Web site, or via fax. I chose the Internet.

When I finally received my reservation date and number, I arrived to find one of the most tastefully decorated and comfortable restaurants in the city. There was no bar and therefore no "bar scene" and zero pickup action (thank God!). The main dining room was arranged so that every table was an intimate corner for two. This was achieved by a clever arrangement of the comfortable banquettes that were shielded from each other by Art Deco etched-glass panels framed in wood. Creatively placed potted trees and large vases of fresh flowers, paneled screens and draperies, added to the intimacy and privacy—as did the soft peach-colored lighting that is most favorable to a lady's complexion. Classical piano music, performed live by one of the partners, Trevor Weymouth, completed the romantic mood. The food leans toward the Italian, with chef Julio Benvenuti showing a knowledgeable hand in the kitchen. I had his signature dish, *trofie alla Genovese*: tiny morsels of pasta bathed in a *pesto* sauce of fresh basil, garlic, pine nuts, and extra virgin olive oil. Julio poaches the garlic first, which gives it a more gentle flavor and, most importantly, doesn't give you the dreaded garlic breath. Take my word for it—it's safe for a first date. As a main course I had the *osso bucco alla Milanese*, which was moist and tender with a lemony sauce that complemented the shank of veal perfectly (I also like the fact that they give you those special forks to get the marrow out). The meal is prix fixe and each diner is billed separately on his and her previously taken credit card. Tips are included. I liked the fact that no awkward bill was presented to fight over. A star just for that. Prices were high enough to keep out the beer-and-pizza trade but reasonable, given the quality and service.

Now for the real reason to come here: I was greeted by another of the partners, a charming Frenchman, Jean-Jacques Lacoste, who previously worked at the prestigious Hermitage Hotel in Monte Carlo. After taking an imprint of my credit card, he typed my reservation number into his computer. I was instantly paired with a diner of the opposite sex, who, apparently, mirrored favorably with my preference list. I was given a card with his name, Bernard Robbins, and told nothing more than my table number. The charming Maurice Gerard, one of the best *maître d*'s in town, led me to my table, took a drink order, and left Mr. R. and me with the menus and each other. It turned out that he was an attorney and a foodie, so we had lots to talk about. I probably won't see him again, but I must

admit that I had a wonderful time and could
not have asked for a more companionable dinner partner. Who knows, maybe next time it'll
be love at first bite? (Sorry! couldn't resist.)

I learned that there was a separate dining
room for couples who had met and wanted to
dine again. Neither dining room is open to
the general public without going through the
formalities. So whether you're looking for
an evening's company or the possibility of a
longer-term relationship, I highly recommend
you give it a try. All things considered, it's a
very classy operation.

As convicted larcenists, the men had had little choice
but to leave the principality, since their chances of gar-
nering meaningful employment there were rather slim.
Julio considered going back to Italy and opening a coffee
bar—but this seemed more an end to a life than a new
beginning. He found a job as a part-time pizza chef in
Nice. Jean-Jacques had wasted so much of his life opening
doors only to find no doors were open to him. Even in
Marseilles the best he was offered was a job as night
watchman at the soccer stadium. He took it. At least no
one would see how low he had sunk. Trevor Weymouth's
previous employer at the Villa la Fortunata refused to take
him back and the best he could do was find freelance work
playing cocktail piano here and there in Cannes; but it led
nowhere and he was barely able to support himself. Maurice Gerard was, in a way, the saddest case of all. Whatever elegance he had managed to salvage after taking
leave of the Hotel de Paris had vanished, and in its place
stood a beaten man who rarely remembered to shave. He
was supported, minimally, by old friends, unable to do
any sort of meaningful work. So, when Pierre Goujon
found Maurice and gave him the letter, he immediately
brightened and found the other three men. They all instantly agreed to the proposal. Individually they may have

been worth little, but together they could probably do one thing pretty well: run a restaurant. In two weeks they were on their way to New York—putting one foot in front of the other and hoping for the best. At least it was a change. Maybe fate had a second swing at life in store for them.

The women

A week before the one-year anniversary of the four lucky women's trip to Monte Carlo, they decided that a celebration was in order.

"Let's call Hollywood CastAways and see if we can get the old dresses again."

"Think they'll remember us?"

"Are you kidding? Our pictures, in their dresses, are up all over the shop."

"Where should we go to celebrate?"

"Sure as hell not back to Monte Carlo."

"You have to admit it would be fun to go back one day—as ourselves."

"You never know."

"So, where are we going to hold this bash?"

"How about the club?"

"Yeah. They'll fucking die when they see us in those getups."

"We strike fear in the hearts of men—cloud the minds of concierges everywhere—breaking banks from Monte Carlo to Vegas. The Rhinestone Cowgirls strike again."

"Shall we rent horses or limos?"

"Get the biggest damned Rolls-Royce you can find."

"Just one?"

"Hey, remember: this time *we're* paying for it."

"I'll sit up front; I'm not proud."

"Think we can find some white caviar?"

"In New Jersey? Are you kidding?"

"Ever heard of FedEx?"

"Right. Fax the Hotel de Paris and have them ship us a can."

"Hell, we can afford it now."

"And hire a small band."

"Great idea."

"Who would have believed we'd come home with almost a quarter-million *profit*?"

"What were the odds?"

"Nobody would have taken the bet."

"Just shows to go you that when you stick together you can do anything."

"Okay. Saturday night—that gives us a week to get organized."

Of course, after the magazine and newspaper articles came out, the hotel had received irate letters from all of the *real* rich women. Fortunately, Pierre had intercepted them and written soothing replies himself, thereby saving his *Monégasque* ass.

34
"Just Deserts"

*If you've got the money, honey,
I've got the time.*

MAURICE AND THE others couldn't believe their eyes
when Georges Delarue walked into the restaurant
with Sophie. After kisses and hugs all around Maurice
took them into the couples' dining room and broke the
rules by putting some tables together at the back.

As they walked through the restaurant, Maurice
stopped and took Delarue to one side as the others proceeded. "Georges, I've never been able to thank you for
what you did. Without your testimony I would still be in
that jail." Delarue had volunteered to be a character witness for the defense—despite the fact that he was the arresting officer. Maurice recalled his impassioned plea to
the court.

"The Bible tells us, 'Thou shalt not steal.' Maurice
Gerard stole and was found out. Another commandment
tells us, 'Thou shalt not bear false witness against thy
neighbor.' To know that a man is basically a decent
man—albeit a man who has made a false step—and not
to testify on his behalf about all of his *good* characteristics
would, in my mind, be bearing false witness, for the court

would be left with a distorted impression of his character. It is true that Maurice Gerard did not devote his life to worthy causes that benefited mankind—but he was a good neighbor and a good friend and his record prior to this arrest was unblemished. When he committed the crime, and he has always admitted his culpability, he was not the man I had known for twenty-five years. Rather, he was a man who, out of desperation and a momentary slip in his sense of values, plotted to take that which was not his because he had just lost his home, his job, and his self-esteem. A troubled man simply fell apart. For that he deserves to be punished. But keep in mind when you mete out his punishment that the women he tried to steal from have all refused to testify against him or to file any claims or complaint for loss or injury. I have spoken to them and can report that they have forgiven Gerard and the others. So, I say again: Punish him, yes, but allow him to be reborn out of the darkness into which, by law, you will have to remand him. Before today, Maurice Gerard was a man I would have trusted to hold uncounted money. If you can find it in your hearts to be lenient in sentencing, I can personally guarantee that you will never see him before you, in this court, again. Punish him, but in doing so, I beg you to allow him to retain some measure of pride."

The judge was moved by the speech—and gave the men reduced sentences of six months each.

Maurice had cried then and his eyes misted over now.

"Why did you do it, Georges?"

"It was because of Trevor. When he refused to sign the paper and testify against Eleanor, I knew that there was more love than larceny in all of your hearts. And, being French . . ." Georges Delarue shrugged and Maurice grasped him tightly around the shoulders and led him to the table where the others were seated.

"I have an announcement to make," said Delarue. "Sophie, this lovely lady, is now my wife. We were married two days ago, in Paris—and are here in New York for our *lune de miel,* our honeymoon."

Maurice looked at Sophie, who was blushing, and they both began to cry shamelessly as he kissed her on both damp cheeks.

"If I'd known you were coming, I would have, as they say in America, baked a cake," said Julio, "but as it is, you will have to be satisfied with my *tiramisu*."

"What a fabulous place you have here, Maurice. How did you do it?"

"You mean how did we do it so fast? Well, it was a restaurant before and so it was simply a matter of decorating. I fell back on my experience as a ship's steward, Julio has met the challenge of running the kitchen to perfection—as you will see. Trevor was skilled at throwing big parties and at entertainment, not to mention his ability as a pianist, and Jean-Jacques is not only the best greeter in the business but has taken to the computer like a fish to *bouillabaisse*. Individually, we were barely surviving, but together we are fifty percent owners of the hottest restaurant in town."

Like old friends who hadn't seen each other for a long time, the conversation flowed and overflowed with reminiscing. "Whatever happened to that Detective Obolensky?" asked Julio at one point.

"Ola? You'd never believe it." Delarue went on to relate how Ola had traced her roots, changed her name to Anna-Maria, and married Benny the Horse. "She is now Mrs. Luigi di Capodanno, happily raising babies and grapes in Montepulciano."

"And you?" asked Maurice.

"I am retired. We've found a small place in Provence that we are renovating into a bistro with a few rooms."

"And Pierre?"

"Pierre is Pierre. He's the same as ever."

"Whatever happened to those women?" asked Sophie.

"It's a year today that we first met them," answered Jean-Jacques. "We should be celebrating but we've been too busy to think about it."

Suddenly the room became oddly quiet as a waiter

pushed a rolling cart laden with champagne, a large tin of white beluga caviar, and all the accoutrements, to the table.

"You were reading my mind," Maurice said, to the waiter.

"Champagne and white beluga caviar, compliments of—" He made a sweeping gesture toward the doorway, where four elegantly gowned and rhinestone-bejeweled women were making their entrance.

"Ah, I see they haven't forgotten. What a surprise—and what great timing," said Maurice as they all rose to greet the women.

"Allow me to introduce our business partners—and our *wives*," said a beaming Maurice.

The kissing was endless, tears flowed along with the champagne, Delarue had his first taste of the wildly expensive white beluga caviar, Trevor played the "Wedding March" by Mendelssohn, Julio served a fabulous meal, and afterward, when the restaurant had closed, Maurice turned off the outside sign that read:

HEADHUNTERS
Good Food and Company

There was a big red neon heart around the letter *H* with an arrow piercing its center.

THE TABLES WERE pushed back and the trio the women had hired played their favorite songs. Everyone danced; the party lasted into the wee hours of the night.

The women never looked more beautiful.

Reader, what were the odds that all of these people would have shared happy endings? The only answer is that sometimes long shots come in—and when they do, they pay off . . . *big*.

CURTAIN

To the disbelieving ladies among you (and those who may be considering repeating the escapades contained in this book): All I can say is rent a room at the Hotel de Paris, borrow some expensive jewelry from Bulgari, dress to kill, and sit in the bar—facing the front—on a Friday evening at around eight-thirty. Someone will definitely send you a bottle of champagne and some white caviar. Trust me; it happens all the time.